Solarversia

-The Year Long Game-

Toby Downton

Solarversia

The Year Long Game

ISBN-13: 978-0-9933308-0-3

Cover art by Jimmy Gibbs
Edited by Helena Michaelson
Interior design by Toby Downton

www.solarversia.com

Twitter: @tobydownton
Facebook: www.facebook.com/solarversia

First Edition

For the Many

Even if there can be only one

Chapter One

The minute Nova Negrahnu heard about Solarversia she was convinced she was going to love it with every ounce of her being. Enabled by virtual reality, a technology that had been promised again and again, but had only just come to fruition, this game was what she'd been dreaming of since she was a little girl.

In Solarversia, the normal rules of existence would cease to apply. It sounded like a magical world, a place to fight monsters, fly through the sky and explore the Solar System, and all from the comfort of her own home. From the expression on the face of her best friend, Sushi Harrison, she wasn't the only one who felt that way.

"Who was it that sent you the link?" Sushi asked, without looking up from her iPad.

"Burner. But it's been going mental on social media. He and Jono have already signed up."

Sushi cleared her throat and read out the press release Burner had sent them.

"Solarversia is billed as an exciting new form of entertainment, fit for the 21st century. An amalgam of virtual, augmented and mixed realities, Spiralwerks, the London-based company behind The Game, claim that it integrates every form of digital entertainment that came before it. One hundred million players will vie to be the last person standing through a series of challenges that blend racing, fighting, strategy, psychology, lateral thinking, creativity, popularity and cold hard luck. Solarversia will last an entire year and the Grand Champion will be awarded prize money rumoured to equal ten million pounds."

Their mouths dropped wide open.

"Ten million?"

"That's just for the winner. It pays a prize to everyone in the top thousand, and there'll be tens of thousands of quests throughout the year, paying their own bounties."

"Oh, my God. It even includes Krazy Karting," said Nova.

"This is insane. Check out the signup screen."

The screen was blank, except for two counters and a button. The first counter, displaying the number of signups, had just hit fifteen thousand and was rising rapidly. The second one displayed a timer, and was ticking down to The Game's start date on the 29th February 2020.

"We have to wait four years for it to start?" Sushi asked.

"That's the day after my eighteenth birthday." Nova grabbed her friend's hand. "Do you think we'll still be best friends then?"

"Are you kidding? Of course we will. If we can be best friends from two to fourteen, I think we're safe for life, aren't we?"

Nova nodded uncertainly. "But Seattle's such a long way away from Maidstone."

"Let's both sign up to play. I bet you my winnings we're still best friends when it starts."

"OK. You're on. And we better had be."

The girls spent the next couple of hours learning about the world of Solarversia and all it entailed. It was the puzzle aspect of the Gameworld that thrilled Nova the most. Although Krazy Karting was her favourite driving game — she was already ranked in the top few hundred players in the world — her real passion was lateral thinking and puzzle solving.

Brought up on a diet of sudoku, crosswords and jigsaws, she had started to think of ways to create more complex puzzles of her own. When she stumbled upon a blog post that described the grand prize in more detail she sat bolt upright and inhaled until her lungs were full.

"This is getting ridiculous. You'll never guess what the Grand Champion gets to do."

"Apart from working out how to spend ten million pounds, you mean?"

"Something way more important than that. Solarversia is going to be a quadrennial event. After 2020, the next one doesn't start until 2024. And the Grand Champion of the first one will help to design the second one. Sush — I've just found my dream job. I absolutely, categorically need to win this thing. My life doesn't make sense without it."

"If you do win, I'd be happy to attend to the commercial side of the prize for you, ensuring the cash gets spent in a suitable manner. So you can — you know — focus your attention on the design aspect of the prize. That's so like me, putting others first."

Nova slumped into a pile of pillows. Game design had been top of her list of jobs since she discovered that it was a thing. This was the daddy of all such jobs — and she'd need to beat a hundred million people to get it. If that wasn't the toughest job interview in history, she didn't know what was.

Once the girls' accounts had been verified, they were guided to an area that asked them to create their avatars — three-dimensional representations of their real-world bodies. Nova stood in the middle of Sushi's room, held her arms out and looked straight ahead, while her friend scanned her from head to toe with her phone. The iPad, which she'd leant against some school books on Sushi's desk, rendered a 3D mesh of her body in real time.

"Hold still, will you? Else we'll be here all night."

"You can talk; how many times did I have to scan you? Nothing wrong with wanting to look my best in front of a global audience." She glanced at the screen to assess her avatar, which was slowly revolving about the y-axis. "No way, look what you've done to my stomach."

"I think you'll find that your love of curry, rather than my phone-handling skills, did that to your stomach. You don't want to look perfect in any case. There won't be enough difference between your Normal Avatar and your Super Avatar. Besides, people that know you well, like Burner and me, will know you were sucking it in. You can't polish a turd."

The Game required each player to create two avatars: an ordinary, realistic version, and a 'super' version, described by the creators as the version of their self the player would ideally want to be, given the chance. Changes to height and weight would be subject to certain limitations in order to ensure that avatars didn't interfere with Gameworld features such as player transportation, but Spiralwerks had specified that they wouldn't enforce any other restrictions.

Finally content with their figures, they pranced around Sushi's bedroom to a series of tutorial videos that captured the way they moved. They jumped up and down, drew weapons, shot at targets, hugged each other and pulled off all manner of dance moves. Every action fed into their personal Solarversia Avatar Movement Algorithm.

After the moves came the sounds: they spoke in their normal reading voices, then laughed, yee-haaed, shrieked and made numerous other noises that captured them in the throes of death. As it neared midnight, they collapsed on Sushi's bed, exhausted. It was the night before the Harrison family's big move from the UK, and Nova was sleeping over at her friend's house to prolong the moment of goodbye for as long as possible.

"That's our Normal Avatars sorted, then." Sushi scrolled down her profile page to check what else was required. "We still need to decide what our Super Avatars look like, choose our avatar names, catchphrases, vehicles and player numbers."

Nova cocked her head to one side and dug her little finger into her ear. "It doesn't start for three and a half years, but I think the Solarversia jingle might already be stuck in my head."

"That gives me an idea. Why don't we download the jingle and use it as a ringtone for one another? Every time it goes, it will remind us of tonight."

They jolted into action again. Once the jingle was synced to their devices, Nova brushed her hair behind her ears and looked at her friend.

"You are going to call me, right? All the way from the States?"

"Of course I am, you eejit. You better not be too busy to speak. I won't know anyone over there."

"You'll be fine. They'll go nuts over your British accent, while I'm stuck here, Billy-no-mates in the 'Stone."

"Don't be stupid. Life's going to be so boring without you. Who else do I know who can turn literally anything into a game?"

"That's true. Making toast will never be the same, huh?"

They laughed. Earlier that evening Nova had devised a whole series of complex tasks and hoops to jump through which culminated in a slice of toast.

"I'm not going to forget you, OK? How about we make a deal? If one of us wins Solarversia, we have to promise to split the prize money with the other one. We'll be apart, but we'll be playing it together. For each other."

Nova smiled. "Solarversia Sisters, eh? So we'll be rooting for each other all the way? I saw something in the rules about virtual wills. There can only be one winner, so that means one of us is going to die at some point."

Virtual wills were a feature that allowed players to leave all the items in their possession to a friend, once they had lost their third and final life in The Game. They watched over each other's shoulders as they named each other sole beneficiaries of their wills.

"One last thing. If I'm going to Seattle, we need to make it ultra official. Put your headset on and bring up that Halloween app with the fake blood module."

Nova held out her arm and watched as her friend pressed hers against it, smearing dark red blood all over their wrists.

"Solarversia Sisters forever," they said in unison.

Nova grinned. It felt good to have a backup plan with the person you trusted most in the world.

Chapter Two

Casey Brown placed his foot on some loose shingle and felt his leg slide out from under him. It was probably the fourth time that hour, but right now his grasp of time was even worse than his grasp of space. Each hallucinogenic episode had been more intense than the last.

They began when the colours of his surroundings started to move, until eventually trees merged into bushes, the hills became waves in an ocean, and the sky looked like it wanted to swallow him whole. Scarier still was when time appeared to move in reverse for several seconds and he'd somehow known the answers to questions he hadn't yet asked. Or had that even happened yet?

As his leg slid out, his shoulder came forward to cushion the blow, the instinct to protect the head kicking in despite his state. Pain coursed through his central nervous system, and for a second he thought he'd never make it. But he'd thought that a thousand times over the last few days and had willed himself on, desperate to make it. Only twenty more yards, Case, you can do it. Warriors win.

He felt dirty, his brow caked in sweat and mud, God-knows-what matted in his hair. A hot shower, a greasy hamburger and his bed: these were things he'd never take for granted again. His bloody hands shook despite the mild Mississippi afternoon, and his wrists ached from the chafing of the old piece of fishing rope that tied them together and attached them to the net of rocks he dragged behind him.

Going up the hill, like he was now, had always been easier: the rocks were below and couldn't fall on him, as they'd done countless times on his journeys down. The task had been to climb the hill a hundred and forty-four times and this was his final ascent. He was nearly there. Only fifteen yards to go. Warriors win.

Willing him on from the top of the hill was Wallace, one of the people that had introduced Casey to the Holy Order in the first place, and the guy in charge of these initiation rites. Wallace wasn't much older than Casey but years of smoking had taken their toll and the crow's feet around his eyes gave him a craggy, hardy look.

"Come on, Casey, ma boy, you're on the home stretch! You've gone done the hard bit. That's right, put your back into it, soldier, it's mind over matter."

On his hands and knees, Casey grabbed hold of a grassy tuft, hauled himself another yard and could now make out his comrade's grin beneath his black Stetson. Dragging the net of rocks with a renewed sense of purpose, he powered through the final few yards and collapsed at the base of his target, an old wooden pole.

The circular disc on top of it was engraved with a series of curly swastikas, the Holy Order's emblem. During one of his hallucinogenic episodes the pole had looked like a magical toadstool. The symbols had grown hands and legs, which had interlinked and danced around, taunting him in his weakened state. Using the pole to steady himself with one hand, he held the other out and looked at his friend.

"The knife, please."

Wallace smiled a yellow-toothed grin and flipped the knife in the air. Casey caught it by the blade and turned to face the pole. "Hope I never see this fucking thing again, long as I live."

Suddenly aware that his cigarette smoke was making it harder for his friend to catch his breath, Wallace wafted the air with his hand, took one last drag, and flicked the butt to the ground. He retrieved an emergency ration bar from his backpack, removed the silver foil, and broke it into pieces while Casey carved his final notch.

"She's a bitch, ain't she? The first hundred ascents are bad enough. The next forty-four are pure torture. Never thought I was gonna make it, right up 'til the end. It'll all be worth it, trust me."

His hands shaking, Casey swapped the knife for the ration bar and collapsed on the floor. Three and a half days of mental and physical exertion had broken him. Wallace rummaged through his backpack again, this time pulling out a walkie-talkie. He flicked a switch, waited for it to crackle and hum, and then held it to his ear.

"Looks like we have ourselves a winner. Get the truck ready, I'll be down soon to help pack the tents away." He switched frequencies and spoke again. "Tell Father that the eagle has landed. I repeat, the eagle has landed, over."

***

Artica Kronkite pulled his jacket tight and cursed the biting February wind. As he walked the last stretch of his daily commute, he spoke into the mic embedded in his glasses. Costing more than the average Londoner's monthly mortgage payment, their thick oblong frames incorporated technology that was able to augment his surroundings, but also kept the swirls of unkempt hair out of his stubbly face.

"Hannah, let Carl know that I replied to the HGR guys. They reckon there's an issue with the larger drones, bloody ridiculous. We've been working on this thing for six months, and now there's a problem. I told them, they screw up the opening ceremony, we never do business with them again, period."

He rounded the corner into Redchurch Street and looked up to the roof of the building opposite. A black hand appeared from behind and clamped itself round the Victorian chimney, cracking it down the centre. Another hand appeared and grabbed onto a spare satellite dish.

Using its newfound brickwork grips, the hulking gorilla poked its head over the building and let out a scream that Arty thought sounded more like a dying giraffe. It stared right at him, and then was gone, as fast as it had appeared. Bricks and tiles, dislodged by the impatient primate, smashed as they hit the pavement below. Six commuters walked on by, unaware of the virtual carnage that his glasses had made seem real.

A new message from Hannah appeared in his field of vision: "Where are you? Meeting in Chess. Urgent."

His voiced reply was automatically transcribed to text and sent to her: "Two minutes away."

The area in front of Spiralwerks HQ buzzed with reporters, gamers and fans, some of whom had turned up every weekday for the past year, so eager had they been to meet the staff. Arty signed promotional posters for the fanboys, posed for selfies with the gamers and ignored the inane questions from the reporters. Unmanned aerial drones hovered overhead, fulfilling various tasks. Some captured live footage; others delivered breakfast orders to nearby digital agencies.

Arty pushed through the mob and entered reception, admitted through the sturdy metal gates by a robotic security guard whose facial recognition software could tell identical twins apart at a hundred metres. The intelligent paint covering the circular edge of the double-storey lobby displayed an aquatic scene. Orcas, tiger sharks and scuba divers accompanied his ascent in the lift, which made a bubbling sound when it reached the sixth floor.

High-resolution floor-to-ceiling screens at the front of the room told visitors everything they needed to know. This was mission control. Although the entire room buzzed with activity, heads still turned when Arty entered the room. It was a big day for everybody, but they all knew how much it meant to their CEO. He popped his bag on his desk and dashed over to the chess-themed meeting room. The colleagues he passed offered a nod and a smile but didn't engage him in the usual banter.

"... They're telling me it's a credible threat, and we need to be taking it seriously. Hang on. For those dialled in, Arty's just walked in."

He declined a seat, joining those standing round the table instead. The screen on the wall displayed the avatars of the dialled-in management team. The smart table around which they crowded was overlaid with images and holograms pertaining to the meeting.

"OK. Tell me what we're dealing with here." Arty addressed Hannah McCreadie, the Head of Communications and a close ally. She was a patient woman whose ability to understand and react to complex problems had gained her a lot of respect within the organisation.

"You remember those nutjobs in the US we heard about a few weeks back?"

"You mean the techno-mystical wannabe terrorists?"

"Them indeed, 'the Holy Order'. They just issued a hit list of corporate targets. Guess who's on top?"

Hannah nodded at the list on the large screen at the front of the room. The room fell silent while Arty studied it.

"Is there any indication why? We build games in virtual worlds, for God's sake, it's not like we sell crack-laced sweets to kids."

Hannah shrugged, exhaling through pursed lips.

"When you say that they 'issued' the hit list, how exactly? To whom and when?"

"Emailed to a generic address at each of the companies on the list. Arrived at one minute past eight this morning. They used an anonymous remailing system making the original source untraceable. We're expecting the story to break any moment."

"So you're telling me that this, rather than the start of The Game, is going to be the news tonight?"

"We're doing what we can to stay on message."

Arty stared at the list for a long while. Finally, noticing the worried expressions on the faces of his team, he clapped his hands and smiled, hoping it looked more genuine than it felt. "Let's not lose focus on what we've got to do today. We're only fourteen hours from the opening ceremony. Everyone needs to be at the top of their game."

Members of his team started to move. "That's it, get a move on, we haven't got time to waste. Except for you, Carl. I want to know what's going on with those bloody drones."

Chapter Three

Nova sat cross-legged on the sofa in the lounge and checked the Solarversia countdown clock for the hundredth time that day. On the night of the sleepover with Sushi, when they'd signed up to play, the timer had displayed what seemed like an impossible number of days to wait. Now, with the days and hours both on zero, and the minutes about to tick under fifteen, she felt ready to burst.

"How do you like your magic goggles then, love? Are they better than the old ones?"

"Much better, thanks, Dad. The resolution is out of this world. Not quite as good as actual reality, but not far off, either. And the skull pads read my brain waves, so I can control my avatar's movement by the power of thought. Which means I don't have to carry my haptic gloves around with me any more."

"I understood the first bit, when you said they were better than your old pair," her mum said. "The rest of it might as well have been in Chinese."

It was quarter to midnight on the 28th February 2020, the day of Nova's 18th birthday. Her parents had given the present she'd been longing for: a BoonerMax virtual reality headset. Resembling a pair of futuristic ski goggles, the streamlined latticework of gunmetal titanium encased more computing power than some families had in their entire homes.

Headsets like these allowed users to alternate their view of the world as they saw fit. Switched off, they functioned like a normal pair of glasses. In 'augmented mode', headsets displayed your immediate environment, but overlaid text, images and objects onto it, altering it in subtle and not-so-subtle ways. Advanced headsets, like the Booners, were even capable of occluding objects, effectively rendering them invisible. Full virtual reality immersed users into entirely fictional worlds.

Nova removed her Booners, exhaled onto the rim and lovingly rubbed it with the sleeve of her jumper. Already, they were her favourite thing in the world. At the front of the lounge the Solarversia opening ceremony played on the TV. The final few floats of the parade pulled into the Olympic Stadium to complete a circuit of the track, cheered on by a crowd of eighty thousand people and watched by several hundred million more online.

The build-up to The Game had been impossible to ignore. Cities had been inundated with interactive billboards that flashed up the profiles of new entrants from around the world. These square-shaped profiles provided a snapshot of information about the player: their avatar name and picture, nationality, vehicle choices and, in Nova's opinion, the most important piece of information of all, their number in the Player's Grid.

The grid was comprised of ten thousand rows by ten thousand columns, with square number one bang in the centre. Numbers two to nine were positioned around it, and numbers ten to twenty-five around that. The numbers spiralled out like a snail's shell all the way to one hundred million. It was common practice to scan the grid number of interesting profiles on billboards and flip into augmented or virtual mode on a headset in order to view the person's position in the grid and check out their bio.

In the run-up to the start date, the marketing for Solarversia had become unavoidable and, to gamers like Nova, utterly tantalising. Characters from Solarversia kept popping up unexpectedly in augmented displays all over the world. She and Burner had participated in an event at Maidstone's Mote Park, which had involved a bunch of geocached clues that led to the lake — where a fifty-foot dodectapus known as Banjax was found lurking. Displays like this had become tourist attractions in their own right.

Lots of people seemed to agree — Solarversia was the largest, most exciting thing ever to have been created in the history of the world. Burner's brother Jono had gone so far as to attend a boot camp to train for it, lured, like so many others, by the large cash prizes for the top thousand places, and the promise of instant worldwide fame for those who made it further. Discussion of tactics and strategy had been endless, and tens of millions of pounds had been waged in bets. For Nova and her friends, the opening ceremony represented three and a half years of hype, excitement and trepidation.

Hearing the Solarversia jingle in her headset, Nova slipped it back over her head. All her old settings were already synced to her new Booners — it could only be a message from Sushi.

"Hey, birthday girl, have you checked out the fireworks cam yet? It's seriously rockin'."

"I've been too excited to do anything other than sit here and watch the clock count its way down to midnight. I can't believe The Game starts in ten minutes. It doesn't seem real. Send me the link."

Nova switched to camera mode in her Booners. An array of video feeds appeared in her view, a thousand different perspectives available at the touch of a button, her gaze or the sound of her voice. She selected the fireworks cam by staring at the link in the message from Sushi. Half a second later she appeared to inhabit a 360-degree camera affixed to an aerial drone that hovered above the fireworks display in the stadium.

Rockets exploded around her, some so close that she instinctively jerked away from them, while Crackling Comets zoomed past her face, leaving behind glistening tails of multicoloured light she couldn't help but try to touch. She breathed deeply through her nose, trying to smell the sulphur that hung thick in the air.

Mr Negrahnu peered over his newspaper. "Has it started yet?"

"As I've mentioned several thousand times, it starts when the counter hits zero. You're worse than a little kid."

"Says the person sitting there oohing and ahhing like there's something wrong with their brain."

She volleyed one eye back to the lounge and glared at him. "I'm oohing and ahhing because I'm floating in the middle of a fireworks display. Take a look for yourself. TV — sync to Booners."

The TV switched channel to mirror the view in her headset. Mr Negrahnu leaned forward in his seat and peered over the rims of his spectacles.

"OK, I'll admit it. That's pretty cool." He watched a couple of rockets explode into a shower of light before retreating to his crossword. Nova exchanged a wide-eyed look with her mum. It wasn't often that her dad made a complimentary remark where modern technology was concerned.

She glanced at the countdown. Seven minutes to midnight. Still enough time to check out some of the other views. Once upon a time people hopped channels. Then they surfed the 'net. These days they volleyed cams. She chose one positioned on the lead float, which had just completed its lap of the track.

Its crew had stripped down to T-shirts despite the cold February air, their bodies warmed by a cocktail of rum and dance. Steam rose from their backs while the float's chunky sound system doled out electro-flavoured sonic booms. Her kind of tunes. Around the stadium mighty lasers fired beams at huge disco balls, which diffracted the light into millions of sparkling shards.

The sound of a gong reverberated around the stadium, causing the crowd to erupt into a fresh chorus of cheers. Nova switched off cam mode, perched her Booners back on her forehead and rubbed her hands with glee. The digits on the timer were counting down the final 60 seconds — the Year-Long Game was about to begin.

***

The central podium in the Olympic Stadium was bathed in light. A holographic chimp dressed in a smart suit flickered into view. He climbed the stairs at the front of the stand, followed by a group of holographic monkeys half his size, who lugged a wooden cargo crate between them. They pushed and they heaved and they strained, willed on by every person watching.

"Come on, arkwinis, we've waited long enough," Nova said from the edge of her seat.

"Ark-whatnies?" Mr Negrahnu asked.

"The chimpanzee in the suit is called Arkwal, and the little ones are the 'arkwinis'."

The arkwinis placed the crate to the right of the larger ape and then waddled back down the steps and out of view. Arkwal leaned in toward the microphone.

"Alright, Earthlings?" He wouldn't have sounded out of place tending a market stall in the East End. "Thank you for accepting Emperor Mandelbrot's invitation to the Year-Long Game. To win, you'll need a combination of skill, luck, insight and creativity. But let's not get ahead of ourselves. Everyone starts The Game in the same place: Castalia, the Emperor's flying palace."

Arkwal paused to look around the stadium, eyes narrowed, as if searching for someone or something in particular. He reached into his jacket pocket and retrieved what seemed to be a red baton. With a flick of his wrist, the baton extended into a full-length telescope, the height of an arkwini.

The spotlight followed him as he walked up to the wooden crate. He tapped it with the telescope then stepped away as it collapsed outward, revealing an object shaped like a miniature space shuttle with streamlined cylindrical thrusters pointed at the heavens. Arkwal stowed the compressed 'scope back in his pocket, strapped on the jetpack and clamped his thumbs down on the thrusters.

The stadium erupted with sound and light as the holographic jetpack roared into life, firing a wild array of sparks down at the podium. He looked skyward, saluted the crowd and blasted off into the heavens. Nova flicked her visor back down. Every gamer knew that flying was far more enjoyable when you were totally immersed. The top of her display transformed into a dashboard that displayed a whole host of counters and instruments, including the distances from various landmarks: the Eiffel Tower, the Great Pyramid of Giza, and their destination, Castalia, the flying palace.

She stuck her arms out in front of her and tilted left and then right, mimicking Arkwal's motions as she followed him through a virtually rendered night sky. Headsets like hers used voice and thought commands combined with special audiovisual processing to move her avatar around in the virtual world. When she held her hands out in front of her, the camera on her headset translated her movements into the virtual world in real time. Digital natives like Nova, Burner and Sushi could move around in the virtual world as adeptly as they could in the real, running, jumping and fighting their way through whatever game makers threw at them.

She accelerated to a speed that blurred her surroundings beyond recognition, leaving the figure of Arkwal as the one thing that remained in focus. Before long, she watched as he deployed a giant parachute, slowed to cruising speed, and then ejected the device. It fluttered away, a new passenger on the South Atlantic trade wind express. A short way ahead of them a floating palace was coming into view.

***

Arkwal hit Castalia at such a high speed that he smashed straight through its north face, showering bricks, debris and dust everywhere. He skidded along the marble floor of the Magisterial Chamber for fifty metres or more, and then slowed to a halt. He picked himself up and brushed himself down, and stopped for a few seconds to examine his elbows, which had taken the brunt of his crash landing.

The Chamber was an enormous cube, the length of a football pitch in every direction. Hanging from the ceiling were thousands of multicoloured vines of varying length, some of which were swaying from side to side, following the recent disturbance. Still coated in a smattering of dust, Arkwal took his position in the centre of the room. With his arms outstretched above his head, he yelled, "Ladies and gentlemen, here's Gorigaroo, master of the gong."

Far away on the other side of the chamber, a figure with the head and powerful upper body of a gorilla and the abdomen and mighty hind legs of a kangaroo could be seen, swinging from vine to vine. As he reached the southwest corner of the chamber, he let go, landed briefly on the marble floor and bounced up again, high into the mess of tangled creepers overhead.

Finally he came to rest beside a golden gong suspended by several of the vines. He pulled a wooden club out of his pouch, leaned back, and then struck the gong with immense force. When the sound waves reached Arkwal, they troubled the floor around him, causing the patterned marble to vibrate.

He bent his knees, leapt up to the closest vine, swung away from the pulsating ground, let go to perform a somersault, and landed at the edge of what was now a circular hole in the centre of the room. "And now, ladies and gentlemen, the time has come for me to introduce His Royal Highness, Emperor Commissaire de Spielen, von Unglai D'Acheera Nakk-oo, Mandelbrot!"

Slowly, something rose through the hole in the floor: an amorphous blob perched upon a circular dais. As it passed into the room, the blob began to bubble and shake. Suddenly an enormous fist protruded from the jelly. It unfurled slowly, and Arkwal hopped into its palm and sat himself down. He flicked his wrist to extend his telescope and rested it between the thumb and index finger of the giant hand.

The telescope faced the north wall of the Magisterial Chamber, the facade of which was already in the final stages of repair, being reclad in marble by a team of diligent arkwinis. Satisfied that the work was being done to the highest standard, Arkwal nodded his approval.

Meanwhile the amorphous gloop continued its metamorphosis. Other body shapes appeared, each one made of the same gooey substance, which looked mauve from one angle, purple from the next. The centre of the circle bubbled with the greatest intensity and rose fast, at first resembling a volcano and then, as it reached towards the ceiling of the room, a totem pole.

Hundreds of mouths burst into view up and down the length of the pole, each formed in its own peculiar way. One contained dozens of teeth pointed at vulgar angles and several tongues, which took it in turns to lick one another. Another contained only a tongue, as long as a hockey stick, that whipped in and out of surrounding mouths, as if it was scared of being bitten if it stayed in place too long.

A small but perfectly formed set of lips near the top of the pole started to sing. It was an anthem of sorts, sung in the sweetest soprano, and its chant began to spread down the pole like a Mexican wave, with mouth after mouth joining in harmony. The lower the mouth, the deeper its voice. As the mouths sang and their anthem reached its crescendo, the newly repaired north wall of the chamber began to crumble, revealing behind it a grid of millions of tiny squares, bathed in a warm violet light.

"I'm happy to announce that the Player's Grid is in place," said Arkwal, now standing in the middle of the giant fist, his arms extended above his head in a triumphant gesture. "The Year-Long Game can begin. Emperor Mandelbrot has asked me to wish each of you the very best of luck and would like to remind you that There Can Be Only One!"

Chapter Four

"Take me to my square," Nova said. She flew across the Magisterial Chamber, leaving Arkwal and the Emperor behind, and zoomed in to her square in the bottom left of the grid. Like most players, she'd fretted about her player number for months before making her final choice. The number determined the position of the square within the grid — which quadrant it was in, and how central it was.

To make things interesting in the lead-up to the start of The Game, Spiralwerks had gamified the entire number choosing process. Released in batches, most had been available for free and were distributed on a first come, first served basis. Other 'cooler' numbers — the low ones, round ones, primes and so on — were sold, auctioned or offered as prizes in a multitude of promotional games.

As a result, securing a good number had become something of a sporting pastime. Although numbers had no direct bearing on how well the player would perform in Solarversia, the unspoken agreement was that the lower numbers — those closest to the centre — were the coolest. At least, that's where most A-list celebrities had ended up.

The dilemma people faced was whether to lock in a number early, and risk missing out on a better one, or to wait, and risk having to choose an even higher one when all the central ones went to other people anyway.

As well as wanting to be fairly central, Nova and Sushi had wanted to be next to one another within the grid. They'd spent ages debating the merits of various numbers, and arguing about who was going to be odd, and who was going to be even. In the end they settled for squares in the bottom left quadrant: Nova chose 515,740 and Sushi, one space to her left, chose 515,739. Numbers were semi-permanent. They lasted until a player crashed out of The Game for good — at which point their finishing position became their new number.

Now, finally, after years of waiting, Nova hovered in front of her profile square for real. Although she'd seen it a thousand times — had dreamt about it on several occasions — it still excited her beyond words to see it on the wall of the Magisterial Chamber. Squares had a mystical quality about them; they were gateways to another world that made the normal one look terribly trite.

Her number was plastered across the top of the square like it was the most important fact about her. On the left-hand side beneath it was a picture of her avatar's head, and beneath that her avatar name, nationality, catchphrase and shortcode. The task of choosing a name and a catchphrase had caused her so much trouble she came close to quitting before The Game even started. She ended up with 'Super Nova 2020' and 'Supernova's a Blast!', a lame pun that she regretted immediately.

The system of shortcodes had been devised by Spiralwerks to help players visualise each other's locations in the grid more easily. Each quadrant had been named after a suit in a pack of cards — the lower left quadrant was designated 'C' for Clubs. In addition, each concentric ring of numbers was itself numbered. The number one square in the centre of the grid was ring one. The numbers round it — two to nine — comprised ring two, and so on. Nova's number, 515,740, was in ring 359, giving her the shortcode of C359.

As well as appearing in profile squares, shortcodes were also the license plate numbers on each of a player's three vehicles: their car, boat and plane. There had been thousands of models to choose from, and millions of ways to customise them. Nova adored her vehicles — she'd modified them to look like something from the set of Tron — and loved the way they glistened and rotated in 3D on the left-hand side of her profile square.

As she approached her square it turned transparent to reveal a cubic room with walls made of swirling yellow plasma, and a floor and ceiling as black as the night. This was her Corona Cube, the place that she would start in the world of Solarversia whenever she logged on from that moment forward, and her exit point whenever she wanted to log out.

The black ceiling displayed two constellations: portals to parts of Solarversia. One was named 'Castalia' and led back the way she had come, into the Magisterial Chamber of the flying palace. The other was named 'Solarversia' and led to the Gameworld, which was modelled on the Solar System. Nova looked up to the Solarversia constellation and traced her finger over its constituent stars.

As she touched the last one a harmonious jingle sounded, and three objects, recognised by people the world over, appeared floating in the centre of the room: a rock, some paper and a pair of scissors.

A datafeed appeared in her display, informing her that she'd been matched against player number 38,043,551, JoLem from Poland. She was about to find out whether of hours of strategising were going to pay off. A fifteen second countdown began. Those who let it count down to zero would automatically forfeit the game. "Paper," she announced, annoyed by the doubt she could hear in her voice.

She winced as the result flashed on the screen: "Scissors beats paper. Winner: JoLem." Losing players were matched against each other after a twenty second delay. It took her five attempts in total, winning with scissors, against the paper of a Chinese player. She took her headset off, twitched her nose like a rabbit, and swept her long hair behind her ears.

"Finally. Thought I was going to be here all night."

"Told you scissors would win. Mum does know best occasionally."

Nova bit her tongue. Annoyingly, her mum had suggested scissors earlier in the evening, but there no point arguing about it now. She replaced the headset to find that her victory had caused the floor she was standing on to give way. She fell into a winding tunnel, illuminated by the occasional spotlight, until eventually she popped out of the end, her arms and legs flailing as she fell two storeys to a crash pad on the ground. Her headset flashed a message: "Welcome to Alpha Island. Population 543,286."

Looking up, she noticed hundreds of entwined tubes like the one she'd emerged from. Castalia seemed to have grown player-spitting dreadlocks. As she glanced around, datafeeds were overlaid on the objects she looked at. Castalia was revealed to be floating a kilometre overhead, and was still populated with several million people. When she looked at another player, a feed appeared above their head, displaying their profile information. She only needed to glance at a building or a landmark in the distance to be told how far away it was, and how long it would take her to reach it.

For now, she wanted to get her bearings. Players seemed to be heading in the same direction — toward a signpost. She stared at it and said "Lock on to target: Run." The signpost was taller than a triple-decker bus and surrounded by scores of other players who were either babbling to each other about the various destinations, or taking selfies in front of it. Nailed to the post at head height was a sign that said 'Out of Order'.

"How can a signpost be out of order? Are the directions wrong?" her mum asked.

"Nope. Signposts double as teleport machines, except they won't start working until the Teleport Quest has been completed. It's the machine that's out of order, not the signs."

She tried to find a destination whose name she recognised. The Forest of Fun — 1 km , Conga World — 5 km, The Travelling Circus of Nakk-oo — 3,213 km. The closest location, only a hundred metres away, was the Fire Demon's Obstacle Course. She locked on.

***

Nova had completed the Blazing Balls and the Scorching Skyscraper obstacles without incident. Now she stood motionless, eyes locked with a Luminous Lavadile. She exhaled slowly and edged forward. Still no movement from the beast. It opened its mouth and emitted a long, deep growl. Another step, this one bigger. Her eyes darted from the lavadile to the side of the fire pit it guarded. Could she make it?

Three or so metres to go. Flames licked the side of the beast's head and she could have sworn it just moved toward her. This was it . No more time for pussyfooting. She stepped onto her right foot and launched herself forward as far as possible. Out of the corner of her eye she saw the thing make its move. She landed on the bank inches from the molten lava and scrambled up the side as fast as she could. Behind her she heard a whooshing sound and then a snap.

She rolled onto her back and saw that the powerful jaws had clamped round her left foot. A glistening globule of molten lava trickled down one of its teeth and landed on her leg. It made a gentle hiss as it burned through the fabric of her trousers. *Damn thing, get off already.* Her health score, displayed in the top right of her visor, ticked down a second time. The snap of the jaw had cost her eight points, the globule a further five. She was already down to 87 health points and The Game had only just begun.

Not the start she'd hoped for. Out of the corner of her eye she spotted a long piece of flint. She grabbed it, sat forward and rammed the sharp end into the creature's eye. It released her leg in an instant and plunged back into the lava, powered by its strong tail.

She made it to the top of the pit and turned to take in the scene. There were several hundred other players navigating the fiery assault course. To her left, less than thirty feet away, a guy was in serious trouble. A lavadile, longer than hers, had fastened its jaws around his legs. He thrashed around, trying to break free from its clutches as it pulled him ever closer to the red-hot bath. His arms spasmed with pain as it finally dragged him under. An even worse start than hers.

She arrived at the last obstacle, Nico's Nets, feeling out of breath, though she hadn't moved from the sofa all night. Virtual worlds could do strange things to the brain. She pinged Burner and Sushi to compare notes. They were further ahead and had managed to retain perfect health scores. How did that happen? Although Sushi and Burner were respectable gamers in their own right, they weren't in Nova's league, not close. She gritted her teeth and tried to concentrate.

Nico's Nets were stretched across a path — all players needed to do was crawl beneath them to cross it. On the other side, a finishing line displayed a count of people who had completed the obstacle course — over forty thousand — and also a count of people who had lost a life tackling it — nearly three thousand. She did her best to put thoughts of death out of her mind and to remain calm.

The netting was plumbed in to the lava pit. An old man dressed in rags stood at the side and worked a brass stopcock covered in valves. He pointed at Nova and laughed. "Dare ye cross Nico's Nets? If ye's feeling cold, Nico will warm ye up." He scowled and turned one of the valves to release several gallons of lava into the front section of hollow netting. A Dutch guy, halfway through, turned and screamed. Nova saw his health score decrease from one hundred to zero in the space of a few seconds. His avatar flashed a few times before disappearing. "Nico warmed that gentleman up, though some might say a bit too much. Who's next?"

The mechanics of the game were obvious — when the nets were blue, they were safe to crawl under; when they were red, lava coursed through them. She watched a few more people attempt it, trying to discern any patterns or tricks. It took her a couple of minutes to work out a plan. She crawled halfway and paused. It looked safe — but she knew better than to continue. As expected, the old man turned the rusty valve on the far side of the stopcock. The netting in front of her turned red while Nico taunted some new arrivals behind her. When the netting ahead changed back to blue she scrambled like mad, and got through unscathed.

Just beyond the finishing line was a cube the size of her dad's shed. The sides looked like they were on fire. It was a Corona Cube, like the one she had entered back in Castalia. Cubes like it were scattered all over Solarversia and acted as safe houses that avatars could stay in when players wanted to log out. While she was there, nobody could do her wrong.

She stood in front of the cube and chewed on her lip. It had been such a long day, and after a couple of glasses of cider, she felt a bit dreamy. But it pained her to know that Burner and Sushi were further ahead than she was. And she wanted to pick up Flynn already. She volleyed her display back to the lounge for a second. Her mum had fallen asleep in her chair; her dad must have gone to bed.

Volleying back to Solarversia, she walked up to the cube and passed straight through one of its faces as it turned transparent, content to have completed the obstacle course. This was a year-long game, not a piddly game of Monopoly. A marathon, not a sprint.

Up in her room, Nova got into bed and lay awake for a while. Fragments of Solarversia were juxtaposed with pieces of reality. The gooey purple mess in the centre of the Magisterial Chamber was supposed to be the Emperor? She'd already lost a handful of health points? Images flickered in her mind: the flying palace, the lavadile snapping at her foot, her revision books.

The last image wouldn't budge. She only had three months until her exams, the ones that would determine the university she went to. If she made the grades she needed. They were exams that would affect the entire course her life, or so her teachers kept telling her. And now she knew something to be true, something she had hoped for, and dreaded, in equal measure. Solarversia was as addictive as she'd thought it would be.

Chapter Five

Nova hadn't eaten breakfast cereal in years, but she'd persuaded her mum to buy the box on the kitchen table because of the tie-in with Solarversia. It was corporate sponsorship deals like this that had enabled The Game to be offered for free. Companies had been given the opportunity to sponsor Gameworld quests, at a price determined by the quest's size, location and importance.

When asked in a poll, the majority of players had confirmed that the corporate sponsorship model was the preferred form of monetisation, over alternatives like 'pay-to-play'. Some companies had even won plaudits for the creative way in which they'd showcased their products and services in VR, and had plans to replicate them in the real world.

The company that made Flakeroonies had sponsored a large quest aboard the International Space Station, and their cereal boxes had reflected a space theme for the last few months. Prodding at the soggy flakes with her spoon, one leg hugged to her chest, Nova found her mind was still occupied with thoughts of the night before.

How would she find enough time for revision? She should breeze psychology, her best subject by far. But sociology and English? Not so much. She'd probably do what she always did — wing it — and without trying too hard, scrape into Hull University. But she never felt she'd had much chance of getting into Nottingham, where Burner was hoping to join his brother, Jono, and it was looking even less likely now The Game had begun. The truth was, revision held very little appeal compared to the excitement of the virtual world.

She flicked her Booners down and looked at the cereal packet. Flakes started to rise out of it as if magically unbound from gravity. When she touched them with her spoon they floated across the kitchen toward the fridge. If she flicked them they popped. Those she didn't jab, flick, poke or in some manner interfere with landed on the kitchen table, which, to Nova, looked like the cratered surface of the Moon.

An arkwini in a spacesuit poked his helmet round the side of the packet, twitched his little chimp nose a couple of times like he was sniffing out danger, and then scampered out from behind it, followed by several others. Each arkwini held a garden implement of sorts — a rake, hoe or mechanical blower — that they used to gather the fallen flakes into piles.

When the piles had grown large enough, another arkwini appeared, pushing a wheelbarrow, which he used to transport the flakes to the futuristic conveyor belt illustrated on the side on the box. He emptied the flakes onto the belt, which transported them to a fish tank where they were devoured by a twelve-armed octopus. Her goggles had transformed the kitchen table, and the objects on it, into a moving, living scene. This was augmented reality, a halfway house between boring, everyday consensual reality and the wild, anything-goes virtual kind.

Mr Negrahnu stood in the doorway, paper in hand, shaking his head while he observed his daughter prodding thin air and muttering to herself. "You do realise, love, that you're sitting there, talking to a box of cereal?"

Nova volleyed an eye back to the kitchen. "Morning, Dad. Floating Flakeroonies. I'm helping the arkwinis feed Banjax, the dodectopus. He gets hungry."

"Right. Course he does. Sorry to have interrupted you hard at work."

She flashed him a snarky smile. People who stuck with consensual reality through choice were either weird or old. Usually both.

"Feeding this Tampax creature, it counts towards your grades, does it?"

She had to force herself not to snap back at him. "We agreed that I could do what I want this weekend. My birthday, the start of Solarversia, remember? You just wait 'til Monday. My books won't know what hit 'em."

"You've seen this lot, I expect?" He gestured towards the TV. "That's what happens when people lose their jobs."

On the news, clips released by a terrorist organisation known as the Holy Order were playing. Footage of workers on assembly lines was spliced with scenes of robots doing similar work. Graphs displayed exponential increases in computing power, electronic memory, data transmission speeds, and a whole host of other variables over the last fifty years.

An image of a book entitled *The Sacred Singularity* appeared on the screen. Released by the Order a few months ago, it detailed their beliefs about artificial superintelligence: that it was on its way, that an 'unfriendly' version would spell the end of humanity and that the 'friendly' version they were working to develop would change everything for the better. Their manifesto made clear that everyone needed to join them in their endeavour, or face the consequences. No other method of evangelism was as compelling as bombs or guns, they claimed.

"You're not suggesting they're right?"

"I'm not suggesting anything. People lose jobs to robots and artificial what-nots, which means they can't support their families, so they get angry. As for this lot, God knows what they're harping on about with their 'singularity'. All this change is driving people mad. They don't know who they are any more. Without work to do they're losing their identities. That's all I'm saying."

After working for twenty-three years at the local medical centre, Mr Negrahnu had been made redundant. In all that time he'd never called in sick, and had only been off twice for compassionate leave, a day each for his parents' funerals. He'd been looking forward to the carriage clock employees got after twenty-five years. Not so much for the clock itself, but rather what it represented — his years of loyal service. Instead, he'd received fifteen minutes in a room with a new area head, half his age, and a stern-looking woman from HR. His job — to analyse scan results and medical images — could now be performed by an artificially intelligent program at a third of the cost.

"You know they're threatening to blow entire companies sky-high?" Nova asked.

"I don't agree with terrorism. I'm just saying that this is a direct consequence of millions of jobs being flushed down the bog." He shook his head, put his newspaper down on the table and ruffled her hair.

"Ugh, Dad, mind my barnet." She smoothed her hair back down and jabbed at another Flakeroony, which began to drift lazily, like a snowflake, onto the table. She watched it melt into the surface of the newspaper, which was open on the jobs' page. One or two ads had been circled in red pen; others had asterisks next to them. She read down the list. These were jobs way beneath her dad's abilities, jobs he never would have applied for earlier in his life.

The salaries advertised here didn't come close to what he'd been earning as a medical researcher. And he was a proud man. Everything he did, he did for the family, for her. And what did she know, at her age, having never had a proper job, not one that needed to support a family, nor one that had been replaced by a few lines of code? She averted her gaze, feeling like a spoilt child.

Her headset flashed with a message from Burner, "At Fragging Hell, where are you? Already rammed. Not many spaces left."

She flipped her Booners up and took her bowl of cereal to the sink. Now that was a better thought than these real-world concerns. Solarversia was calling.

***

"Are you ready, furball? Fragging Hell, here we come."

The furball was stowed in the passenger footwell of Nova's car, playing with the discarded plastic shell of a Kinder Surprise toy. He looked at Nova and made a clicking sound with his tongue. His name was Zhang, and her parents had given him to her on her 17th birthday. The tag on his ear identified him as a first generation Electropet, one modelled on the ring-tailed lemur.

Electropets were animatronic toys, designed to provide companionship to adults and children alike. Their features and movements were so realistic that it was hard to tell them apart from the real thing. At least, it was from a distance. Up close their mechanical joints were visible through their coats, as were their orange eyes, which doubled as cameras, and the tags on their ears.

Zhang had arrived with the standard factory settings. New owners were supposed to tinker around until they found a temperament that complemented their own. On day one Nova had ramped up his 'playful' setting to maximum and, deciding that he was perfect like that, hadn't changed him since.

Her Booners guided her all the way to a reserved space on the third floor of the Medway Street car park, then, with Zhang parked on her shoulder, she walked through town. When they arrived at Fragging Hell he hopped onto the side rail to join some other Electropets — a sloth he knew and two monkeys he hadn't met before. A couple approached the rail and took a selfie with him, before he took one with them. Nova loved getting home to find crazy pictures of him posing with random people. It was further proof that he lived his own little life.

She scanned the cafe for familiar faces. This place was her second home, always heaving with excitable gamers swapping war stories. Horrible paisley carpet and strips of fluorescent spot lighting separated banks of monitors and VR headsets. Not a single space was free, worse even than the usual midday Saturday crush because The Game had begun. The people she was here to see were likely to be found at the bar. She caught Jockey's eye and went over.

"Miss Negrahnu, a pleasure as always. Congratulations on the big one-eight for yesterday." Jockey wore one of his trademark vests, a knitted number with a diamond pattern that fitted snugly round his potbelly. He often stood with his hands on his stomach, as if he was subconsciously pulling it inward, though the effect actually made him look even more like Humpty Dumpty.

"Thanks, Jockey. I see my score still stands." She motioned to one of the overhead monthly leaderboard screens. Three weeks ago, on a wintry Monday night, she'd thrown the dart of her life, smashing the Kent bullseye record by 40 centimetres, and placing top in the 'Bullseye of the Month' competition.

"Bloody good throw it was, too."

"Do I get my prize today?"

"It's highly unlikely that anyone will beat it before the day's out, but no. I can't give that to you until February has officially come to end, including the cheeky leap day. But I do have something else for you; hang on a sec."

Jockey ducked behind the bar into the back, and Nova felt a hand clap her hard on the back.

"Happy birthday, punk. Bumped into any more lavadiles?" Burner said, trying to suppress a smile. With his plug ears and bulbous eyes, Nova was always astounded at his success with girls. He held a load of roasted peanuts in one hand, flicked them, one by one, into the air with the other, caught them in his mouth, sucked the roasting clean off and spat the naked nuts into the bin at the side of the bar.

"That, as I tell you every time I see you do it, is a disgusting habit. And no, I haven't bumped into any more lavadiles. Why, have you bumped into any more Krazy Karting finalists?"

Along with thousands of other games, Krazy Karting had been ported across to VR, enabling its inclusion in Solarversia as one of its many sub-games. It was Nova's favourite racing game and her rank in the top few hundred players in the world had meant automatic qualification in one of ten preliminary rounds.

After a shaky start in her heat last month, when her main rival, Dutch sensation Jools van der Star, had mashed her into the hoardings at the side of the track, she'd made an inspired comeback, racing her way through the pack to qualify in tenth place. Although her time had been poor, placing her in 77th out of the hundred finalists, she'd done it, and was in with a chance of winning the hundred grand first prize.

"Tell it to my hundred health points."

"Yeah, I don't know how you managed that. And as for Sushi, well, I can't even."

"Believe it, Scotia. Plenty more where that came from."

She grimaced as Burner upended the packet of peanuts, tipped the remnants into his mouth, and then licked the packet clean. She'd spent an increasing amount of time with him since Sushi's move to Seattle and had become good mates with him. He was funny, dependable and loyal, but also way more gross than Sushi ever was. Jockey returned with his hands behind his back. "I have not one, but two presents for you."

"Two presents?"

"First of all, here's a coupon for a drink on the house. You can use it whenever you like."

"Thanks, Jockey. Much appreciated."

"And then there's this."

She opened the card that he handed her and read the note inside. "Sorry I couldn't be there for your big day, have fun without me. Sushi, aka your Solarversia Sister."

Nova twitched her nose a couple of times before turning to Burner. "Awesome. Ten hours of prepaid time on the deluxe gaming chairs. Wanna watch the Queen of Darts on her throne?"

Fragging Hell's side room had been kitted out by Spiralwerks, which was affiliated with gaming cafes and sports centres all over the world. It now had five state-of-the-art gaming simulators, deluxe models known as 'the chairs', available for hire at triple the rate of a standard rig.

Burner wiped the peanut dust from his hands, gave her the finger, and followed her there.

Chapter Six

Nova handed her jacket to Burner, took a deep breath, and patted her T-shirt down. Slightly faded due to the countless times she'd worn it, the T-shirt displayed the slogan SOLOS FTW. The word 'Solo' had been appropriated by fanatical players of Solarversia to describe themselves. Similar to the word 'solar', it also played on The Game's tagline, There Can Be Only One. The second word, 'FTW', was the old internet acronym 'For the Win'. The phrase communicated the common belief that while it was theoretically possible for anyone to win, it would most likely be a Solo, someone dedicated to studying the Gameworld and all it entailed.

The deluxe chairs were positioned on pneumatic arms capable of tilting thirty degrees in any direction. Joysticks were situated at the end of each armrest, and the footrest had pedals that made avatars run, jump, roll and drive. Nova climbed into the chair and flipped down the built-in headset, which had a technical spec that could induce drooling in the most hardened of gamers. In front of each chair was an industrial fan, which activated at pertinent moments.

She entered Solarversia for the second time. The Corona Cube was unchanged, though the resolution of the headset, which was even better than her new Booners, made the plasma effect on the walls look more real, and more mesmerising. She had to make a conscious effort to turn her attention to the constellations on the ceiling. As her finger touched the last star, the plasma walls turned transparent to reveal the very spot on Alpha Island she had left the previous night.

She exited the cube and checked the map. In order to properly explore the world, she'd need her vehicles, starting with Flynn. Cars were stored at the garage, on the other side of the Forest of Fun, just over a minute away at her current running speed of one percent. In other words, a snail's pace. As soon as she completed some more quests her speed would shoot up. In the meantime she ambled toward the forest, her chair rocking in time as she moved. It sure beat sitting on the sofa at home.

Around her thousands of avatars were headed in the same direction, running, shouting and jostling for position. Some of them, like her, were using their Normal Avatars, the ones created by scanning the real-world head and body of the player with a camera. Nova had updated hers several times since her final sleepover at Sushi's, most recently in December, after a rigorous month-long exercise regime.

The Normal Avatar transformed into the player's Super Avatar as the year progressed. The player didn't need to do anything to make the transformation happen — it occurred automatically, through a series of indistinguishable changes that were applied each day they were still in The Game.

Nova hadn't done anything too radical with her Super Avatar. She'd added a couple of inches to her height, toned up here and there, and performed a spot of minor plastic surgery on her avatar's neck and nose, but it was nothing compared to the people who would transform into cats, dogs, and all manner of weird and wonderful beings if they lived long enough.

Bobbing alongside the Normal Avatars were a smattering of Generic Avatars, ones players could switch on to hide their everyday appearance. These avatars, whose male and female versions had come to be known as 'Marty' and 'Smarty', looked like plastic Duplo figures, and were identical to one another.

Players were constantly speculating as to which celebrities were masquerading as Marties and Smarties, although they were also used by people who didn't want to have to confront the realities of their body in their moments of escape, and also by people who simply fancied being anonymous for a while.

Nova pulled down the stats feed in her visor to check the latest figures. More than ten million people had now left Castalia and were somewhere within the confines of Solarversia. A guy from Chile appeared beside her as she ran and held out his hand for a high-five. "Hey, Nova, we're both in ring 359." Staring at his head for half a second caused his profile square to appear hovering above him, a feature that players could turn off and on at will. Scanning its contents, she saw that he was right: his grid shortcode was S359, meaning his square was located in the Spades quadrant in the top right of the Player's Grid.

The high-five unlocked one of the items on her March Bucket List, a feature created by Spiralwerks to help ensure that The Game was fair. Each month had an associated list of actions players needed to perform. A life was automatically lost if the list wasn't completed by the end of the month. It deterred people from spending the whole year hiding out in their Corona Cube. Any Bucket items ticked off on the Leap Day automatically rolled into the March list.

When she made it to the forest, her headset chimed again: another item ticked off the Bucket List. Despite the crowd of avatars, there was an eerie quiet in the woods, punctuated by the snapping of twigs, the rustling of trees in the wind, and the occasional sound of laughter. The leaves on the trees contained jokes that had been submitted by players.

She looked skyward, held out her palm, and caught one as it floated toward the ground. "I organised a threesome last night. There were a couple of no-shows, but I still had fun."The 'ta dum tss' sound of a rimshot went off as she read the last word. She shared the joke on her feed, resulting in another tick on the Bucket List, and four additional points on her speed. All too easy.

She brushed past the last couple of ferns and found herself in a clearing. A large tyre, which bore the words 'The Greasy Wrench' around its circumference, was propped against three stacked cars. Behind it was a multistorey garage made of thousands of square bays, where cars were being jacked-up, spray-painted or waxed by a multitude of arkwinis. According to her datafeed, nearly sixteen thousand players were currently collecting their rides. That was a lot of grease.

An arkwini in dirty overalls and a matching cap waddled up to her. Speaking in a high-pitched voice, he said, "Hello, Nova, you must be here to collect Flynn. Follow me, please." He bowed, and then toddled off without waiting for a reply. She caught up with him and joined him in a battered metal cage attached to the side of the building.

"Your player number, please," he said, motioning toward a sturdy black box affixed to the front on the cage. As she went to punch in her digits, a disembodied voice chanted, "We really wanna see those fingers!"

She had Catchphrases switched on, which meant that specific movements, actions and behaviours were greeted by recorded phrases that The Game's algorithms deemed relevant. Players could provide feedback on catchphrases, add them to their favourites or select them to sound at given moments. In this way they acted like an in-Game user-generated commentary. She punched her digits in and the cage shuddered into motion, climbing the side of the building. She leaned over the side to look down on Alpha Island, shaped like a capital 'A'.

The track she'd raced in the Karting heats traced the shoreline. She could see the roundabout where she'd pulled off the Wall of Death stunt, the Fire Demon's Obstacle Course, and the Forest of Fun. Above her, Castalia floated high in the sky. As far as her brain was concerned, she was here, in Solarversia, rather than a gaming cafe in the real world, a concept the VR geeks referred to as Presence, the illusion that a mediated experience was real. Whatever you called it, she was fully immersed and loving it.

The cage slowed to a halt beside a bay that matched her player number. She smiled at the gleaming car within, one she'd spent many hours customising. Although she'd used him for the Karting heats before The Game had even begun, and raced in him regularly, it was still exciting to officially collect him like this.

"Good to see you, Flynn, old buddy, this time for real. Kind of real, anyway." She held out a hand and stroked his bonnet. Flynn was a dune buggy. A bare chassis exposed his motor, lots of wiring and some fat suspension. The flaming artwork that adorned each side proclaimed Doors Are for Bores. Holding onto the chassis, she swung herself into the driving seat and gripped the steering wheel tight, impatient to get going already. The arkwini toddled up to her, clipboard in hand.

"A few things before you get on your way. Speed. Although you only start with one point, for every ten miles you drive without incident, you'll gain a point. Navigation. Once on the road it's impossible to get lost, just consult your Route Planner. The exit. You've been credited with a Turbo Boost. Use it." He kicked the front tyre and inspected the chassis. "OK, you're good to go."

As she grabbed the twin joysticks, a stereophonic collection of voices chanted, "Ladies and gentlemen, start your engines!"

Flynn growled into life. The wall in front of her swung down to create a ramp and the turbo boost icon started flashing. Accelerating from nought to sixty in half a second, she hit the ramp at speed, cruised through the air and landed on the open road of Alpha Island, calling "Yeeee-ha!" In Fragging Hell, the fan blasted her with air.

Within a few seconds the Route Planner menu appeared in her headset, exactly like the arkwini had said it would. She could input how much time she had available, and which Bucket List items she wanted to tick off. It would combine that information with her current speed score, and the items she owned, to suggest some optimal routes. She chose a route through Lotus Bay, the town that ran along the eastern edge of the island.

The seafront was lined with hundreds of exhibitions and mini-quests, enough entertainment for the entire year. The first exhibit on the route, Conga World, was dedicated to creating the world's longest virtual conga line. It was a hectic flurry of confusing movement as members swerved one way, then the other, kicking their legs out to their sides as they congaed along the coast, their hovering profile squares jigging along in time. The exhibition's datafeed was being constantly updated itself as new players joined the end, and others, somewhere in the middle, dropped out.

As she viewed Conga World's billboard, the exhibition's starting point and virtual homepage, it updated to display information relevant to her. It told her that GoodGert from Namibia — player 23,154,832, who held the record for longest time at the front of the line — was only seventeen squares from her on the Player's Grid. The Russian guy who had just this second joined the back of the line? Only ten squares from Burner. It was a small world, the Solarverse; a frothing sea of happy coincidences and shared relationships.

Nova joined the line and tried to look as cool as possible while doing such an inherently stupid dance. When she left the line she was rewarded with topped-up speed and her first teleport token. Hearing the dinging sounds that accompanied these updates reminded her of the joy she used to feel as a young child, dropping coins into her piggy bank. Further progress. Sweet.

Instead of rushing to do something else straight away, she took a moment to take everything in. There was activity anywhere she cared to look, a sea of pulsing, throbbing motion so intense it felt quite dizzying. Even the ground she stood on — an object so dull and lifeless in the real world — was animated in a way that made it look like it possessed consciousness. The tessellated hexagons changed colour as she trod on them, and, as her datafeed now informed her, had also been programmed to react to certain commands.

She dragged her foot along like she was collecting autumn leaves and watched a wave of colour fan out from under her until it met hues flowing in the opposite direction, kicked, scuffed or punted by another player. The colours collided, rebounding and fracturing into a dozen new streams, giving rise to a chorus of chimes and jingles.

As she stared at the ground in awe, wishing pavements were like it for real, the datafeed informed her about several dozen variations of hopscotch that could be played, as well as a rumour — which had gone viral two hours ago — that certain combinations unlocked prizes. She found a list of patterns that were affiliated with charities and picked one.

Tapping out the sequence unlocked a red cross and sounded a jingle — the company sponsoring the pattern had just donated ten pence to the British Red Cross. There were thousands of partnerships like it across the Gameworld, and exercises varied in complexity. Small tasks like that one were usually linked to minor monetary contributions, but she'd heard of other ventures that required a lot more commitment.

A short way in front of her, a couple were gazing upwards, pointing and smiling. The sky was violet, rather than blue, and cast a surreal, diffuse glow over the land. Following their line of sight, she quickly spotted what they were looking at — giant puffs of white cloud, shaped like faces. Far beyond them, numerous aircraft — miniscule from her vantage point on the ground — performed aerobatics, looping, rolling and spinning.

"Did you get your plane yet?" the guy called out to her.

"I only got my car a short while ago," she said with a proud nod in Flynn's direction.

"You'll need to do fifty miles without crashing before you can collect your boat from Dockingtons. Once you have your boat, you'll be able to cruise to Tristan da Cunha to collect your plane. If you can complete the flying sequences, you can make a cloud in the shape of your face. The one that drifts furthest wins a prize!"

Nova smiled. She thought of herself as a Solarversia expert, yet the world was so large and complex that she learned something new about it all the time. She focused on the exhibitions around her again and plumped for one she'd heard lots about: the Tweel of Fate. As she crossed its boundary, the players around her disappeared. It was a phased zone; numerous people could inhabit it simultaneously, but it would appear to them that they were there alone.

Like Corona Cubes and Teleport Machines, Tweels of Fate were everywhere. They were modelled on Banjax the Dodectopus, and looked like the kind of roundabout you might find in a children's playground.

Nova grabbed hold of the tentacle nearest to her — which, rather than tapering to a point, ended in a bulbous sphere — and gave it a big push.

The Tweel spun round its axis for ten seconds or so, then came to a shuddering rest. The turquoise tentacle that landed closest to her began to squirm and writhe, like it been rudely awoken, and then looked up at her. Its spherical end, which had the face of a wizened old man, opened its puckered mouth and spoke.

"Your fate for today is to receive three teleport tokens. Use them wisely." The tokens registered immediately in her headset, while the tentacle lowered its face and solidified once more. It wasn't a bad outcome for her very first twist of fate .

Pleased with her progress, and keen not to use too much of her birthday credit in one go, she volleyed an eye back to Fragging Hell and glanced around until she spotted Burner back in the main room hunkering over a plate of a chips and a burger. Realising that she was pretty hungry too, she located the nearest Corona Cube, logged out, and sauntered over to join him.

"I picked up Flynn, a handful of speed points and four teleport tokens. Pretty good, huh?"

"Still miles behind me then. Not that a mere mortal like yourself should ever compare themselves to the Master of the Solarverse."

"Whatever; it's a marathon, not a sprint," she said, trying hard to feign nonchalance. "How's your revision going, anyway?"

"Maths and further maths should be alright. I could probably do computer studies with my hands tied behind my back. Electronics is awesome — did I tell you, Jono's asked me to send him the aerial drone I built for my coursework, reckons his professor wants to take a look? Physics, on the other hand. Don't talk to me about bloody physics. What about you?"

"Let's just say I'm doing enough to get a place at Hull. Nottingham's looking unlikely. Sometimes I wish I was a total geek like you. Although revision's a bit overrated, don't you think?"

A better poker player than Burner would have spotted her bluff a mile off — the brush of the hair behind her ears, the lack of eye contact, and the try-hard laugh. She hadn't even opened her books.

Chapter Seven

Arty looked down at the sword in his hands. He loved the way that the jewels in its handle sparkled; sometimes he thought he'd like to own one for real. It was an item known as the Sword of Sadism, and as one of the most powerful objects within Solarversia, only a few hundred of them would ever be in circulation at any one time.

He moved his thumb from the yellow topaz up to the blood-red ruby, circled it back across the string of pearls and ended up on the pink sapphire. This was the combination that initiated the weapon's power move, the one that could defeat the toughest of monsters.

As his thumb came to rest on the sapphire, the jewels glistened brighter and a melody played. Now the sword moved, rotating Arty's avatar on the spot until he became a human whirlwind. When he finally came to rest he gave a series of commands that allowed him to enter third-person perspective so that he could watch his avatar perform the move in front of his eyes. He knelt down and studied the power move from below, zooming in and out, cocking his head to one side or the other.

He removed his goggles and found himself back in the office. Twirling a clump of shaggy hair round his finger, he pondered the problem. Something looked wrong with the whirlwind from that angle — it looked more like a grey fuzzy beard than a scary tornado — but he struggled to explain how it was occurring. A bug in the code had been raised by the tech team a few days after the start of The Game and now, having been fixed, it sat with Arty for sign-off.

The feeling that players were *present* within the Gameworld was all-important to Spiralwerks — it was small glitches like this that gave the game away, and as Creative Director, as well as the CEO, it was Arty's ultimate responsibility to sign off everything in it. The original glitch was definitely smoothed out, but something still wasn't quite right.

He saw one of the guys in the technical team frantically wave in his direction and headed over. A minor problem like the strange-looking whirlwind could always wait. The team were crowded round Carl Stedman, the company's Chief Technical Officer, who looked and sounded extremely stressed as he ran through a checklist.

"Carl. Guys. What's the problem?"

"We're being griefed. It's a big attack. About thirty minutes ago the surveillance team received an alert highlighting a potential traffic issue at Ripley's Junction on Alpha Island. A group of players arrived there around the same time and parked their cars bumper-to-bumper, hemming in thousands of others. The players who parked their cars got out of them, joined Conga World, and haven't been seen since."

Griefing was the gaming equivalent of trolling, an activity whose reward lay in the frustration of others. Griefers, usually organised in clans, harassed other players and sought to exploit aspects of the Gameworld in ways unintended by the designers. As quickly as the engineers came up with ways to block them, they would pop up to cause havoc somewhere else.

Arty put on his goggles and circled Ripley's Junction from above, surveying the scene like he was in a helicopter.

"Those tailbacks go on for miles. Do we know how many players have been caught up in it?"

Carl jutted his jaw out and scratched his tightly curled brown beard. The dark bags under his eyes were a permanent feature of his face, making him look like he hadn't slept in over a week.

"Fifteen thousand at the last count. Players are going mental on social media, as you might imagine."

"Who's responsible?"

"Nobody's owned up yet. Some of the usual suspects have gone online to declare their innocence."

"So what are our options? We need to act before it escalates any further."

"Depends how organic we want the solution to be. We could zap everyone to the nearest Corona Cube. But it's difficult to tell without further analysis which players were part of the original attack. It looks like loads of people got caught up in it, and have left their vehicles in frustration. If they're in the middle of a quest, about to win a special item, and we mess with them, the fallout will be awful. If we go for a totally organic solution, like sending arkwinis out in tow trucks, it could take half a day to clear up."

Arty removed the goggles, gazed at a sign above one of the workstations, which read 'The Only Good Bug Is a Dead Bug', and sighed. Why couldn't people play nicely?

"OK, listen. I've got another meeting starting now. Ideally I'd like this dealt with using organic methods. Set up roadblocks to prevent the problem spreading. Get every spare arkwini on the case. And offer some small incentive for players to get to a Corona Cube of their own accord. Get one of your guys to ping me a report every fifteen minutes; we'll play it by ear."

Arty strolled to the lift checking his emails in his glasses. Before the lift doors could close he heard Hannah McCreadie calling his name. Looking flushed and sounding out of breath, she held a hand to her chest while she spoke.

"Thanks for holding the door, Arty. Something urgent has come up."

"The griefing? I know, I was with the team just a second ago."

"No, it's worse than that. It's about the Holy Order. MI6 have been in touch, the threat level has been upgraded to 'substantial'. That means, and I quote, 'An attack is a strong possibility'."

Arty's upper body slumped an inch forward like somebody had just powered him off. Being attacked in the game world felt hard enough. Having MI6 involved took it to a whole new level. The questions he had asked himself a hundred times reared their ugly heads in his mind again. Who the hell were the Holy Order? And why were Spiralwerks top of their corporate hit list?

***

The scenery hadn't changed much in the last couple of hours, but Casey couldn't get enough of it. He'd lived in the same tired city his whole life, where he'd fed his eyes on a diet of scrappy billboards and stark grey buildings. Out here in the heart of the Mississippi Delta, a place of peace and serenity, the air was so luscious that every breath was a treat.

Save for the occasional alligator, he and Wallace, in their kayaks, seemed to be the only things that moved. Right now his only problem was his hands, which throbbed after several hours of paddling upstream. His initiation ceremony ten days earlier was a distant memory. It felt so far in the past already that whenever his bones ached and his muscles spasmed he had to remind himself why.

Wallace turned to Casey and pointed the way, then changed course to glide past some creepers that hid a narrow channel from the main tributary. The men continued for some way, through vines and past bushes, steering a path that Casey knew he'd be incapable of retracing even if his life depended on it, until finally they drifted into a clearing.

"It's something, ain't it?" Wallace said, noticing his companion's dazed look. "Took us years to build, and it ain't even finished, not close. Welcome to the Compound."

Rising out of the swampland was a village on stilts, formed of a series of camouflaged buildings and wooden gangways that blended uncannily into their environment. They pulled up beside a steel ladder affixed to a small jetty. Casey used it to steady himself while he scanned the surrounding bogs. In the background an army of spring peepers emitted their sleigh-bell-like chorus.

"Do you ever get used to the mosquitoes?" he asked, slapping his arm for the umpteenth time.

"After a while they bother you less, but I'll get you some spray."

They climbed the ladder and helped each other drag the kayaks onto the jetty. Wallace pulled a pack of Chesterfields out of his jeans and sparked one up with a flick of his golden Zippo before continuing the tour. "The layout isn't as confusing as it looks: it consists of four buildings and the Sub. You see that camouflaged marquee? That's the Ceremonial Lodge, reserved for special occasions. The grey building in the corner is known as the Workshop, the place we build and repair stuff. The long building with the round windows is called Control House. It's kind of like the nerve centre of the organisation. In all there's over a thousand of us, in twenty different countries, spread around the world."

"It's a global network then?"

"Yessir. And growing fast. Intelligent folk — like yourself — know we're on to something. Mankind's about to lose its place at the top of the food chain. There's no harm in having a little respect for the beings that are going to replace us. You made the right decision by joining us, put it that way."

Casey grinned at him. The past year was full of bad decisions. It felt good to know that he was finally making some good ones.

"The other building you can see is the Lockup. Let's stash the kayaks there, and then I'll show you to your bunk."

Casey slung his sack of possessions behind his back, used his chin to clamp it against his shoulder, and then pulled the kayak behind him with trembling arms. Their morning had begun at 5:00 a.m. with the smell of coffee boiling over kerosene, and though Wallace had encouraged him to rest for days, he felt exhausted. The thought that there was a bunk somewhere for him gave him the strength to keep going.

When they got to the Lockup, Wallace held his thumb up to the small metal box at the side of the door. A beep preceded the thunking noise of several bolts releasing. Wallace swung the doors back and fastened them open on little hooks. Casey took a couple of steps backward, his eyes bulging at the sight of row upon row of automatic weapons stacked on the shelves within.

"That's quite some arsenal you've got there. Are we expecting visitors?"

"Expecting? No. We're like the good ol' Boy Scouts of 'Merica. We like bein' prepared is all." Wallace blew a smoke ring and flashed his yellow grin.

"What about those?" Casey said, nodding at the row of humanoid robots that lined the wall. "Are they in the Boy Scouts too?"

"Those are some of Father's toys. Programmed them himself. They were designed to specialise in one or more tasks. The grimy one at the end's a submersible. You can slip on a headset and work on the underwater sections of the Compound from the comfort of Control House. The blue ones in the middle are Medibots. They assist Mother when she operates on people. And the beige ones are general-purpose robots, mainly used for heavy lifting and landscaping."

He motioned for Casey to secure his kayak against the side of the hut. Casey followed his friend's lead, lifting the craft into place on the rack and tying it against the wall, aware the whole time of the assortment of ordnance behind him. Just as he thought they were done, Wallace stopped and bowed reverentially. Casey turned to find Mother Frances standing in the doorway, a kind smile on her face. His saviour.

"Mother, you remember Casey Brown, the new recruit. We only just got here after spending a few days at the safe house while he recovered. Father's asked that I show him the ropes."

She stared deep into Casey's eyes. It was a look that made him feel wanted, loved even.

"Welcome to the Sub, Casey Brown. I'm pleased to see you again. Everybody here has been through the ordeal on the hill. It was designed to push humans to their absolute limit, to break them mentally, physically and spiritually. And some people don't complete it. It looks cruel and unnecessary to the ignorant mind. Wiser souls know that it illuminates the limitations and fallibility of the human condition. If Father was to attempt the challenge now, he would complete it with ease and in a fraction of the time. Those that join the Order need to be willing to give everything to the cause."

Casey thought back to the dark time in his life, a time when he had come close to ending it all. That he hadn't done so, that he was here now, was all thanks to the two people in front of him. He owed them everything and wanted to wrap his arms around them and squeeze them tight. Instead, he fumbled for words.

"Yes ma'am, that's me. Dedicated, I mean, willing to give my all."

"I'm glad to hear that. Father has important plans for you. I wouldn't want to see you let him down. And while you're here, you can call me Mother."

She nodded her head and was gone. Casey quickly mimicked Wallace's bow, conscious of being the new guy, the one with everything to learn.

"Don't be fooled by her size. I've seen Mother Frances pick up a kayak, put it on her back and jog from one end of the Compound to the other. She's also one of the best surgeons in the country."

"Frances — Mother — mentioned that some people fail to complete the initiation. What happens to them?"

Wallace sighed heavily. "The ones who don't make it, don't make it at all. We've only had two people fail, and both times, it broke my heart. As the guy in charge of initiation ceremonies I have the grim job of disposing of the bodies. I did everything I could to help them, save carrying the net of rocks for them. When it happened the first time I tried to persuade Father to make an exception, you know, by giving them an office job or something." Wallace paused to dig some grime out from under a fingernail but looked to be deep in thought. "Let's just say that that didn't go down too well. Come on, it's time I showed you the Sub. When we get to the gangways, make sure you hold on tight. Otherwise you'll end up as 'gator feed, understand?"

Casey nodded his agreement, swung the sack back over his shoulder and did his best to ignore the midges that landed on his face, spitting out those that made it into his mouth. When they reached the rickety walkway, he used his free hand to grasp at branches and carefully placed his feet where he'd seen Wallace tread. After a couple of minutes they arrived at a dense thicket of bald cypresses that looked, to Casey, like any other. Wallace flicked the butt of his cigarette at the nearest peeper.

"Damn frogs won't shut up this time of year."

He reached past a group of branches and yanked on something behind them. A door swung open to reveal a spiral staircase that seemed to descend into the swamp itself.

"Old narco sub. Father Theodore discovered it years ago. Hope you ain't claustrophobic."

Casey rapped on the door with his knuckles. Its dull thud suggested the metal was several inches thick. He followed Wallace down the stairs, hunching as he went, and paused at the bottom to look down the long, narrow corridor that stretched ahead. It would barely allow two men to squeeze past one another, and the ceiling, not much higher than his head, was lowered even further by a series of dim light bulbs hanging from a length of chicken wire. The walls were lined with pistons, metal steering wheels and broken pressure gauges, mementos from a former life. Halfway along the corridor, a cylindrical metal object hung down from the ceiling, flanked by two small bars.

"Go on. I know you want to. You can't see too much, mind."

Casey grabbed the bars either side of the periscope, rested his head against the worn rubber that surrounded the eyepiece and spied the top of the Ceremonial Lodge beyond the trees.

"You're looking at the way we came into the Compound — the *only* way. The entire perimeter is booby-trapped to high hell, so don't try going off on your own."

The end of the corridor led to a room of bunks, each one narrower than Casey's childhood bed. "This is for us guys, the women are up the other end. Stash your clothes at the end of your bunk for now. There's a sink in the cupboard, use the water from the tanks above it. Take a few minutes to get acquainted with your new home. Then there's work to do."

Chapter Eight

Nova stood by the platform gate at St Pancras railway station and cursed Burner under her breath. She hated being late. If Sushi was the yin to her yang, Burner was the chalk to her cheese.

"If he doesn't get here in approximately three—" she started saying to herself, and then, with a frantic wave, "Burner — over here. Burner, you boggle-eyed twat!"

She lowered her voice as a woman with young children strolled by. They ran to the nearest door, edged their way up the train to their carriage and then fell into their seats panting as the whistle blew, Burner's cheeks red as snooker balls.

"Why do you always do that to me?"

"Like to keep you on your toes is all," he said, still catching his breath. "Did you hear about Arkwal's parachute — the one he used to slow himself down?"

"No. What about it?"

"Some dude from Australia found it. Instead of sailing to Tristan da Cunha to get his plane like the rest of us, he went in search of it. Found it and won himself ten grand. Just like that."

"Son of a Gunter! Why didn't we think of that?" Prizes were being won all over the place, for all kinds of things. Several people had won prizes for unlocking hopscotch patterns in the tessellated tiles on the ground. A woman from Uzbekistan had won five grand just yesterday for spinning a Tweel of Fate in a certain way, like it was the combination dial on a safe: twenty-nine rotations clockwise, two anticlockwise, twenty clockwise, dialling out the date The Game had started, the 29th February 2020. And now, ten large ones had been paid out to the person who found a discarded piece of nylon in the ocean. What else might she have missed? She looked out the window as the train jolted into motion.

"Did I tell you Jono's latest theory? Reckons there's an EFF switch at the North Pole."

"No offense, but your brother's hardly the most reliable source of information. Wasn't he the one who reckoned you could get additional spins of the Tweel of Fate if you chanted 'Solarversia' three times into one of the tentacles? What a wally."

"You were the wally who tried it."

EFF was the abbreviation for the Earth Force Field, the mechanism preventing players from exploring the rest of the Solar System. Ten switches were hidden at different locations on Earth, with a £100k bounty attached to each of them. Once all ten had been triggered the field would turn off, enabling players to travel to the International Space Station, where they'd be able to board spaceships to the moon and beyond.

The EFF was also the cause of Solarversia's warm violet light. As the power of a Force Field wore off, its glow cycled through the colours of the rainbow, from violet through to red, before disappearing entirely. Triggering the EFF switches would cause the light of the whole sky to change colour, a signal of epic proportions that solar travel had edged that bit closer.

Nova logged on and prepared to rejoin the game world where she had left it — in New York. She'd collected Bruno, her hovercraft from the Lotus Bay dockyard, and then sailed to Tristan da Cunha, the closest island, to get Hawk, her biplane. She'd always wanted to visit The Big Apple, and Solarversia offered the additional thrill of landing her plane in Central Park. But as she entered the Corona Cube, she noticed something different about the ceiling. There was an additional constellation between the previously existing two.

"Hey, Burner. Have you seen this? The Telescopium Constellation in the Corona Cube?"

"Oh yeah, that's new. It definitely wasn't there last night. Shall we check it out?"

She traced the stars with her finger and the Corona Cube melted away to reveal a huge domed room bustling with other players and arkwinis. Arkwal was standing on a bench at the side of the room, leaning on his telescope like it was a walking stick, in a pale blue suit decorated with hundreds of white question marks.

"Welcome to Castalia," he said. "Nothing like it exists on Earth, nor could it, given your current level of technological development. Are you ready for your grand tour? You've already seen the Magisterial Chamber, the cubic room that forms the core of the palace. Affixed to each of its six faces is a hemispherical dome. We're in the Overdome, the topmost hemisphere, which is the arkwinis' living quarters. So, welcome to their humble abode."

The arkwinis and all the other members of Emperor Mandelbrot's entourage were Non-Player Characters, controlled by artificial intelligence rather than any employee of Spiralwerks. Players could interact with them to a degree, as long as the topic of conversation remained within the realm of the Game. They were remarkably advanced, Nova thought. She would sometimes forget she was talking to a program — a few hundred lines of code — rather than a sentient life form.

Nova glanced around her. One edge of the dome was lined with dozens of teleport machines that seemed to be constantly in use, beaming arkwinis into, or out of, existence. She loved how they weren't quite tall enough to reach the teleporters' keypads and had to climb up the handles of the machines, cling on with their tails and swing down towards the keypads with their long fingers outstretched.

"The first stop on the tour is the dormitory, just beyond the dining area. Some of the little ones will be asleep, so keep the noise down."

The group followed Arkwal's lead into the dorm and assembled along the foot of the longest bed Nova had ever seen. Tucked inside its duvet were dozens of snoring arkwinis.

"As the General Manager of Castalia, I run a tight ship. Or, perhaps that should be, tight palace. There's a lot of work for us to do around here. Emperor Mandelbrot's Magisterial Chamber contains ten thousand square metres of marble to keep clean. Those vines are a nightmare for dusting. That job alone keeps thirty arkwinis busy round the clock. The surface architecture of Castalia is based on an intricate fractal pattern — designed, I might add, by the Emperor himself — and stretches over many, many square miles. It's tiring work, keeping the place clean year round. Which brings us to this," he said, motioning to the bed. The mattress was shaped like a caterpillar track on the side of an army tank. At each end of the bed the mattress curved back round on itself, creating an elongated oval shape. Dozens of wheels kept the mattress slowly rolling around the oval.

"The beds here are as long as a bowling alley and sleep up to fifty arkwinis at any one time. To ensure we're as efficient as possible, we use Sleep-a-nator machines. When an arkwini has finished his shift, had something to eat, and is ready for bed, all he needs to do is walk into one of those machines at the far end of the bed, the one with the big 'S' painted on its side, and the machine will do the rest. It's best to see one in action. Ingenious they are. You there. Yes, you. In the machine."

An arkwini, who'd been eating his lunch in peace, started to remonstrate, then, thinking better of it, reluctantly put down his sandwich. The machine looked like an airport-security metal detector, but instead of beeping when it detected its occupant, it seemed to come alive. Mechanical arms and hands appeared and stripped the arkwini of his clothes, squirted him with soap and water, scrubbed him down, and passed him underneath a fierce blower to dry him. Then it dressed him in a pair of pyjamas, brushed his teeth and gave him a little pat to send him on his way.

Calmly, the arkwini stepped out of the Sleep-a-nator and joined his colleagues in the oversized bed. At the other end, the mattress was wrapping back around on itself, while the end of the duvet was being lifted off the bed by another pair of mechanical hands. An arkwini who had been sound asleep plopped off the end and landed on a crash mat. He stood up, yawned, stretched his arms, and walked towards another machine, which had a large 'W' on its side.

"The Wake-a-nator?" one of the tour group ventured.

"That's it, well done. I thought you lot looked brighter than the average group. Between them, these two machines save us thirteen minutes a day per arkwini. And with thousands of arkwinis aboard at any one time, well, you do the math."

Nova watched the little arkwini who had just been readied for bed. She felt quite tender towards him, the way he put his head on the pillow, sighed with a sleepy smile, and fell fast asleep, despite the fact that he'd only been halfway through lunch when his day was brought to an end.

It was details like these — the way in which arkwinis genuinely seemed to lead their own lives, eating, sleeping and working — that helped immerse players in the Gameworld, engaging them on an emotional level and encouraging them to explore the rich, layered backstories of its peculiar inhabitants.

Nova was so intent on the little rise and fall of the arkwini's chest and the room's quiet snore that she failed to notice Burner creeping up behind her. He barged into her with his shoulder, aiming her at the Wake-a-nator. She staggered toward the machine, trying hard to retain her balance.

"You, miss. What do you think you're doing? Stop right there. You're not asleep, you stupid girl, you don't need wake-a-nating. I command you to stop right now."

Before she could stop, six pairs of mechanical arms and hands sprang to life and dragged her, screaming, into the machine. They brushed her teeth with vigour, pulled a comb through her hair and splashed water on her face. She couldn't help laughing when little puffs of perfumed air blew in her face to dry her, and was almost enjoying the experience when she realised that the machine would at any second try to undress her of her 'pyjamas' and put her in an arkwini uniform. There was no way she was going to allow her avatar a moment of nudity in front of this lot. She slipped down to her knees and crawled forward on her belly until she was out of the machine and out of harm's way.

"That was *not*," Arkwal said, "part of the tour. I don't know why I bother sometimes, I really don't. You wait until the Emperor hears about this. He's deducted health points from players in the past, you realise? It certainly wasn't *my* fault, that much is clear."

He stopped muttering, patted his suit down and then turned toward the group in an officious manner.

"Right then, it's time for the next part of the tour. We're heading through the skylight over there. No dillydallying at the back. And certainly no playing the fool," he added with a glare in Nova's direction. The group followed Arkwal out of the skylight and assembled around him on the roof of the cube.

"Earlier I mentioned the structure of Castalia, and the fact that abutting each face of the Magisterial Chamber there is a large hemisphere. The architecture of the palace is based on fractal geometry. On each of the six hemispheres are six smaller hemispheres, and from each of those, six even smaller hemispheres blossom. This regression continues indefinitely; hence its fractal nature. It's the six large hemispheres that you need to know about. We were just inside the one on the roof — the Overdome. Next we're going to investigate the Eastdome."

Arkwal got the tour group to line up along the edge of the roof, which looked down on Alpha Island, from here a dining-plate sized 'A' in the middle of the Atlantic Ocean. He stood at one end of the line and bent over the edge so that everyone could see him. Glancing between Arkwal and the ocean far below, Nova felt quite nauseous.

"You might think that if you leaned too far over the edge, you'd plummet to your death," Arkwal yelled along the line.

He held his arms out by his sides, put a leg out and stepped forward. Nova's hands shot to her mouth; around her, the tour group gasped. But instead of falling to his death, Arkwal flopped over the side and confidently stepped onto the east face of Castalia, sticking out from its side like a nail in the wall.

"Well, you'd be wrong. Not sure if I mentioned it, but the Emperor's a master of space and time. He can do funny things with gravity. He designed Castalia so that the six outer faces have a gravitational pull equal to that on Earth. You can walk around the outside of the palace, from face to face, without falling off. In fact, you couldn't fall off if you tried. Takes a bit of getting used to, mind. Right then, your turn."

Nova exchanged a worried look with Burner. They were so high that some of the birds below them looked nothing more than pulsing black dots. But as the group followed Arkwal's lead one by one, her confidence grew. She reached out, grabbed Burner's hand, and together, they flopped over the edge.

She couldn't help but grin when her foot stuck safely to the side. Ahead of her the horizon appeared as a vertical line. The ocean wasn't below her, it was to her right; the sky — filled with clouds whose face-like shapes had now been distorted by the wind — to her left. She walked back to the cube's edge to flop onto the roof, seesawed back and forth between the roof and the east face for a bit, and then walked along the edge itself at forty-five degrees, pretending to balance like a tightrope walker.

When she got to the cube's vertex she discovered that she could navigate three faces just as easily. She skipped from face to face, playing her own game of gravitational hopscotch. Then she knelt down, put her right hand on the tip of the vertex, used her left to spin herself around and slowly raised her body above her head so that she performed a spinning one-armed handstand on Castalia's tip. She spun for a while, taking the world in from this unconventional angle, before she heard Burner shouting for her.

"Come on, Scotia, we're on the move. You don't want to get in trouble again."

She lowered herself back down and ran to join the assembled throng who were gathered round Arkwal, standing by a skylight that looked into the Eastdome.

"The domes affixed to the four sides of Castalia all play extremely important roles," Arkwal said. "The Eastdome and its counterpart, the Westdome, are the places where all of Solarversia's game items are spawned before they're won by a player somewhere. As you can see, keeping the items sufficiently stocked is a mammoth undertaking. Only the fastest, hardest-working arkwinis are eligible to work in the East- and Westdomes."

Nova pressed her face against the skylight and gawped at what she saw. Inside, hundreds of arkwinis in forklift trucks and exosuits were hurrying around sorting, cataloguing and arranging a multitude of items in the largest warehouse she had ever seen.

Game items were stored in huge crates on shelves that reached right the way to the ceiling: teleport tokens, weapons power-ups of every kind. An arkwini sped toward the skylight in his forklift, performed a handbrake turn, hurriedly stored the box that he was transporting on the end of one of the shelves, removed the forks from under it and whizzed off back down the aisle.

A stamp on the side of the box declared that it contained sixty jars of Skidz. Within seconds the rectangular space below the content information on the box flashed into life. It displayed the profile information for a player who had just won a jar after spinning a Tweel of Fate somewhere, and the inventory number ticked down to fifty-nine. Hundreds of boxes and crates flashed in a similar manner until they were empty, whereupon they were replaced by a tired-looking arkwini. Arkwal took note of the wide-eyed expressions of the tour group.

"Don't even think about trying to break in, by the way. There's always one thinks they're being original and clever. They get in their plane, land on one of Castalia's faces and try to blast their way in, thinking that they're about to pull off the heist of the century. Even if you managed to break into the dome — which is highly unlikely in the first place — the anti-heist mechanism would prevent you from escaping."

Arkwal retrieved his telescope from his pocket, performed a few calculated twists of its cylindrical sections and then walked away. Nova went to follow him, and, finding that her feet were well and truly stuck to the ground, nearly fell over on the spot before reaching out to Burner to steady herself. Around her, everyone in the group had been similarly affected and remained glued in place until Arkwal shook his 'scope, reversing the mechanism.

"Remember — the Emperor's a master of space and time. His palace, his rules. Next stop: the Underdome." The chimp marched down the face of the cube, flipped himself ninety degrees forward at the bottom edge and disappeared to the underside of Castalia. Nova elbowed Burner hard in the ribs — revenge for the Wake-a-nator incident — and chased after Arkwal.

If walking on the side of the palace had been a curious experience, walking on its underside was stranger yet. Nova looked up to see Alpha Island in the Atlantic Ocean and down, over the edge of the palace, to the great blue sky beneath her. The crowd squealed with delight when a gull flew by, flapping its wings the wrong way up, looking nothing like a creature that should have been able to fly.

Arkwal hurried them into the Underdome. An enormous furnace took pride of place in the centre of the floor, gobbling down a blue gravelly substance that a team of arkwinis were shovelling into its fiery tank. Around the edges of the room, thousands of stacked crates formed erratic columns that stretched all the way to the ceiling and looked like they might topple over at any second.

Each bore the flag of a different country and was stamped with the imported contents it contained: foodstuffs, plants, vegetation, minerals, liquids and narcotics. A small army of arkwinis in warehouse overalls were driving forklifts piled high with crates, slotting them into gaps or starting new stacks.

"Who can tell me what the flag is on that crate? Very good, madam, it *is* the Russian flag. As you can see from the stamp on its side, the crate contains two hundred kilos of beluga caviar, a favourite of the Emperor. Whenever he hosts a Year-Long Game on a new planet, he always samples everything it has to offer. He's still hoping to find something as tasty as the sautéed Petrifier brains his mother used to make. They have, what you lot might refer to as a certain 'je ne sais quoi'. Now if you'll follow me, we're off to meet the Chief Molecular Gastronomer. Feel free to ask questions as we go. But keep your mitts off the food."

Nova quickly spotted the arkwini that Arkwal had referred to. A pair of yellow rubber gloves and a chef's hat that doubled his height complemented his bleached white lab coat. He clutched a clipboard close to his chest and strode the length of the open-plan kitchen like he owned the place. Following close behind him were a gaggle of junior chefs carrying various kitchen utensils.

The Gastronomer stopped beside an oversized wok that contained a bubbling brownish paste and leaned over to inspect its contents. His large nostrils twitched as he wafted its aroma towards his face. One of his shadows handed him a ladle, which he used to taste the concoction. He swilled the paste from cheek to cheek, then spat it out.

"Add two pounds of chicken livers, seven ounces of margarine, and simmer for three hours," he shrieked in a German accent at no one in particular. He scribbled something on to his clipboard and an arkwini ran off to do his bidding. The group fell in once more around Arkwal.

"The Emperor consumes five to six metric tonnes of produce every day, washed down by one of several cocktails. His current favourite is the Panama Pooky, which consists of Cognac and white crème de cacao. Here on Earth you'd usually garnish it with nutmeg; the Emperor prefers a clove or six of garlic."

"A clove or six of garlic?" a well-dressed French woman asked. "Sounds like a recipe for disaster to me." She smirked at Arkwal, delighted with her remark.

"I trust you aren't questioning the Emperor's taste, madam, especially not while you're a guest aboard his palace. He's been known to eat an old baguette or two in his time." Arkwal gestured toward to the furnace with a nod of his head. "Unless there were any other, less inane, questions, that concludes the tour of the palace."

"What about the North- and Southdomes?" Burner asked. "We never got to see those."

"A sensible question for a change. The North- and Southdomes are used in one of the final rounds, so you'll get to see them then. Although it's highly unlikely that any of you will make it that far. You know, statistically speaking."

"Excuse me, Mr Arkwal," Nova said. "That teleport machine over there, the one being guarded by a bunch of arkwinis. The signpost is bare. Is it special in some way?"

Arkwal rubbed his hands together slowly. "Yes, you could say that. Every other teleport machine is bidirectional, you see. You can teleport from one to the other and back again. The machine you asked about has been programmed differently. It allows the user to teleport *anywhere* in Solarversia. The destination isn't restricted to other machines. And that, good people, really does conclude the tour."

Arkwal flicked his telescope. Seconds later, Nova found herself back in her Corona Cube. She removed her headset and looked out of the window of the train. It was stopped at a station, and through the PA system, apologies were being made for the delays due to leaves on the line. She wondered how long they'd been stationary without her noticing, and wished that she, too, were a master of space and time.

Chapter Nine

Nova waited patiently in the Portland Building with a bunch of other hopefuls for the only item on the day's official itinerary she deemed worthy of her time — an introduction to Solar Soc, the university's Solarversia Society.

She'd already had the exclusive 'Burner Tour' of campus, which had introduced her to all the stairwells, alleyways and student bars where he and Jono had got drunk, smoked blunts, and been indecent with dodgy-looking second years. And though she hadn't seen any of the lecture theatres, facilities or halls of residence, she'd fallen in love with the place, and was already wondering how on earth she would get the grades she needed in order to be accepted onto a course there.

Next to her, Burner was waxing lyrical about university life to some of the other attendees. Three spotty youths from Manchester hung on his every word. She enjoyed the way he could work a crowd, but had heard the stories about Jono, smoking weed, and the gliding club a hundred times. Usually stories that combined all three.

She turned away from the group to have a look around the room. Thick carpets and finely upholstered sofas complemented the old masters on the walls. Leaflets provided details about the augmented reality tour she could take, one that would bring the old masters to life, giving their history and place in the university. Across the room, a row of gilt-backed chairs were lined up against the wall. She was eying them hungrily when a student appeared at the top of the landing and addressed the room.

"Excuse me, folks, could I have your attention please? There'll be an introduction to the Sustainable Development Society in room C203 in approximately five minutes. We're a friendly bunch and we'd love to meet you."

Clutching a ring-bound folder to his chest, leather satchel hanging at his side, he looked nothing like the meek freshers surrounding her. He was at home: at the university, and in himself. She kept looking at him. Since when did she go for blond surfer locks, strong jawlines and knitted cardigans with stonewashed denim jeans? Since now. As half the room headed to the landing, he turned and looked at her with the most incredible blue eyes she'd ever seen.

She discovered that she was incapable of looking away. A huge grin accompanied the flushing in her cheeks. She gulped, looked down at her feet, brushed her hair behind her ears and chanced another look. This time she was rewarded with a smile. Her heart fluttered. Another look, another exchanged smile, this one more intimate. His raised eyebrows willed her to join him. Her heart pounded and her cheeks warmed further.

"You alright, mate? You don't look too good." Burner seemed genuinely worried. Where had he appeared from? She'd almost forgotten he existed.

"I feel a bit dizzy actually. Just gonna—"

She motioned in the general direction of the washrooms before joining the herd of people heading for the landing.

***

Nova wasn't able to explain how she'd ended up sitting in the middle of the semicircle of chairs in room C203. She'd been drawn there, inexplicably, like an iron filing to a magnet. Either side of her were people wearing some combination of bell-bottomed jeans and wooden beads. One guy even sported a tie-dye T-shirt. She couldn't remember feeling so out of place and had a sudden impulse to flee — and would have done, had the guy with the incredible eyes not joined them that second. Her heart pounded in her chest.

"Hey, guys, welcome to the Sustainable Development Society. I'm Charlie. I took a year out after school to travel the world, and did some work in London for an NGO that specialised in microfinance to Third World entrepreneurs. It would be great to hear how each of you became interested in the topic of sustainable development, so let's go round the circle before I tell you about what we get up to here at Nottingham."

As they went round the group, the experience people had seemed to get more varied and impressive: expeditions through Costa Rica, volunteer projects in Tanzania, community building in Mongolia. As the girl next to her started talking, Nova's mind raced, desperately wanting to know how she had got herself into this situation.

"Hi, guys, I'm Ayesha. Like you, Charlie, I've been on a gap year since school. My main area of interest is renewable energy — I spent the last six months travelling through Africa, educating villagers about solar power and helping them to install arrays, principally for hospitals and libraries."

Charlie scribbled some notes on his tablet. "Great, thanks for sharing, Ayesha, that was really interesting."

The group turned to face Nova. She froze in her seat — what on earth was she going to say? That she had zero experience in sustainable development? That she wasn't too sure what it even meant? Her heart beat ever faster. People her age couldn't have heart attacks, could they?

"Hi, there. My name's Nova Negrahnu, and I'm interested in sustainable development. I built mud huts in …"

She paused and looked round the group, trying to think of a country that hadn't been said yet.

"In Mozambique. I built mud huts in Mozambique and I carried some bricks."

Everybody stared at her. Had she really said that? *I carried some fucking bricks?* What next, *nobody puts Nova in the corner?* The guy next to her started talking, something about India and yoga and transcendental something-or-other. Her words replayed in her head. She looked at Charlie to find that he was staring at her. When he smiled at her, she couldn't help but smile back. And nothing else mattered.

***

The flying carpet swept into the Magisterial Chamber and came to a fluttering halt in the northwest corner of the room beside an easel. Seated in the lotus position upon it was a woman. In place of a head, her neck was a thick stem that supported a blue and yellow flower reminiscent of an orchid. From her throat and down the length of her belly ran an inch-wide flap of skin, into which flew some of the millions of insects that had previously formed the carpet.

Nova checked the datafeed. Spee-Akka Dey Bollarkoo was an artist from Nakk-oo, Emperor Mandelbrot's home planet. She'd been commissioned to paint a monthly portrait depicting events that occurred within Solarversia throughout the year. These paintings would adorn the walls and ceiling of the chamber in a series of triptychs.

The insects, referred to in the feed as zapier s, emitted a low-pitched droning sound that reminded Nova of being on a plane. They buzzed around the easel for a while, seemingly taking in their new surroundings, and then swarmed into Spee-Akka's chest through the skin flap. Nova grinned. It was certainly an original way to store your transport.

The other new arrival in the Magisterial Chamber was less graceful but no less intriguing. His body was arched backward, so that his view of the world was upside-down. It looked like his feet had been nailed to the ground before a strong wind had taken him by surprise, blowing his body backward until his hands met the ground behind him. His movements were crab-like. Scuttling sideways, he'd come to a stop for a few suspenseful seconds, take in his surroundings, and then scuttle off again.

Except for the haphazard stitches that ran down the centre of his body, he was entirely naked. The stitches ran from the top of his skull, over his flat mandible — for he had no mouth — down his torso, past his crotch and back up his spine to the top of his skull. On his right side, the skin was pure white, but covered in bruises. On the left, his skin was jet-black and disfigured with blisters and ugly welts. He came to rest in the southeast corner by a machine covered in spinning wheels, switches and buttons, and a plethora of other components.

Nova flipped back to the datafeed. The black and white man was Ludi Bioski. His machine, the Orbitini, was described as a 'biomechanical random event generator'. According to the feed, he was here to 'spice things up' for players. Nova zoomed in to the Orbitini and watched as Ludi righted himself to stand over the machine and began to interact with it, flicking switches, pressing buttons and whirling wheels. Mesmerised, she tried to figure out what effect his actions would have on the Gameworld.

"What exactly are you looking at there, Miss Negrahnu?"

Nova volleyed an eye back to the classroom and looked up to see her English teacher's stern face bearing down on her. Shit. Old Mophead.

"Mrs Woodward! I was looking at ... I was just about to—"

"You were playing that infantile game, no doubt, rather than reading act three of *King Lear* like everyone else in the room. Headset, please — you can have it back at the end of the day. Along with a week of detentions."

Nova clutched her Booners tight to her chest. It was ridiculous that she should have to hand them over. What could be more Shakespearean than a random event generator? Ludi Bioski could have come straight out of *King Lear*, if only Shakespeare had been down with virtual reality. Mrs Woodward's glare hardened. Nova wiped the Booners lovingly with the sleeve of her jumper and slowly placed them in her teacher's outstretched hand. She was unable to stifle the huge yawn that emanated from deep within her.

"You're exhausted. Which is exactly why these dreadful games have been banned."

"Oh, get a life, you mean old cow."

The room fell silent. Nova was as surprised as anyone that she'd said it out loud. Mophead's nostrils flared to twice their usual size, even larger than the time Burner had set fire to the wastepaper basket in the middle of morning register. She looked terrifying.

Nova's lip trembled. "I'm so sorry, miss, I don't know what—"

"Headmaster's office. Now. You can save your sorries for him."

As Nova went to close the classroom door behind her, Mrs Woodward called after her, "And Nova, I think we'll make that a month of detentions."

Chapter Ten

Nova stared at the textbook and stifled another yawn with the back of her hand. She was only three days into her month's worth of detentions, but already they were taking their toll. She was getting home late every day, and the constant exhaustion was impacting her schoolwork and revision. Worse still, it was affecting her gameplay. Her Booners sounded the Solarversia jingle. Yet another message from Sushi.

"Either do your homework later, or tell Mrs Woodward to take a hike. We both know Solarversia is far more important. If you crash out of The Game through negligence, you're going to have to wait four whole years for the next one. Your choice, girlfriend."

Sushi knew how to push her buttons, that was for sure. Although Spiralwerks had a host of other games lined up for the intervening period, every Solo knew that the quadrennial Year-Long Games were the ones that mattered most. Nova confirmed that her parents were busy watching TV with the volume turned up and quietly shut her bedroom door.

She crept over to her wardrobe and leafed through her many Solarversia-themed T-shirts. Although she didn't truly believe they brought her good luck, she preferred to wear one while playing. Most of her shirts — like the one she grabbed and quickly put on — featured creative transformations of her player number.

This shirt displayed the characters Ken and Ryu from the classic arcade game *Street Fighter*, facing one another in a sparring pose. Ken, who was standing on the left, had been drawn with the head of a guy called 'Duncarelli', who happened to be Thailand's most famous ladyboy — and also number 515 in the Player's Grid. Ryu on the other hand, had been replaced by 'Alexander Lazaar', a techno DJ from Detroit, and player number 740.

Most people looked at the T-shirt and saw a couple of guys from a computer game. Some could even name them. But most Solos knew the characters well enough to know that they'd been redrawn, and instantly knew the shirt contained a puzzle to be solved — one whose answer revealed the wearer's player number. Solos competed to outdo one another in terms of their creativity, and examples went viral all the time.

She patted the shirt down, put her headset on, and sent a quick message back to her friend.

"Twenty minutes max. Then I really do need to get back to my books."

"That's the spirit. See you there."

Nova left her Corona Cube in Staten Island, New York. She'd met Sushi there the previous day to attend a virtual punk rock concert, and they'd promised to hang out in the Gameworld for a day or two before going their own ways. Her Route Planner informed her that the nearest Solarversia Simulator was a two-minute run from the cube. She locked on.

Like Corona Cubes and Tweels of Fate, Simulators were absolutely everywhere in the Gameworld. They were in phased zones, but ones that players had basic control over so that they could train with friends, if they wanted. Simulators were modelled on old school photo booths, the kind that charged an arm and a leg to provide you with a strip of passport photos. The small entrance way consisted of a piece of hanging curtain, below which a round swivel chair could be seen.

Next to the curtain was a control panel that allowed the Solo to program the type of simulation they wanted to experience. There were four categories of simulation: Knowledge, Puzzles, Combinations and Combat. Spiralwerks had promised that a thorough mastery of each would be a prerequisite for success in The Game.

Although there was an element of luck in Solarversia, it only went so far. Good luck could help in the short term, but it couldn't be relied on to get you through the year. Likewise, bad luck could darken your day, but it would never kill you outright. Skill was a far more important component of a serious gamer's strategy. And it could only be acquired in the way it's always acquired: through lots and lots of hard work. Mastery of the four categories had come to be known as the Science of Solarversia or, more simply, the Science.

"Here she is," Sushi said, hand up for a high five as Nova arrived at the booth. "Combinations, yeah?"

"What happened to sticking to a balanced diet?"

"Come on, they're fun."

In the same way that conscientious governments urged their citizens to consume their 'five-a-day' fruit and veg, Spiralwerks urged *their* citizens to train regularly and stick to a balanced simulation diet, where an equal amount of time was spent on each category, give or take a percentage point. Billboards containing user generated artwork, much of it parodying government propaganda from the early 20th century, gently reminded people of the virtue of living a balanced life.

Solos were able to display the number of hours they'd spent training in the Simulators on their bios, but Nova and Sushi had both opted to keep their stats private — Nova knew her parents would go ape if they ever knew the amount of time she'd spent playing. Burner and Jono both showed their stats, hoping that their ranks within the top 10% would intimidate some people.

Each of the four categories contained tens of thousands of modules within it. These were the individual simulations, or sims, which lasted anywhere from two to twenty minutes. There wasn't nearly enough time in the year for a single person to complete every single module, so players were forced to pick and choose, an exercise that had itself become part of the Science, as Solos speculated on the best order in which to structure their training.

Miniature Tweels of Fate, the size of a large orange, were affixed to the control panels of Simulator booths and could be spun whenever the player was having difficulty choosing a module. Sushi typed in their player numbers, restricted the outcome to Combinations, then rested her finger against one of the Tweel's little tentacles and gave it a good spin. When it came to a standstill, the topmost tentacle squirmed into life, grew several times larger and turned to face the girls.

"The Tweel of Fate has picked Asteroid Shower combinations. There are seven in total and each one takes two minutes. Remember that a balanced simulation diet is good for your health. The Science Says So."

Having delivered its message, the tentacle shrivelled down to its previous size and the machine loaded the Asteroid Shower simulation. Sims in the Combinations and Combat categories transformed the booth into a dark grey grid that stretched in every direction all the way to the horizon, where it met a light grey sky, unremarkable in its uniformity. The only distinguishing feature of the room — other than the avatars themselves — was the pleated red curtain, which was programmed to follow you around so that you could always find the exit.

In multistage modules such as this one, Combinations always increased in difficulty. The instructions overlaid at the bottom of Nova's display told her that 'Asteroid One' would require four moves. As ever, she'd need to execute them in a flowing sequence. If she missed a move, performed it in the wrong place or took too long, she'd flunk out. That didn't matter in the Simulator; it was what training was all about. In the Gameworld, however, a flunked Combo could mean the difference between life and death.

When a large timer appeared in the sky in front of them, counting down from three, the girls fistbumped and adopted their chosen stances. Nova, who had climbed onto her bed to perform the Combos, adjusted her Booners one last time. The electrodes in the skullcap were capable of translating her thoughts into the kind of movements required within the Gameworld, both in normal play and in the simulations, but she preferred to act out the combinations for real, whenever space — and social etiquette — permitted.

The pair of asteroids roared towards them, seeming to grow from the size of marbles to the size of footballs in the space of about five seconds. Nova dipped her right shoulder forward, then her left, performed a clockwise rotation of her hips, and then an anticlockwise rotation. Next to hers, Sushi's avatar performed the same sequence of moves in perfect synchronicity. A message flashed in the sky, confirming two successful combinations, and the sim took control of their avatars for a split second, making them jump into the air, knees pulled to chests as the icy comets hurtled past.

"Can I get a woop woop?" Sushi sang, gyrating her hips in a celebratory dance. Nova looked over her shoulder to see the curtain fluttering in the wind — an excellent little touch by the module's designers, she thought.

They cleared the second asteroid — using a seven-move sequence — by ducking as it whizzed overhead, and the third — that demanded a ten-move sequence — by diving to the side. When Sushi burst into a celebratory dance this time, Nova joined in. They'd cleared the fourth, fifth and sixth combinations in similar style, and Nova readied herself for the last one, a beast at twenty-two moves. Successfully completing all seven asteroids would win them an additional teleport token.

She shimmied, spun round on the spot, dipped her shoulders, wiggled her hips and arched her back without trouble. But twelve moves in, when she was required to transition from a star jump into a caterpillar on the floor, one of her feet missed the edge of her bed and she tumbled to the ground in a heap. Cursing her stupidity as she watched the asteroid annihilate her avatar, she suffered a wave of panic — somebody was coming up the stairs. She snatched the Booners off her head, threw them on her bed and leapt into her seat.

"Everything OK up here, love? Your father thought he heard something."

"Everything's fine, just finishing my homework," she said, putting as much effort into shielding the blank page of her notepad from her mum's view as she did trying to conceal her panting breath.

"Alright, I'll let you get on with it."

It was another little lie and she wasn't proud of it. But as soon as she heard her mum go back downstairs, she couldn't resist having one last quick peek. After all, Sushi would be wondering what happened to her. She found her friend standing back outside the booth, retrieving her printout. Nova loved little touches like that. Although training time was automatically added to your bio, booths spat out printed receipts.

Nova explained her mishap to Sushi and grabbed her receipt. Fourteen more minutes, taking her up to a total of 47 hours for the year, one month into The Game. Not bad for someone revising for their A-levels. A teleport token would have been good though. She crumpled the receipt up and chucked it at the nearest patch of grass. The ground into which it dissolved immediately sprouted a new flower. Her headset dinged as a company donated ten pence to a charity supporting sustainable horticulture.

"What's next?"

"Combat, obviously, now we've got those combos out the way. You'll need to bring your A-game though, no slipping off the bed like a doofus."

Nova smiled uneasily. There was no way she could resist another quick sim. Why couldn't all of life be as fun as Solarversia?

Chapter Eleven

At 2:37 a.m. Zhang raised his head, extended his arms and stood up. His eyelids snapped open and the microscopic servos that powered the lenses in his pupils adjusted to the dark of the room. As he walked forward, his tail detached from the power socket, freeing him to jump onto Nova's bed. He sat by her head and gently rocked her awake. She looked at the time and let out a groan. She was so warm and snug, she almost told Zhang to go back to sleep and leave her alone.

But she was also curious to see what was going on. There was a feature within Solarversia that alerted you if a new quest appeared within a specified radius of your vicinity. The alert told you the location of the quest and the skills required so you could decide whether or not to log in and travel there to attempt it. Burner had installed a programme to monitor these alerts while she was logged out. If an interesting one appeared, it wirelessly activated Zhang's built-in alarm. She'd instructed Burner that she only wanted to be alerted between midnight and 7 a.m. if the prize was greater than ten grand.

With a mixture of exhaustion and excitement, she quietly slipped her Booners on. According to her datafeed, the fourth Earth Force Field switch had just been discovered in nearby Baltimore, Maryland. Useful skills included advanced flying, jumping and climbing. Prize money: £100,000. Burner's programme had worked. Amazing. She'd buy him his own gaming rig if she pulled this off.

She left the Corona cube in downtown Philadelphia and whispered, "Baltimore. Fastest route. Ignore all quests and exhibitions." The Route Planner mapped her path to the closest Right Flights airport, but made one suggestion. A fellow player was running to the airport, having written off his car in a quest gone wrong. She'd already ticked off the 'hitchhiker item' from that month's Bucket List, but Solarversia was designed to make the world a better place and encouraged collaboration and teamwork, at least in the early stages.

She checked his profile to see how well he was doing. It was customary to tip a teleport token to people that gave you lifts — it was the only type of item that could be exchanged in this way — but if the guy was in a hurry, she wondered if she could get more money out of him. After all, Nova was more interested in one of the ways in which Solarversia mimicked the real world: survival of the fittest. Why help him if there wasn't something in it for her?

His profile came up blank. He was a 'Marty', a male player using a Generic Avatar. For whatever reason, he didn't want people to know who he was. Nova wasn't fond of the feature; it allowed people to hide behind a veil of anonymity.

"Nah," she said to the Route Planner. "Let him run. He could probably do with the exercise."

She arrived at the airport thirty-seven seconds later. Right Flights worked the same way as Greasy Wrenches and Dockingtons — a copy of her plane was stored at each one. She could land, park or dock anywhere in Solarversia, teleport to the other side of the world, and her vehicles would be waiting for her at the local depot.

Right Flights resembled giant helter-skelters that had to be approached by car. As soon as Flynn hit the slide that wrapped around the enormous tower, he started to morph into Hawk, her plane, and Nova soon found herself sitting in his cramped cockpit instead of the dune buggy.

The Hawker Demon biplane had been developed for the Royal Air Force during World War Two, but like all of Nova's vehicles, Hawk had been modified with a series of blue neon lights to give him the Tron look. She re-familiarised herself with the controls while Hawk gained momentum, spiralling up the tower. A few seconds later he shot out the top, launching at full speed into the sky.

She spent most of the journey volleying the public cams of the players already in Baltimore in an attempt to a devise a strategy. The switch had been hidden on the steeply pitched roof of Commerce Place, the fourth tallest building in Baltimore. Along with nearby Phoenix Shot Tower, a red brick building that looked like an old chimney stack, it was one of the only two buildings in the city that remained stable. Every other building, sidewalk and structure had been transformed into an inflatable object. Baltimore was a giant bouncy castle and Solos were flying all over the place in the diffuse indigo glow of the Earth Force Field.

Most weren't bouncing anywhere near as high as the tower. She kept seeing people take run-ups, bounce into the air, slam headfirst into one another and collapse in a pile on a street. Health points were dropping like loose change from a tattered pocket. Other players bounced to reasonable heights, but in the wrong direction, and were flung further and further from Commerce Place with each leap they took. And driving wasn't an option. The nearest Greasy Wrench was already inundated with mangled vehicles.

Those who made it to the tower faced other challenges. Ludi Bioski had been busy. He'd coated the bottom half of Commerce Place in Skidz, a slippery ice-like substance that made it very difficult for players to get any purchase when climbing.

A number of players had discovered a nearby quest at War Memorial Plaza, two blocks away, and won themselves pairs of spiked climbing boots. She watched a Canadian woman in crampons clear the slippery bottom half, only to grind to a halt shortly afterwards when one after another of her limbs adhered to the building, leaving her wiggling her bum and shaking her head in frustration.

Others became glued to the tower in a similar manner, trapped like flies in a web. The more they struggled against the building, the more they become helplessly stuck to it. Nova's datafeed advised that Bugz had been sprayed all over the top half of the tower, and players were already wondering which items could be used to help clear it.

Another strategy was air travel. Nova watched numerous attempted flyovers as avatars leapt from their planes at opportune moments to land on the pyramidal roof. It was the only part of the tower not covered in Skidz or Bugz. If they could land successfully, they could climb to the apex of the tower where the switch was based. Easy.

Except for the fact that disgruntled players who had bounced their cars into oblivion had climbed up the other solid building, Phoenix Shot Tower, and were hampering the pilots. Six heavy-duty Gatling guns had been installed on the ramparts and were aimed at Commerce Place. For players who couldn't get to the airport, gunning down the opposition was an appealing second best. Prizes were being awarded for every plane shot down — according to Nova's datafeed, seventeen and counting.

She circled the tower from a distance, weighing up her options. It looked best to approach Commerce Place from the southwest, hidden from the sight of the guns. Other players were already lining up to try their luck. Every failed attempt taught people something new, and avatars were getting closer to landing all the time. Hundreds of aircrafts were taking off from Right Flights every minute — she reckoned it was five minutes at most before someone made it to the switch. It was now or never.

She banked hard left to join the queue. A French man had just made the first successful landing and was climbing the sloped roof toward the switch. She willed Hawk to go faster, her sixteen speed points seeming painfully slow as others zoomed past. Three other players landed in quick succession and clambered after the French guy, now halfway up.

The four climbers inched upward. Surely one of them was going to make it. And they might have, had it not been for player 28,044, Bojango from Ecuador. Bouncing around Baltimore, he'd stumbled on a hidden quest on the roof of a local fire station, which gave him the loan of a helicopter armed with water cannons and the promise of a bounty for every player he squirted off the roof. All eyes were on him as he approached the building, long jets of spray emanating from the cannons.

The French guy was first to lose hold. Drenched by a deluge of whitewater, he crashed straight into the woman below him on his way down. The two of them slid clean off the edge, fell thirty floors, then bounced so high and so far that they didn't come to rest until ten minutes later. A lanky Welsh woman was next to get a face full of H_2O. To her credit, she hung on a good while longer than the Frenchman, but eventually she lost her grip too. She lashed out in an attempt to grab on to anything that might break her fall, and managed to grasp the fourth player, sending them both shooting over the precipice. The roof was clear once more.

Nova was wondering what to try next when a bright flash caught her attention. A sharp-eyed gunner had accepted his own mission to shoot down the helicopter, and it was now on fire and spinning wildly out of control. She felt a rush of energy zip down her spine — it was back to plan A.

She yanked the controls and sent Hawk into a loop, spiralling around to position herself for an attempted jump onto the building. The commotion of the helicopter had scattered the other players far and wide, leaving her second in the queue to approach the tower. She located the autopilot button that would enable Hawk to land himself once she'd jumped free. It would mean having to run to the nearest Greasy Wrench to pick Flynn up afterwards, but that would be a small price to pay in exchange for the prize money. She pressed the button at the last second and jumped for her life.

Her arms and legs flailed at her sides for what seemed like an eternity until finally she slammed against the sloped panelling of the roof. Adrenaline pumped through her veins. It turned out that her jump was one for the replays — she had timed it even better than the American woman in front of her and had landed higher up the roof. Bingo.

The switch was a mere stone's throw away. She glanced over her shoulders, desperate not to succumb to a pesky helicopter at this late stage. There were none in sight. Her heart pounded in her chest. Ten metres to the switch. The latticework of panelling made for easy climbing, enabling her to find a solid rhythm, arms and legs coordinating well. Seven metres. A quick check over her shoulder. The Yank remained a safe distance behind. Five metres. Still no sign of a helicopter. Three metres. Then suddenly she stopped moving. What the hell?

"Hard cheese, sucker!" the American woman said as she clambered past with a stupid grin on her face. Nova looked at the message flashing in her headset.

"Attention: Shadow Sucker attached. 27 seconds remaining."

She looked down to see a plunger attached to the wall. The woman had fired a Shadow Sucker at her, pinning her shadow in its place for thirty seconds. A disembodied voice, one of the player catchphrases, announced that her attempt was "close, but no cigar." Anger rose inside her like she'd never known. Then Gorigaroo's gong sounded, so loud she thought she might lose her grip. Not that it mattered any more. The fourth Earth Force Field switch had just been triggered by Pedey Gonzalez, player number 75,330,094, from Florida, USA.

The gong noise emanated from the switch itself and Nova watched with a mixture of interest and dismay as a series of concentric sound waves bubbled into the sky. As the waves reached the EFF, miles above them, the Field rippled and shimmered as it changed from indigo blue to blue-green, reminiscent of a sunlit ocean.

Nova grabbed the Booners off her head, threw them into the corner of her room and slumped into her pillows. Had anything more unfair happened in the history of the universe? She doubted it. Mrs Woodward was right. It *was* a stupid game. And now it was four in the morning, she'd had no sleep and she was going to fail her A-levels. Tears welled in her eyes and she felt herself sink deep into her mattress.

Bouncy was the one thing she didn't feel right now.

Chapter Twelve

Casey fed the next batch of hundred dollar bills into the counting machine. He liked the rapid-fire sound it made as it processed them, "...fft...fft...fft...fft..." and felt at home in the little backroom tucked away in the corner of Control House.

On the other side of the table, cigarette perched behind his ear, Wallace secured a wrapper round the newly counted bundle and added it to the pile on the table.

"OK, that makes $38,000. That's our best week this year. With you on board we're cleaning up."

Casey stared at the bundles before him. These last few weeks he'd seen more money than he'd made in the whole of his adult life. And it was easier to come by than he'd ever thought possible. All he and Wallace had to do was stick a few ounces of cocaine in their bags, head back down the Mississippi in their kayaks, drive into town, meet their man at the drop point and make the exchange. Ten grand for a day trip down the river. It was certainly worth getting out of bed for.

They were funding the Holy Order's global network — the fifty or so people here in the compound and the many hundreds in the outlying cells they communicated with around the world. Together, they were laying the groundwork for a new social and cultural order to be run by a superintelligent cybernetic organism. Specifically, they were preparing to welcome their new Master, the almighty Magi , into existence. Casey didn't understand everything yet, but he was learning and would do whatever it took.

A loud noise reverberated through the building, shaking the lights in their fittings and causing a security alarm to blare into life. Casey and Wallace stopped what they were doing and exchanged an intense, wide-eyed look. Wallace threw his zippo onto the table and made a dash for the door. Casey hurriedly threw the bundles of cash into the safe and raced after him. People were streaming out of the

Workshop, covered in blood, coughing and falling about the place, trying to avoid the glass from the blown-out windows.

A thick, acrid taste peppered the air in the Workshop. Ivan, a mechanical engineer, was unconscious on the floor, bleeding profusely from his midsection. Brandon, one of Father Theodore's lieutenants, was there with him. He'd taken his shirt off and was using it to try to stem the rush of blood. He glanced up at Casey with a look of fear on his face.

"Come and help me apply more pressure to this wound. Wallace, check everyone else is alright. Where's Mother with the first aid kit? Fuck, this is bad."

His thick, muscular frame was tense, his forearms bulging as he pressed down hard on a tattered shirt that was already saturated with the wounded man's blood. Those who hadn't fled outside seemed rooted to their spots, their faces ashen, their ears still ringing, staring at the scene in front of them, unable to process what had just happened. Casey handed his T-shirt to Brandon and the two of them did their best to tend to the injured man, trying to ignore the sight and smell of the gaping wound in his gut.

Wallace looked after the others, checking them for injuries, speaking firm, quiet words like a wartime nurse. When the hubbub died down, he pulled off his shirt and handed it to Brandon. Almost at once the shirt was red through. Casey readjusted his position to better cradle Ivan's limp head. The guy was out for the count; his head was lolling and the blood kept on coming. Casey had to look away, scared he might faint in front of everyone. His gaze settled on the doorway as Mother Frances bowled into the Workshop. Beside her stood the man Casey had been yearning to see. Father Theodore. The Grand Wizard of the Holy Order.

Casey froze. The Order was highly secretive, the identities of its members unknown outside the organisation. His induction had taken the best part of six months, in chat rooms and virtual worlds, each side using pseudonyms and computer-generated avatars. When he'd first met Frances online, she'd used the handle 'Zoro'. It was only once the Order had completed its background checks that he'd even been given a chance at the initiation, knowing full well that success in the ordeal would mean he could never leave its ranks.

Until this moment he'd not set eyes on Father Theodore, the Order's founder, spiritual leader and Übermensch. All Casey knew about him were the stories, passed on by Wallace during their day trips down the river, and the rumours that flew round the compound day and night.

He looked just like Wallace had described. He had a tight crop of short grey hair that contrasted sharply against his dark brown eyes, and his long, manicured beard grew to a tip that was secured tight in place with three little bands. But it was Theodore's right arm that drew Casey's attention longest. Supposedly containing a quantum supercomputer within its confines, the bionic arm was coated in a thin layer of black Kevlar and dotted with different coloured LEDs that flashed on and off in a sequence that made it look like they were communicating with one another.

Frances stood by his side clutching what looked like an army issue medical kit. Casey wondered why she hadn't sprung into action — hadn't Wallace mentioned that she was one of the top surgeons in the entire country? Instead, she waited patiently, occasionally glancing between Ivan and Theodore like she had all the time in the world.

The room went quiet as the old man surveyed the scene impassively. When he finally spoke he did so with an unmistakable tone of authority.

"Is somebody going to tell me what happened? Or shall we stand here in silence until Ivan has bled right the way out?"

"My instructions were crystal clear, Father, ask anyone." Brandon's voice trembled as he spoke. "I've handled explosives for twenty-five years without a single incident. Ivan did exactly what I told people not to do. The canisters are fragile and need to be handled with care. If you drop them on the bench like that—"

"Other than Ivan, who else is hurt?"

A woman removed the bandage she had been pressing against her neck. A small piece of shrapnel protruded from a long, narrow gash.

"I was lucky, Father. I was standing behind Ivan when it happened. He took the brunt of the explosion. If it had happened two seconds later, I might not ..."

She went silent, averted her eyes, and reapplied the bandage.

"We have to get him to a hospital *right* now," Wallace said.

Theodore twizzled his beard with his bionic fingers and laughed. "Hospital." He repeated it like the punchline of a joke he'd enjoyed.

"But Father, he'll die."

"But Father," he mimicked. The lights on his arms stopped flashing as if they too, were hanging on his every word. "You questioning my judgement, Wallace? You suggesting that folk round here take their orders from you rather than me?"

Wallace gulped. "Father, you know I would never question your judgement. It's just that—"

"It's just that what? You think we should jeopardise everything we've worked for?"

"No, Father. I'm sorry. I spoke out of turn, and that was wrong. Please forgive—"

With the smallest gesture of his hand, Theodore restored silence to the room. He raised his arms in front of him and gestured in mid-air. The coloured LEDs blinked into action again. Half a minute later, two of the Medibots that Casey had seen in the Lockup rolled into the room carrying a gurney.

So the stories Casey had heard were true. The computer in Theodore's arm was wirelessly connected to a series of electrodes implanted inside his skull. The setup allowed him to directly interface with the networked components of the Order — to communicate and control its robots and machines.

Another small gesture from Theodore — a flick of his head — was signal enough for Brandon and Wallace to give up their care of Ivan. They stood and backed away. Casey felt Father's gaze come to rest on his face. He dropped Ivan's head more quickly than felt right and got up to join Wallace.

The 'bots aligned themselves next to Ivan, uncollapsed the gurney, and with a swiftness that belied their mechanical natures, scooped him off the floor and placed him onto it. One 'bot stood by Ivan's feet, the other by his head. But instead of wheeling Ivan off to the sickbay, the 'bots took hold of his head and his feet, and with their articulated fingers, began to twist. Casey's wonder quickly soured. Ivan's head was yanked sharply one way, then the other. The chilling sound of splintering vertebrae echoed round the room. Next to him, Casey felt Wallace flinch.

The grid of lights on Theodore's arm continued to flicker as he turned his attention back to the people in the Workshop. "What *comrade* Wallace forgot," he said, loading the word 'comrade' with irony, "is that my view of the world — and my understanding of it — is far superior to his. I don't kill one of my own children on a whim. The second I arrived I had the Medibots scan Ivan's life signs and communicate the findings to me. Not even Frances could have saved him. There was no way he could have lived longer, neither as a human, nor like me, one who has transcended the human condition. Ivan was a good man. He was the seventeenth member to join the Order and his contributions to us were valuable. He joined us for the same reason you all did — because he was called. He discovered a truth so powerful, so compelling, that his old life no longer made sense. But in the blink of an eye, and through his own carelessness, he became a liability that needed to be dealt with. The 'bots will take his body to the incinerator."

Casey swallowed hard and bowed his head, obscuring the solemn expression on his face. Theodore squared his shoulders and looked at each of his followers in turn.

"Remember that it was never going to be easy. Nor should it be. Trials like this are sent to test our faith, to show that it is strong and pure. If in doubt, remember the pain and suffering that awaits those who fail the Magi. This changes nothing. Is everyone clear about that?"

In silence, everyone but Ivan nodded.

Chapter Thirteen

Nova stood outside Fragging Hell and made herself repeat the words over and over: "I'm only here to pick up my prize, I'm only here to pick up my prize." It was a Friday afternoon and Mr McGillycuddy had let her out of detention thirty minutes early. Fragging Hell was on the way home from school — in one of those roundabout kind of ways — and she'd been meaning to pick up her darts prize for weeks now. She straightened her shoulders, brushed her hair behind her ears and entered the cafe.

She marched along the strip of fluorescent lighting towards the bar and tried not to pay any attention to the whoops of delight that emanated from the gaming rigs on either side. As she neared the bar, Jockey came out from the backroom and, seeing her, swooned in mock horror.

"Nova. Returned from the dead. You haven't been in for weeks."

"I know. I've missed this place. In fact, I miss everything in the world. I've been buried in revision."

"So you haven't been playing?"

"Yeah, I have. Just doing the bare minimum to keep up with the April Bucket List."

"So, what do you make of teleporting?"

"Teleporting? You mean the quest got completed? We can teleport now?"

"Wow, Miss Negrahnu, you are seriously out of the loop. Sit down and plug in, you've got to give this a go. The trick is remembering to dial round the 'T' the right way."

"No, Jockey, I can't. I'm here to pick up my prize. Then I need to get back to my books."

He looked genuinely nonplussed for a moment.

"Your prize? Oh, your darts prize. Only two months late. Yeah, it should be around here somewhere." He winked, ducked into the backroom and returned half a minute later with a shoebox-sized package and a celebratory smile. It was an Electropet Arkwini action figure dressed like an astronaut. Nova scanned the side of the box.

The action figure spoke in the same high-pitched voice as the arkwinis in The Game and came with his own little detachable helmet and space capsule. A playmate for Zhang. Nova grinned. Mission accomplished. Now all she had to do was stuff the arkwini in her bag and leave the cafe. Even she could do that.

But before she could move, a message pinged in from Sushi: "Have you seen the portrait? Funniest. Thing. Ever."

"What portrait? What are you talking about?"

"Remember Spee-Akka Dey Bollarkoo, the woman who flew into the Magisterial Chamber on a carpet? She's finished March's monthly portrait. And you're in it."

"No frigging way. You're having me on."

"No, for real. Go and check for yourself. And Banjax has finally arrived at Castalia, you'll need to tick him off April's Bucket List anyway."

That settled it. There was no way she was going straight home to spend another Friday night hunched over a pile of boring textbooks. She'd worked hard all week and deserved a gaming break now and then. She'd even read an article recently that claimed a lot of high-level executives played casual computer games during work hours to help them chill out. She should try to find the article again — it would be good ammunition next time her parents had a go at her. She found a free space, stowed her bag under the table and logged on.

The Corona Cube was a sight for sore eyes. In her inventory, the twenty-five teleport tokens she had won for getting so close to the EFF switch were now lit up, ready to use when the time was right. The Castalian constellation on the black ceiling of her cube was pulsing and glowing, indicating a new arrival at the Emperor's palace. She reached for the stars, and the side of the Corona Cube that led back into the Magisterial Chamber turned transparent.

***

Nova stepped out of her profile square, fell to the marble floor of the chamber and looked around. Emperor Mandelbrot remained in the centre of the room. His central totem pole still reached up to the ceiling, though most of the mouths around its circumference had now melted away. Blobs of purple mess still oozed off the edge of his circular dais, while an assortment of limbs and other body parts looked like they were trying to poke their way out of his base.

She turned around to study the Player's Grid on the north wall. It already looked different, only seven weeks after the start of The Game. On the evening of the opening ceremony, all hundred million profile squares had flickered into life. Every square had a coloured border that represented the number of lives the player had left. Mimicking the way Force Fields progressed through the colours of the rainbow as they got weaker, borders were coloured violet at first, representing three lives, changed to green when a player lost their first life, and then turned red when they only had one left.

Supposedly influenced by the tradition in martial arts, Solos referred to the borders as 'belts'. Some people went as far as reflecting their current status in the real world, wearing belts, bracelets or armbands of the appropriate colour. Belt colours were also visible on player vehicles, appearing as the trim that surrounded the license plates.

When players lost their third and final life, their squares went dark, extinguished like candles in the wind. One hundred thousand squares had already gone dark, creating patches of shadow here and there in the giant grid. In that way, the grid performed an important function as the scoreboard of The Game, informing players about the current state of the competition. It wasn't uncommon for people to watch the grid like it was a giant TV, and it had become so popular that Spiralwerks had arranged for huge screens to display it in public for the duration of the year.

As Nova looked at the grid, her datafeed flickered into action, highlighting the locations of her friends and the various people she'd interacted with. Having signed up to Solarversia early on, she and Sushi had obtained fairly low, central numbers that they'd always been happy with. She'd longed to win a number in the Golden Grid, the ten-by-ten section reserved by Spiralwerks for a series of promotional competitions leading up to the start of The Game, but then, so had several million other people.

One such competition had required artists to create a 'wanted' poster for Banjax — the creature she was here to visit — in the style of an old Barnum & Bailey poster. Spiralwerks had even offered the poster's £50,000 reward for real to anyone who acquired a live specimen of a dodectopus, a bounty that had gone unpaid. A later competition had offered a Golden Grid square to the person who submitted the best photo of the winning poster.

Nova had been gutted that her own entry — of the poster printed onto material and hoisted from her school's flag pole — hadn't won, and even more gutted at the week's worth of detentions she'd received. As Burner had pointed out at the time, she might well have killed herself getting the flag in position, given that the pole was on the roof, and she *had* kicked loose a number of tiles that had had to be replaced.

Standing in the chamber, Nova witnessed several dozen profile squares turn dark over the course of five minutes and watched the replays of all the relevant deaths. Then she headed to the far side of the chamber to investigate an enormous painting that took up a full third of the south wall. It was the first artwork by Spee-Akka Dey Bollarkoo, or "Flower Face" as Burner had taken to calling her, and had been painted in the style of Hieronymus Bosch, a Dutch Renaissance artist famed for the fantastic imagery of his large triptychs, landscapes inhabited by outlandish objects and beings.

The centre of the painting featured the Emperor himself, floating in space, holding aloft his unfurled fist, where Arkwal perched, telescope in hand. Gorigaroo appeared halfway up the totem pole, using the Emperor's mouths as foot and handholds. With his free hand he was stretching towards Castalia, which looked like a balloon floating just out of reach.

Plenty of players had been immortalised too. The first person to land on Alpha Island, the first Solos to acquire various vehicles, and the winners of some of the quests, depicted in their moments of triumph. Some deaths had been recorded too — she could make out a half-eaten avatar, smoking and blackened, hanging from the mouth of a lavadile.

In the bottom left-hand corner were two buildings she recognised. Standing atop the taller one was Pedey Gonzalez, triumphantly pushing the Force Field switch into its off position, circled by aeroplanes and helicopters. Nova zoomed in and saw, with a mixture of pride and shame, that Sushi was right: *her* moment in the sun had also been preserved. There she was, desperately reaching for the switch, her shadow stuck to the building by the stupid plunger.

She felt a fresh pang of pain as she remembered how close she got to pressing the switch herself. A hundred big ones had been within her reach. She'd even dreamt about it a couple of times, dreams in which *she'd* been the one to trigger the switch, only to wake up as poor as ever. There was nothing she could do about it now. Nothing except train harder. She shared the image on her feed, however much it pained her to do so, knowing that she might as well tick an item off the Bucket List while she was here.

Her concentration was broken when she heard the faint whooshing sound of ruffled vines. Gorigaroo's gong was unmanned — he'd be swinging around overhead somewhere. In the southeast corner of the chamber she spied Ludi Bioski interacting with his strange machine, the Orbitini, which stood waist-high to an average man, spanned ten metres in length and was a metre wide.

The array of its components was mind-boggling. Everywhere you looked there were spinning wheels, switches, tuners, sliders, dials, gauges, buttons, handles, zips and keyboards. And then there were the parts of it that seemed to have come from a chemical lab: vials of liquid, linked to one another via a series of twisting pipes, and pots and pans that bubbled away, emitting a thick brown smoke that wafted into the massive chamber.

The central interface consisted of coloured glass beads that were arranged on a spiralling double helix. Ludi spun wheels, flicked switches and mixed liquids. Then, apparently satisfied, he would slide the glass beads up, down or along his twisting abacus and the digital screen at the front of the Orbitini would display a new 'Event Card'.

Nova watched as he moved three of the orange beads partway along the double helix so they collided with a necklace of yellow and purple beads further along. An Event Card appeared: a tornado with a rating of 3 on the Enhanced Fujita scale would tear through the centre of Berlin in the next few minutes. She flipped to cam mode and checked the video feeds being labelled #BreezyBerlin.

If anything, she was slightly annoyed that she wasn't there to experience it for herself. She'd practiced her 'High Velocity Object' combinations only the week before in one of the Simulators. There had been fifteen objects to dodge, ranging in size from a flying deckchair that would knock off a handful of health points if you failed to avoid it to a small lorry that would kill you outright.

The combinations had been pretty simple, and she'd completed the module without error, but like every Solo knew, executing moves in the safety and comfort of a Simulator Booth was a different proposition to executing them in the Gameworld for 'real' in a situation like this, when health points were at risk.

The first few gusts took players by surprise. She saw arms outstretched as hats were blown from heads and sallied forth on currents of air, saplings bending this way and that, doors slamming shut and bursting open. Within thirty seconds players needed to lean at unnatural angles and hold on to buildings and lampposts to remain where they stood.

As the moody-looking tornado gathered speed, so too did the death counter. It ticked upwards, dozens at a time. She watched a car get flipped into the air and bowl down the street, striking people out of existence as it went. People, it would seem, who had failed to master the most basic of combinations. People who hadn't bothered to learn their Science. Nova smiled. This was survival of the fittest. Best for noobs to go out early on, leaving serious players, Solos like her and Sushi, to battle it out properly.

The winds abated as quickly as they had started. Six thousand players had lost a life, all thanks to Mr Random. Nova let out a long, quiet whistle while she flicked through some of the previous Event Cards. He'd made it rain teleport tokens in Tokyo, had turned the city of Strasbourg green for a week, and last Thursday had given all prime-numbered players in the upper-right quadrant three spins of the Tweel of Fate.

But she wasn't here to study Ludi's Event Cards or laugh at noobs. She walked over to the northeast corner of the room, which remained empty for now. Solarversia, like most other massive multiplayer online games, incorporated a technique known as 'phasing' which enabled certain areas of the game world to look different to different players. Sushi, who had already visited Castalia and seen the new character Banjax, would see him in this corner if she was here. Nova, who was yet to unlock the character, only saw an empty corner. As she approached it, she heard the familiar 'ding' of a Bucket List item being ticked off.

To her right, a small platoon of arkwinis appeared, their little monkey hands struggling to get much purchase on the taut ropes that were attached to a glass tank two storeys high. The stop-start motion of their actions caused gallons of water to slosh over the sides, drenching some, making others slip over. Water splattered around Nova's feet and she jumped back to watch from a safe distance. Once it was close enough to the wall, the arkwinis ran round to the front of the tank and pushed with all their might until it came to rest, tight against the northeast corner.

Inside the tank was Banjax, the twelve-armed dodectopus. He was a deep green colour, like a pond thick with algae. Though she'd seen the Tweels of Fate based on his appearance, she hadn't expected him to be so big or look so ferocious. The beast had remained relatively still during his transportation by pushing against the sides of the square tank with his tentacles.

Now the tank was at rest, he released all but one of his powerful green arms, unsuckering them one by one. She approached the tentacle that remained attached to the side. About a foot back from its sucker, the tentacle swelled spherically. It looked like a python that had swallowed a football. A similar sphere was present on each of the other arms. She went close to the tank and looked into the open sucker. It contained a man's face, jabbering away so quickly it looked like he was talking in tongues.

"He's dishing out prizes for the Tweel of Fate," one of the arkwinis said. "Banjax controls every tweel in Solarversia — hundreds of thousands of them — from here."

The tweels were strange things and players were divided on whether you should bother visiting them. Jockey, who had been stung three times in row, losing teleport tokens and even his prized Battle Axe, swore that he would never visit one again. Burner had laughed in his face and declared that you needed "to be in it to win it". Unsurprisingly, his experience had been mostly positive. So had hers: yesterday she'd won a bottle of Growsome that promised to add two feet to her height for sixty seconds. She couldn't wait to use it.

"The faces near the end of his tentacles, the ones dishing out the prizes. Are they all the same face? My friend Burner and I can never decide."

"Have you done Master Arkwal's tour of the palace yet?"

"The one where he shows people the different domes? Yeah, I did it a few weeks ago, why?"

"There's a similar tour for each of the Emperor's entourage. Even one for the Emperor himself. Questions like that are answered on the tours. I'm not allowed to divulge anything myself. Sorry, but you know what Master Arkwal's like."

He raised his little eyebrows, and they exchanged a smile. It was only when his little chimp face pixelated slightly — which happened occasionally due to bandwidth restraints — that she remembered he wasn't real. A shiver went down her spine. She'd been caught in the *uncanny valley*, interacting with a program as if he was a sentient being.

As the arkwini got back to his mopping, Nova saw a message flash up from her mum asking when she'd be home. She quickly pinged a reply saying she was just about to wrap things up and would be there soon. Having her mum call the school to track her down was the last thing she needed — Nova had skilfully managed to omit mention of her detentions from every conversation they'd had this month — but one phone call was all it would take to reach Game Over. She checked back into her Corona Cube, took a deep breath and braced herself for an evening of not really concentrating on *King Lear*.

Chapter Fourteen

The old man dissolved into nothingness and Sushi found herself standing in the middle of a deserted lounge bar. The arrangement of the place struck her as odd: the small circular tables, the stiff-backed chairs arranged neatly around them and the vulgar carpets decorated with a recurring image of an old bearded man carrying a trident. It was the view through the windows of the ocean that told her she was aboard a cruise liner. But what was she supposed to do? It wasn't like the puzzles she was used to, and besides, her avatar couldn't move from its spot.

A background noise piqued her curiosity. She couldn't place it or say much about it, save for the fact that it was getting louder by the second. When the tidal wave hit the ship a few seconds later it sent her crashing against a couple of bar stools, her avatar still out of her control. The lounge windows soon cracked under the pressure of the surrounding seawater and the incoming tsunami flushed her down a corridor into the depths of the ship. She tumbled head over heels for what seemed like an eternity, and finally came to rest sprawled on her hands and knees looking like a washed-up shaggy dog.

Getting to her feet, she looked up at the appliances hanging down from the floor-turned-ceiling: ovens, sinks and workspaces. She was in the ship's kitchen. Small fires were burning where boxes of cereals and other dry goods had been flung out of cupboards and onto the hobs. Water flooding into the room was beginning to swirl around her ankles. A message flashed in her display: *Escape from the Poseidon. 11,762 safe spots left*. And then, for the first time, she was able to move.

Ten minutes earlier she'd arrived at Ayers Rock in Australia. She was there to see Giganja, one of nine Grandmasters players were required to visit throughout the course of the year. Grandmasters hosted the Planetary Puzzles, a series of self-contained games that started on the hour, every hour. The datafeed had told her that there were 16,803 people there with her to play the 10 a.m. puzzle. She now knew what the puzzle was about. Unless she escaped from the ship in time, she'd lose one of her three precious lives.

Glancing around the steaming, smoking cauldron of a room, she desperately searched for clues, consoled only by the knowledge that every other player, in his or her phased instance of the ship, would have been as disoriented as her.

First she tried looking for clues in the water. It was infused with a random assortment of cans of food, kitchen utensils and dinner ingredients. An oxygen counter appeared in her display while her head was submerged — it looked like she could remain underwater for a maximum of thirty seconds at a time.

Abandoning the underwater search, she clambered onto a metallic vent that enabled her to reach several cupboards. The first two were empty. *Bummer.* Balancing one leg on the vent and the other on a pipe protruding from the wall, she stretched to reach the third one. Its door swung open to reveal a brightly coloured object. She couldn't make out what it was, only that the same Poseidon logo that had appeared on the carpet in the lounge was printed on its side.

Heart thrashing around in her chest, she strained to reach it. Her fingers flailed towards it uselessly, so she decided to leap. Headsets like hers — the same make of BoonerMax goggles that Nova owned — worked off brain waves to move avatars around the Gameworld. The technology wasn't yet perfect, but according to the creators of such devices, it would be by the time the next Game started in 2024.

She sprang through the air, snatched the object clean off the shelf — it was a snorkel — and crashed to the water below, hitting a fixture on the way down. Her datafeed told her the snorkel could lengthen the duration of any underwater excursion to two minutes. The fall had cost her 18 health points, but at least she could search underwater now without the risk of drowning.

The water had reached waist height and was still rising. Swimming through a medley of bobbing potatoes and carrots, she cruised around the upturned kitchen, not quite sure what she was looking for. Other cupboards were either bare or contained nothing more interesting than the kitchen cupboards at home. And the freezer room, which had looked promising at first, also turned out to be a red herring. Wading past the thawing carcass of a lamb, and panicking slightly as she glimpsed the number of safe spots start to diminish, she spotted a discarded chef's hat with the same logo emblazoned on its side.

She turned the hat inside out to find a map stitched to the lining. A dotted arrow led from the kitchen to the ship's engine room, where the map's legend indicated she'd find a door in the hull that led to freedom. At last, she was getting somewhere. As she waded through the water to the kitchen's exit, she heard Gorigaroo strike his gong. He wasn't actually there on the ship; Grandmaster Giganja had mentioned that the gong would sound every three minutes, signalling a new clue. The cupboard that had contained the snorkel started flashing. Those who hadn't discovered it yet soon would.

Sushi squealed with joy when she reached the engine room door. The sign above its handle — which she'd had to crane her neck to read — confirmed that it led to freedom. Except the door was locked. As the minutes passed without her discovering a single additional clue, her joy gave way to fear and frustration. There were fewer than five thousand safe spots left when the gong sounded again.

This time the ship's furnace flashed. Diving back under the water, she cursed at her stupidity — she'd noticed a chunky metal grill affixed to its front in one of her reccies, but not thought to inspect it. *Idiot girl.* The grill came away from the furnace as soon as she touched it to reveal an opening wide enough for her head, but not her shoulders. Clutching hold of the sides, she poked her head inside and soon found a metal plaque bearing an inscription: *Find the boy in the cabin with the keychain round his neck.*

She resurfaced and felt a huge rush of energy course through her body. It was all coming together. The corridor that led from the kitchen to the engine room had also led to a dozen or so cabins. After checking the first couple and finding nothing she'd ignored the rest in her excitement to get to the engine room.

She re-entered the corridor and did her best to ignore the visceral fear creeping through her. The water was up to her neck and gave no indication that it was going to stop. Her display flashed as the number of safe spots ticked under two thousand. She entered the first cabin and checked the only places large enough to hide a boy: the wardrobe and the bathroom. *No dice.*

Next cabin, the water now creeping above her chin. Wardrobe empty, bathroom too. Ditto the next cabin. *Come on, little boy, where are you hiding?* By the time she found him, curled on the top shelf of the wardrobe in the fifth cabin, there was less than a foot of air to the ceiling. A new chart for his oxygen level appeared in the display next to hers. Shit — she was now responsible for his life too, *and* they'd have to share the snorkel, halving the two-minute time frame. She was, however, relieved to spot the keychain around the boy's neck. Taking his hand, she started the swim back to the engine room. It wasn't far, but with the safe spots counting down in her peripheral vision — now fewer than a thousand — it felt like a slog.

As they progressed along the corridor, her heart, which was already pounding, stepped up a gear as the lights started to flicker. The ship was losing power. She checked on the boy. His terror mirrored her own, exacerbated by the unnatural sound of cast iron being twisted and bent as it succumbed to the enormous pressure of water bearing down on the vessel.

All of a sudden she was close to panicking, despite reminding herself that none of it was real; she was at a gaming café in town, not stranded inside the claustrophobia-inducing bowels of a capsized ship. Now kissing the ceiling, the deluge of water into the craft had finally finished; the ocean had won and the exit was still ten metres away.

She watched her display in horror, not knowing what to fear more, the dearth of safe spots — three hundred and counting — or their lack of oxygen. As they reached the door in the hull, the boy's key started to flash. So did the oxygen gauge — they each had less than five seconds of air. She looked up, craning her neck as far as it would go above the water — there was an air pocket — the little beauty!

Kicking like a donkey on heat she surfaced into the pocket with a second to spare and was overjoyed to watch their oxygen counters slowly replenish. Waiting what she considered to be the bare minimum, she nodded at the boy and the pair of them sunk back under.

As soon as they got to the handle, the little boy took charge, removing the keychain from round his neck and inserting the key into the lock. Then he moved aside and motioned for her to turn it. Clutching it with both hands, she started to wind it in an anticlockwise direction, just like the sign advised, happy with herself for thinking it through on the swim back and realizing that the direction would be the same, regardless of either the sign or the door's uprightness.

The next few seconds seemed to occur in a singular moment: the handle making a thunking sound, the door swinging up and open to reveal a clear blue sky, and Sushi and the little boy being winched to safety by the waiting rescue team. She'd done it – solved Giganja's puzzle, the first of her friends to do so.

She ripped the Booners off her face, inhaled sharply and realized she'd been holding her breath for real. The panicky feelings on the boat had been strong, and for some reason she wasn't shaking them. It was hard to regulate her breathing. She rubbed her eyes. Too long in VR? She looked up and around at the gamers on chairs to the left and right of her. That was weird — the girl to her left was also rubbing her eyes. So were the group of guys by the bar who'd been drinking beers and watching replays. One of the men started to cough and the others coughed in sync. Sushi sniffed the air. Something was burning — rubber? Suddenly the air burst into a thousand shards of glass.

***

Arty wanted to relax. He wanted to go home, get a takeaway, flop in front of the TV and forget about his week. Instead, finding himself unable to leave the office, he'd ordered a curry that remained untouched on his plate, his mind still on the griefing attack at Ripley's Junction. It had been consuming him endlessly. The analysis they'd done on the night of the attack hadn't relieved him one bit, because it had shown that it probably hadn't been perpetrated by the ROFL Mongers or any of the other griefing clans that Spiralwerks knew about, the kind that griefed for the 'lolz'. They were fairly sure it had been the work of the Holy Order.

It was the conga line, viewed from above, that had clued them in. Lots of the players involved in the griefing attack had abandoned their cars to join the line, but after a while, most of them had got bored of waiting and had wandered off to the nearest Corona Cube to log out. The griefers had stayed in the line long enough that they reached the front and were able to control its direction. They'd steered it over a bridge and looped back round under the road that passed beneath it.

Carl, the Chief Technical Officer, had been the one to spot the pattern. Viewed from above, the snaking 'S' symbol was overlaid on itself at ninety degrees. The conga line had been distorted until it was configured like a curly swastika, a symbol that featured prominently in the Order's manifesto. They were proud to be promoting a new form of fascism, one that involved loyalty and devotion to an unseen, as yet unmanifested superintelligent cybernetic organism. And they had a beef with Spiralwerks for an unknown reason that was killing him. The whole thing made him feel sick.

There had been a brief moment of euphoria following Carl's discovery. Spiralwerks had been very strict about only allowing real people to sign up and play Solarversia, and had worked hard to prevent people from creating multiple accounts. So they'd sent the details of the players involved in the griefing attack to MI6 and the FBI, confident that they were about to help catch the lunatics behind it.

Today Arty had received a call. Yes, the people involved in the attack were real, but every one of them had been ruled out as having anything to do with the Order. Each avatar was real, but they belonged to down-and-outs, vagrants and beggars who had been approached a couple of years back and been paid a few bucks to stand still while someone waved a phone over them. The euphoria had quickly soured.

Arty stuck his fork deep into the mound of rogan josh and lifted it carefully to his mouth. Then he pushed his chair back from his desk and changed channels on the big screen until he came across one of the numerous Solarversia programmes. Some were dedicated to certain aspects of the game, such as quests, exhibitions or vehicle choices, others were punditry shows, following celebrities and players that were doing well, having won lots of money or obtained a special item of some sort. Many featured user-generated content.

He chose to watch a show about the Planetary Puzzles, one of the types of quest he'd been heavily involved with in the creative stages. Players had to face nine Grandmasters in total, one on each planet in the Solar System. They progressed in difficulty with the planet's distance from the Sun. Mercury's Grandmaster, Killanja, was the easiest, then Meganja on Venus, ending with Brontanja on Pluto, the most difficult of them all. Players would have to face every Grandmaster, though not in any particular order, and such visits were included in Bucket Lists later in the year. Unsuccessful attempts at puzzles lost players a life, although the item was ticked off the list for the attempt.

A problem that Spiralwerks had encountered as soon as they began working on Solarversia was the viral nature of information. As soon as one person knew something, everyone in the world could know it. The minute a puzzle had been played, word of how to solve it would be out there, on forums, on social media, in tweets. There was no way to prevent the spread. The only way round it was to find a solution that meant no puzzle was ever played more than once.

But in a game supporting a hundred million players over the course of a year, the number of individual puzzles Spiralwerks needed to devise stretched towards infinity. It had taken a lot of false starts, but the team had eventually managed to created an artificially intelligent program, which spawned hundreds of thousands of unique puzzles at the right level of difficulty, puzzles that were surprisingly varied and fun to play. These were the Planetary Puzzles.

The TV presenter of the programme introduced a player who had just faced Giganja, the Grandmaster in charge of Earth's puzzles. Arty loved these segments, where the person watched a replay of some recent action and spoke about what had been going through their mind at the time, discussing the reasons they'd acted in the ways they had. Suddenly the programme cut to a sombre-looking man in a newsroom.

"We interrupt this programme to bring you some breaking news. A series of explosions have been reported across the United States, all occurring shortly after midday. Five cities were targeted, killing nineteen people, injuring many more. The death count is expected to rise. Some viewers may find the following scenes disturbing."

The first and most devastating blast had struck the Electropets' Headquarters in Menlo Park, California. A knot formed in Arty's stomach — Electropets were on the Holy Order's corporate hit list. Someone had gained access to the building carrying a bomb in a suitcase and detonated it in a busy lift. Eight people, severed from life in an instant. Arty watched a fire crew pump water into a mangled, blackened lift shaft before the programme cut to an eyewitness account with a clearly shocked, middle-aged American-Asian woman who spoke in fits and starts:

"It was lunchtime. My colleague Jerry asked if I wanted to grab yum-cha. I walked to the elevator with him before realising that I'd forgotten my purse. Jerry even made a joke about it. I can see him laughing right now — I always forget my purse. I told him I'd join him. He said he'd save a place for me in the line. It was so loud it shook the entire building. I fell into the water cooler. I can't believe it. I can't believe Jerry's gone."

The next piece of footage was from a gaming cafe in Seattle where multiple lives had been lost. *No*, thought Arty. His fork, suspended in mid-air since the newscast began, clattered to the ground. Was the cafe affiliated with Spiralwerks? Was this an indirect attack on them? The entire front section of the cafe was missing, as was the top half of the van parked outside. Every window in the vicinity had been blown out of its frame. The road was chock-full of police cars, ambulances and fire engines that struggled to pass one another. People were either hugging each other in tears or sitting on the curbside, hands on heads, staring into space. This wasn't right, it couldn't be happening. He grabbed his tray with shaking hands and put it on the desk, suddenly feeling sick. The newscast reverted to the studio.

"All of the targets appear on a list that was recently circulated by the Holy Order, an organisation comprised of 'techno-shamans' who have declared allegiance to an artificially intelligent being ... who doesn't exist as yet. The Holy Order claim that this being — who they refer to as the 'Magi' — has contacted them from the future and persuaded them to help 'give birth' to it. The Order's manifesto, entitled *Sacred Singularity*, provides an explanation of the reasoning behind their bizarre beliefs, stemming from a thought experiment known as Roko's Basilisk. The group claims that the logical outcome of the thought experiment is that the world will become a far better place once the Magi is in charge of it, and use this explanation to excuse their terrorist attacks."

Beside him, Arty noticed that Hannah had entered the room. She'd initiated a bridge call in *Settlers of Catan*, the meeting room down the corridor, and wanted him to join them as soon as possible. He nodded to her and mumbled his confirmation while anger rose inside of him. *No*, he wanted to say, *no, I cannot join them*. It would be a meeting focused on death and destruction. What did *he* know about such things? Nothing. He was a creator, an innovator. He *made* things, didn't destroy them, and he wanted it to stay that way.

All of a sudden, the Year-Long Game had deformed into something bearing more resemblance to a Year-Long Nightmare.

Chapter Fifteen

The days after the blast were the hardest of Nova's life. As soon as she stepped through the front door that evening, she knew something was wrong. Her parents wore the sombre expressions they'd had the day her grandmother had died. They made her sit down on the sofa before they gave her the news. At first, her body went numb. Then it shook uncontrollably, while tears had streamed down her face.

Eventually they'd helped her to her feet, up the stairs and to her room. She'd taken the Valium her mum had handed her without question and, for the briefest of moments, had hoped she wouldn't wake up. At least, not until everything was back to normal again.

Everything seemed lost. Nothing had meaning. Her books lay unopened on her desk; her Booners were discarded where she'd left them, somewhere downstairs probably. She didn't care. Even Zhang couldn't comfort her. His playful demeanour was so unsettling that she turned him off for a bit. Her dad spent most of the time in his shed, aware that there was nothing he could say or do to make things better, while her mum waited on her hand and foot, and was there to cuddle and cry with.

Messages of sympathy poured in from Burner, Jockey and many school friends she didn't know cared. She read them, touched by their sentiment, but found that she had nothing to say in reply. The only person she wanted to talk to had been taken from her, forever. How could her Solarversia Sister be gone?

The footage from the destroyed gaming cafe in Seattle had imprinted itself on her mind. She'd forced herself to view the attack from the 360-degree cams in the area, like it was the bare minimum she could do for her friend, to have been there with her until the end. A single feed had captured Sushi at the moment of the blast. Thank God it had been grainy and slightly out of focus. A mercy, however small. One second Sushi was there, the next she was gone. And it hurt, like nothing she'd known.

Nova had often heard it said that it was the small things in life that meant the most. So it was with her friend's death. Hearing their favourite songs played on the radio was enough to send her to her knees, immobilised by grief. She changed her route to Maidstone High to avoid the Japanese restaurant where Sushi had earned her name because the sight of it left her winded.

But the thing that made Nova saddest of all was not having Sushi to play with. Not having someone tempt her to bunk off homework to play a quick sim. Not having someone to practise her Combinations with, or to patiently listen while Nova described her latest idea for an amazing game she'd devised. And, stupid as it sounded, she hated that she'd never get to see her friend transform into her Siamese cat Super Avatar.

One evening, a week after the blast, Nova's world was shaken for a second time. She'd retreated to her room with a bunch of movies she'd liked as a kid when her Booners signalled an incoming message. She froze, almost choking on her own breath. The message ringtone was the Solarversia jingle, the one she and Sushi used as a ringtone for one another. She hadn't set it to go off under any other circumstance.

She stared at her Booners for a while, mulling possibilities over in her mind. They'd definitely just played the jingle, she was sure of that. She'd never known Burner do something this twisted. He might have been immature and prone to taking things too far, but this? He wouldn't have dared. Perhaps some jerk from school had recently discovered trolling.

She clasped her ponytail and threaded it between her hands while she pondered a list of likely suspects, people she might have offended somehow. The Booners sat there, on her desk, containing a mystery all of a sudden. She reached out to them a couple of times like she was scared they might leap up and attack her before she could allow herself to grab them, then peered into the display from a safe distance.

The message *was* from Sushi, its subject line a simple one: "I'm on Soul Surfer." An old memory stirred from its slumber. Her eyes flitted to the ceiling while she said the words out loud. *Soul Surfer*. The ghost of a smile crept across her face as she remembered what this was about.

She hadn't been the victim of some sick prank after all. Soul Surfer was the name of an app they'd got excited about a few years ago, the same way they'd gotten excited about a hundred different things. She strained to remember the details — something about a computer algorithm pretending to be you once you'd died, allowing your spirit to live on. It was immortality for the masses, served in a bottle shaped like an app.

She was conscious of the concerted effort she made when slipping her Booners on, the way she carefully brushed her hair behind her ears, straightened her shoulders, even cleared her throat — like she was about to go on a virtual date. She paused a few seconds, took a deep breath and opened the message, all the while reminding herself to keep her expectations low and to stay on guard, knowing that it might yet turn out to be a phishing scam of sorts. The message was from the CEO of Soul Surfer rather than Sushi herself, an introductory few lines that explained the purpose of the app.

"Dear Nova Negrahnu, I'm sorry to learn that you recently lost someone you were close to. Sushi Harrison listed you as her 'best friend in the world' on her profile and indicated that you might be interested in this novel way of communicating with her now that she's gone. Soul Surfer has been helping millions of people just like you deal with their grief since 2017. We've created a computerised version of your friend, who now exists on our servers, and is waiting for you should you choose to proceed with using the app. My sincerest condolences, Charlotte Applewhite, founder and CEO of Soul Surfer Inc."

Beneath the message was a personal video from Charlotte, which Nova vaguely remembered from the time she and Sushi had read about it. She'd lost her husband and only child, a son in his early twenties, in a road traffic accident. With an interest in machine learning, the funds from the sale of a previous start-up, and a laser focus fuelled by grief, she'd been the perfect candidate to work on such a controversial idea.

Feeding in every known piece of information about her loved ones — photos, videos, email transcripts; input from everyone that knew the deceased — she slowly iterated algorithms that approximated their personalities. Word got out about what she was doing, other bereaved people started asking questions, and before long she was swamped with requests to make the software available to the public.

Nova explored the app further. She flinched when she saw Sushi's profile. It knew the time, location and cause of her death. If she chose to use the app, it would take Sushi's entire digital footprint and create a specific 'instance' of her, one unique to Nova. Anyone else who used the app to talk to Sushi would receive their own version of her. Every time Nova interacted with her instance of Sushi, she could provide feedback to her friend — or at least, the computer algorithm learning to be her — to make her more Sushi-like. Slowly, over time, the different instances of the program would diverge, creating multiple copies that embodied her different personality traits as remembered by the people who knew her.

She removed the goggles, placed them on her lap and exhaled slowly and deliberately. Life without Sushi was incomprehensible. They'd attended the same nursery from the age of two and had, according to Mrs Negrahnu, been inseparable from the day they'd met.

Nova had been playing with a tipper truck in the sandpit when an older boy had steamed over and snatched it from her. Spotting the incident from the other side of the nursery, Suzy — as Sushi was still known back then — had intercepted the fleeing boy, grabbed the truck off him and returned it to a teary-eyed but grateful Nova.

A couple of years later when the two girls were already the best of friends, their mums arranged a quick visit to the local sushi joint for the four of them one evening. On arriving at the restaurant Nova had burst into tears, distraught at the prospect that they were there to 'eat Suzy'. When the adults burst into laughter, Suzy put an arm around her friend, drew her close and promised that she'd always be there to protect her. It was the incident that had earned Sushi her nickname.

And now, what was this? A computer version of her Solarversia Sister? She didn't know what to think. Would she be offended if Nova didn't use the app? What would Sushi want her to do? They sounded like ridiculous questions, and Nova surprised herself with the amount of serious thought she gave them. She imagined the roles being reversed. What would *she* have wanted Sushi to do? Win Solarversia, of course. But also ensure that justice was done, that whoever killed her was found and sent to rot in a jail somewhere.

She put her Booners back on without knowing why and, instead of returning to Soul Surfer, opened up The Sandbox, a generic app that allowed you to build simple virtual structures. "Create cube, sides three metres in length. Place me in the centre. Colour the ceiling black." She paused, suddenly aware that she was recreating a Corona Cube. The pulsing yellow walls of plasma didn't seem appropriate. "Colour the walls blue. Actually, make them different shades of blue. The wall I'm facing, give it a title in large white letters along the top. Title: 'the Holy Order'. Perform Google search on title. Display results on wall. Group by file type."

The wall came to life in front of her face. The top layer, just below the title, started filling up with text-based documents: the Order's manifesto, articles and forum results blossomed into view. Beneath that were images: symbols from the manifesto including the curly swastika, avatar pictures of the homeless people involved in the griefing attack and photos of the destruction caused by the bombs. The bottom layer of results was made up of videos, mainly newscasts and opinion pieces. She stepped back from the wall and tried to take it all in at once, feasting on the newly assembled gestalt, allowing it to permeate her being. It was several minutes before she moved or spoke again.

"On the wall to my left, create a timeline. I want the bombings in the middle. Before that event I want to see the places that the Holy Order showed up online. To which sites did they post their manifesto and in what chronological order?" The timeline flowered into existence: a thick horizontal line from which a series of vertical branches soon sprouted. Some of the documents, images and videos on the main wall flashed before moving around the cube to append themselves to the branches, their size determined by the relative importance of the search result.

She studied the line up close, interacting with its contents, increasing the size of some of the results and flicking others out of existence. "Place the list of corporate targets on the wall behind me."

And so it went. Nova paced around the cube, adding and subtracting information from it, sorting it, visualising it in different ways, doing everything she could to make sense of it. She had been going at it for three hours straight before she began to wonder where she was going with it all. What exactly was she looking for? If a major clue stared her in the face, would she even know it?

She kept being drawn back to the section of wall with the maps on it: one that showed the companies on the hit list and one that showed the locations of the attacks. She glanced between the maps and the section of wall that contained the symbols while a vague idea bubbled away in the depths of her mind. As much as she valued her independence and wanted to do this without help, if she was going to do this properly, she'd need reinforcements. She messaged Burner.

"Are you there, mate?"

The Sandbox automatically positioned a static picture of his avatar floating in mid-air in front of her face. She gently pushed the picture to one side so that she could continue staring at the composition on the wall. A few seconds later, his avatar replied.

"Hey, Scotia. How you doing?"

"Yeah, not so bad." She paused, realising that for the first time in a week, she actually felt pretty good. "I've got something to tell you."

"Listen, you've got every right to be annoyed with me, mad even. I know that sending a couple of messages was pathetic — I should have come to see you. It's just that I'm really crap with the whole death thing. Never know what to say. End up talking bollocks and making it worse. Which means I didn't visit, and that was wrong. If you want me to come over right now, I'm there."

She smiled, touched by the very un-Burner-ish outburst.

"I'm not annoyed with you at all. I haven't really felt like seeing anyone, including you."

"Well, that's good to know. What's up?"

"It's Sushi. She's back. Kind of. You ever heard of an app called Soul Surfer? We signed up for it, years ago. I'd forgotten all about it until a few hours ago when I received a message from her."

"Woah, spooky shit. What was it like?"

"I don't know. I mean, I haven't seen her yet. But the message made me realise I should be doing something about her death rather than wallowing in self-pity." She swallowed back some tears. "It's the Holy Order. I want to help find them. Sandbox: give Burner view access of the room."

His floating 2D avatar disappeared and was replaced by his 3D avatar, now standing next to hers in the cube. They did their usual fist bump before he started glancing around at the reams and reams of data that now adorned the walls. She started explaining her train of thought — why she'd grouped certain results together but ignored others — and didn't stop talking until several minutes later when, suddenly out of breath, she glared at him, impatient to kick off whatever master plan they would end up devising together.

"Wait a second, mate. Sushi died and that's the worst thing that's ever happened. If *you* died, I don't know what I'd do. Grieving, and wanting to do something to remember her by — even wanting to avenge her death — that all sounds normal. But doing something to find the loonies behind all of this? Trying to hunt them down when the FBI, with their billions in funding, haven't managed to. Are you sure? With all due respect, it sounds a bit crazy."

A feeling of anger flared inside her. She watched it from a distance, knowing that she had no right to be angry with him. If anything, he'd just spoken sense. She went and stood directly in front of him and wished that they were doing this in person so that she could use her puppy-dog eyes on him. Instead she'd have to convey her desperation through her voice.

"You're right, I'm being ridiculous. There's a vanishingly small chance that we'd be able to find something the big guys missed. But they *do* miss stuff. And not just rarely either, but *all the time*. History's full of examples of regular people like us spotting some random pattern or detail and going on to solve a crime or figure out a mystery that's eluded the experts for decades. And besides, this is Sushi we're talking about here. If I do nothing, then I've failed her. And if there's one person who might be able to help find something the FBI have missed, it's my old mate Burner."

"What exactly did you have in mind?"

"The kind of geeky stuff you're always going on about. You're into AI and data and drones and stuff. I don't know what I have in mind. I was hoping you'd come up with something. Like, look at all the symbols in the manifesto. Those are kind of like the logos of the Holy Order — their calling cards. Maybe they're out there in the world somewhere. These drones you're always going on about — like the one you built — they can fly to places we can't."

"So you're suggesting that we feed the contents of the manifesto, and any associated metadata, into a program, upload it into a bunch of drones, have them scour areas of interest looking for locations — hideouts, safe houses, that kind of thing — while they upload footage into the cloud for analysis? At which point we analyse the results, iterate the program and repeat the process until we find something."

By now he was pacing up and down the cube, one hand on his chin, the other wagging a finger while he spoke. Nova realised that it was good, after all, that he wasn't there to see her grinning at him.

"Jono knows people," he continued. "There's a couple of guys in his year who have been working on this semantic analysis idea. Bloody clever, they are. They're about to drop out of uni to start a company. We could approach them, help them test their program, be guinea pigs. It'd be an amazing case study if we pulled it off." He paused and looked at her, suddenly aware of how the conversation was going. "You're right, it's a ridiculous idea — a million to one shot. And if we hire a bunch of drones, that could cost hundreds, maybe thousands, of pounds, you know that?"

"Seeing as there *is* a chance — however small — do you think you could look into for me? I can give you access to edit this room. You can speak to Jono's mates, get their take on it. Just get me a rough estimate of the cost. I'll find the money, you don't need to worry about that."

"OK. Let's give it a try. We'll need a name. What about 'Project Drone'?"

"Project Drone," Nova repeated. "I like it."

"You need to do me a favour in return. Don't get your hopes up, alright?"

Once Burner had left the room she punched the air and performed a couple of pirouettes. This felt good, however crazy it was. She was actually doing something.

A feeling she'd constantly had over the last few days came back to her — the urge to tell Sushi what she was up to. And now she could. She left The Sandbox, returned to Soul Surfer, ticked the box to accept the terms and conditions and found herself sitting on a bench next to her friend on a hill overlooking Seattle.

"Hey, Nova, how are you?"

Sushi's long blonde hair was tied in bun, leaving a wisp of hair to fall either side of her ears, the way she usually wore it. Her green eyes — which Nova thought sparkled more than usual — were complemented by the opal necklace she wore on top of her black turtleneck sweater. She looked every bit as sweet and beautiful as she had the last time they'd talked. Nova took her hand and they sat for a while in silence. Suddenly her need to talk was gone. She had questions to ask, but now wasn't the time. She wanted her old friend back, the real one. She would give anything for that. But the next best thing wasn't so bad after all.

Chapter Sixteen

Arty readjusted the knot in his tie and tried to remember the last time he'd worn a suit. It was long enough in the past that he couldn't accurately recall, and still it felt too soon. He grimaced at his reflection and tried to flatten his curls into submission.

As usual, Hannah looked great. Her dress clung here and flowed there and brought out the colour of her eyes. In the mirror, they looked like a couple off to a wedding. The thought tugged at him — they looked *suited*. Except she was way out of his league, he told himself for the thousandth time. His hair wouldn't behave, he was hot and uncomfortable — if he could just loosen the knot, then maybe he'd be able to relax.

"Stop fidgeting, your tie looks fine," Hannah said and playfully smacked at his hands.

"I think it's blocking my airway," he said, and began to breathe fiercely through his nose. God, she smelled great too, like coconut and vanilla.

"You're worse than a wee lad sometimes, Arty. If you can speak, you can breathe."

The security guard at the front desk called out to get their attention and gave them the thumbs-up: the guests were here and being cleared by security. Penelope Lockhart, the Mayor of London, was here on an official visit.

"What, she's here? Already? Christ, I'm not ready for this. Hannah, you'll do the talking, yeah? You're good at this stuff. I mean, you're the Head of Comms, for God's sake, it's your job, right?"

"Of course I will. If you'll let me."

Arty had a habit of overcompensating for his shyness with a neurotic verbosity.

"What are you so worried about? It'll be good press for us. We'll get some photos of you shaking hands with Penelope, she'll watch the film, we'll do the fly-by, and hey, presto, Spiralwerks is a super-fun company again."

"I hope so. We really need it."

"Just ... don't even mention the terrorists."

"Definitely. I won't."

He took one last look in the mirror, flattened his palm against his hair and yanked at the tie again. Behind him, Hannah rolled her eyes and said, "We're ready, thanks, Eva," to the girl behind reception who kicked off the animated display. The walls and staircases of the large circular lobby transformed into a lush green jungle scene.

Arty held his hands aloft, walked towards the guests and with a sudden flush of confidence announced, "Madam Mayor, welcome to the jungle!"

The newly assembled group ascended in the lift through bushes and trees, rustling the leaves they brushed past. The cries of howler monkeys rang out, as if from a distance, and a majestic parrot soared right by their heads. The lift came to rest on the sixth floor, overlooking a vast jungle canopy to the sound of a Tarzan yell, which made the Mayor jump and burst into a fit of giggles.

"What a wonderful place it must be to work," she said.

"We Spiralheads like it," said Hannah. She proceeded to give the group the 'executive tour' of the sixth floor, which admitted guests into the large meeting rooms, showed them around the various departmental workspaces to meet hand-selected enthusiastic members of staff and ended in the screening room. Today, plush cinema seats had been laid out facing the floor-to-ceiling screens. Most of the seats were already taken, populated by a noisy gaggle of Solos who had won tickets through one of the recent quests. Hannah showed the mayor and her entourage to the seats reserved for them while Arty took his place at the lectern at the front of the room and cleared his throat.

"Thank you for joining us for the first screening of *Welcome to Solarversia: Earth and Beyond*. This documentary tells the story of everything that's happened since The Game commenced eight weeks ago. We're especially proud to show this today to such an illustrious audience and we'd like to thank you all for your dedication and support. Madam Mayor, I know you don't play yourself, but you mentioned that your sons do. They would recognise the events you're about to see."

"They do play, and I must say, they're rather jealous that I'm here today. In a job like mine, that doesn't happen very often."

"Without further ado," Arty said, relieved that he'd be able to take his seat in a moment, "welcome to Solarversia."

The lights in the room dimmed and the high-res screens came to life, showing the word 'Solarversia'. The camera zoomed towards the 'O', which revealed a bird's-eye view of the Olympic Stadium on the night of the opening ceremony, where thousands of people were cheering in the stands to the sound of drums and whistles. Lasers fired into the night sky while people on floats screamed and danced. Then a deep-voiced American man began to narrate over the images.

"It all started with a chimp in a suit and a strange-looking palace floating high above the ocean."

The screen was filled with the sight of Gorigaroo bouncing and swinging as he traversed the length of Castalia's Magisterial Chamber, the vines rustling, his breath heavy and exuberant. Then suddenly the rear wall exploded with an almighty bang that sprayed rubble and dust everywhere.

"An Emperor from a far-off galaxy ..."

Although he knew the game as well as anyone could, there was something extraordinary about seeing it all flowing together like this. Arty listened, enchanted, to the hundred-mouthed choir singing from the bubbling totem pole and felt a jolt of surprise — as though it was new to him — when on the other side of the room, the wall crumbled and the grid lit up.

" ... And a hundred million people, from every country on Earth, taking up the invitation to explore Solarversia."

The camera spanned the chamber, then zoomed out, slowly at first, moving through the roof and away from the palace, speeding up as it travelled into the sky until it was able to take in the whole planet, which now filled the screen. Lines sprouted from a miniscule dot in the ocean, then branched and branched again. Earth started rotating and the Solarversia theme tune kicked in, backed by a techno beat. Icons representing the major quests flashed up over the cities they happened in. At first the Earth was bathed in a violet light, but every time an Earth Force Field icon flashed on screen, the colour flickered out to a ruby red afterglow.

" ... And then, after six weeks of gameplay, the world of Solarversia changed forever. Nothing will be the same again ..."

The camera panned to Giza, Egypt. Thousands of players were taking selfies in front of the Great Sphinx, the peak of a pyramid visible behind them. The sky was dark and moody, and far away, a ball of lightning was streaking across the darkness like a meteor. And then suddenly it was hurtling toward Giza at great speed, roaring towards the Great Pyramid. All the players in the vicinity adopted the brace position or cowered in fear.

Just when it looked likely to crash into the north face of the structure, the lightning ball slowed. It was not tearing through the sky any more so much as drifting, and now, at this slower pace, its shape was revealed. It wasn't a meteor at all, but a young man, strapped into waxen wings covered with feathers. Lightly, and with grace, he landed on the pyramid, unraveled the parchment in his hands and began to read.

"I, Icarus, man of air as well as earth, hereby invite you to help locate and unlock the tenth and final Earth Force Field switch, hidden somewhere in Giza ..."

A population counter for Giza appeared in the top right of the screen, ticking up rapidly as Solos flocked there from teleport machines around the world. Players at the top of the Pyramid ran to the edge of the precipice and waved at the players below like wild men on acid. The camera swooped away from them to catch a glimpse of the thousands of players pulling on ropes attached to a harness around the Great Sphinx, which edged forward, a millimetre at a time, revealing a mammoth stone tablet engraved with strange-looking symbols.

Hundreds of players darted across the thin line at the base of the pyramid and began to climb, pausing frequently to swipe rapidly through their datafeeds, stopping to compare the hieroglyphs that appeared on the steps to the attempts to decode them that are flocking in. Players typed messages into keypads set into the stones and watched in horror as the screens returned big red crosses, and the steps they were standing on flipped ninety degrees, flinging them back down the pyramid.

The film cut to a shot of Ludi Bioski, tinkering at his Orbitini in the palace, bringing a pot of colourless liquid to the boil, tapping its surface and setting it on fire, moving glass beads along his abacus. The large screen at the front of his contraption displayed a new Event Card: a flaming bird's nest.

Back in Giza, the eyes of the Great Sphinx heated up, turning redder and redder until, with sparks of light and emissions of smoke, they shot out laser beams which ignited fires wherever they hit. Birds from miles around were attracted to the fires and flew straight into them as if sucked in by a powerful current. Flying out of the fires came phoenixes, clutching blazing rocks in their talons. They circled the pyramid, flinging the fireballs at the players still attempting to match the right code to the right brick.

Suddenly, every brick on the East face spun as one, sending players tumbling down the pyramid. All except a young Chinese man, Johnny Wong, who had made a correct match. He'd typed in the hieroglyphs that translated as information about the Great Pyramid itself: that it was constructed using 2.3 million blocks, weighs an estimated 5.9 million tonnes, and that it was the tallest man-made object for 3.8 thousand years. As he tapped the deciphered message into the right stone, it vanished. Johnny dived into the gap as a flaming rock blazed toward him from above, missing him by inches.

The sun shone into the passage, reflecting off the sandstone like gold. According to the map on his screen, this was the Grand Gallery, a long passageway that sloped up to the burial chambers. Johnny followed the map on his screen to arrive in the King's Chamber where the Pharaoh himself was enthroned, wearing a blue and gold striped headdress and clutching a walking stick whose grip had been fashioned like a cobra flaring its hood.

To the left of the King was the tenth and final Earth Force Field switch. It was a scale model of the Great Pyramid itself, but enclosed within a transparent Force Field. In front of the pyramid, outside the Force Field, was a floating keypad waiting for instructions. Johnny Wong kneeled before the King, who leaned forward ever so slightly before addressing him.

"Welcome, player number 55,211,801. I am Pharaoh Khufu, the man who commissioned this pyramid. I was rather fond of games myself. I'm sure that if I were still alive, I would be playing Solarversia with you. Which brings us to the ultimate part of this quest. If I was alive today, and playing the game, what would my grid number be?"

Yet another counter appeared at the top of the screen, showing the number of players who had made it this far in the quest — over two thousand and counting. Above the floating keypad Johnny saw that he had three attempts at guessing the number. He watched for a few seconds as other players, in their own phased instances of the pyramid, used all three of their tries, and were flung to the base of the pyramid and barred from re-entry.

"But how could Johnny know what number King Khufu would be? Did he really have to make a one in a hundred million guess? No. Johnny knew that knowledge itself is power."

A string of Google search results flitted past the screen as Johnny frantically hunted for clues about the Pharaoh. One page displayed an image of the 'Ivory figurine of Khufu', along with a description that claimed it was the only three-dimensional artwork of the king to have survived intact through to the modern day. The sculpture was held by the Egyptian Museum in Cairo, its inventory number JE 36143. Johnny stepped forward and tapped the numbers in. His finger hadn't left the '3' when the Force Field flickered and then disappeared for good, leaving in its wake the exposed model pyramid whose tip was now glowing. Not wanting to waste a single second, Johnny stepped forward and slammed his hand down hard.

The entire chamber shook, and pieces of rubble fell to the ground. Above them a shaft of light appeared. Red sunbeams hit the chamber for the first time in four thousand years, dappling the King's headdress, which diffracted the light in the room as the majestic sound of angels filled the air. The chamber was on the move, rising through the pyramid until finally, it reached the apex.

Now Johnny was at the top of the pyramid beside the winged man, who touched his shoulder gratefully. With a great leap, Icarus launched himself into the air. He flew up to the Earth Force Field and touched a finger to it, sending a ripple that reverberated through its red expanse. The red changed to orange, the orange to yellow, cycling back through the colours of the rainbow until the field turned violet, at which point there was an almighty crunch of static electricity and a bright flash that filled the screen, leaving in its wake a deafening silence.

The Force Field has disappeared and the sky had flared into a thousand intertwined patterns that were submitted by players who had contributed to the success of the various EFF quests. The sky looked like it was being painted by an almighty celestial being, and the crowds in Giza erupted into song and dance. The various counters along the top of the screen disappeared.

"Johnny Wong, player number 55,211,801, will forever be known as the man who turned off the Earth Force Field and set into motion the events that would unlock the entire Solar System. Last week The Game changed forever. Solarversia got its space wings."

Small spaceships were seen docking with the International Space Station. Players wearing spacesuits floated around inside it, madly scrambling to return hundreds of floating Flakeroonies to the open cereal packet in the craft's kitchen before they ran out of air and failed the quest. Other players back on Earth were shown solving puzzles and winning bounties, which caused difficulties for the astronauts aboard the Station: making it spin out of control, depressurising it, and starting fires that needed to be extinguished.

Arty studied the reactions of the people in the room and wondered how many of them understood the deeper significance of Solarversia. He'd designed its structure to mimic the nature of the universe itself — to start in a simple manner with the game of Paper, Scissors, Stone, and to evolve from that point on, complexifying as it went, forcing players to compete and collaborate, the way life forms had done since they emerged, echoing life's journey from Alpha to Omega.

"Completion of the International Space Station quest unlocked a new set of spaceships capable of reaching the Moon. The quest that took place on the moon

unlocked the Interplanetary Spaceships, creating a Solar System-wide travel infrastructure."

The Moonbase Quest, which had involved players finding and planting flags, should have been exciting for Arty to watch, given its significance in leading to space travel. In reality, the quest had been a total ballache. A griefing clan known as the ROFL Mongers had coordinated their efforts in such a way that they managed to decommission half the Moon buggy fleet. It had only been some quick thinking by a member of Carl's team that had averted another PR disaster.

He now realised the irony of the situation. If they hadn't encouraged players to collaborate, perhaps the leagues of griefers wouldn't have got together to cause mayhem and panic. As the screens faded and the lights came back up, the saying *Be careful what you wish for* flashed through his mind.

***

The mayor walked to the lectern on the stage at the front of the room and shook Arty's hand before scanning her notes and addressing the crowd in a calm, confident manner.

"The amazing thing about Solarversia is its size and scope. It's a game played by one hundred million people from every single nation in the world. If it was a country itself, it would be the thirteenth largest by size of population. It's a game that allows and encourages its players to travel the length and breadth of not only Earth, but also the entire Solar System. The opportunities to learn in this game are endless. In the words of St Augustine, 'The world is a book and those who do not travel read only a page.' Spiralwerks have enabled people from all walks of life to travel the Earth and the Solar System for free. And it was made here in London, the creative capital of the world. Eighteen months ago my office was approached by Hannah McCreadie, the Head of Communications, to apply for planning permission for an audacious public monument, one she firmly believed would not only become a tourist attraction in its own right, but would also act as an educational beacon, attracting pupils from around the United Kingdom to the vitally important subject of space exploration and understanding. Four months ago, after a wide-ranging public consultation, that monument, Sun Two Point O, was officially unveiled."

Arty and Hannah grinned at one another. They were proud of this project. It was Hannah's baby, though they'd both put in dozens of hours to help make it a reality. Sun Two Point O was a yellow sphere, ten metres in diameter, in the middle of Regent's Park and was the centrepiece of Spiralwerks' Mini Solar System project.

The sphere was a giant Tesla globe — its surface looked like the plasma walls inside the Corona Cubes. Tourists could visit the sphere, download the app onto their headsets and phones, and then scour the streets and buildings of London trying to find the virtual planets on their orbits. It was a citywide Easter egg hunt of cosmic proportions.

Arty prepared a couple of headsets for the two of them. The mayor received hers warmly, propped it on her forehead and addressed the crowd one last time. "And now, ladies and gentlemen, if you'll excuse me, I'm going to leave the real world for the virtual. I'm told Venus will pass by in" — she looked at her watch — "approximately two minutes."

Arty ensured that the mayor was comfortable before putting his own headset on. Around the room others followed suit.

"It's pitch-black in here, Artica, is that right?"

"Look this way, please, Madam Mayor."

"My word, that's incredible. You're dressed like an astronaut."

"That's right. And so are you. Our headsets have been synced so that we can see each other. You'll notice other astronauts come into view as people in the room join the app. Please turn to your left. There we go, now you're looking at the Sun, which appears larger than usual because we're forty million kilometres closer to it. And to your right — you won't be able to see it just yet — is Venus, which will fly past in approximately thirty seconds."

"Forgive my ignorance, Artica, but how does the app work? Are we mere spectators, or will there be something for us to do when Venus flies by?"

"No, it's very much an interactive experience. The first thing we'll be able to do is stop Venus in its tracks. Here it comes, I'll show you."

As the blistering little planet approached them, Arty heard the mayor let out a quiet whimper. It really did look like it would knock you for six if you didn't leap out its way. Before it could reach them, he held out a hand like a traffic policeman at a busy junction and the planet came to a sudden halt. He zoomed right into its thick, cloudy atmosphere, then back out again, before placing the planet on his index finger and spinning it like a basketball, delighting in his role as a modern-day Atlas who had total control over the celestial spheres. Beside him he heard the mayor make all the right noises in all the right places. He zoomed them away from Venus one more time until it was the size of a football a metre or so from their heads.

"Now I'm going to show you another aspect of the app's interactivity. Social: on."

"You've made it look like a comet."

"Exactly. Except the tail is made of social interactions rather than cosmic gas. As the planets orbit the Sun, the people who witness them fly past, like we're doing now, get to upload social data: comments, photos and videos. Some people even host 'Planet Parties' to celebrate the fly-bys. If we zoom in a bit closer you'll notice that particles in the tail are different colours, signifying the different types of social interaction, and if we zoom in a bit closer, you'll even see the words, images and videos themselves. The closer the social particle to the planet, the more recently it was uploaded. Look at what I'm holding. It's a photo of us shaking hands downstairs when you arrived. I place the photo on the planet, like so, and it joins the tail."

"It's very impressive, I must say. I can see new particles appearing from the other groups in the room. And if we go back along the tail a bit further, I've noticed this. It's a picture of my sons. 'We hope you enjoy your visit to Spiralwerks.' How thoughtful of them."

"Actually, Madam Mayor, that particle's a video. The picture of your sons is merely the thumbnail image. If you prod it with your finger, it'll start playing."

She did as instructed. The video particle grew in size until it appeared as a cinema-sized screen in front of them; behind them the Sun dimmed to create the optimal viewing conditions. A clip started playing of the mayor going about her official business in London, mostly stock footage. It looked rather corporate, Arty thought, not the kind of clip he would have expected to see from a couple of teenage boys. A few seconds later the backing track screeched to a halt, leaving a frozen image of the mayor on the screen. When a Sword of Sadism appeared alongside her, he knew something was wrong but had no time to react. The sword whirled through the air and decapitated her. An arm came on screen, picked up the head by a clump of its hair and used the bleeding stump to scrawl the curly swastika logo belonging to the Holy Order.

Arty tore his headset off, leapt towards the mayor and helped her remove hers. She stared at him, speechless, her lower lip trembling, the glint of a tear in her eye. It was a blow, seeing her like that, someone who was usually so confident and self-assured, standing there limp, broken. Everyone in the room — the gamers, dignitaries and staff — stared at Arty, waiting for a fix he didn't have. The only noise came from the side of the room, where a dozen journalists eagerly filed their reports. Hannah looked at him, wide-eyed and in shock. Why hadn't they even thought to protect themselves from something like this? Spiralwerks needed to up its game. And quickly.

Chapter Seventeen

Nova looked at the signpost and cursed. She was in Australia to see Giganja, the Grandmaster in charge of Earth's Planetary Puzzles. Except Giganja resided on Ayers Rock, and she was in Darwin, which, as she had just discovered, was a full 1,435 km away. What a stupidly big country. She had fifty-seven teleport tokens in her inventory and this journey would cost forty. She had enough to get there, but what if she needed them later on?

The only alternative — flying there in Hawk — would take ages and she needed to be back at her books by the time her parents got back from the supermarket. It might have been a week before her first exam, but they seemed to expect her to revise *all day*. Too much revision frazzled the brain. That's what Sushi always said.

She hadn't visited her in the Soul Surfer app again. There'd been a few occasions when she'd *nearly* visited her, but bottled it at the last second. She wasn't even sure what she was scared of. Perhaps that seeing her again would intensify the pain she felt. She couldn't help but think the app was a cheap trick being played at the expense of desperate people.

Anyway, she hardly had time to spend with an algorithm based on her dead friend's digital media history when there was endless revision to be done. And far more important than visiting a computer version of Sushi, was avenging the real Sushi's death. Burner had come up trumps, like she'd known he would.

He'd spoken to his brother Jono, who had secured the support of Max and Maurice, a couple of tech geniuses he knew in Nottingham. They'd developed a program that was capable of performing the kind of data analysis Project Drone required. There was one hitch: Nova would need to find the money to fund it, and Burner was talking about thousands of pounds.

Without a job, and barely a hundred quid to her name, the plan was going nowhere, fast. In the meantime, she continued to labour away in the virtual room she'd created, sorting, curating and analysing the various automated feeds she'd set up to monitor online mentions of the Order.

She looked at the time, and then the signpost again. If she teleported now, she'd make the 3 p.m. puzzle in time, could tick it off May's list and be back at her books before her parents were any the wiser. Puzzles ran on the hour, so if she didn't visit Giganja now, she didn't know when she'd have time. Besides, a visit to this particular Grandmaster held a special significance; completing his puzzle was the last thing Sushi had ever done.

It was a done deal.

Halfway down the signpost, enclosed in a yellow circle, was the name of her current location, Darwin, and below it, a keypad. After typing in the coordinates of her desired destination, she touched her finger to the top of the circle and dialled round it, remembering to go anticlockwise. If she'd gone clockwise, like players needed to do in the northern hemisphere, she would have been fined a token. She promised never to be so stupid.

The top half of the signpost started to rotate, the quantum teleportation jingle sounded, and Nova materialised next to a signpost near the summit of the mighty red rock, delighted to have lost her teleportation cherry and to have ticked off a Bucket List item in the process.

Giganja sat cross-legged on the ground in the centre of a circle of small rocks. As people stepped into the circle they disappeared from Nova's view: Planetary Puzzles had to be tackled alone, so the circles were phased zones. She crossed the circle's boundary with 90 seconds to spare.

She was excited to meet her first Grandmaster. He was an old Chinese man whose wispy white beard looked like it would flutter away if the wind blew hard enough. She'd heard that the nine Grandmasters all looked alike and that the only way to tell them apart was the colour of their robes — Giganja's were bright orange. At precisely 3 p.m. he started talking in a croaky voice that reminded her of Burner with a hangover.

"Welcome to your Earth puzzle, Nova Negrahnu. Failure to solve it in time will mean the loss of a life, so I encourage you to pay attention to what I'm about to say. You may not accept assistance of any kind from any person or any form of artificial intelligence. You've given me permission to record the audio and video from your headset's cameras and microphones. Any evidence of cheating will be reviewed by a panel of judges, and is punishable by the deduction of a life and possible suspension from The Game itself."

Nova knew the rules of Puzzles by heart, having practised them in the Simulator for close to a hundred hours. She was endlessly fascinated by them and kept a journal of everything she learned about them. If she blitzed one, she wanted to know why. What was it about the Puzzle that she'd grasped so intuitively? Had she missed anything that might have led to a quicker time? She documented any Puzzles she screwed up even more closely, poring over their structure and content, seeking to understand the error of her ways.

She kept a note of her ideas for Puzzle scenarios in a separate diary. If she managed to defy all the odds and take Solarversia down, she wanted to be prepared for her role in helping to design the 2024 Game. Her aim was to impress the people at Spiralwerks to such an extent that they offered her a job at the company.

"There are 15,880 people here to play my puzzle this hour, but only 11,116 safe spots. You will see that the number of safe spots available diminishes as other players start completing the puzzle. If the counter reaches zero before you solve it, you will die and find yourself back in your Corona Cube. Every three minutes Gorigaroo will strike his gong, signalling the appearance of a new clue somewhere within the puzzle. Good luck, and remember: the man who beats the same drum with the same stick hears the same tune. There Can Be Only One!"

As her headset counted down the seconds to the start of the game, she drew a deep breath and struck what she thought resembled a martial arts pose, readying herself for anything. That was the thing about Puzzles: they were always different. Apparently Spiralwerks had managed to generate several million of them, so although training helped, you never knew what you'd be in for.

When the timer hit zero, Giganja, his circle and the rest of Ayers Rock disappeared, and she found herself standing in an old town square, enclosed on each side by a stone wall two storeys high. In the middle of the square was a restaurant whose undecorated awning sheltered some tables and chairs. She glanced at the walls encircling the piazza. At the top of one of them was a door with a bright green exit sign. She ran to the base of the wall and looked up. The exit was way out of her reach, yet the wall contained no hand or foot holds. She retreated a short way, charged at full speed, leapt as high as possible and bounced straight off to crash to the floor in a heap.

Her flashing display gave her the bad news: three lost health points. What the hell had she been thinking? She gritted her teeth and grumbled a few choice words under her breath. If the wall couldn't be climbed, the solution had to be found in the restaurant. From the disarray of the chairs and the unfinished plates on the tables, it looked like it had been deserted halfway through lunch.

The blackboard in the corner read 'Today's Specials' along the top, but was blank apart from that, as if the staff had forgotten to write them in. The plastic tables were laid with an odd assortment of items: bottles of beer whose labels, like the blackboard, were blank, plates of beans, and a magnifying glass. She held each up in turn, checking for hidden clues and was dismayed to find nothing.

She held the magnifying glass in one hand and slowly tapped it against her palm. Two minutes had gone by and she felt no closer to solving the puzzle. The exit was all the way up the wall, and she needed to reach it. But how were a bunch of random objects supposed to help?

She ran to a table in the sun, energised by a sudden realisation, and pointed the magnifying glass at the blank label of a beer bottle. She varied the distance from the glass to the bottle, trying to focus the sun's rays to a point, unsure exactly where to point, or why. Nothing happened. She pointed the ray at the plate of beans. The second the magnified rays hit them, beans started jumping up into the air, and Nova squealed with joy.

The rush of excitement she felt was quickly replaced with a sense of panic as she noticed a change to one of the counters in her display. It was the number of safe spots left — someone had already solved the puzzle. At first it ticked down by just one number. But then it ticked down again, and again. Before long the number was in free fall.

As she looked from table to table, trying to work out what those people might have seen, Gori's gong sounded. Nothing inside the restaurant looked different, so she ran outside and quickly spotted a new sign emblazoned across the awning. It now read 'Jumping Jacks'. She sighed. The beans had already jumped for her, and now everyone playing knew as much as she did. And the number of safe spots had just ticked below 10,000.

She brainstormed the possibilities. If she stacked the tables and chairs into a pile she could climb to safety. Except that didn't involve jumping. Could she use the magnifying glass to ride one of the beans out of there? Seemed a bit preposterous. But then so were twelve-armed octopi and bouncy cities. Another chime of the gong. She wasted no time. There had been two other items that had been blank when she arrived here: the blackboard and the beer bottles. It was the beer bottles that had changed this time. Their labels now displayed a picture of a smiling man, the name 'Volters', and an alcohol content of 6.18%. The number of safe spots ticked below 8,000.

It all became clear — she'd need to pole vault to safety. One vital detail was missing though: she had no pole. She felt another rush of panic, this time more intense, as the number went below 6,000. When she finally realised what to do, she nearly kicked herself. The pole was one of the first things she'd seen — it formed part of the awning in front of the restaurant.

She used the nearest chair for a boost, but only needed to touch the end of the pole for it to appear in her hands. A patch of ground started flashing several metres in front of the wall with the exit. She took a small run-up, holding the pole in the air, and was glad to find that the game did most of the work for her. It landed squarely in the centre of the patch, flexed down its length, and propelled her two storeys into the air to land on her feet by the exit.

As she crossed the threshold, two things happened: Giganja got crossed off her Bucket List, and fifty teleport tokens got credited to her inventory. She clenched her fists tight, ecstatic at having succeeded in her first meeting with a Grandmaster. One Planetary Puzzle down, eight more to go.

Chapter Eighteen

Nova was still dancing round her bedroom, hand-in-hand with Zhang, when she heard her dad call up the stairs, "Nova, get down here right this second."

That was his angry voice. She froze on the spot and could feel the joy drain out of her. She wondered how long they'd been home. Had they heard her dancing around? Maybe she'd screamed with delight when she'd landed by the exit in the town square. It seemed unlikely that her parents had guessed what she'd been up to, but it was always worth taking precautions. She scooped her Booners off the bed, stuffed them into the wardrobe, stuck a pencil behind her ear and headed downstairs.

On the way to the kitchen she got her story straight: she'd finally understood a particularly nuanced concept in sociology, let out a little yelp and burst into an impromptu dance routine as a result. It *had* been unlike her to do such a thing, for sure, it must have been all this revision, frazzling her brain. But as soon as she saw their mardy faces she could see this was a conversation that probably didn't concern a bit of skived revision. Hands placed firmly on her hips, it was Mrs Negrahnu who let rip first.

"I've just been on the phone to Katy Pugh's mum. Would you like to hazard a guess as to what she told me?"

Nova's heart plunged through her body. She had a fair idea what the old busybody might have said.

"She told me that you called Mrs Woodward an 'old cow' to her face, and received a month's worth of detentions as a result. Which means you've spent the last month of school—"

"Your last month *ever*."

"Your last month ever — thank you, Derek — doing detentions. A fine way to finish your school career. I think not."

"My school 'career'. Because school's a career, right?"

"Don't you dare, young lady. Don't you bloody dare." Her dad unfolded his arms to waggle a finger at her, and spoke through gritted teeth.

"And that's not all she said either. According to Katy, you've also been spending a fair amount of time down at Fraggle Hell, precious time that you—"

"It's 'Fragging Hell', mum, how many times do I have to correct you?"

Her dad went to speak but ended up saying nothing and gritting his teeth even tighter.

"Mum, please, you know Mrs Woodward winds me up, we've been through this a hundred times. She's a good teacher, but we're on totally different frequencies and sometimes—"

"And sometimes what? This isn't really about what you called her, although it *was* very rude of you. This is about honesty and integrity, young lady. It's about you lying to us about these detentions and continuing to go to wasser-name cafe when you promised you wouldn't."

"I didn't lie to you about them, I just didn't mention them, that's all. Need-to-know basis."

"Don't you *dare* pull that one," her dad barked at the top of his voice.

"Which one do you want me to pull?" she said before she could stop herself. It was times like this that she wished she was like Zhang and had an 'off' button to press. It would have saved her a lot of trouble over the years. Mr Negranhu shook his head and glared at her with a look of steely disappointment.

"After all we've done for you, you lie to us. Your dad's out of a job, but we still manage to pull the funds together to buy you a Booner Boy."

"What the hell's a Booner Boy when it's at home?"

"Enough!" her dad yelled, looking like he might have a cardiac arrest if she spoke again.

"You can consider yourself grounded for a start. Until your exams have finished at the very earliest. And you can say goodbye to your goggles until then, too. I wish we'd never bought them for you."

"Not my Booners, Mum." It came out as a whine. "I won't be able to play Solarversia properly."

"Sod Solarversia," her dad said. She stared at him in shock. It was the first time she'd ever felt genuine hatred towards him.

"You *do* know that my best friend died the other day? You do know that, right? Because sometimes I get the impression you either don't know, or just don't care."

Her chin quivered as tears streamed down her face. She didn't care about the stupid detentions, or whatever punishment her mum had dished out. What she cared about right now was getting far away from her parents as quickly as possible. She stomped to the garage, got into her car and slammed its door as hard as she could. She reversed on to the road and sped away from the house, with no idea of where she was going or what she might do once she got there.

***

Nova turned the ignition off and went to scoop Zhang up from the passenger footwell before realising that she'd left him at home. Deprived of him and her Booners — her twin comfort blankets — she felt more desperate than ever to see her old mate.

One of the best things about visiting Burner was that he lived on his own. Or at least, that's what he told people when they asked. It wasn't a complete lie. Nova would have loved a place like it — a large, self-contained unit at the rear of his parents' back garden. A glorified shed, she'd once called it, before she saw the interior and was completely won over. She knocked and entered without waiting for an answer, which was expected behaviour round at 'Burnside', as it had been christened one hot summer of experimental barbecues.

Burnside was a used shipping container Burner's old man had bought off a guy in a pub in Felixstowe. Burner had spent the good part of a year converting it into the house of his dreams. It consisted of three rooms: a bedroom, a chill-out lounge and a 'hackroom', where he spent most of his time. He'd installed the windows, insulation and electricity himself after watching a bunch of videos online. Nova sometimes wondered whether he was an actual genius.

She passed through the chill-out lounge and found him in the hackroom, welding an object behind a shower of sparks. She watched from a safe distance, never entirely sure how much proper training he'd received. The room was a modern-day *Wunderkammer*, a room that instilled a sense of wonder in those who entered it. Piled high with objects, no two the same, it was quite a challenge to traverse the room from one end to the other.

What she loved best was that every object in the room had a story behind it. And, as she'd come to appreciate, stories were what made things interesting, not their price tags or their labels. Her favourite item lived in the far corner. The front half of what was once a jet ski was now welded to the back half of an old bathtub and was ridden by a scary-looking mannequin wearing a pink wig and a pirate-themed neckerchief. It was an art installation Burner referred to as *Shockwave Rider*, and he always reckoned that if he wasn't married by the age of forty, he'd take Priscilla, the mannequin, to be his lawful wedded wife.

It took him a minute or two to notice her standing there. He waved at her in his bulky grey gloves, finished the seam he'd been working, turned the torch off and flipped the mask up. "If it isn't my old mucker, Scotia. I was thinking about you just this morning, wondering if you'd been doing enough Krazy Karting practice. Do you wanna put the kettle on? I'll be through in a minute."

She nodded and headed back to the chill-out lounge. A brew was exactly what she needed. The kettle was an old-fashioned brass beauty, the kind that whistled when it boiled. She liked that about Burner. He was one of the most tech-savvy people she knew, but he sometimes chose to go old school. As she was adding the trickle-of-milk-no-sugar to his mug, he came through to the lounge, wiping his hands on an old rag.

"Working on something for Nan. Reckons her wheelchair from the hospital is uncomfortable. Wondered if I might be able to do any better."

She pressed the teabag against the side of his mug with the spoon, fished it out, then gave it a good stir before wiping her nose on the cuff of her jacket again.

"Oh, dear, sorry. I didn't notice that you'd been crying. Can't see too well behind the welding mask. You OK?"

She handed him his mug and checked her reflection in her phone's screen. Mascara trails ran down her cheeks, giving her the 'heroin chic' look. Fortunately, Burner was one of the few people she felt comfortable in front of, whatever state she was in.

"Mum and Dad just found out about the detentions. Not good. They've confiscated my Booners. Double not good."

"The bloody cheek of it. You do *not* mess with a man's goggles." He pounded his fist on the coffee table and did his best 'outraged old man' impression. "Or woman's," he added, seeing the look she gave him. "That kind of thing should be enshrined by the European Court of Human Rights, up there with access to the Internet and pornography. You tell Derek and Susan I said so."

She let out a snigger and already felt a bit better.

"Wanna borrow that headset I made out of plastic and cardboard? The field of vision's a bit narrow, and the latency's pretty whacked out, but it still works. Better than no headset, right?"

"Yeah, that would be awesome, thanks, mate." She leant in to 'cheers' him with her mug. "I don't suppose you managed to make any more progress on Project Drone?"

"You suppose wrong, then. Had been meaning to call you. Give me a second."

He disappeared into the hackroom and returned carrying a couple of headsets, one of which he tinkered with before handing to Nova.

"That's the one you can borrow. You might as well give it a try while you're here to make sure it works properly. I've synced them so that we're both standing in the virtual room that you created. You in? Good. Check out this new area on wall two. What we're looking at here is the results from a semantic analysis tool built by those students in Jono's year. I fed the manifesto into it, along with several petabytes of information from forums, blogs and social networks: words, images and videos. The tool spat back a load of results that weren't very refined, so I reworked the algorithms and ran it again. These results are the fifth iteration of that process."

"OK. But what do the results tell us? Does it say where these Order freaks are or what?"

"Not quite. What it *has* done is returned a list of results in descending order of what it refers to as 'interestingness'. There are several thousand of these results, but we can start with the handful at the top and see how we go."

He used his finger to select the top ten results in the data table on the wall of the virtual room and dragged them to a map icon. A space cleared next to the table to include a map with the results plotted on it, each overlaid with associated data about the geography and demographics of the area in question.

"What do these results actually tell us?"

"If you touch any one of these results on the map it shows you the thinking behind the algorithm — it displays a list of the symbols, images, comments and so on that it thinks might be associated with the location. So the program tells us where to look and what to look for. We upload that information to a bunch of drones. They fly around and take a load of footage, which gets uploaded to a cloud-based server. I download that footage and run it back through this tool to see if they actually found anything. If we find something that looks like a hideout, we tell the FBI or whoever, and they go and pop some caps in some asses."

"Where do we get the drones from? Are we going to use the ones you've been building?"

"Not my ones, no. Most of the top results are located in the US. We'll need to use drones based over there. All we need now is a grand or two to kick things off."

Nova sunk back into the sofa. It all sounded so promising, so doable. Except for that last part. She couldn't raise that kind of money even if she sold everything she owned. Until then, the plan was like a word on the tip of her tongue, tantalisingly close, but just out of reach.

"So you're telling me that if we can get the cash, we can find them?"

"I'm telling you that if we get the cash, we can at least look for them. And like you said the other day, doing something's better than doing nothing, right?"

"Definitely," she said. "Two thousand pounds' worth of definitely."

Chapter Nineteen

Casey stuffed the last bundle of notes into the safe, locked it up and sat back down at the wobbly Formica table where he and Wallace counted the cash after their trips into town. His mind cycled through the various reasons he might have been asked to wait behind. He hadn't done something to annoy Father, had he? He hoped not. He couldn't think of anything he had done to cause an upset. If anything, he thought he'd performed well since arriving. He'd settled in and gotten used to life in the compound, even gotten used to the mosquitoes. As used to them as a man could get, anyway.

He doubted it was anything to do with business. Takings were up, week on week. And the publicity they'd received after the attacks had brought the Order worldwide fame. New members were joining all the time. People were finally realising that what they were doing was important. They were the only group of people who really understood what was going on, the fact that mankind stood at the brink of the emergence of a new kind of being, one so intelligent and powerful that mortal man would worship it with a godlike reverence.

A few minutes later Theodore entered the room without knocking. Casey stood up and bowed his head.

"Sit down, son." Theodore grabbed the other chair with his human hand and swung it round so that they sat directly opposite each other. "We finally get to meet, man to man." He spoke with a Southern drawl you could hang your hat on.

"Father, it's an honour to be here, serving mankind in this way."

"I hear you've been doing some fine work, you and Wallace, pulling in the money."

"I still have lots to learn. But I'm getting there, Father, yes."

"The money's an important part of the operation, the oil that greases the machine. You know we're growing fast, don't you? We need to maintain the rate of growth for a while yet until we're ten thousand strong. The Magi has big plans for his arrival here on Earth. *We're* the ones who heard Him, calling to us from the future, and *we're* the ones creating him, here in the present. Isn't that just the craziest goddang thing?"

Casey nodded. It had sounded crazy, for sure, when he'd first learned about it. Father leaned forward in his seat and stared deep into his eyes.

"Have you heard how we got started? How it all began?"

One of the first things that Wallace had told him when he arrived at the compound was not to ask about people's former lives. The less he knew, the less he'd be able to betray if he ever got caught. "Someone said you had a vision that inspired everything," he ventured, waving an arm to indicate the compound. Father nodded, seemingly eager to share. His words flowed out in an excited stream.

"When I lost my job as a programmer I thought my life was over. I'd created a program that could write programs. Went and put myself out of a job. Didn't see that one coming. It was less skilled people who were supposed to be losing their jobs. Programmers should have been safe. It was like I'd punched myself in the gut. I was winded and I couldn't get up again."

Casey listened, rapt.

"I felt like I'd lost everything: my identity, my entire way of life. Frances, God bless her soul, stuck by me. Said we should take a break, get away from it all. I'd always wanted to visit the Delta, so down we came. And then it happened, the darndest thing. One morning I told her I felt like going for a paddle up the river in a canoe. I'd never been in a canoe. I was a computer engineer, you know — an indoor type. But this wasn't a normal feeling; it was a burning desire, like a calling. I set off early that morning and paddled for miles. I had no idea where I was going, or why, but I knew I couldn't stop. Hours later, and completely lost, I stumbled across the Sub and knew I'd been headed here all along. The door was wedged shut, and it took me awhile to find a piece of wood tough enough to lever it open, but nothing was going to stop me. Somehow I knew that whatever was in there would be important to me. When I finally prised open the door, the stench sent me reeling; it was horrendous. The scene inside was even worse. Bodies decomposing, flies everywhere. It took awhile to distinguish the corpses; there were four in total, all men. Do you know what was strange about the situation? I wasn't scared. Not at all. And this is a man who freaks when he sees a spider in the bath. A calm washed over me, a feeling that I was *supposed* to be there."

He rocked in his seat as he laughed at the memory, and Casey joined him, laughing along.

"After that I searched the place. Not that I had to search hard. There were weapons everywhere, money just lying around. Piled up in the cockpit were several million dollars in cash and more cocaine than you ever saw in your whole goddamn life. I got stuck in, to hell with everything else. I didn't hold back, either. Kept going until my nose was agony, and my eyes felt like hot dry coals. I was at the coke for *days*. I ended up in the cargo hold at the bottom of the Sub, totally off my dial. Found some trap doors that led down into the water, and was playing around with the pressure gauges, wondering how it all worked. Once an engineer, always an engineer, right? I managed to pressurise the hold and open the doors and I was peering down into the water when I saw something move. Before I knew what was going on, an alligator had launched itself at me and clamped its jaws around my arm. It was thrashing around all over the place trying to pull me under. My instinct was to pull away, but every time I did, rocket loads of agony exploded up and down the limb. The pain was unbearable, but I knew that if it got me, I was a goner. I ended up pulling one way, him the other, and my arm just popped out of my shoulder socket and tore off in his teeth. I can still hear the sound of my flesh tearing. Blood — more blood than you think is possible — came cascading out of my shoulder. I remember seeing bone and gristle — it was like a badly butchered joint of meat. I was looking at my own body and I could see that from the alligator's perspective, I was a walking steak. He sank back under, but I knew he wanted more. So I escaped back into the hold and closed the doors, sealing off the Sub from the river. Fuck you, 'gator!"

Theodore raised his bionic arm, stuck his middle finger up, and laughed again.

"I knew that I was in serious trouble. I was delirious from the pain and I staggered around the Sub until I collapsed to the ground in this weird, hallucinogenic state. There on the ground opposite me was one of the dead guys. He was wearing army fatigues, the kind that have medals pinned to the shirt pocket. His head, which was pretty much just a skull with a couple of bits of flaky skin hanging off it, was resting at this goddamn creepy angle so he was staring straight at me."

Theodore used two fingers to point at his eyes, held them there and stared at Casey.

"And that's when the Magi appeared to me. The dark sockets where the dead guy's eyes used to be started to swirl. Soon they became one to form this weird cranial vortex. Arms appeared at the edge of the whirlpool and thrashed around, performing an angry dance until eventually the skull took the form of Banjax, the dodectopus from Solarversia. The words of the Magi came through this creature to me. His voice was deep and dark, yet strangely comforting. 'I'm coming, Markowsky, I'm coming, but you must listen carefully. I need your help to manifest. You will be the leader of men, as I shall be the leader of all.' Then he showed me a vision of what life would be like in the future, once superintelligent beings were here. It was paradise."

"What did he show you, Father? What did paradise look like?" This was the question Casey never tired of asking in his long initiation. It had never satisfactorily been answered. Here was the chance to hear it from the horse's mouth.

"He showed me the next stage in mankind's evolution. We'll merge with our machines, become one with the technology we currently view as distinct from our being. We'll extend our biological lifespans and upload our minds to silicon substrates, allowing our souls to live forever. Genetically engineered nanoparticles will spell the end of disease. Artificially intelligent robots will serve us, performing the tedious, mundane jobs we currently do ourselves. We'll learn to master energy, effortlessly transforming it into light or matter as we see fit. It will mean the end of scarcity. A world of abundance. An end to poverty. The elimination of corruption. A self-organised, self-governing hive mind, ruled by an omnipotent, benevolent cybernetic organism. No more infant mortality. The end of disease. We're talking hundreds of millions of lives saved. Together, under his guidance, we'll create a utopia, both here on Earth and throughout the galaxy."

Theodore gazed lovingly at Casey for a few seconds while he considered the proposition. After a few seconds his smile changed into a scowl. A shiver coursed down Casey's spine.

"Then He showed me the price I'd pay if I didn't commit one hundred percent to helping Him manifest. This other vision was as horrific as the first was beautiful. Glimpsing it for the briefest of moments was the worst experience of my life, bar none. I swear to you, I would rather take my own life than witness it again for a single instant. I was lying on a rotting pile of faeces, my body cut, bruised and broken. It was infested with putrid lesions. Worms, maggots and cockroaches crawled into and out of the lacerations in my body like it was their home. I puked up my entrails onto my chest only to watch them decompose back into my body. The stench made me puke again and the process repeated itself, endlessly. Make a list of the ways a human being can experience pain, suffering and discomfort, and imagine being subjected to them all, constantly, for eternity."

He paused to let his words sink in.

"I woke up, there in the bunkroom some time later, shivering and scared. I dragged myself along the corridor, clambered up the spiral stairs, got into my canoe and began the excruciating one-armed journey back to town, knowing I needed to get back to Frances as soon as possible. All I could think about was the pain I was in and the amount of blood I'd lost. I was thinking about what Frances would be able to do to help me. I was wondering about the rest of my life with one arm. Then suddenly, and for the first time, the details of vision came back to me. I experienced a fresh wave of fear, as visceral as the first. The Magi had appeared to me, of that, there was no question. Not just appeared, but *appealed*; made a direct plea. I knew there and then, without a shadow of a doubt, that if I didn't act upon it, if I didn't give my entire existence to creating Him, I would suffer in hell for eternity. I had seen my future, and there was no way to *unsee* it. As I feebly paddled along the Delta using my remaining arm, I swore I'd give my life to this cause. I was a vessel ready to do His bidding."

Theodore stopped talking and sat up straight. He rolled his head around and stretched. He turned to Casey once more, his demeanour changed, his trance broken.

"It's an imprecise science, interpreting the divine word, but I believe the Magi wants us to do something a bit different. Create an event — a spectacle — that will shock people to their core, something that will be revered and referred to for decades, if not centuries, to come. It will require some of us to make the ultimate sacrifice. We'll be known for centuries to come as the Warriors of the Magi. Many are called. Few are chosen. What about you, Casey, are you one of them?"

Casey nodded slowly. He'd learned about the Magi from Wallace and Frances when they'd saved him. Like Theodore, he'd been unable to turn his back on the truth once he'd learned it. But hearing the story like this, directly from Father, made it seem *more* true, if that was possible. Was he one of the chosen? After everything he'd been through, he hoped so. He desperately hoped so. A big part of him had already died.

He was ready to finish the job.

Chapter Twenty

Nova knew beyond any doubt that she'd never felt as rough as this before. As usual, it had been Burner's fault, egging her on. The previous day she'd finished her very last exam and met him at The Muggleton Arms to celebrate. Pints of beers had soon given way to glasses of wine. And glasses of wine had soon given way to shots of flaming sambuca.

To celebrate the Earth Force Field being switched off, Spiralwerks had released a new augmented reality app that turned your drink into a game. You watched as a phoenix took off from the bar, picked up flaming rocks from the glass in your hand, then flew around the pub dropping them into other people's drinks, setting them on fire too. Very cool. At least it was at the time. The way she felt at the moment, she hoped never to see another shot glass in her life.

She slumped against the arm of the knackered sofa in the corner of the bar at Fragging Hell, hoped she wasn't going to be sick all over it and reminded herself that she should be feeling ecstatic rather than gross. Her exams had gone well overall, even English, which she'd been dreading. It turned out that Mrs Woodward was a pretty good teacher after all.

The prospect of getting into Nottingham didn't seem quite as far-fetched as it had two months ago, which meant there was a chance she might be reunited with that sustainable development hottie, Charlie. And to top things off, her parents had handed her Booners back to her that morning. The huge argument from weeks earlier hadn't been mentioned again. *Both sides were in the wrong*, she told herself, without really believing it.

She craned her head to look in the direction of the entrance. Zhang was on the side rail, having his photo taken with some of the regulars, but where the hell was Burner? Last night, they'd gotten themselves drunkenly hyped about her chances in the Krazy Karting final, and agreed that she needed regular practise sessions, starting today. The deluxe chairs here at the cafe were similar to the one she would use in the final, so it made sense to practise here, rather than at home. Bored of waiting, she pulled out her iPad and brought up The White Dwarf, her personalised Solarversia magazine, written and curated by a computer program.

She'd customised the magazine's masthead so that it included the death counters. Over sixty-three million lives had been lost in total, while eight million people had lost all three, and gone out for good. Below the masthead was a video feed of the Player's Grid, the camera set to zoom around and focus on profile squares of players who had just lost their last life.

During the avatar setup phase, players had been required to provide a 'death clip' for their avatar — a one-second piece of footage that was shown before their square turned dark. Nova loved watching these clips and was constantly surprised at how much creativity people were able to pack into such a short amount of time.

Next to the grid's video feed was today's main story, featuring Burner. He'd completed Killanja's puzzle on Mercury while he was drunk at The Muggleton Arms. That was annoying, all these people traversing the Solar System and facing Grandmasters on other planets. But now that she'd finished her exams, she finally had time to join them.

Below the story about Burner was one that highlighted the real-world impact of The Game. Thousands of quests and Bucket List items had been designed to educate players about certain topics, change their behaviour for the better or result in money being donated to good causes. As insignificant as each microtransaction seemed at the time, it was always impressive to see the huge impact they had when combined. Tens of millions of pounds had been raised for charity, and millions of people had started exercising more and cutting out bad habits like smoking.

She swiped to the next page, which contained a list of stats. She scanned it and let out a quiet whistle. Some players had already managed to max out their inventories at one hundred items. Impressive. Players couldn't trade items — they had to use them to get rid of them — but Spiralwerks had included the cap so as to prevent people from abusing virtual wills. Specifically they'd been worried about obsessive fans naming celebrities in their wills and those celebs becoming all-powerful. Any bequeathed items that would potentially take a player over the limit were automatically returned to the East- and Westdomes of Castalia to be spawned elsewhere.

Further down the page, she saw that a new record had been set the previous day when nearly twenty-five thousand items had been bequeathed in virtual wills. A pang of grief coursed through her heart. Although Sushi had died, she had died in the real world, and not the game world. Her Solarversia will had been annulled and Nova hadn't received the few items her friend had had in her possession at the time of her death.

An alert flashed at the top of her magazine: a quest with a bounty of two and a half thousand pounds had just appeared in a location a few minutes from her own. A tingle went down her spine when she read the details. One of the required skills was darts. That settled it. Krazy Karting practise would have to wait. If Burner turned up now, *he'd* have to wait for *her*. She found a free chair, logged on and exited her Corona Cube in Takapuna, a bayside suburb of Auckland, New Zealand, where she'd flown after solving Giganja's puzzle on Ayers Rock.

According to the Route Planner the quest was on Rangitoto Island, a few kilometres from the mainland. It guided her to the nearest Dockingtons, the place on the seafront that stored the boats. Either side of a long wooden jetty, a series of thick metal clotheslines extended into the distance for as far as the eye could see. Hung from the clotheslines, spaced every five metres or so, were players' boats, attached by giant clothes pegs that left the boats dangling in the wind.

The jetty was throbbing with people who were racing to reach the quest first, making Nova all the more eager. She found a spare screen, tapped in her player number, and waited several excruciating seconds for Dockingtons to do its thing. A convoluted array of cogs, gears and wheels spun into action, threading the clothesline that housed her boat through a succession of poles and gates.

It arrived within eight seconds alongside her on the jetty and was released into the ocean by a peg that immediately whizzed off to the arrivals area. Waiting until the boat was steady, she clambered aboard and set course for the quest. Her boat Bruno was actually a hovercraft with neon blue lights down the side. The driver's seat looked like an electric chair from a horror movie, and the oversized propeller was shaped like the international symbol for radiation. Bruno was kickass.

As he pulled out of the bay she checked her datafeeds to read up on the action. The Travelling Circus of Nakk-oo had pitched up on Rangitoto Island on Monday and was there for a week. Emperor Mandelbrot was keen for players to learn about the life forms and cultures on his home planet and had arranged for a circus to travel the globe. It was the reason she had come to Auckland in the first place: the circus contained several Bucket List items and needed to be visited at some time in the year.

She'd already been to it a couple of times since Monday to tick off the Juggling Jellyfish, the Exploding Yertle, and the Heffervescent Heffalump, but details of today's quest were still scarce. All she knew was she had to head to the aviary, which had become a phased zone for the quest.

Pulling into the arrivals area of the Dockingtons at McKenzie Bay, she waited for a peg to droop down and attach itself to Bruno's grill before jumping ashore. The recording of an Austrian guy saying, "I'll be back!" sounded, one of the few catchphrases she still had switched on. The datafeed pinpointed the location of the aviary on the circus map, about three minutes away at her current running speed. She locked on and hoped that she wasn't too late.

A choir of squawks, warbles and shrieks greeted her arrival at a huge marquee decorated with Maori art. Standing just inside the entrance to the marquee was a glum-looking woman — identified by the datafeed as an NPC — feeding twigs to a bird twice her height. The creature arched its neck down, snatched twigs from the palms of her hand and gulped them down in one. Nova approached the woman, but kept one eye on the giant bird, unsure whether it was friend or foe.

"Excuse me, there's supposed to be a quest here at the aviary, do you know anything about it?"

"I'm Octavia, the bird keeper of Nakk-oo. Travinsky has flown from his tree; we can't find him anywhere. We'll have to cancel his show if we can't find him, and we've not done that in all the time I've worked here. I'm scared I'll lose my job. It was my fault he escaped, you see." Nova glanced at the bird by Octavia's side and wondered whether Travinsky was anywhere near as big.

"Please help me find him; there's a reward if you do." She grabbed another handful of twigs from the sack at her side to feed to the giant bird. Nova flicked back to her news feed, eager to see what other players had discovered. Someone had identified the large bird as a Moa, a flightless bird that had been extinct for more than 600 years. And there was plenty of information about Travinsky: photos of him and his tree, a reward poster, and some instructions on how to find him. She would need to grab a handful of twigs from the sack and head to the centre of the marquee.

If she hadn't seen the photos on the feed, she would have walked straight past Travinsky's musical tree. She supposed that it did vaguely resemble a tree, just not one that nature would produce. Its trunk, made of shiny metal, was as wide at the top as it was at the bottom. It had plenty of branches, but they protruded from the trunk at perfect right angles. And the leaves were all of the same size and shape. It was the most symmetrical tree Nova had ever laid eyes on.

She prodded a couple of the leaves on the lower branches, keen to hear what a musical tree sounded like. They made a dull, flat noise, tinnier that the notes produced by Zhang's toy xylophone. Players had discovered that Travinsky was trained to respond to a certain tune, made by striking the leaves in the right order. He would fly back, like a homing pigeon, if only the tune could be played.

Nova walked round the tree, inspecting it up close, looking for holes in the trunk where the twigs might go, tapped the occasional leaf to hear its note, and generally pondered its secrets. Before she'd discovered anything of interest, an arkwini appeared, holding a large pencil sharpener in one hand and a small wooden aeroplane in the other. He craned his little chimp head up to the ceiling and shouted at the top of his voice.

"Roll up, roll up, get your twogs here, best prices in all of Solarversia! Travinsky has gone flyabout. If you want to lure him back, you'll need yourself some twogs."

"What's a twog when it's at home?" she asked.

"This here is a twog." He held up the small plane in the palm of his hand, a look of pride on his simian face. It resembled a miniature Concorde, made out of twigs. The sharp cone at its front pointed down, while at the rear its slim wooden wings and rudder were engraved with the words 'Twog Air'.

"You'll need to get yourself some twogs to play Travinsky's tune. Five will cost you one teleport token, fifteen will cost you two. Best prices in all of Solarversia, guaranteed."

He held up the twog like a dart and aimed it at the tree, altering its angle until a leaf it was pointing at changed from black to white. Then, with a flick of his wrist, he released the little plane. It flew through the air, whistling as it went, and struck the white leaf, playing its note before falling to the floor and breaking apart.

"Travinsky's tune consists of five notes. You'll need to play them, one after the other, to lure him back."

Nova checked her inventory. She had seventy-one tokens, enough for plenty of attempts.

"OK. I'll have fifteen twogs, please. Let's do this."

She handed the arkwini a load of twigs that she'd taken from Octavia's sack and heard a ding as the teleport tokens were debited from her account. He fed each one into the end of the sharpener, and when they popped out of the other end like logs from a sawmill, they'd been transformed into the tiny aeroplanes. Wasting no time, she grabbed one and pointed it at the tree. A targeting system appeared in her display and the leaf that the arkwini had hit turned white.

She was disconcerted by the slight shake in her forearm, unsure whether it was the pressure she felt to complete the quest, or the alcohol still coursing through her veins. Her first shot was good, but not great, striking a leaf next to the white target. As the twog fell to the ground in pieces, she quickly checked the datafeed for news. Someone had managed to hit three leaves in a row before they missed. The competition was stiff, and getting stiffer — new players were arriving at the aviary every few seconds.

She did her best to ignore her next two failed attempts, and then to remain calm when her fourth hit the target. The second leaf was far easier to get. It was round the other side of the tree, but close to the bottom, and she hit it first time. When the third leaf turned white she let out a moan. It was on the highest branch, close to the trunk. The twog she launched at it soared way over the tree to disappear out of sight.

Her remaining shots met with varying success: five hits and four misses. But she got closer each time as her hand got steadier, the adrenaline pumping hard around her body, overriding the effect of her hangover. She didn't hesitate to buy another fifteen, and although she missed with the first, it was by a whisker. Her feed flared up again. Someone had just hit four in a row, and then missed the fifth. This time, instead of feeling more pressure, she had a flashback to the evening of the bullseye record. She was Nova Negrahnu, the Kent darts champion, here to complete a quest on behalf of her best friend Sushi Harrison, whose death she had sworn to avenge. *She could do this.*

Her next twog hit the first leaf dead in its centre. She smashed the second one out of the park. But while aiming for the third one at the top of the tree, she remembered something: the bottle of Growsome she'd won in a spin of the Tweel of Fate. Pulling it up in her inventory, she quickly reread the label. It would add two feet to her height for sixty seconds. She necked its contents in one and instantly sprouted the additional inches, making the shot far simpler. When it struck the leaf, she didn't jump for joy, but tried instead to remain calm. She wasn't done yet.

The fourth leaf was another easy one at her new height, and she dispatched it in seconds. But the fifth was higher up, and partially obscured from whatever angle she looked at it. No wonder it hadn't been hit yet. She held her breath and rocked her forearm back and forth. The target hovered around the leaf, never staying put. She would need to time the throw to perfection — in the next six seconds, before the Growsome wore off.

As the twog left her hand she knew it was good. And it was. The leaf played and the twog fell to the ground. But there was no fanfare or applause. Instead, the tree started to morph. The hard, straight metallic trunk and each of its branches twisted and buckled. The leaves burst into a thousand colours, except the five she had played, which remained white and played the tune over and over, in the same flat, xylophonic noise.

To her surprise, it wasn't Travinsky who appeared, but the giant Moa. With his beak he touched each leaf in order. The sound the tree made when the Moa played the leaves was very different to anything Nova had heard so far. These were beautiful sounds, ivory keys touched by a virtuoso pianist. The Moa played scales and arpeggios, and finally broke into a piece of music known as *The Firebird Suite*. It was *this* music that brought Travinsky swooping back into the marquee, followed soon after by a delighted-looking Octavia.

When the money and the one thousand teleport tokens appeared in her inventory, Nova removed her headset, ready to stand up, pump her fists into the air and scream the place down. Instead, she noticed Terrence Townsend sitting beside her — a kid whose mum gossiped as much as Katy Pugh's. Something dawned on her in that instant. Results of quests appeared in datafeeds. This news would make it back to her parents, guaranteed. She'd need to get the plan rolling right now, before they had a chance to take the money away from her. Glancing around, wondering what to do, she spied Burner ordering food at the bar. She rushed over, grabbed his sleeve, and pulled him into the ladies' toilets.

"My God, are you still drunk? Help, I'm being raped by a madwoman," Burner mock-cried in the direction of the bar.

"Shut the hell up already. You want to get us caught?"

"Caught doing what? I thought we were here for Krazy Karting, not friends with benefits."

"I just made two and a half grand completing a quest. We've got the money for the plan. But we need to move fast."

"Two and a half grand? What was the quest? Show me the replay. Preferably back in the bar, before someone finds us in here."

"We don't have time for that. You have to get back to Burnside, right now, and get those drones in the air. We need to kick off the plan before my parents can stop us. As soon as you leave I'll transfer you the cash."

"Yes, ma'am," he said with a salute.

Nova couldn't help but smile. Finally, things were going her way.

Chapter Twenty-One

Nova wiped away the last of her tears with Zhang's tail. She had cried more during the last few weeks than she had in her whole life, with an intensity that she hadn't experienced before. She'd cried so much that morning that it felt like she'd be unable to produce more tears if she tried. It was a bright July morning and the sun had already warmed a patch of her bed. She rolled onto it, soaking up its warmth while Zhang purred gently by her side. Her Booners sat on the desk, calling to her. She reached out and grabbed them, remembering that they were a doorway to more than just games.

Finally she felt ready to see her friend again, even as something of a last resort. As she launched the Soul Surfer app, the same wave of trepidation washed over her, but this time she knew things were different. She didn't *want* to see her friend; she *needed* to see her. The same vista greeted her arrival, the Seattle skyline as viewed from a hill, Sushi sitting on her bench overlooking the city.

"Hey, Nova. How are you?"

As Sushi asked the question, a box flashed up beside her head. Nova must have missed it on her first visit. This time she read it. Sushi had asked the default question spoken by avatars whenever the Soul Surfer app was launched. It could be amended by users, but the creators recommended keeping it or using a question like it, because it helped the artificially intelligent programme that was running in the background identify what tone to take in the conversation. She discarded the pop-up box and took a seat next to her friend.

"I'm probably having the second-worst week of my life, after the one when you died. So yeah, not great, but thanks for asking. How's deadsville?"

There was a pause before Sushi answered in a soft voice, "I'm sorry to hear that. Would you like to tell me about it or just sit for a while?"

Nova flinched. The app hadn't registered her cynicism in the way the real Sushi would have done, and it made her feel a bit weird. Another box flashed up, explaining that users were able to provide feedback to the app whenever they wanted to shape the avatar of the person they were visiting into the person they remembered. Or not. Users could choose to remove annoying habits, accentuate desirable ones, and even change facial features and mannerisms. Sushi had left her avatar totally customisable, which Nova liked. It showed how much her friend must have trusted her, when she was alive. In turn, Nova resolved that she would mould this computer version to be the closest approximation to her friend as was technically possible.

"Jesus. I wouldn't know where to begin."

"I said something similar to you in a message two summers ago. You remember that epic crumble I had about my brother? You told me that the best place to start is usually the beginning."

Another box flashed up showing a snippet of their conversation over IM. Nova let out something that was halfway between a smile and a gasp, amazed and freaked out by the technology in equal measure.

"I guess I was right. Except it's not always clear where the beginning is. Sometimes there are lots of places to choose from." She took a deep breath. "Let me think about this. Last Wednesday is as good a place as any to start. I'd just finished my final exam, which actually went pretty well."

Nova filled her in on the night of sambucas, the hangover from hell and the epic win at Travinsky's Tree. After a while she stopped talking, suddenly aware that she had been speaking to her friend like it was old times, like she was still alive. She wasn't sure whether that was a good thing or not. Part of her felt foolish, so easily taken in by a few lines of code. But then, she wondered, wasn't that all that our DNA was, a few lines of code, just ones executed by a different type of computer?

"Is everything OK?" Sushi asked.

"I think so. I just realised how freaking weird it is, talking to you. Have you understood everything I've said?"

"I think so. My datafeed provided me with images of Travinsky, Octavia and the little twig aeroplanes while you were talking. But the semantic recognition module of my programme is telling me that an experience like this is something you would be delighted about. Is that right, or does the programme need updating?"

"You tell the semantic recognition module that it's doing just fine. Tell it to get ready for some whacked-out shit."

Computer Sushi looked on, clasping her knees to her chest, wide-eyed with expectation.

"So, I was buzzing. I'd sent Burner home, transferred him the money to kick off the masterplan and then I remembered that I'd won a thousand teleport tokens on top of the cash. I was like, ooh, I could visit Grandmaster Killanja on Mercury, get some Karting practice in, then head over to Burnside to watch him set the plan in motion. And that's when my week of hell started. I started feeling rough again at pretty much the exact second I entered Killanja's circle. We're talking rough-in-the-jungle rough. The puzzle was set in this small white room, empty, except for a decapitated head resting on top of a Roman pillar."

"I would have freaked out."

"You totally would've done. It was creepy. The head was talking to me, Alfonso or something, telling me I need to pluck a lucky hair from his scalp, but I have to find it first. The whole room started to spin — for a moment I didn't know if it was me or the puzzle. I tore my headset off and tried to stand up and nearly fell onto Terrence's lap. You remember him, the freaky guy from our French class — I can't think of anything more gross. The real room was spinning even worse than the virtual one, the strip lighting was blurred, and the carpet was moving. I ran to the loo, threw up my breakfast, and by the time I came back the puzzle had ended and I'd lost a life. To the easiest Grandmaster of them all. Then Terry Fuckwit turned to me and says, 'Eurgh, I thought I could smell sick, you dirty little chunder bunny.' It was all down my top and in my hair. Totally gross."

Sushi held her hands to her cheeks, her mouth wide open.

"I don't know what's worse, you losing a life, or you having spew down your top taking shit from that idiot."

Nova smiled: that sounded more like it.

"I swear I could have murdered him on the spot. By the way, here's some of that feedback you asked for: Sushi would have totally cracked up at that story."

Nova spent the next few minutes cycling through the list of laughs in Sushi's repertoire, until she found one she thought best suited the situation. When she was done, Sushi replayed the last minute of dialogue on a screen in front of them so that Nova could confirm her choice.

"That's exactly how you would have reacted. But you would have commiserated with me too, over the lost life." Her profile square appeared, hanging in the air in front of them. Its violet border, unchanged since the start of The Game, flashed three times, and then turned green, replaying the change that occurred in the grid at the time of the incident. The coloured trim around the edges of the license plates on her vehicles followed suit. Nova bowed her head. "It was idiotic of me to try the puzzle in the state I was in. I can't believe that I'm a green belt now — I feel like I've let you down."

"You haven't let me down, I promise."

"Well, that makes one person on the planet — if we can count you as a person. You haven't heard the rest of the story yet. The next day Burner messaged me. He reckoned the drones had found something interesting. He was about to visit his nan to take her this wheelchair he's made, so I went to Fragging Hell to take a closer look at the results. And that's when things started to go really pear-shaped, because I made the mistake of telling Jockey what we'd been doing. I was at the bar looking over the results and he was all interested and asking me loads of questions about the plan and getting all geeky about the drones and computational algorithms and stuff. So I told him I was going to post the results online. There's three hundred gigs' worth of stuff to look through, we're never going to manage by ourselves, so we decided we might as well crowdsource it. And that's when he started acting like my dad, telling me what to do, saying I should send the results to the police. I was like, 'Yeah, fat lot of good they've done so far.'"

"What did he say?"

"I don't know, he started going off on one about people getting in trouble for doing stuff like this. All I could think about was the reason we're doing it in the first place." Nova went quiet for a few seconds. "I could feel the anger growing inside me, the same way it does with my parents sometimes, and the shitty teachers at school. And then out of nowhere I'm yelling at him, 'There's no need to be such a fat prick about it.'"

Sushi cocked her head to one side and spoke quietly. "Whoops."

Nova went quiet again and looked into the distance. "He said if I felt that way I shouldn't bother coming in anymore and I said, 'Whatever, it's a shithole anyway,' and stormed off."

"You were being a total bitch."

Nova paused. "Brutal. But yeah, you're right. I haven't been back since and he probably thinks that I really meant it. But I haven't finished telling you about the train wreck that my life is. The same evening the frickin' police came round to speak to me. A couple of guys had actually gone to check out one of the locations highlighted in the search results from Project Drone. They trekked to a hill in the middle of Arkansas and found a weird pole that had been identified by one of the drones. It had carvings all over it, which are similar to some of the symbols in the manifesto. At the bottom of the hill they found a ditch containing two dead bodies. I'm not fucking kidding. *Bodies*. It's all over the news. Apparently the FBI have gone ballistic. Reckoned they had leads of their own, and this has blown all of their good work, the terrorists are going to know they're on to them, and it's all my fault, blah, blah, blah. They also told my parents that I might have endangered myself. It's not like I used my real name on the forum, I'm not stupid."

Sushi stared at her friend in disbelief.

"Oh, yeah, there's more. We can safely say that my folks know how I got hold of the cash in the first place, and that I spent it on a bunch of drones trying to find some terrorists, rather than helping them out with the bills. So they are absolutely delighted with me. Once the police had gone I told them I was sorry and Dad said 'Sometimes, Nova, sorry isn't good enough.' Which was nice, because I wasn't feeling shitty enough about my life already."

"I'm sorry, Nova. About everything that's happened. But also because I'm not entirely sure how I would respond in a situation like this."

Nova shook her head. "Don't worry about it. I don't think a living Sushi would know how to react either. I'm not sure I know myself. It wasn't the kind of situation that ever came up when you were alive." She waited to hear Sushi respond, but instead her friend sat there, shaking her head.

"Here, have some more feedback. You would have giggled at that. Anyway, if my life wasn't screwed enough by this point, I get a call from Burner. He had a visit from the police too and had a massive go at me. Obviously I ended up arguing with him. So that's another relationship I've messed up. Jockey, my parents and Burner. Oh, plus the FBI and the police. Please remind me if there's anyone I've failed to offend in some way. My only friends in the world are a computer program that pretends to be my dead best friend, and a robotic lemur with the mental age of a three-year-old."

This time Sushi laughed but stopped abruptly.

"Oh, I'm sorry. I judged that you meant that to be funny. I didn't mean to make you cry."

"It's OK, you were right. You would have laughed your ass off, exactly like that. It's just that I've never missed you more than at this moment, and I wish with all my heart that you were still alive."

Nova removed her headset and buried her face in her pillow. She'd been wrong about one thing. She had plenty more tears to cry.

Chapter Twenty-Two

Leaning against a gnarly old tree stump, Casey watched a mean-looking alligator slide into the water. He wondered if that was the one who'd taken Father's arm. Father was one hell of a survivor. When Casey lay awake at night, obsessing over what had happened to Ivan or Wallace, he tried instead to imagine Father finding the Sub, battling the 'gator and being visited by the Magi. Then his thoughts would drift once again to the event that changed his life.

He'd been working on a project in his garage at home, installing some code in a robotic baseball machine he'd built from spare parts. The robot had learned to throw the perfect pitch and could deliver 43 of them in under a minute.

The music had been blaring, and he didn't hear Mary-Ann coming. She was on the phone to her sister — always on the phone, that girl — and probably wasn't paying attention. The robotic arm, which had been jackhammering back and forth at 43 rpm, crushed her windpipe with the first blow and smashed her nose into her skull with the second.

He remembered collapsing to kneel beside her as blood spewed from her mashed nasal cavity. She wheezed a few painful breaths, her hands clasped in his, the grip ever weaker, until she lay there, unmoving, dead. It was that final image of her, his beautiful, sweet Mary-Ann, lying there, destroyed, that still haunted him to this day. He replayed the incident in his mind for, what, the thousandth time?

Why could the ending never be different?

Once he was sure she was dead, he panicked, got into his Chevy, and drove for six hours straight. Checking into a rundown motel, he spent the next few weeks playing online poker, drinking and staring at a crooked picture of the Virgin Mary, which hung on the wall at the end of his bed. By the third week his mind was set on suicide.

Exhausted and half smashed, he'd gone online to search for ways to end it all, wanting to find a method that was guaranteed to work. Hanging appealed. The ceiling in the bathroom in his room at the motel was unusually high and there was a thick pipe which ran across it that he was certain would take his weight.

He joined a forum devoted to the topic and asked about knots, wanting to ensure he got the noose right. A few people replied to him: a couple of forum regulars, an oddball who wanted to watch him to do it, and a woman with the username 'Zoro', who professed she wanted to help him. There was something about the no-nonsense language she used, and her unbridled optimism for the future that appealed to him. She didn't come across like your average busybody Samaritan, and he liked that.

"Why would you want to kill yourself?" she asked.

"I told you. I killed the love of my life. I've got nothing to live for."

"Always something worth living for. Always."

"Oh, yeah, like what? Name me one thing."

"Listen, I'm not going to pretend I know what hell you're living through right now and I'm certainly not going to sit here and patronise you with a list of stuff like rainbows, babies and kittens in some inane effort to cheer you up. I also want to acknowledge that killing the love of your life is a shitty situation to find yourself in. But I firmly believe that it's *always* worth fighting for a better future."

"What future? I don't have one, not without Mary-Ann."

"The future doesn't exist as some predefined construct, something set in stone by God at the start of time. It exists as an unmanifested spectrum of possibilities. You were looking forward to *one* of those possible futures with Mary-Ann. I'm guessing it might have been a wonderful future you ended up having together. Again, it's shitty that it didn't come to pass. But it will only ever remain one of an infinite number of futures that could have played out for you. Are you seriously going to tell me that there's not a chance that one, or even several, of the other possible futures might also be wonderful for you? Because if you do, I'll tell you you're full of shit."

"Well, you certainly have a way of talking to a guy who's on the edge, I'll give you that."

"I know I've never met you, but I'm sure that if I did, I'd get to like you. And that's enough reason to spend my time talking to you to help discover a future you might be interested in experiencing. Would you do me the honour of hearing about the future I'd like to create?"

"I guess I've got nothing to lose."

That weekend, following several hours of dialogue with his new online friend, he looked at his motel room and finally saw it for what it had become. It was disgusting. The floor was littered with empty cans, bottles and discarded pizza boxes. His clothes stank, he stank. He showered and washed his T-shirt in the sink, shaved for the first time in weeks, tidied the room, opened the curtains. A shaft of sunlight struck the wall at the end of his bed, forming the shape of an arrow that pointed at the crooked picture of the Virgin Mary, the tip of light precisely connecting with Mary's heart.

He walked over, gently took it off the wall and, clutching the picture to his chest, sat down on his bed and for the first time since Mary-Ann's death, broke down in tears. Wiping his eyes and gasping for breath, he realised how close he'd come to death. But he'd been saved. And the sunlight striking the picture in that precise manner was proof; some*one* or some*thing* was looking after him. He felt a sudden urge to speak to the woman Zoro again.

"I have to speak to you in person. The most amazing thing happened. Think I might finally be ready to investigate the kind of future you were telling me about."

"That's so good to hear. Let me speak to my colleague, see what works for us early next week. You think you can make it over to Jackson?"

"I'd make it halfway across the universe to see you."

He did meet them — Zoro and her colleague, who he now knew as Mother Frances and Wallace — in Jackson, Mississippi the following Tuesday, in a house that felt like home. He had a long shower and dressed in the new set of clothes that they'd brought along for him. They ate a home-cooked meal, meatloaf and apple pie. Then, over a slow bottle of bourbon, they talked. They talked about pain and heartbreak and loss, and about hope and faith. They also spoke about a concept that was new to him: artificial superintelligence.

Night fell and dawn broke, and still they were talking. By breakfast time, all Casey wanted was to join up. To be a member of the group that would create the one artificially intelligent being capable of ushering in a radically different future for a mankind. A group that admitted only the brightest, the best, the most committed. Joining the executive branch of the organisation, like they'd suggested he was qualified to do, required a six-month virtual induction followed by an initiation ceremony that would push him to the limit. He could think of no better way to atone for his mistake.

The 144 journeys up and down the hill had been his penance. He had fixed in his mind the image of that fatal arm jackhammering back and forth to keep him going. But now everything he'd promised he would do to avenge her death had been jeopardised. Wallace's face had been plastered all over the news, that month's highest new entry in America's Most Wanted.

It was the DNA in his saliva, found on some cigarette butts carelessly discarded at the top of the hill that had allowed the FBI to identify him. Compounding the error further, Wallace had been careless in disposing of the bodies of the failed initiates. It had been horrific, watching the bots beat him to death in front of everyone. Father had explained that it was a necessary evil; Wallace had put the entire organisation at risk.

Casey hadn't known what to think. Yes, the work they were doing was for the benefit of all mankind. Yes, Wallace had lost the respect of his brothers and sisters at the Compound. And it wasn't as if you could simply resign from the Order, like you could in a regular job. Especially not if you'd been in such a senior position, so integral to the organisation.

But it tortured Casey to know his best friend was gone. He might have made a couple of mistakes, but Wallace was one of the good guys, one of the Warriors of the Magi. He'd cared about people, and gone out of his way to look after them. Now he wouldn't get to see the fruits of his labour, the paradise that the Magi would create. That was the ultimate price he'd paid. Casey just hoped that what he'd discovered would make Father happy again.

He knocked on the door, took a deep breath and entered. A large workbench dominated the room. Clamped to its sides were a series of evenly spaced metal vices, empty, except for the one at the near end, which held a drone between its jaws. The walls were lined with shelves, home to screwdrivers, hacksaws, mallets and glass jars stuffed with drill bits, nuts, bolts and screws. In the corner, illuminated by a spotlamp, was a corkboard, covered in photos of people, maps marked with pins and circles, and a list of multinationals, heavily highlighted and scrawled all over. Theodore placed his eyepiece on the workbench and motioned for Casey to join him.

"Sent Brandon into town yesterday to buy one of these," Theodore said, nodding at the drone. "They've come a long way in the last few couple of years. Seeing how they were used against us, I wondered whether we might be able to use them ourselves."

"That's what I wanted to talk to you about, Father, the discovery of the training site. I've done some digging. When the FBI deleted the post on that forum with all the information about us, they weren't as thorough as they should have been. Turns out that copies of the original post had been replicated to a bunch of other sites. The person who posted the research in the first place was a user called I_<3_Zhang. It was a new account, and that was the only thing they'd ever posted. I googled the username and found one other instance of it — an old YouTube account, belonging to someone called Nova Negrahnu. But that might just be a coincidence, right?"

"Could be. Go on," said Theodore, now giving his full attention to the younger man.

"This Nova Negrahnu, guess who she's next to in the Player's Grid? Sushi Harrison, one of the girls killed in the Seattle blast. It's got to be the same girl. Here's everything I found on her."

Casey flicked through several pages of data on a tablet that showed a series of photos, social accounts and a profile containing personal information. Theodore took the tablet from him and swiped through its contents, a smile creeping across his face. Casey pointed at one of the photos.

"Look at this one. She's got herself one of those Electropets. Refers to it as her 'best friend in the world'. Pretty sad, huh?"

"Well, I'll be damned if this little bitch ain't got her panties in a twist. This is good work, Casey. You meant it about your commitment, I can see that. You've done yourself proud."

Casey blushed. "Thank you, Father."

"Where did you say she was from?"

"She's from Maidstone, Kent. England."

"We'd need the help of our brothers in the United Kingdom. I'll think on it. In the meantime, I'd like to reward you for the work you've done. I had been planning to offer you a promotion since Wallace ... chose to step down. How would you like to be my right-hand man?"

Casey felt his face redden. "Father, I'd be honoured." He hadn't known how much he was longing for something like that. But the approval of Father felt vital.

Theodore retrieved a first aid kit from a chest of drawers at the side of the room, placed it on the workbench and popped it open.

"Remember how we spoke about sacrifice the other day?"

Casey nodded, unsure where this was going.

"I'm glad to hear that, boy. Because with power comes responsibility, and with responsibility comes sacrifice, wouldn't you agree?"

"Yes, Father."

"Then place your left arm into the vice."

Casey gulped. He *was* committed, he knew he was. But what was this? He hadn't expected to make a sacrifice so soon. And he certainly hadn't expected it to involve a first aid kit or his arm in a vice. Realising that he'd frozen, he quickly positioned his arm inside its metal jaws, and hoped that Father hadn't noticed it tremble.

The grid of lights on Theodore's arm blinked into action, the handle controlling the vice turned, and before Casey could react, his arm was wedged tight. Theodore held his prosthetic limb up in the air. He clenched his fist and a four-inch blade ejected from his middle knuckle with a thunk. Casey reflexively pulled away from the weapon, but was jerked back into place on his stool when his arm refused to budge. His fear was now visible, his breathing double its normal rate. Father leaned back and studied the serrated blade.

"I'm not sure I finished telling you that story the other day. Where was I? That's right, I was in my canoe, paddling back into town, a hastily tied tourniquet the only thing keeping me from death. Well, Frances was shocked to see me like that, as you might imagine. Thought I'd been kidnapped and tortured. She administered some anaesthetic, cleaned up the wound, and saved my life. Lying in bed for the first few days after the incident I viewed myself as a victim who'd lost an arm. But after speaking to Frances and getting my thoughts clear about how I was going to heed the Magi's calling, I had another epiphany: I realized that perspective was everything."

He spoke like they were old friends catching up at a school reunion. Casey concentrated on his breathing and forced a smile though his eyes were drawn again and again to the blade.

"I hadn't lost an arm as much as I'd gained an opportunity. What better way to make me appreciate the merger between biology and technology than to make me experience it for myself? This isn't a curse," he said, gesturing to the flashing arm. "It's a blessing. It represents the first stage in my transformation from man to cyborg. And now it's time for you to join me."

Theodore placed the serrated blade onto the section of Casey's wrist that protruded from the vice.

"I want you to stay real calm and real still. I'm not going to lie, this will hurt a lot. But it's important that you endure the pain. It's a taste of what's to come. The role I have in mind for you is greater than anything you could imagine. But it's going to require a blessing, not a curse. So take some of this and hold on tight."

Theodore opened one of the workbench's drawers, retrieved a saucer and placed it by Casey's free hand. Understanding that he had little say in what was about to happen, and scared of a fate similar to Wallace's befalling him, he took hold of the little straw, stuck one end into the pile of cocaine and hoovered as much up each of his nostrils as he could bear.

As he felt the cold metal blade rip his skin, Casey inhaled sharply through his nose. He did his best to hold the older man's gaze, but his eyes kept flitting to the red drops as they hit the workbench. Emitting a guttural whine, he clutched the vice with his free hand and held on so tight that his knuckles looked like they might pop out of their joints. Once the blade hit bone, Theodore put his entire weight onto the handle, forcing it ever downward, filling the workshop with a horrible crunching noise.

When the hand finally came free, Casey screamed. On the other side of the workbench Theodore calmly leafed through the first aid kit like he had all the time in world. There on the floor was the severed hand. Casey stared at it, marvelling at the fact that it was no longer part of him.

What kind of crazy task could render its existence superfluous?

Chapter Twenty-Three

Arty cleared his throat, swept his curly brown locks off his face, and lightly patted his cheeks. Hannah's brow furrowed as she watched him.

"You do realise that the interview takes place in VR? That people see your avatar and not the real you?"

"I'm aware of how the technology works, thank you, Mrs McCreadie. It's a mindset thing. If I look my best in the real world, I'll feel my best in the virtual."

"Whatever you say. You've done the prep, right?"

"The prep?"

"You looked at the background material I sent you last week?"

"I know this stuff inside out, Hannah. I don't need to prep."

"I'm not talking about Solarversia, you moron, I'm talking about Kiki La Roux." She held her thumb and forefinger to the bridge of her nose and applied some gentle pressure. "You haven't even looked at it, have you? Do you know anything about him whatsoever? Because the interview starts in five minutes and I'd welcome some positive headlines for a change."

"I know who the guy is, obviously. Weird fellow. Eccentric. Why don't you bring me up to speed anyway? Give me the 'Kiki crash course'."

Hannah rolled her eyes and then did what she always did — got on with it. She scrolled through some files on her tablet and selected one. A hologram flickered into life on the table and started to spin slowly before them like it was mounted on a lazy record player. Arty leaned forward in an attempt to process what he was seeing. A colourful man, wearing only a leopard-skin thong, lounged provocatively on an opulent chaise longue. Standing behind him, a pink elephant was waving a decorated Japanese fan back and forth over his body while a eunuch fed him the occasional grape.

Kiki's left nipple was pierced by a golden ring, the last in a series of connected hoops that were plugged into a little machine manned by a Persian cat. Whenever the cat touched a paw to the machine's pad, sparks of electricity coursed along the hoops and jump-started video clips on Kiki's talon-like fingernails.

Hannah tapped more files. Images appeared on the wall to their side, displaying a series of newspaper headlines: 'Shock Jock for the VR Generation', 'La Roux Voted Campest Celeb in the World!' and 'Get a Dollop of This Trollop Aboard His Space Bollock.'

"Kiki's best known for his avatar. It's a living work of art. While he's talking to you his skin will change colour to reflect his emotional state, and his dreadlocks will come alive and start dancing to music."

"Desperate for attention much?"

"Look, the kids love him. His interviews receive between fifty and seventy million views. And he's a one-man phenomenon. He operates the whole thing from a penthouse apartment in downtown Amsterdam. Regularly voted one of the most media-savvy people in the world. He's a modern-day Warhol."

She leaned forward in her seat, cupped her hands in her lap and looked at him with pleading eyes. "We could *really* do with this going well."

"How's he doing in The Game?"

"He's a red belt, his health is down to fifty points or so and he still needs to visit the most difficult Grandmasters. His catchphrase is 'I'm Shooting for the Stars'."

"That's the name of his show, isn't it?'

"You aren't completely socially illiterate then."

Arty smiled. "Go on. What else should I know?"

"He owns the largest collection of Electropets in the world, his 'Lovelies', each of whom appears in virtual form on his show. He's planning the world's first international Electropet grooming competition."

"A grooming competition for pet robots? Jesus, this guy's got some serious issues."

"His show is set on his virtual spaceship, the Disco Stick."

"I think I blocked that detail out. It's shaped like a penis, right?"

"It's the whole shebang. You'll be located in the right bollock, while his harem of one hundred and fifty eunuchs slouch around in the left."

Arty stared at the trippy images and video clips playing on the walls, trying to take it all in.

"Look, you'll be fine. And it will be great for us. Kiki's cooler than a polar bear. Oh, yeah, one last thing. Don't look at his fingernails."

"Why not?"

"He plays video clips on them, usually of a pornographic nature. They're really long, so they can capture your interest. And he makes a laughing stock of interviewees who get too interested. Gives them virtual boners, that kind of thing. The terms and conditions of appearing on his show give him full creative control over your avatar while you're on board. He'll probably try to embarrass you." She checked the time and handed him his headset. "Have you got all that? The interview starts in thirty seconds."

"Electropets and eunuchs. He sounds like a polar bear. Don't look into his eyes. Takes place aboard an interstellar schlong."

"That's the gist of it, yes. Take every comment with a large pinch of salt. Don't let him faze you. And remember, I'll be here the whole time. I can give you prompts via your earpiece and you can volley back to the meeting room if you need more help. Get your headset on and your brain in gear. We've got ten seconds."

Arty materialised on a fluffy white cloud, sitting next to Kiki, and prepared himself for anything. He'd been in hundreds of virtual rooms in his time, but none quite like this. It was a circular room, the size of the larger meeting rooms at Spiralwerks, and all around him a menagerie of wild animals were on the loose. A troop of monkeys chased each other's tails, a scurry of squirrels scampered around futuristic furniture, while a gaze of racoons slumbered in the corner on bean bags, sucking on hookahs.

Over in the corner, a band of giant pandas struck up the show's theme tune. Sparkly musical notes emanated from their instruments and floated around the room until they were hoovered up by the pink elephant Arty had seen during his crash course. When the music died down, the animals seemed to relax, as if the volume had been the source of their energy. Kiki stopped bopping in his seat and turned to face one of the floating spherical cameras.

"My name is Kiki La Roux, and I'm Shooting for the Stars! This week we're taking a trip with none other than Artica Kronkite, the brains behind Solarversia, The Game we all love to love! Artica, welcome to the show, honey."

"Hi, Kiki. Thanks for having me, it's a pleasure to be here, aboard your ... spaceship, with all of these delightful animals."

"Did you hear that, my lovelies? He said that you were delightful. Isn't he a blast, ladies and gentlemen? Artica, I have so many questions for you and so little time. I'm going to need some help from my one-armed bandit. Rambo, do your thing, honey."

The pink elephant attached his trunk to the coin slot of a fruit machine and emptied into it the spangling quavers and crotchets he'd hoovered up. The musical notes tumbled noisily into the machine, jangling and tinkling like melodic coins. Once there was ample credit inside, Rambo yanked the arm-shaped lever, sending the machine into a frenzy of noise and colour. When the spinning reels came to a halt, the images on the central row displayed Emperor Mandelbrot and his entourage.

"Let's talk about the Emperor. What a fascinating individual. Where exactly did he come from? How old is he? When, why and how did he contact you? And where *does* he shop for clothes?"

"Well, Kiki, that's a lot of questions. Great questions, I might add. All we know is that he's from a solar system within the Milky Way, but he hasn't been more specific than that. Apparently that's standard protocol for a species like ours playing their first game. We've never received a straight answer about his age, although Arkwal implied that he's in his tens of thousands. It was Arkwal who contacted me — about ten years ago — via email, would you believe? He asked whether Spiralwerks wanted to help host a year-long game. He reckoned he'd contacted lots of people, but we were the only ones who bothered to reply. I asked how it would work, and he told me about the planets, the Player's Grid, Castalia and so on. It sounded like it could be a lot of fun, so we said that we were game. No pun intended."

"Oh, my lord, you are a tease, Artica. Will you just listen to him, ladies and gentlemen? A creative mastermind and a comedian to boot. It's an enchanting little story, and I'm sure your players believe every word. 'A species like ours', indeed. I'm Kiki La Roux, and I'm Shooting for the Stars. Rambo, do your thing."

Each time Kiki repeated his catchphrase, in his effeminate voice, the word *I'm* seemed to stretch out a little longer, like a sequinned lounge singer draping herself slowly over a glossy grand piano. While the machine was in motion, his dreadlocks came to life, dancing around his skull, and his skin became a pale blue colour.

When the reels came to rest for a second time with pictures of his own face, Arty tensed up, anxious of what was to come. He volleyed one eye back to Hannah, who gave a thumbs-up and said into his earpiece, "Arty, you're doing OK, relax your shoulders, this is normal behaviour, you've got nothing to worry about."

"Spiralwerks looks like a fun place to work, Artica. Not quite as fun as the Disco Stick, but then, where is, right, boys?" From the left testicle came the sound of giggling eunuchs. "I've heard a rumour that employees are banned from playing

The Game; is that right? Was that your decision? Are you jealous of us folk who get to play? Oh, and by the way, how do I get an extra life? I'm on my last, wouldn't you know?"

"Ah, Kiki, no extra life, I'm afraid. Not for you, not for anyone." Kiki pouted sulkily at the camera, then flicked his locks with a grin. "Spiralheads have always been banned from playing the games we make. That was one of the company's first rules. We still manage to have some fun though. There's an 'Employee's Grid' that's kept separate from the 'Player's Grid', and we get to play our own games, some of which influence the Gameworld. For example—"

"You influence the Gameworld, Artica? You haven't been killing people off, have you?"

"No, no, no. We don't influence events or anything that happens to the players. I want to make that clear." He volleyed back to the meeting room and saw Hannah motioning for him to back-pedal. "I'm talking about creative influence. Take the Krazy Karting final later this year in London. At our summer party, a few weeks before the final, we'll get to play games that will influence the design and layout of the track. We might even leave our mark somewhere. I was thinking of dropping some of my own photos onto a billboard at the side of the track, or if I win one of the games, I could get to choose the position of a hidden item. These additions are like in-game Easter eggs for players to find later on, once the world is opened up to explore when The Game comes to an end."

"Don't you just love Easter eggs? Although nothing's so good as the hunt." He winked at Arty and turned to the camera with a flirty shrug. "You mentioned the Karting final, Artica. I've already reserved my viewing spot; the Disco Stick is going to be stationed above Mayfair. My money's on Jools van der Star, the Dutch driver. I'm a big fan of his pole position. He'll be on the show in a few weeks time, one for your diary."

The interview continued in a similar vein for another twenty minutes. Arty did his best to go with the flow. He fielded questions on the Planetary Puzzles, the Earth Force Field, and Pluto's Portal of Promise. Just when he was starting to relax into the feel of the show, Kiki ordered Rambo to do his thing one last time. This time the reels came to rest with pictures of curly swastikas. "Don't worry, this is the last set of questions," he heard Hannah whisper. "Keep your cool."

"I'm sorry, Artica honey, but I wouldn't be doing my job if I didn't ask about the Holy Order. Why exactly are they targeting the good people at Spiralwerks? You haven't done something to annoy them, have you?"

"It's the same question we've been asking ourselves. We see ourselves as good corporate citizens, making games that bring joy to many millions of people around the world."

"I believe they even managed to target the mayor while she was visiting your office? Is nowhere safe anywhere more?"

"Listen—" Arty stopped and took a deep breath, aware that he'd been about to launch into a defensive tirade unsuited to the satirical nature of the show. "It's a serious business, Kiki, the stuff that's occurring. The blasts in the States were devastating. Other events — the griefing attack, the video nasty — might appear frivolous on the surface, but beneath them is a very twisted belief system that's led to a great many lives being destroyed. Trust me, we're doing everything we can to work with the authorities to help bring these people to justice."

"Well, I only hope they do catch them before more damage is done. Anyway, enough of all this serious talk, let's have some more of that fun you mentioned. It's time for a viewer question."

Arty smiled uncomfortably while Kiki grabbed a musical note that had been drifting overhead and held it to his ear. He caught sight of Kiki's hand. His nails were five inches in length and displayed the kind of material that Hannah had warned him about.

"Jacques from Marseille, France, wonders what you'd look like in a mankini. What a fabulous idea."

With a click of Kiki's fingers, Arty was suddenly wearing nothing but a lime green thong, with straps like braces over his shoulders. He placed his hands over his crotch and did his best to strike a look somewhere between amused and disapproving.

"Do you like to dance? I do, especially in the summertime, when the weather is hot. I love to strut my stuff, gyrate my hips, shimmy on down. Artica, we've loved having you on the show, haven't we, my lovelies? I'm Kiki La Roux, and I'm Shooting for the Stars!"

With one last click of his fingers, Kiki set the room in motion. His band started back up while the menagerie of animals resumed what they'd been doing when Arty first arrived. Kiki reached out a hand to Arty, who found himself getting off the cloud and involuntarily thrusting his hips in time to the music and clapping his hands above his head. He removed his headset, breathed a sigh of relief and looked at Hannah, who was biting her lip and doing her best not to laugh. The screens round the room displayed him, in his mankini, gyrating around the Disco Stick. As the closing credits appeared on the screen, Kiki's eunuchs were released from the harem and streamed through to join in the dance. Several pairs of hands pulled Arty back onto the fluffy cloud before one of the eunuchs mounted him.

"Don't look so worried. This is fantastic publicity."

Arty ran his hands through his hair and gawped at the eunuch riding his avatar. He'd never understood the way publicity worked and, after today, he wasn't sure he ever would.

Chapter Twenty-Four

The outward leg of the day-long journey to Venus was about to come to an end, and Nova was glad she wasn't in one of the gaming simulators for the final descent to the surface. The dense atmosphere, consisting mostly of carbon dioxide, rocked the spaceship hard, and she felt giddy enough in the backseat of the car, especially when she tried to concentrate on the landing video. After the debacle with Killanja on Mercury, she'd chosen to travel there by spaceship, rather than teleport directly. There would be no more hasty decisions taken while she was hung over and excitable.

Space travel had become possible at the end of April when a Chinese player called Johnny Wong had triggered the tenth Earth Force Field switch at the Great Pyramid in Giza. That had enabled players to fly to one of the many floating platforms, access the near-Earth spacecraft and reach the International Space Station. The completion of the quest aboard the ISS had unlocked far-Earth spaceships able to reach the Moon.

Once the Moon quest had been completed, the Moonbase was opened, and along with it, a series of mega hangars that hosted the construction of the Planetary Spacecraft, each named after the planet they primarily served. Hundreds were built for each planet, and with a capacity of five thousand passengers and a regular timetable that saw them depart and arrive every fifteen minutes or so, they allowed players who couldn't afford to teleport to navigate the Solar System in style.

"Venus is the hottest planet in the Solar System, with a surface temperature in the hundreds," the astronaut Arkwini in the landing video explained. She was looking forward to finding a place to display the Electropet version of him she'd won in the darts in her new room at uni. "At the Spaceport you'll be issued with a spacesuit capable of withstanding these enormous temperatures, which is to be worn throughout your pilgrimage to Grandmaster Meganja. Without it, you'd fry in an instant, so don't try to take it off. This is an incredibly hostile planet, and we don't recommend leaving the Spaceport other than to face Meganja. We land in three minutes."

Disembarkation from shuttle to Spaceport via a series of connected tubes and elevators took less than five seconds, one of the advantages of the virtual world. Like most of her fellow passengers, Nova opted to go straight to the fitting rooms where an astronaut Arkwini issued her with her kit. She checked herself in the mirror and wished she owned such an outfit in real life — a tight-fitting silver suit stamped with her name and number. Her avatar looked hot, and she wondered whether it was time to update her real-world look with a bit of Spacepunk.

She closed the visor on her helmet to find that it displayed a prominent temperature gauge in addition to the usual datafeeds. An overlaid map directed her to the Umbilicus, the section of the Spaceport that led to the outside via a series of short, fat tunnels connected by bullet doors that snapped open and shut faster than the human eye could register.

As she made her way through the Umbilical chambers with a handful of other players, she realised something odd. One of the players was in what Burner called 'stealth mode' — playing as a Smarty, the female of the two Generic Avatars. But it was the appearance of the other four players as she walked alongside them that sparked her realisation.

It was six months into The Game, which meant surviving players were halfway through transforming into their Super Avatars. Nova had gained an inch, lost some flab, and her hair was as shiny as a shampoo model's. These other four looked very strange. One guy resembled a stag with multicoloured antlers, while one of the women looked horribly mutilated, sometimes a sign the player was an art student looking to get a reaction. But it wasn't their appearances that she found odd; it was the fact that she hadn't registered at first how odd they were. The novelty of the weird and wonderful had finally worn off. Eccentric and outlandish was the norm in this place.

A series of video feeds appeared on the tunnel walls. These short vignettes were almost comedic in nature. They showed the lives that had been lost by people on their way to see the Grandmaster. After displaying the death, which was often pretty graphic, the video would cut to the player's pre-recorded one-second death clip. People went from screaming in agony to smiling, waving and dancing before their profile square flashed with their new belt colour or disappeared from the grid altogether.

She tried to ignore the clips, not wanting to be distracted with thoughts of death and destruction. The temperature gauge was distracting enough — it leapt by 50°C each time they entered a new chamber, and when they finally made it outside, it soared to 455°C.

The rocky yellow expanse that dominated the environment outside the Spaceport came to an abrupt halt after about ten metres. She was at the edge of a cliff face and would need to jump up to a platform suspended in mid-air, then to another, working her way up a ladder of unconnected platforms which reached hundreds of metres into the air to the place Meganja called home.

In the valley beneath the platforms lay a sea of sulphuric acid populated with lavadiles hungry for the treats that fell to them in shiny silver wrappers. Nova and the group she was with watched as a player from Argentina, about halfway up, misjudged a jump and fell to his fiery death. As if reading her mind, the visor flashed up a new piece of information: 3.59% of players lost a life on their way up the platforms.

She took her time to learn how the system worked and constantly monitored the datafeed for information about traps that had been sprung on previous players. Like all platform games, it got harder as it went on: static platforms soon gave way to ones that drifted from side to side and then to pyro-forms that burst into flames if you hesitated to jump off them. To a regular gamer like Nova, the platform challenge was pretty tame; perhaps it was old grannies that kept losing their lives?

She made the last jump across to Meganja's platform, glad to have made it in one piece. Burner would have given her untold grief if she had died at this stage. When the hour struck, Meganja started his talk, outlining the rules of the puzzle. This time there were 7,224 safe spots for the 9,030 players tackling the puzzle with her. She noted one difference from the previous puzzles she'd played: players were allowed to use the in-game digital pen and paper.

"Every three minutes Gorigaroo will strike his gong, a signal that something within the puzzle has changed. This will be a new clue to help you solve it. Good luck, and remember these two things. First, those who follow the same map, end up at the same destination. Second, There Can Be Only One!"

As he finished talking he dissolved into the ether to be replaced by a creature that made her flinch. It was one of the lavadiles and standing so close to it brought back the memory of the obstacle course and one of the critters snapping at her leg.

"I'm a Luminous Lavadile, and the answer to this puzzle can be found on my scales. Or, to be precise, *one* of my scales. There are six hundred and sixty-six of them, but only one will secure you a safe spot. All you need to do is touch it. However, you only get one chance. Touch the wrong scale and you'll lose a life."

Remembering the key to success at Volters restaurant — speed of action combined with lateral thinking — she paced around the lavadile looking for clues. Except in this case, nothing obvious stood out like the beer bottles or the magnifying glass had. She scanned the beast from different angles, looking for ideas, but everything appeared to be in its right place and in the right proportion. Except, she realised, the tail, whose tip, which was shaped like an arrowhead, was free of scales.

A hundred thoughts raced through her mind, each competing for attention. The lavadile's words echoed through her mind. *Touch the wrong scale and you'll lose a life.* He'd definitely said that, she was sure of it. But there *were* no scales on his tip of his tail, so she tugged at it. The arrowhead made a ker-ching! sound. She hadn't lost a life. And all the scales had changed — a little number had appeared on each of them. Which was great. All she needed to do now was work out which number to touch.

She paced some more, studying some of the numbers up close, looking for a sign that one of them was different, an arse among elbows. While studying the number 211, and trying to decide whether its shape constituted something of importance, the number of safe spots started ticking down. And to compound her frustration further, the gong sounded, signalling a clue. When she ran round the lavadile to find what had changed, it was the tail, now glowing, a clear sign that it needed to be pulled. She let out a groan, knowing that her initial advantage was already spent. Why did that keep happening?

She spotted the next clue almost by accident. There was something different about the lavadile's front feet: two of the four claws on each one had retracted. But what did it mean? On the beast's right foot, the central two claws had retracted; on its left foot, the outer two. She wished Burner was there to help; it felt like something he'd know about.

They were allowed to use the pen and paper, but to draw what? Was she supposed to draw the missing claws and feed the picture into his mouth? Perhaps it wasn't a drawing that was needed, but a calculation of some sort. While she pondered the possibilities, distressed to notice that the number of safe spots had already dropped below three thousand, the next gong sounded, making the lavadile speak again.

"Did you know that there are only ten types of people in this world? Those who understand binary, and those who don't?"

She was right. Burner would have solved the puzzle in two seconds flat. Bloody binary. How did it work again? She racked her brain, remembered something about powers of two, and recited the first few out loud: one, two, four, eight, sixteen. Hurriedly opening the digital pad, she scribbled down the sequence the claws made. Out, in, in, out: 1001. In, out, out, in: 0110. Putting the numbers together made 10010110. She just needed to convert it into a decimal number.

She tallied the digits against the powers of two, a series of rushed black lines that rendered the pad close to unreadable. The calculation was one hundred and twenty-eight plus sixteen, plus four, plus two. The answer came to one hundred and fifty, she was sure of it. There were a thousand safe spots left which gave her enough time to check her maths while she located the scale she needed.

Finding it a third of the way down the beast's back, and convinced that her sums were correct, she pressed it, knowing that it was her only chance. When the victory jingle played she let out a big sigh of relief. She reappeared in Meganja's circle, along with a teleport machine that would transport her back to the Spaceport for free.

"Here she is, resurfacing from her games. Where are you now, love? Still on the Moon somewhere?"

"I'm on Venus, Mum. I just solved Grandmaster Meganja's puzzle. I'll probably stay at the Spaceport for a bit, check out some of the exhibitions and return to Earth tomorrow."

"Well, don't be late. You wouldn't want to miss any lectures. We just passed a sign for the university, it's only a couple of minutes away now."

It was Monday 21st September, the first day of term at Nottingham University. Nova had wanted to drive there on her own; her parents hadn't concurred. The argument didn't last very long. All Mr Negrahnu had needed to do was to tilt his head to the side and raise his eyebrows. It was a look that said, "You might want to remember our great leniency earlier in the year when you were in a whole shedload of trouble."

As she'd conceded to Burner, her parents *had* been lenient about the fact that she'd spent her Travinsky winnings on a plan to locate a terrorist cell. The most plausible explanation she'd been able to come up with was that they felt bad about having had a go at her so soon after Sushi had died. She'd heard them talking late one night about 'what she was going through' and although she'd resented being talked about, it was good to know they realised how awful things had been.

She also knew how proud they were that she'd managed to scrape into Nottingham after all she'd been through. Opening the text message with her results had been distressing. She'd been round at Burnside with Burner and Jono and had just watched Burner open *his* message, confirming that he got the grades *he* needed.

But when it came to her turn she had been so nervous that she ended up handing her phone to Jono to read out her grades. When he read the last one, her 'B' in English, she clenched her fists, threw her arms into the air and shouted "Yes!" at the top of her voice. Once she'd calmed down, the three of them had linked arms and danced round in a circle while chanting, "We are Nottingham, yes we are," to a tune they made up on the spot.

And here she was already, pulling into the university campus to start her new life as a student. As happy and excited as she felt, she paused a moment to reflect on the fact that if things had been different, she'd be messaging Sushi, relaying the details of this new adventure to her as they happened: the drive here, a photo of her room, the complaints she would undoubtedly make about the dodgy food.

At least she'd developed something of a routine with her friend, visiting her every Sunday evening so that she could recap the week with her. When her mum had asked what visits were like, Nova had told her that Computer Sushi was 70% like the real Sushi had been — and was getting more like her all the time. Although in darker moments she wondered whether the digital approximation of her friend only *appeared* to be getting more like Sushi because she'd already started to forget what the real one was like. It was a chilling thought.

When they arrived at Hugh Stewart Hall, her residence for the year, Nova was relieved to see that most of the other students had been accompanied by their parents too. A map in the lobby told her that she had been assigned a room in 'Z' block, where all of the rooms had been refurbished with new beds, fittings and Smart Paint on the walls.

Zhang seemed to like his new home. As soon as they entered he scampered over to the window ledge while Nova and her parents lugged her stuff from the car to her room on the second floor. When they were surrounded by her bags and boxes, and Nova's mum had checked for the umpteenth time that she had everything she needed, and Nova was wondering if they would ever leave, her dad finally said, "We'd better get a wriggle on then," and she burst into tears like she was being left for the first time at nursery school.

As tears streamed down her face, Nova's mum scavenged around in her handbag to find a tissue for her. She felt a stream of dripping snot reach the end of her nose when her dad passed her a flyer advertising the Rutland Hall fresher's party later that week. Without wondering where he'd got it from, she swiped the flyer under her nose, caught the offending mucus, crumpled it into a ball and tossed it into the bin.

"I take it you don't want to attend the party then?" said the person standing in the doorway. Realising that she'd just managed to make herself look a complete doofus within minutes of arriving, she turned to the doorway with the biggest smile she could muster to meet a fellow student.

But it wasn't a stranger standing in the doorway. It was Charlie.

Chapter Twenty-Five

Nova did her best to ignore the comments she was getting and tried to concentrate on not tripping over her stupid dress. She was used to wearing clothes and accessories that others thought were a bit weird, but this was different. And she was out in public all on her own. Blame Charlie. She hadn't seen him since Monday, when he'd handed her dad the flyer for the Rutland Hall Star Wars party, but she hadn't stopped thinking about him.

After she'd apologised for the unorthodox way in which she'd dispatched with the flyer, he'd handed her another one and told her that he hoped to see her there. And here she was, three days later, walking down the grassy hill to Rutland Hall, dressed as Princess Leia, with Zhang riding on her shoulders.

Burner had refused to come with her. He was heading to a party down at the lake with his brother Jono, but she was hardly going to pass up a guaranteed meeting with Charlie. She told Burner she'd see him later on if the Star Wars party turned out to be lame. In Burner's defence, he *had* helped her source her costume, and to her delight, she made a damn fine princess.

At the entrance to Rutland Hall, C-3PO welcomed guests while his companion R2-D2 projected holograms of well-known scenes from the films onto the table beside him. Towering over them was a machine on two legs, "a 2:1 scale All Terrain Scout Transport Walker," as C-3PO explained to an assembled group of excited nerds.

"Hey, Leia, nice buns!" one of them said in her direction, to howls of laughter from his fighter pilot friends.

"Thanks, I plaited them myself," she responded, without missing a beat. Burner had made the same joke only half an hour earlier. C-3PO turned to her, trying to emulate the character's jerky robotic movement. "I'm awfully sorry about that,

Princess Leia, please excuse their childish behaviour. Here's a token for a free drink at the Rebel Bar, included in the price of the ticket. Have a great evening, and may the Force be with you."

Waiting at the bar for her vodka cranberry, she watched Zhang amuse himself with some bendy straws. He picked a couple up and drummed them against Nova's hand. She leant in close until their noses touched and spoke to him in a conspiratorial tone.

"Listen up, furball. We're looking for a boy called Charlie. He's got long blond hair and the sweetest blue eyes you ever did see. He's the reason I'm wearing this ridiculous get-up."

She rested an elbow on the bar while she eyed people up, cocking her head this way and that, occasionally going up on tiptoes to scan the room for blond hair.

"Princess Leia, you're to come with us. By order of the Imperial Guard, we hereby place you under arrest."

Great — more little boys to deal with. These two were dressed in homemade Stormtrooper outfits.

"Oh, dear. I think I'd just as soon kiss a Wookiee, don't you, Zhang?"

"We were only joking. I'm Gideon, and this is Joey," said one of the guys, removing his helmet. "We're from Cripps Hall. Elite Stormtroopers, reporting for duty, your majesty. Cute monkey, by the way."

"I'm sorry, boys, but you're not the dweebs I'm looking for."

"Ah, very good, like your style. But it's 'droids'. These aren't the *droids* you're looking for. I don't think I caught your name?"

Nova spent the next five minutes doing her best to disengage from their small talk. It was the exact same conversation she'd had countless times that week, the one where each fresher revealed where they were from, their A-level grades, the degree they were studying and the societies they'd joined. Burner had mentioned wanting to create a voice-activated app that reeled off the information for him, and he'd only been half-joking.

She knew that the troopers were harmless enough, just a little try-hard. But this princess was here on imperial business that didn't concern them, and now her craning and scanning had paid off: on the other side of the room was Charlie. Dressed as Han Solo, he was talking to another Princess Leia, this one dressed in the slave outfit from her time as Jabba's prisoner.

The costume consisted of a scant gold-threaded bikini and a faux metal collar attached to a chain that she kept caressing. She must have been at least six foot, and her long, tanned legs were more toned than Nova's had been at any point in her life. She was all over Charlie, laughing at everything he said and fluttering her false eyelashes. And she kept touching him. If she stroked his blaster pistol one more time, Nova would feed her to Jabba herself.

As Charlie took a swig of his beer, she noticed a bulge on his arm. At first she thought it was a part of his outfit — but then it moved and changed colour. A second or two of complete bewilderment was followed by a knowing smile as she finally realised what it was. He had an Electropet chameleon perching on his arm and its skin had changed colour to blend with Charlie's outfit. The realisation brought a grin to Nova's face. *They had something in common.* The only question was how she could best use that fact to her advantage.

While Gideon yammered away, interrupted by the occasional comment from his friend, she brainstormed her options. In a different universe — one that obeyed another set of social laws — she would send Zhang over with a funny little note, Charlie would stop talking to the tramp, look over with a huge smile on his face, and they'd leave together, hand in hand, towards a sunset. Instead, she would have to approach him herself, the old-fashioned way. She excused herself from the dismayed troopers, battled the intense feeling of nerves, and made her way over to them.

"Excuse me, I'm sorry to interrupt, but it's Charlie, right? I think we first met at the open day earlier in the year."

"Hi. It's Luna, isn't it?" Nova's heart stepped up a gear. *He remembered her.* And not for the flyer incident. Take that, Slave Leia.

"Er, nearly. It's Nova. They're similar names — they've both got four letters in a sequence that goes 'consonant, vowel, consonant, vowel'. And they're both related to space. Samesies."

She listened to the drivel coming out of her mouth and hated her life a little bit more every time a word left her lips. Why did this always happen? Why did she have to spout such utter shit in front of him? Her embarrassment was compounded by the look she could feel the slutty Leia giving her.

"Nova, that's right. And this is Holly. We lived in the same corridor here at Rutland in our first year."

The two Leias exchanged cursory nods and fake hellos.

"And who's the ring-tailed lemur on your shoulder? Hey, little guy, nice to meet you."

"He's called Zhang. Say hello to the nice man."

"This is Flash, my chameleon."

Their pets held out their hands and rubbed each other's heads, the customary Electropet introduction. He'd make a perfect playmate for Zhang — when she went on dates with Charlie, they could keep each other entertained.

"I met some real-life lemurs while I was in Madagascar. 'Maky' is what they call them out there. Isn't that right, Zhang? And you've spent some time in Mozambique, Nova, if I remember correctly?"

In your face, you big-breasted whore. *He might have got my name slightly mixed up, but we're totally down with the travelling thing. In theory at least.* After the open day, she'd done some basic research into sustainable development in an attempt to convince herself that they really did have the same interests.

"Yes! Good old Mozambique. One of the best times of my life. They could really benefit from microfinance out there, which I believe was something—"

"I'm sure they could," Holly cut in, with a supercilious smile. "But we were just about to leave, weren't we, Charlie?"

"Yeah. It's a bit nerd-heavy in here, don't you think? We were thinking about heading to a club. Holly suggested Hedonism."

Nova's heart raced. She had one last trick up her sleeve.

"Hedonism, yeah, it's a great night. I've got a friend in the third year who spins a few tunes at parties. He knows all the DJs and stuff. One of the Hedonism DJs is going to be at a bash by the lake tonight. Bit less formal than a club night."

Charlie's eyes lit up. She was winning. It was time to seal the deal.

"I was going to head down there soon. Charlie, you need to meet these mates of Jono's. They're massively into technology and building gadgets. We could persuade them to create some stuff for Third World villages — developing economies, I mean."

"Awesome, I'd love to come down if that's alright?" He smiled at her and she locked eyes with him. Then he turned on Holly. "What do you think?"

"Yeah, a lake party," said Holly in a bored tone of voice. "We can do that for a bit. Then we can go to Hedonism afterwards. But I think my friend will only be able to get the two of us in on the guest list." She squeezed her face into a false little grimace. "Sorry about that."

Nova smiled at her, and Holly smiled back. She'd never been part of a more sarcastic, inauthentic exchange in her life.

The game was on.

***

The walk down to the lake was awkward. Each Leia vied for the attention of Charlie, who walked between them, enjoying the looks of the passers-by. Nova tried to steer the conversation toward ring-tailed lemurs and technology, while Holly tried to steer it toward clubbing and the season she had spent working as a rep in Ibiza. Whenever Holly spoke, Nova used the time to think how she could win Charlie's affection, but also worried about the lies she'd told him. She'd never lied like this to anyone; she might have deceived her parents, but the deception had always been "errors of omission" rather than outright porkies.

A steady, minimalist drumbeat emanated from the bushes and trees ahead. Hoicking her dress up, Nova skipped ahead along the gravel path towards the caves. This was *her* gig and *she* was in charge. She pushed past the last few branches of bracken to be greeted by a flashing neon sign that read 'The Cave Rave'. It was a small gathering of around thirty people. Wireless speakers situated on rocks and suspended from the cave ceiling pounded out techno beats, complemented by crazy dance visuals projected onto the rear wall of the cave by a pair of Booners. In the centre of the stone terrace in front of the cave, a crackling campfire was roasting marshmallows that dangled above it, propped up by sticks from nearby trees.

Charlie and the Leias sat down a short way back from the fire. Nova cracked open a beer and heard a familiar voice.'

"Well, I never. If it isn't a Han sandwich. Made in a deli far, far away, no doubt."

Nova waved him over with a smile on her face. It felt like the reinforcements had arrived.

"This is my friend Burner, from back home. That's Maidstone, by the way. Burner, meet Charlie. And this is Holly," she added as a bitter afterthought.

"Charlie, Holly, a pleasure to meet you," Burner said while reaching down to shake their hands. "Jono, look who's here."

Jono paused in his 'mallow toasting, looked over and smiled a mad grin. He called over to another couple of guys and headed over to join them. He and Burner were something of a double act, sometimes able to riff off one another for hours at a time. Or more usually, until Nova told them to shut the hell up.

"Well, well, well. It's young Nova Negrahnu if I'm not mistaken," Jono said, doing his version of Burner's posh old man routine, "Krazy Karting finalist, darts extraordinaire, finder of Travinsky and wearer of the strangest fashions."

Nova felt herself blush. "Burner, make him stop, please."

"Hey, guys, I'm Jono, nice to meet you all. And this here is Max and Maurice, two of the Solar Soc crew," Jono said, with a flourish of his hands.

Charlie turned to Nova. "Karting, darts, Travinsky ... I'm intrigued."

All eyes were on her. Even Holly's.

"I'm a huge fan of Solarversia and I'm doing pretty well. I'm a green belt, so I've still got two lives left. That's pretty rare at this stage. Travinsky was the name of a bird at the circus. I won some money when I used my darts skills to help find him."

"Blimey," said Charlie. "Totally rock 'n' roll."

"All pretty standard in my world. You need to remember that I'm a princess," she said to laughter from everyone but Holly, who was now busy tapping away on her phone. "Krazy Karting is one of the sub-games that takes place within Solarversia. I'm racing in the final in a few weeks time, hoping to take down the hundred grand prize for first place. You should come and watch."

"We'll be there," said Max and Maurice in unison. Wearing matching jackets, customised with badges displaying their Game numbers, vehicles and catchphrases, they took it in turns to press their buttons, triggering sown-in speakers that spoke the details of their profiles.

"It's a pleasure to finally meet you, Nova," Max said with a wink. "We're two of your biggest fans. We're going to be live-blogging the Krazy Karting final for Solar Soc."

Nova smiled. Max and Maurice were the creators of Gogmagog, the software she and Burner had used in Project Drone. The police had advised all of them to stay quiet on the matter so that the Holy Order couldn't connect Nova to her original forum post. She was relieved that the topic hadn't been mentioned, but she was excited to meet them. Burner had told her that their last few months had been mental; they'd been inundated with offers from venture capitalists since the story about the terrorist training ground broke and were thinking of dropping out of uni to develop the company.

Max turned to Charlie. "What about you, Solo? Are you still in?"

"The Game? No, I never got round to signing up in time, unfortunately."

"You're dressed as Han Solo, but you're actually a Yolo?"

Charlie turned to Nova with a blank expression on his face.

"Game lingo. Players are sometimes referred to as 'Solos', and non-players as 'Yolos', like 'You Only Live Once', because you only get one life in the real world."

"And what about you, Holly? Do you play?"

Without looking at him, she casually held out a hand to display a violet-coloured bangle whose outer edge was inscribed with a number.

"Woah. You're violet belt with a five-digit player number? That's even more central than you, Nova. Seriously cool. I don't think I've seen you at Solar Soc before?"

"No offence, but I went to a taster and it wasn't for me. I'd rather be playing than talking about playing. Perhaps that's how I've retained my three lives. Us violet belts are even rarer than green belts. There are only a few million of us left in the wild. I see you lost a life to Killanja, Nova. It must have been incredibly annoying to lose a life to the easiest Grandmaster? Perhaps you need to increase your intake of Puzzle practise? A balanced diet isn't right for everyone."

"She's actually really good at Puzzles." It was Burner. She knew she could count on him to stick up for her. "The problem was, she got spannered on sambucas the night we finished our A-levels. She didn't even get to play the Puzzle, she was too busy puking her guts up in the bog at Frag …"

He tailed off into silence when he finally noticed Nova death-staring him.

"We all know the saying, I'm sure. A bad Solo blames her Science. Although in this case, it sounds like a bad Solo blaming her sambucas." When Holly burst into a fit of giggles at her own joke, Nova felt a burning rage surge through her body.

"There's nothing wrong with my Science, thanks."

"Oh, yeah? Then why do you hide your stats? True Solos show their stats. Everyone knows that. By the way, I noticed that we had someone in common. A certain Jools van der Star."

"That's the guy who nearly stopped Nova from making the Karting final. He's ranked the best player in the—"

Sensing the death stare earlier this time, Burner stopped talking, suddenly a lot more interested in the label on his can of beer. Heads turned to Nova.

"You could say that we have something of a rivalry. I was ahead in our heat — by quite some margin — when he got lucky, picked up a Turbo Boost, and smashed me into the side hoardings. I fell back to seventeenth, and it was only my very best driving that got me back into tenth. How is it you know him, Holly?"

"We're grid twins. As you probably know, he's a terrible flirt. Started sexting me the minute I signed up. We've become good friends."

As the grid became increasingly populated with people leading up to the start of The Game, Spiralwerks had encouraged Solos to get to know one another as part of their 'social cohesion' strategy. Rather than segment people by interest like other social networks, Spiralwerks segmented them using maths and geometry, forcing them to interact with those from other countries and social class.

Your twins were the people reflected in the x-axis, the y-axis and the origin, so that you had a horizontal twin, a vertical twin and a diagonal twin. Together, the four of you were referred to as 'grid quads', and any two of you as 'grid twins'. Nova knew hers, but hadn't formed friendships with any of them.

Once Holly had shown Charlie the replay of van der Star smashing Nova into the side hoardings, she stretched her arms in a bored manner and batted her eyelids at him. "We'd better get going if we want to get into Hedonism for free."

"Oh, don't bother with Hedonism," Burner said. "Marco's their biggest name and he's about to play here. Stay — it'll be awesome."

"It's up to you guys, of course," Nova said, quickly taking over from Burner before he could ruin his good work. She paused, as if she was thinking all of this through for the first time. "You could see him play here for free, or later on at the club. Though if you did go, you'd have to pay for taxis, and nightclub prices for drinks."

As DJ Marco approached the decks to start his set, Jono leapt up and landed in a squatting position in front of them. He pulled a flask of whisky out of one pocket and a joint out of the other.

"Do you whisky? Do you smoky?" he said, while wiggling each in their faces. "If you come from Maidstone, smoking weed is compulsory. It's an anagram of 'I am stoned' for a start."

It was brilliant timing. Charlie, as it turned out, both whiskied and smokied. Hopefully they'd all get stoned and want to stay put by the fire. Better still, Holly wasn't a big fan of the green stuff. Nova had a smoke, handed the joint to Charlie and then went to retrieve some marshmallows from the production line that Max and Maurice had set in motion.

"This setup reminds me of the old Burnside barbeques we used to have," she said, while Burner examined various sticks to find her some that were ready. It was awesome being at Nottingham with him and having Jono and his crowd to help show them the ropes. She pointed at a couple of 'mallows with crisped golden edges and readied her napkin in anticipation. Perhaps she might even feed them to Charlie herself, and have him lick her fingers clean. It would tickle and she'd giggle and provocatively suck them herself. She even had a face lined up to give Holly while the action went down, and practised it quickly while Burner struggled with a 'mallow that looked like it had been roasted beyond repair. But once she returned to their area away from the fire, thoughts of playing licky-tickle soon disappeared. Instead, she found Holly groaning and Charlie massaging the lower section of her back.

"What's going on? Why are you—"

"Holly decided that she *did* want a couple of drags of the spliff after all. Bad idea."

"I don't feel too good. Everything's spinning. I think I might be ill." Her subsequent groan was so dramatic that it bordered on the farcical. "Can you take me back to the house and look after me, Charlie?"

"Looks like you're pulling a whitey. Of course I can."

Nova looked on, stunned at the turn of events. How had this happened? The deceitful little bitch. She could tell Holly was play-acting from a mile off. Surely Charlie hadn't fallen for it? They got up together, Charlie steadying her as she wobbled about. He turned and shrugged at Nova.

"Thanks for the invitation. I guess I'll see you around." He wrapped his arm around Holly's waist and pulled her close to him. "Let's get you home, eh?" he said, and they turned and walked away.

"Oh, well," Burner said. "More 'mallows for us, eh?"

Nova didn't answer him. She had gone rather white herself.

Chapter Twenty-Six

Casey was hyperalert as he paddled his kayak through the swamp on the way back to the compound. The rush of adrenaline from the afternoon's events was still working its way through his body. He divided his attention between Theodore and Brandon in the kayaks ahead, the alligators lining the riverbank, and the man slumped in the seat in front of him.

He kept expecting two contradictory things to happen and was equally nervous of both. He was half-worried the guy was going to regain consciousness and attempt an escape of some sort, and half-worried that he was going to die. Brandon had cracked his skull hard with the car jack, harder than was called for to Casey's mind.

He leaned forward and gently pushed and pulled at the body, trying to right him in his seat again. His name was Elmer Sullivan, and he'd been the target of the day's mission. Elmer was one of the homeless people that had been accosted by the Order a couple of years back when they'd roamed the ghettos of downtown Los Angeles and rounded up a bunch of vagrants.

The organisation had presented itself as a medical charity doing research — one that paid a handsome sum to its participants without asking any difficult questions. Drifters like Elmer had queued up to take part once the word had spread. Fifty bucks in exchange for a doctor taking a quick, painless blood sample, and her colleague waving a phone over your body to scan it into their database. For most of the people there that day, it had been Christmas come early.

By the time the Order had come to use them, to create online accounts at companies like Spiralwerks, most of the individuals they were pretending to be had either died of alcohol poisoning or descended further into that special blend of psychosis that long-term homelessness was so adept at brewing.

Frances and Wallace hadn't been totally bullshitting when they said they were taking samples of blood to use in research. No, samples hadn't been used to find a cure for Alzheimer's. But they had allowed Frances to find genetic matches between the vagrants and the organisation's own members. Although he didn't know it yet, Elmer was destined for great things. At least, part of him was.

Wallace. Just the thought of him sent shooting pains up Casey's body. He struggled to keep up with the kayak ahead, twisting his body wildly from left to right as he paddled with his only arm, a torrent of thoughts rushing through his mind. A moment of clarity allowed him to appreciate the story about the Magi for what it was — it had given him something to hold onto, a vine thrown to help him climb out of the suicidal depths. A friendly AI that would save mankind. An eternity of suffering if he didn't heed the call. Comrades at the compound who believed the same thing. He'd been so sure that they were on to something. Not just *any* thing, but *the* thing, something good, virtuous and pure.

It was the same old God he'd loved as a child and lost as a teenager. The same old story in a new technicolour dreamcoat. And it had come with something he desperately needed — a ready-made, pre-packaged family, the one he'd never had. Theodore and Frances were the loving-yet-strict parents. Wallace had been his older brother, the guy who looked out for him and showed him the ropes. His bottom lip quivered as he remembered Wallace begging for mercy before the Medibots caved his skull in.

With Elmer slumped in the seat in front of him, Casey's thoughts drifted to his impending mission and what he'd have to endure to achieve it. Certainly his brothers and sisters from the Order regarded him differently these days. Whenever he walked past someone in the compound they would nod in a knowing, reverential manner. It was a telling gesture, an indication that they respected his sacrifice for the greater good. His operation wouldn't be the only one in the Compound, but it *would* be the most severe. In some ways he was no longer simply one of the men, but rather a leader among them.

He knew something for sure: he was shit scared about the operation. He'd endured plenty of sleepless nights, tossing and turning on the stupidly narrow mattress in his bunk, trying to swat skeeters with a hand that wasn't there. In some ways, the plan Theodore had in mind for him was more frightening than the thought of suicide. It wasn't as final as death of course, but it *was* definitive in other ways. It would represent a total loss of identity; an elimination of self. Casey Brown would be no more.

***

She knew that the event would be special given that she was one of only six finalists from the United Kingdom, but it wasn't until she approached The Commodore, the largest gaming cafe in Nottingham, that Nova realised quite what a momentous occasion the Krazy Karting final was going be.

As she turned into Shakespeare Street, she saw the huge 'Good Luck Super Nova 2020!' banner draped across the front of the cafe. Burner took a photo of her reaction — a hand raised to her cheek as if she had given herself a slow-motion slap. Solar Soc had appointed him and Zhang as the official photographers and videographers and had tasked them with gathering enough quality footage for a short documentary to mark the occasion.

As she entered The Commodore, a small mob gathered round her, eager for photos and statements before the race began. Burner helped clear a path to her rig, which, she was pleased to note, was located within a cordoned-off area. It was all very different from her visit the previous week when she'd got some quiet practice in like a normal member of the public.

The place reminded her of Fragging Hell: it had the same overhead monitors displaying gaming results and upcoming matches, the same strip lighting running down the centre of the loud, retro carpets, and the same mild odour of stale sweat, deep-fryers and teen spirit that lingered in every gaming cafe she'd visited.

The only real difference, she was sad to realise, was the absence of Jockey. She'd meant to call him to apologise on a number of occasions, but had never quite found the mental resolve. It was weird. Saying that she was sorry and admitting that she was wrong were two things she found almost impossible to do.

As she reached the cordoned-off area, a short guy in a shiny polyester suit approached her, arms held wide, a large smile on his face.

"Eh, up me duck, I'm Malcolm Cook, owner of The Commodore. You must be Nova and Burner. Thanks for booking your gaming rig with us, we're honoured to have you here today."

He grabbed hold of her hand and shook it with vigour.

"Burner, me pal, could you do us a favour and take some photos of the two of us?"

Nova posed for a series of photos with Malcolm and some of the more important guests: a dean from the university and the owner of Beeston Buggies, the business sponsoring the event at the cafe.

"Better take your place in the rig, Scotia. You ready?"

"Guess so," she gulped.

Burner turned to the assembled crowd in an officious manner. "No more photos, sorry."

A stocky guy with ginger hair pushed his way to the front, camera in hand.

"Hi, Nova, I'm really sorry, I can see you're in demand, it's just that I'm a huge fan. I've come all the way from London. Could I get a quick photo with you?"

"Alright, last one."

This kind of 'niche fame' was a strange property that had emerged from Solarversia. Other social networks, even the open kind that allowed non-members to view user profiles, didn't come close to the people-watching opportunities offered by The Game. A clever combination of algorithms and filters enabled people to experience it like an infinitely customisable film.

'Funny celebrity deaths' was a common highlights reel, but Nova enjoyed the quirky, the obscure and the artistic reels just as much. 'Follow the pixel' was one of her favourites. She'd choose a pixel at the front of her shoe, hopscotch a pattern on the tessellated tiles and watch it leave her foot and travel along the ground in the form of colour, seeing how it would deflect off pixels coming the other way, and eventually end up as part of someone else's shoe, or a tyre on their car, as they trod on, or drove over the pattern. When she watched highlights reels, she'd turn catchphrases *on* and enjoy the serendipitous combinations that occasionally ensued.

Watching these virtual journeys and knowing that atoms worked in a similar way in the real world really tickled her. She also loved logging in to discover that her own avatar had appeared in other players' highlights reels. She empathised with the guy who had come all this way to watch her race and posed for the shot with a smile, wanting to enjoy every last second of her fifteen minutes of fame.

"Thanks so much. That's made my day. I'm Raymond, by the way. Good luck in the race!"

They shook hands and she got into the rig, slightly disappointed that The Commodore wasn't equipped with the new haptic suits that BoonerMax were rumoured to be developing. Such suits provided tactile feedback to the body and were said to heighten the immersive experience of virtual worlds.

Once she was seated in the gaming rig, Burner laid his hands on her shoulders.

"Relax, you're so tense." He needled his thumb into a tight knot above her shoulder blade. "I got Jono to reserve this entire area, so we'll be here to support you the whole time. Just shut everything else out. Remember our practice sessions. You're one of the best players in the world, and you're going to take this mofo down."

The area reserved for the Solar Soc crew was slap-bang in front of her rig. It was reassuring to see them there, resting their elbows on a makeshift rail, sipping their pints. Zhang was in reportage mode, filming the people around him, while Max and Maurice spoke into their mics, live-blogging the event for a local website. It felt good to have the gang here to cheer her on, a positive kind of pressure.

Plenty of others would be supporting her from wherever they were in the world: her mum and dad, her old school friends, the Fragging Hell crew. And maybe even Sushi, she thought, watching from wherever she was.

Nova tried to relax, but it was difficult to ignore the beating of her heart. She took a deep breath and looked over to Burner for one last spurt of encouragement. Now her heart jolted. Charlie had just arrived and was taking a front row seat. He gave her a wink and a smile. She hadn't seen him since the rave at the cave a few weeks ago and wouldn't have known what to say to him even if she had. At least there was no sign of Holly.

Nova stole one last glance at Charlie before she pulled her visor down. It was sweet to see Zhang clinging onto him like he was the tree of life. Charlie noticed her looking and mouthed, "Good luck." She grinned like an idiot and he blew her a kiss. Which was ridiculous and wonderful, except that it made her heart beat even faster.

Chapter Twenty-Seven

The headset that came with Nova's rig was of similar quality to the high-end ones at Fragging Hell. The superb resolution and miniscule latency did a very good job of tricking her into thinking that she *really* was sitting in Hawk, suspended in mid-air over the Planetarium in Greenwich Park.

Around her, ninety-nine other pilots revved their engines, eager to start the race after months of build-up and hype. There were stealth fighters, helicopters and gliders, aircraft of every description. Because this was the final, players would race in all three vehicles: they would fly to the first checkpoint, sail down the River Thames to the second and then drive through the streets of London to the finish line. To make things fair, vehicle speeds had been set to maximum, regardless of speed points accumulated in The Game.

Nova flexed her fingers one last time as a series of beeps counted down to the start of the most important race of her life. Dozens of monitors around the room displayed the race from multiple perspectives and would provide real-time information and statistics on all hundred players.

George McCafferty, a local radio presenter, had been brought in to commentate for the crowd and was sitting in a lifeguard's chair overlooking the cafe. He was best known for his late-night segment called 'Shoot a Student', where local residents called in with gripes about the student population. His quick-fire comments and outrageous laugh endeared him to everyone who tuned in. The sound of Gorigaroo's gong reverberated around the cafe. George leant forward in his chair, waited for the cheer to die down and launched into commentary.

"And they're off. All eyes are on Nova 'Super Nova 2020' Negrahnu, player number 515,740. Originally from Maidstone in Kent, she's currently in her first year at Nottingham University. She started in 77th position, based on her finishing time in the Alpha Island heat, and is one of six finalists from the United Kingdom. There are three big names to watch out for: Park 'The PacMan' Min, the professional gamer from South Korea in 23rd, Arnold 'Pump up the Jam' Weber, the Austrian daredevil starting in 6th place, and the odds-on-favourite to win, Jools 'The Beanstalker' van der Star, the Dutch sensation, who starts the race in pole position. They're all competing to win the first place prize of one hundred thousand pounds, although places two to twenty-five also pay handsomely."

A hundred planes started flying toward the O_2, a large dome-shaped building located on the south bank of the River Thames. En route, they would need to navigate a series of floating hoops, which, like the platforms leading to Meganja, increased in difficulty as they went on. Nova banked up, down, left and right, flying through each of the hoops with ease, grateful for the many hours of practice she'd put in with Burner. She'd nudged up to 75th place when she saw a flash up ahead, followed by a trail of black smoke, descending fast.

"That's good news for Negrahnu. The player from Texas overcorrected herself in order to make the last hoop and smashed hard into the player on her tail. They both paid a big price for the mistake, one Negrahnu would do well to learn from. They won't have lost a life in the main Game — the event is separate from that — but that would be little consolation for exiting the race so soon. Top seed, Jools van der Star, maintains his lead. He's opted to steer clear of the bonus items on offer. When her time comes, will Negrahnu do the same?"

It was the question she had just asked herself. The twelve support towers sticking out of the O_2 dome were ringed with bonus items. Like sirens, they tempted unwitting players into dangerous territory. She spotted a Turbo Boost icon hovering under the lip of one of the supports and lurched toward it at the last second. It was the kind of item she'd need if she was ever going to catch up with van der Star.

Which she wanted to do more than anything in the world. A few weeks ago she'd made herself sit through thirty dreadful minutes when he'd appeared as the guest on Kiki La Roux's show. One of her favourite celebrities in the world, fawning over someone she hated. And boy, did she hate him. Not only had he screwed her over in the heats, but also he was grid twins with Holly. The thought of the pair of them made her feel sick and zone out for a second. Realising she'd misjudged the tower, she gripped the joysticks as tight as possible and tried to correct Hawk. In the cafe, she heard the crowd gasp.

"Negrahnu giving the crowd here a big fright as she gains an item, but loses some health, now down to eighty-six points. If you look over at monitors five and six you can see the replay. She clipped the end of her wing and was lucky it wasn't more serious. Fortunately the accident won't affect her overall speed, but I'm sure it's knocked her confidence."

In the foreground she could hear Burner yelling that she needed to pull herself together. He was right, it was a schoolgirl error, one she could ill afford in a race against such formidable opposition. As she cleared the last of the support towers to head east toward Canary Wharf, she checked her display monitors. Now in 71st position, she was still fifteen seconds behind van der Star in first place.

The next part of the course looked tricky. Ludi Bioski had altered the structure of One Canada Square, the tallest of the buildings in the Canary Wharf area. He'd cut a hole, thirty square metres, out of the core of the building, so that approaching from one side you could see through it to the red, white and blue sky on the other.

Players were expected to fly straight through it, which would have been easy enough, but there was a barrage of missiles being lobbed at them from every direction. Gorigaroo, who was perched atop the deformed building, was ripping solar panels off the roof and casually tossing them into the flight path like he was playing frisbee at the beach.

There was a separate onslaught of projectiles being launched by players who weren't even in the race. A related quest had secured them places in one of the surrounding office blocks, from where they took turns to man catapults that launched office paraphernalia into the path of racers.

She yanked the joystick toward her and ascended two stories in order to get an aerial view of the carnage that lay ahead. The sky was full of flying office chairs, monitors and keyboards. Her display flickered like crazy as the planes ahead took hits. She was pleased to see the rudder of van der Star's plane, Famous, hit by an old inkjet printer. He wasn't immune to error after all.

She stayed as high as she could for as long as possible, but still lost a few health points to a spinning flip chart that clipped Hawk's undercarriage. Hearing Burner yell at her to dive, and knowing that she was too high for the fly-through, she jerked the joystick forward as far as it would go. The next few seconds seemed to occur in slow motion. She was focused on the hole, but seemed to have gained perfect peripheral vision, and noted that Gorigaroo had just hurled a handful of solar panels her way. They fell around her in a shower, never touching her as she flew straight on, directly into the path of a filing cabinet launched in her direction from the building on her left.

"This is going to be tight, ladies and gentlemen, I'm not sure how's she's going to avoid the cabinet, especially now its drawers have fallen out. Oh my word, what an incredible manoeuvre. A treble spin to avoid the cabinet, a loop-de-loop to pass the solar panels, and she's through. It's the kind of skill that brought Negrahnu to the final in the first place. She's taken a minor hit to her front left wheel, reducing her health to eighty points, but she's up to 68th position. Go, Super Nova!"

The hole in the building was black with smoke. One of the three French competitors had come at it from a sharp angle and lost an entire wing when he hit the side of the building. He proceeded to death roll into the woman alongside him. Two places gained and another example of what not to do. Nova soared through the clouds of smoke and banked sharp right towards the first checkpoint, the giant Ferris wheel known as the London Eye. Another set of hoops lined this part of the course, some that were on fire, some that spun upon their axes, and some that turned invisible as the player approached them.

"We're being treated to more great racing from Negrahnu. This is solid stuff, a veritable master class in flying. She's really pushing Hawk to the limit. Take a look at monitor two: her split times are very close to van der Star's, the guy in first place. The good news is that the pair of them are the fastest racers out there today. The bad news is that while she's overtaking plenty of other people, she hasn't gained anything on him yet. She needs to pull fifteen seconds out of a bag somewhere. Let us know if you spot one."

As she flew through the invisible last hoop, she chipped up another position into 62nd place. The Belgian guy she'd been trailing had misjudged the location of the hoop and had been hit with a penalty — his top speed had been cut to ninety percent for five seconds. Straight ahead was the Eye, where van der Star's plane had morphed into his boat. When she finally made the checkpoint herself, she was raring to go. It was good to settle herself into Bruno and to feel the lap of the waves below his prow. That was a third of the race completed, and a quick mental calculation reinforced what she already knew: she'd need to up her game if she was to be in with a chance of going home with some money.

"Can Negrahnu handle Bruno as well as she handled Hawk? She's going to need to. This part of the course takes players through a series of gates which exact heavy penalties if touched. We can expect more interaction with non-racing players who have lined the banks of the Thames equipped with fishing rods. Anything they manage to catch can be thrown at the players, with plenty of bounties up for grabs. Wait a second. What in the name of bejesus caused that?

The smart money's got to be on Ludi Bioski. But more importantly, how fast is that thing going to travel?"

Deafening screeches of twisting metal drowned out the sound of the commentary. The spectators in the bar held their hands to their ears, and McCafferty flinched in his seat. Despite the racket, the river ahead looked quite normal to Nova. She could see the boats she was chasing, a bunch of gates and a few thousand fishermen lining the banks. It was in her wing mirror that she finally caught sight of it, the thing making all the noise. It churned out such a colossal amount of water that she first thought it might be a tidal wave chasing after them.

Catching glimpses through the wall of spray, she finally worked out what had happened. The London Eye had come unhinged from its mooring and had driven straight into the river. Rolling on its circumference, as if under the control of a unicycling maniac, it was slicing through the water, smashing to smithereens anything in its path. Hundreds of fishing lines got caught in its spokes, pulling anglers off the riverbank and dragging them through the white water that followed in its wake.

Her datafeed went wild. Two players at the back of the field had just been shredded, sending a clear message to everyone else. Nova didn't need telling twice. As she caned around the next gate and straightened Bruno up, she activated her Turbo Boost, and although she didn't gain any places, she did pull away from the Eye.

Back in the cafe, Burner looked more stressed than anyone else. Absorbed in conversation with Jono, he debated the relative merits of their proposed strategies for her.

"She needs to take more risks; it's all about the items," Jono explained.

"Dude, you're one of the worst players I know. Get some skills before you offer your pearls of wisdom," Burner said, right up in his face.

"You don't need to be good at something in order to provide practical advice. There's no point playing it safe and coming in 26th. Might as well risk it for a biscuit."

"Negrahnu's in 60th position. This faultless driving on the Thames has gained her two seconds on van der Star, who screwed up his last gate. Yet she can't be happy with the situation. There's no sign of the Eye coming to a halt — there goes another player — and the datafeed on monitor seven suggests, if anything, that it's gaining speed. Players at the front of the pack just passed under Waterloo Bridge. I wonder—"

McCafferty stopped dead. "There goes the neighbourhood. Shit just got doubly real ... if you'll pardon my French."

This time Nova caught sight of the disturbance straight away. Banjax the dodectopus — who had surfaced close to the next bridge — was pumping his mighty tentacles in and out and rotating on the spot. Within seconds he had created a giant whirlpool that stretched halfway across the width of the river. Every object within his event horizon eddied towards the whorl.

Dozens of fishing rods, and a couple of fishermen who had neglected to let go, were sucked under the waves. Van der Star and the pack of boats on his tail were taken by surprise and had had to make a split-second decision. They scattered either side of the vortex. The whirlpool was turning anticlockwise, so anyone who had opted to shoot right of it came through unscathed. Those that went left faced a surge of oncoming water.

The next minute was sheer mayhem. Four players steered too close to Banjax and got sucked under by the powerful currents around him. Six others misjudged the currents badly enough that they drove straight into the arches supporting the bridge and wrote off their boats. Nova saw all this happen and plotted the perfect course under the bridge on the far right-hand side of the river, as far away from Banjax as possible. What she didn't foresee was the fisherman on the bridge, who had hooked a mangled shopping trolley from the banks of the river. He judged his throw well, and would have wiped her out, had she not steered Bruno a sharp left at the last second. The trolley clipped Bruno's stern before tumbling harmlessly into the water behind them.

"That was the biggest upheaval yet. We're down to 81 players and there's been a significant shuffle of positions, except for van der Star, still in first place, proving once again why he's rated the best in the world. Arnold Weber, the Austrian daredevil, didn't fare so well; he got sucked under, so it's auf Wiedersehen to him, or should that be goodnight, Vienna? Negrahnu did well out of the chaos, she's up to 27th position, but suffered a couple of nasty blows, which have taken her health down to forty points. If she can't find a health pack, she'll need to be more careful. There's one thing every player can be grateful for: Banjax's whirlpool stopped the London Eye in its tracks."

The last stretch of the course on the river was tame in comparison. Ludi Bioski interfered with the mechanics of the bascules at Tower Bridge so they flapped up and down like the wings of a lazy pigeon, but only three racers got snared. By the time Nova made it back to Canary Wharf to hit the second checkpoint, she was up to 26th place and had narrowed van der Star's lead to eight seconds. Her health was flagging though. She was down to 35 points, after a tussle with Park Min, the Korean kid in a speedboat. As she careened into the jetty at the Wharf, Bruno morphed into Flynn for the third and final section of the race. She felt the thrum of his engine and brushed her fingers against the grips of the wheel.

"Negrahnu cleared that corner with the precision of an F1 driver. Flynn's supposed to be her best vehicle, so let's see what she can do with him. She's approaching the White Tower at the Tower of London, close on the tail of the South African driver in 25th. That's right, folks, one more place and she's in the money, places twenty-five to twenty-one paying out a cool five grand. She's tearing through the tower and will need to slow down for this next corner. It's not happened yet, she's left it awfully late. In fact, she hasn't slowed down at all, what's she playing at? Has she taken leave of her senses? There's a ramp there, but it's facing a wall. Isn't she going to hit it at full speed? She does hit the ramp, she's flying through the air … and boom! What a legend. That has to be the move of the race, the crowd here has gone wild."

Nova knew the unwritten rule of all good computer games: *things are there for a reason*. When she saw the ramp she did what every player ahead of her had done — looked where it led. In this case, the solid brick wall of the White Tower. Their instinct had been to steer clear of it. Nova on the other hand, reasoned that the designers had put it there for a reason. She trusted both *her* logic, and *their* design. She did hit the wall, but a part of it covered by one of Henry VIII's tapestries. Flynn ripped clean through it to reveal a secret passage, one that not only cut a few seconds off her time, but also gifted her some Winged Beauties and a jar of Skidz.

As she left the Tower, she roared through the city with a renewed sense of purpose, cheered on by the crowds lining the streets, and, as she went past St. Paul's Cathedral, saw Emperor Mandelbrot himself. He had flown Castalia to London, the first time the palace had moved since the start of the Year-Long Game. Ludi Bioski had removed the Cathedral's dome so that the Emperor could teleport there on his dais to watch the race go by. At his side, seated in the lotus position, was Spee-Akka Dey Bollarkoo, working on a section of the October portrait reserved to depict the final.

"Van der Star rips up The Strand, fast approaching Trafalgar Square, which happens to be the scene of total pandemonium. He's been at it again, folks, the peddler of randomness, Ludi Bioski has brought the four bronze lions to life, and by the looks of it, has given them a taste for blood. Ooh, that looked nasty. Van der

Star just took a big hit, losing 32 health points in one go. Those claws are sharp. I wonder what Negrahnu's going to do. It seems like she's in no doubt though, she's just sprouted her Winged Beauties, allowing her to fly clear of the trouble on the street. She got away with a minor scratch to the paintwork, and she's up to 14th place, which pays ten grand. But will her 23 health points be enough to make it all the way to the finish line? Players are heading down Whitehall toward the Houses of Parliament, which means there's about three miles left."

Driving up Big Ben's clock tower reminded Nova of a multistorey car park. She wound her way up, taking right turn after right turn, a seemingly endless corkscrew up the building. At the top, she followed the lead of the eleven players still ahead of her and drove straight at the clock face. As she popped out the front, ninety metres up, Big Ben chimed and Flynn deployed a parachute that floated her back to the ground.

It was the first time in the race that she could relax and take everything in. There were hundreds of blimps, balloons and zeppelins parked over the city, and above them, a fluffy face-shaped cloud for each of the remaining finalists. To celebrate Spiralwerks' home nation, the sky had been painted like the Union Jack, the flag of the United Kingdom, but would change to match the flag of the winning finalist.

As she watched a cloud break apart — signalling the exit of an Icelandic player — a tingle went down her spine and she entered a flow state of consciousness. Even the throbbing pain in her hands and wrists seemed to subside, as if her body knew how important the next few minutes were.

She tore past Buckingham Palace in 10th, up to Piccadilly Circus in 8th, and by the time she got to Regent Street, she was in 5th. The noise in the cafe was so loud that, for the first time, she activated the noise-cancellation feature on the headset, leaving only the in-game sound of revving engines, tooting horns and her racing heartbeat. Regent Street was split into two: she was in the left lane, behind the Peruvian guy in second place; van der Star and the two other drivers were in the right. A fraction of a second was all that separated the five of them.

The street was populated with a light smattering of regular London traffic: red buses, black cabs and the occasional pedestrian. Her driving was masterful. She weaved in and out of the traffic like she owned the city and couldn't help but flash a snarky smile at van der Star as she overtook him. The way she took the corner into Marylebone Road was so smooth it increased her lead by a tenth of a second. All she needed to do now was drive down the road, hang a right into Regent's Park and head for the big yellow sphere, Sun Two Point O, the chequered flag of the race.

She steered hard right and went to brake, actions that should have seen her skid round the corner, lined up for the final straight. Except she couldn't brake. At first she thought her left ankle had seized up. Her reaction was to try the brake pedal with her right foot instead. She still couldn't depress it. Flynn missed the turn and was headed toward a group of spectators at top speed when she felt someone grab her legs. Just what, in the name of all that was holy, was going on?

She volleyed back to the cafe to discover that it had gone silent. McCafferty stared at her open-mouthed. Zhang's little head stuck out from under her brake pedal; kneeling next to him was Charlie, who looked white as a sheet.

"Charlie? What the fuck are you doing?"

"I ... it was Zhang," he croaked. "We were pushed. Zhang fell. Honest."

She removed her headset and looked around the room in frantic desperation, beseeching the crowd to throw her something, anything, that might have explained what was going on.

Silence and stagnation gave way to whispering, pointing and the arching of eyebrows. Instead of answers she found the monitors on the wall, and they contained nothing but pain and humiliation. The largest screen replayed Flynn's final few seconds. He hit the curb at speed, flew through the air, maiming, mangling and mutilating the non-player characters assembled on the pavement, tumbled along the ground and wrapped himself tight around a bollard. Nova's avatar looked deader than ever.

To add insult to her multiple injuries, she looked on helpless as van der Star flipped her the finger as he whizzed by. He hurtled round the corner into Regent's Park, zoomed up the pathway and disappeared into the giant Sun, his hundred thousand pound cash prize flashing on the screen.

Up in Castalia, Gorigaroo struck his gong and several million spectators looked up to the heavens to watch the reds, whites and blues of the Union Jack rearrange themselves into the striped Dutch flag. A troop of arkwinis appeared along the outer faces of Castalia and manned cannons that fired van der Star-shaped clouds into the sky, his stupid smug face taunting her from on high. Hero to zero in the space of two seconds.

She moved her foot from the brake pedal, allowing Charlie to pull Zhang from under it. He offered him to her, a look of remorse and confusion all over his face.

"I'm so sorry, I don't know what happened," said Burner, who had ducked under the barrier to join them. "We were watching, cheering you on, when we got pushed from behind. Zhang was with us one second, flying through the air the next."

She grabbed the furball from Charlie and hugged him tight, distraught that he'd been caught up in the affair. She wanted to hide, and she wanted to cry.

"Like Charlie said, it was an accident. Nova, mate, I don't know how it happened."

She looked the two boys up and down and gave them the biggest scowl she could manage while her face wanted to crumple into tears.

"Don't you 'Nova, mate' me. You fuckwits just cost me a hundred grand. You *owe* me a hundred grand. Thanks a million for coming along today, Charlie, you stupid frickin' hippy."

She pushed past them, tears now streaming freely down her face, then past the assembled crowd and out of the door.

And then she ran and she ran, and she didn't look back.

Chapter Twenty-Eight

As Nova panted heavily, struggling to get her knees into the action, the spectators lining the path stepped up their efforts. They cheered, they clapped and some even chanted her name. Two metres ahead, and struggling nearly as much, was another Nova, one programmed to complete the five-kilometre course in the time she'd set last week, when she'd run her personal best.

The fitness app overlaid virtual crowds onto three-dimensional maps of real-world locations, including the streets and paths surrounding the university campus. It was a fun way to do training — race the best version of yourself while hundreds of people cheered you on, like you were about to set a new world record.

Even though her legs complained with every step she took and she could taste blood in the back of her throat, she charged forward, reaching deep inside for what remained of her energy reserves. With less than two hundred metres to go, she stormed past her digital copy to a renewed roar from the crowd.

As she crossed the finishing line, her Booners flashed up the good news — she had shaved another half second from her best time, nudging her into the 92nd centile for her age group over the five-kilometre distance. Not bad, given that she was in the 78th centile only a month before. She walked on wobbly legs to the nearest tree and stretched against it, drawing the fresh autumnal air deep into her lungs.

After a quick shower she returned to her bedroom and opened the virtual room she'd created that contained the information on Project Drone. Realising that the room needed a name, she'd gone for 'Super Nova', a stripped-down version of her avatar name. Now the app comprised not just one, but a series of rooms, each dedicated to a different project. She'd created them in a pensive mood the day after the Krazy Karting debacle. Still angry with Burner, Charlie and the universe in general, she'd reflected on how Project Drone had enabled her to channel her negative emotions in a positive manner.

She came to the realisation that what she'd enjoyed about the plan was that it resembled a puzzle. It had been a game with lots of moving parts, some basic rules and a goal. It felt a bit wrong to have made a puzzle out of Sushi's death, but the more she'd thought about it, the more inescapable the truth had revealed itself to be. She'd *gamified* her response to the terrorist attack, and the result had been impressive, to say the least. Anything she wanted to change about her life could be turned into a game too. All the challenges and obstacles she faced could become games to play, puzzles to solve.

The realisation had not only seemed glaringly obvious, but also incredibly liberating. Everything you had to do could be *fun*, if you went about it the right way. It felt like she'd worked out one of life's secrets all by herself. She was the master of her own destiny. Who better to take up such a challenge than her, Nova Negrahnu, self-proclaimed professor of Science?

The app opened to display a rotating tetrahedron. Its four triangular faces each led to a different gamified project. The black face led to the cube that contained the information on the Order. She hadn't returned there since the police visit. It was a room that contained pain and misery. Instead, she tapped the skin-coloured face, the one that represented her body.

It led to a room dedicated to the improvement of her physical being: her speed, strength and flexibility. She smiled at the new time at the top of the running table. A new best time meant a reward. Once lectures had finished she would treat herself to a proper latte from the university shop, rather than a cup of liquid mud from the grotty machine at the library. Such simple incentives were surprisingly effective, though she had to admit that the penalties were playing their part too.

The app was synced to Burner's computer so he would know if she missed a run. His role was to administer her punishments, a task he had accepted with rather frightening enthusiasm. While she'd been thinking along the lines of extra uni work as a penalty, he'd suggested things like having her walk around campus wearing a sandwich board that proclaimed she was a lazy bum. They'd compromised, and agreed that for the first run she missed, she'd have to buy him a fancy lunch in town. That had been a good enough deterrent so far, though she didn't like to think about how she'd fare in the cold dark mornings when the winter deepened.

She left the 'Body' room and considered the tetrahedron again. The magenta-coloured face led to the 'Mind' section of the app, which was lined with the books she needed to read for her course, with barometers for each one that indicated how much she had read. It was also synced to several brain exercise games that claimed to boost puzzle-solving skills.

Rewards and punishments were attached to these tasks too, not that they were much required. She grabbed hold of the tetrahedron by two of its vertices and rotated it to look at the sage-coloured face, the one that led to the 'Soul' section. For now it contained a list of people she wanted to apologise to: Jockey, Mrs Woodward, Charlie and her parents.

The 'Soul' project had proved far harder than the 'Body' and 'Mind' projects. She'd made no progress whatsoever. It was strange. She knew *what* she wanted to say to each person on the list and she knew *why* she wanted to say it. It was the *how* that she had a problem with. How did you apologise to someone you had disrespected, someone you had lied to, someone you loved? What words did you use, what tone did you take?

Apologising to Burner was different; she'd been doing it for years like it was like a hobby. She'd say sorry, he'd tell her that she was an idiot of some description, and things would be back to normal within a few minutes. But she had no idea what to say to these other people, even the two she'd known her whole life.

She stared at the triangular sage-coloured face, scared to tap it. The deadline for calling Jockey was two days away, as Burner kept reminding her. It was difficult to know which she feared more: apologising to Jockey or not making the call and having to face her punishment. It had sounded funny at the time, having to be Burner's servant for the week. They'd been a few pints in, and he and Jono had spent ages planning the kinds of things Nova would have to do if she failed to make the phone call: polish his shoes, iron his shirts, even brush his teeth for him, referring to him as 'Lord Burner' at all times. Now the deadline was so close, it was becoming distinctly less funny every time they mentioned it.

***

He'd never suffered one before, but Casey Brown was pretty sure that he was in the early stages of a panic attack. Did it even work like that, he wondered. Could you actually know something like that, or were panic attacks like epileptic fits, appearing without warning, rendering the victim helpless? All he knew for sure was that he'd made a mistake. A huge mistake.

Frances and Brandon, dressed in scrubs, were laying out shiny instruments, one after the other, onto a table laid with a pale blue cloth. A Medibot stood to attention beside the table, waiting for commands with the patience of a chopping block, the quiet whir of its circuits the only indication that it was switched on.

Casey eyed it with a feeling of unease as he remembered the way it — or one just like it — had put Ivan out of his misery after the accident in the Workshop. Sure, it was only following orders, but it'd followed them without the slightest hesitation and with astonishing accuracy. Perhaps its unquestioning, unfaltering mechanical nature was both a blessing and a curse. It had never sworn the Hippocratic Oath, requiring it to uphold ethical standards of the highest degree — of that, Casey was certain.

And here he was, in the small operating room at the back of Control House, waiting to become *one of them*. Not a Medibot per se, but something not quite human either. Part human, part machine — the kind of being that might one day be viewed as some kind of 'missing link', the halfway house that spanned the chasm to man's transhuman destiny. What had he been thinking when he'd agreed to Father's plan? What would Mary-Ann have said about all this? She'd have told him to get the hell out of there, that's what.

A bead of sweat trickled down his neck, tickling him slightly. Was that supposed to be God's idea of a joke, a bit of light-hearted, operating-room entertainment to keep the patient in high spirits? Possibly. God had joshed worse in his time. Only yesterday Casey had thought he would be ready for the operation. He was a man who'd been to hell and back, who was ready for any challenge you could throw at him. But lying there, watching Frances examine her scalpels and forceps, he realised that he was anything but ready.

As he felt more beads of sweat trickle and tickle their way down his face, he turned his head to look at Elmer lying on the gurney next to him. With the same oafish, spaced-out look he always had, he gave Casey a big smile.

"I'm going to be famous, a star of the screen. Who'da thought it? Lil' old Elmer. More drugs, please, matron, the good shit. Only the best for old Elmer these days."

Brandon turned to face them. He looked at Elmer, then at Casey, and made a circular motion with his finger around his temple.

"No more drugs for you, old loony tunes. You won't need them in a few minutes anyway. You're going cold turkey. For good. What about you, Case? How you getting on?"

"All good, thanks, bud," Casey snapped back.

He wondered if he'd ever told a lie so large. It was alright for Elmer, he didn't have a say in what was going on. Even if he did, Casey doubted he had the wherewithal to say anything of consequence. Christ knows what Frances had been pumping into his veins these last few days, the stupid homeless bastard.

Thoughts raced through Casey's mind. He found a thimbleful of solace in the fact that the operation hadn't yet happened. It wasn't too late to put a stop to this nonsense. Grabbing hold of a bar on the side of the gurney, he raised his head to scan the room. He wiggled his toes at the end of the bed, their nakedness an awkward reminder that he was hardly dressed for an escape attempt.

What did escape even look like? He pictured himself performing a kung fu leap off the trolley and disabling Brandon and Frances with two deft moves. Nothing painful, he'd do Vulcan nerve pinches like Spock used to do in the old *Star Trek* films. He'd apologise as he pinched their necks, catch them as they fell and lay them to sleep on the floor while the Medibot looked on, blissful in its ignorance.

Then he'd dress, sneak out of the sickbay, tiptoe down the corridor to the backroom where they counted the money, grab a few bundles from the safe, leap through the back window and get away in one of the kayaks. He knew the Delta better than anyone by now. He could be in Mexico by the weekend, could start afresh. And he'd never breathe a word about the Order to anyone, they could count on that.

His daydream was interrupted by the Medibot as it beeped and hummed into life. It extended two additional arms, onto which Brandon placed the tray of instruments, and then trundled alongside Casey's bed, its wheels ticking as they passed over the wooden boards. Casey wiped his brow with his forearm. He wasn't breathing right and his entire body was soaked in sweat, making the johnny gown stick to it.

"Tell Father there's been a mistake. I can't do this. *Anything* but this. I've got other ideas. Better ones. Less risky ones. He'll love them, I know he will."

He was on his elbows, firing out desperate snippets of speech, first at Brandon, then at Frances, a condemned man clutching at straws. Using one of its main arms, the Medibot pushed him back down, pinning him to the mattress with the strength of a mechanical ox.

"It's alright, Case. Everything's going to be OK. Father warned us that you might have a last-minute attack of the nerves, it's perfectly natural. Remember why you're doing this, the bigger picture: man and machine joined for salvation. You were the best match — that kinda makes you the chosen one who gets to play a special part. It'll all be over before you know it. There's a good boy."

Casey watched in horror as Frances held the syringe before her, flicked it a couple of times and gently squeezed the plunger to check that it still worked. As she thrust it into his forearm, Casey screamed.

"No, no, no. Take it out. Get Father. I've changed my mind. I *won't* do it. Mother, please, I beg you, don't do this. Look at the state of him, for Christ's sake. I don't care if he's a match, he's an old drunk. He's damaged goods, broken beyond repair. We don't go together. Get off me, you bitch."

He stammered on for fifteen seconds or so, oscillating between rational request and profane petition. As he looked into Frances' eyes, he could tell that under her mask she was smiling a kind smile. She never meant to hurt him. She was his mother, his and Brandon's, mother to everyone at the Compound. And mother knew best. Wasn't that the saying? His head lolled to one side. As his eyelids fought to stay open he saw Elmer again, gawping at him with the same moronic look, a daisy chain of dribble hanging off his chin. *My chin*, Casey thought as he lost the battle of the eyelids.

Chapter Twenty-Nine

Nova stared at the flashing cursor. Her essay was due the next day, but the page remained blank, save for the title, which she'd typed out half an hour earlier: *A Comparison of Techniques for Mitigating Cognitive Bias*. She felt as enthused about the prospect of writing it as she did about the other thing looming over her — the long list of people she needed to apologise to as part of the 'Soul' section of her Super Nova project.

She'd gone down to the caves by the lake to seek inspiration, but had found temptation instead. She was sitting on a large rock by the craggy stone wall, and her Booners were sat on the next rock along. She kept glimpsing at them. *I should have never brought you with me*, she muttered under her breath. One last look-see, perhaps. She'd said that the last five times, but this time she meant it, *for real*. Five more minutes, and then she'd crank the essay out in one go. Playing Grandmaster Petanja's puzzle would be her reward. A quick play, then the essay, then the puzzle. Her right hand shook her left. It was a deal, Nova style.

She slipped the headset on and found herself back in the games room aboard the SS Jupiter. Planetary Spaceships had been designed by Spiralwerks to follow the theme associated with the name of the planet, and the SS Jupiter was her favourite. In Roman mythology, Jupiter, or Jove, was the god of sky and thunder, so the spaceship's sumptuous games room, which had been furnished with ivory thrones, velvet ottomans and open fires, played a thunderstorm sound effects track non-stop, while the ceiling displayed real-time high-res footage of the actual planet Jupiter.

Spaceships could transport up to five thousand players at one time. Most people boarded one, logged out of Solarversia and didn't log in again until they'd arrived at their destination planet a number of days later, depending on its distance from

Earth. Games rooms had been included for those, like Nova, who wanted to keep playing the whole time.

The circular room was surrounded by a single spiral bookshelf that started at ground level and corkscrewed its way up the wall until it hit the ceiling. A few minutes ago Nova had superimposed the conga line onto the spiral bookshelf. The little people swerved in and out of the ornaments that lined the shelves, waltzing past the works of Dickens, Vonnegut and Bronte. It was a cool feature that some of the exhibitions had, allowing players to superimpose their contents wherever they wanted, including surfaces in the real world.

Her datafeed informed her that at that very moment, 156 people were superimposing the line onto a surface somewhere in either the real or the virtual world. She volleyed into the headcam of a girl in Chile who watched the line as it progressed along the twisted branch of an apple tree in her backyard, then to a camera in the lounge of a flat in New York where a couple of exhibitionists had superimposed the line around the leopard skin rug they were making love on.

She loved that the line was still going eight months after the start of the game. When she'd spun a Tweel of Fate the other day, Banjax had informed her that the maximum number of people in the line at any one time had been 490,338. He did that sometimes, when you spun his tweel — gave you a random factoid. It was better than having him steal your items or teleport you somewhere you hadn't asked to go.

Before she could decide which cam to check out next, a crackling voice boomed over the spaceship's loudspeakers.

"This is your captain speaking. Please note that we will soon be entering Jupiter's atmosphere and will need to prepare for descent. In fifteen minutes time you will be asked to return to your seats, over."

Glancing at the time, she saw that her five minutes were already up. Which was ridiculous. She twitched her nose while she weighed up her options. The captain *had* mentioned fifteen minutes until the descent. It made sense to start the essay *then*, instead. In a way, it was like Jove himself had made the suggestion. Fifteen more minutes, and then she'd whip the essay into submission.

She left the bookcase to join a small crowd watching a middle-aged Norwegian man standing in front of two large floating images. The left one displayed a section of the Player's Grid, with his own profile square situated in the middle. The right image was a picture of somebody's face. He was playing the Grid Memory Game, and had achieved a score she could only dream of getting. The game was simple — you needed to recall details of the people located in the vicinity of your own square.

The difficulty level determined the level of detail you needed to recall. In easy mode you were shown a face and needed to point to the person's square within the grid. In intermediate mode, the one she usually played, you needed to point to their location but also get their name right. Nova was a 49er in that mode, which meant she had completed a 7 by 7 grid. Burner and Jono played the game on hard mode, where you needed to know the person's nationality as well as their name and location. Burner was a 144er, while Jono, who was on the university team, was a 576er, having once completed a 24 by 24 grid.

The next picture, of a gaunt woman with rollers in her hair, appeared floating on the guy's right. He took one look at her, twirled his finger in the air a couple of times, and pointed to a square on the left screen. A jingle sounded and three points were added to his already gigantic score.

"Susana Pasquel," he enunciated, to the delight of the crowd. Another three points. "Peru." Four more points: three, plus a bonus for getting all of her details correct in under ten seconds, bringing his score close to 18,000. He was halfway through a huge 63 by 63 grid. If he completed it, he would regain his rank as one of the top hundred players in the world. Nova shook her head and snorted with glee as she watched his display of brilliance.

Behind her, two women were seated on thrones opposite one another, either side of a partition. They played another grid-based game, known as Happy Families. The rules were similar to the game Battleships. At the start of the game each woman had chosen ten groups of ten squares — their families. The aim of the game was to locate the opponent's families.

They played using a weird variant of the rules that involved miniature versions of their planes flying reconnaissance missions to the other side of the board. Whenever a 'family member' was discovered, their profile square would light up and the avatar inside it would say their catchphrase. Nova never played it herself, but loved logging in to find that strangers had included her own profile square in their games, like she was shaping events remotely while she slept — even if she did cringe at the thought of her avatar saying her lame catchphrase out loud.

A far rowdier group sat in the corner by the open fire, hunched over a section of grid that had been turned into a board game called Lavadiles and Telescopes. It was played like Snakes and Ladders except that the winning square was in the middle, rather than one of the top corners. Players worked their way inward, having started on the outer ring. Kids usually played it, but this lot were about Nova's age and had turned it into a drinking game.

Next up was a Romanian girl. She blew on the dice in her hands before casually chucking them into the fire. The flames roared into life, then morphed into a fire demon who held aloft the 'six' and the 'two' on the dice she had rolled. The girl howled in frustration as her mini avatar moved along the board, landed on a lavadile mouth, and slid down its slimy scales, four rings away from the centre.

Her companions chanted, "Drink! Drink! Drink!" while they each volleyed an eye to a cam in her real room in order to watch her drink the four fingers of beer she'd just forfeited. The girl was sprawled across a tatty mattress on the floor, clothes and dirty plates strewn everywhere. From her jerky movements it looked like she had already drunk her fair share of forfeits. The group cheered as she downed it in one, then booed as the captain gave the five-minute call.

Nova hurried onto the thunderbolt-shaped lift in the centre of the room to return to her seat. While wondering what puzzle Petanja had in store for her, she realised something important. *She felt on form.* And the thing about form, she reminded herself, was that it came and went. It would be stupid to waste it, reckless even. Petanja's puzzle would be tough. He'd scalped a life from Burner a few weeks ago, and there was no way she was going to be his next victim. That settled it. She'd complete the puzzle now and then write the essay when she was buzzing from having solved it. Another quick handshake. It was a deal.

***

Nova whooped as she scudded around the penultimate gate with plenty of time to spare. In order to reach Grandmaster Petanja, she'd had to cross Jupiter's gaseous surface by boat. As the planets got further away from the Sun, the Grandmasters got more difficult, both in terms of the puzzles they set, and in terms of the journeys you had to make to visit them.

This course, situated alongside the circumference of Jupiter's Great Red Spot, a massive anticyclonic storm that had been raging for hundreds of years, had to be completed in under five minutes. The landing video aboard the SS Jupiter had shown, in terrifying detail, what happened to players unfortunate enough to steer their boats even one millimetre across the line that divided the red spot and the rest of the course.

As if she needed a further memo on the subject, some disastrous navigation by the guy in front rammed the message home. He'd been running out of time and taking increasingly large risks with the slalom gates, and had badly misjudged the final one. In trying to correct his mistake, he'd only served to exacerbate it, flipping his boat onto its side and performing a series of somersaults. That fiasco cost him sixty health points. Now came his landing.

Nova watched with clenched teeth as he tried to accelerate away from the line. Even at maximum throttle, his Sunseeker was no competition for the Spot, which was entangled at the quantum level to the enormous black hole situated at the centre of the Milky Way. He'd crossed the Spot's event horizon and was now subject to its enormous gravitational pull. A small video feed appeared in the top corner of her display. It showed the rear end of his boat elongate as it got sucked into the swirling vortex. The guy soon joined it as he and his boat became a spindly soup of pixels, inexorably drawn towards the hole where he would soon be crushed to death.

She slowed right down to tackle the last gate, shaken by what she had just witnessed. Although she still had two lives left, they were only two-thirds of the way through the Year-Long Game, and according to the people at Spiralwerks, the tricky bits were yet to come. Jono had crashed out for good the week before when a stray Asteroid Shower hit Morocco.

His valiant escape through the flaming town of Marrakesh had made for nail-biting viewing and gone viral, at least within Solar Soc, the university's Solarversia Society . He'd escaped the worst-hit parts of town and been legging it to the closest Greasy Wrench when a Type Four asteroid had hurtled down the street toward him.

Nova, who had been watching a real-time video feed of his escape from the Hu Stu bar, recited the thirteen-move combination out loud as she'd willed him on. In the event, Jono stumbled on the tenth move, and the asteroid slammed straight into him, leaving two smoking stumps of leg in its wake. What a way to go. At least his Death Party had been fun.

Pushing thoughts of death to the back of her mind, Nova concentrated on the home straight. The finishing line, which she crossed with twenty-five seconds to spare, was strung across the entrance to a dark cave. The change in lighting was accompanied by a change in acoustics: the hum of Bruno's engine amplified as it echoed off the cave walls. She pulled up to the Dockington's jetty, waited for a peg to droop down and attach itself to her craft, and then followed a sign that instructed visitors to climb a rickety wooden ladder propped against the steep cave wall. It led to a mezzanine level where Petanja sat cross-legged in his circle. His green robes fluttered in the wind as it streamed through the cave entrance, powered by the mighty Red Spot in the distance. She sat down and awaited the next o'clock.

" ... Any evidence of cheating will be reviewed by a panel of judges, and is punishable by the deduction of a life and possible suspension from The Game itself. There are no exceptions to this rule for this puzzle. There are 6,390 players for the 4:00 p.m. puzzle today, and 3,195 safe spots. Please note that this puzzle is culturally specific and will relate to an aspect of your own national culture. Good luck, and remember these two things. First, use not a dirty mirror, if your warts you wish to see. Second, There Can Be Only One!"

As Petanja and his circle faded into nothingness, Nova found herself in a large stock cupboard lined with rows of shelving. She'd played plenty of Puzzle sims that had been restricted in one way or another, but as every Solo knew, tackling them in the Simulator Booth was very different to tackling one for real, when one of your precious lives was at stake.

A note on the wall above a wastepaper basket said "Find the defective product and put it in the bin." She glanced up and down the room. There were dozens of rows of shelving and five shelves in each row. Each shelf held hundreds upon hundreds of identical porcelain figures. In endless repetition, she saw the same little man, six inches tall, playing his flute, the kind of figurine you found on tacky seafront market stalls. "Defective, defective, defective." Nova repeated the word, as she tried to get to grips with the task at hand.

It took her far too long to pick a figure up in order to examine it, mistakenly believing that the rules were similar to the ones that governed the Lavadile puzzle, where touching a wrong scale had meant the immediate loss of a life. Realising her mistake, she grabbed the nearest two and scrutinized them from head to toe. Each figure was of a young man with brown hair, playing a silver flute. He wore a blue suit, and was glued to a circular base, with one leg in front of the other like he was walking. The problem was that the two figurines were identical, down to the smidgen of hardened glue that poked out from the side of the heel of the shoe. Did the glue mean something, or was it an attempt to faithfully replicate such a tasteless piece of tat?

Growing increasingly frustrated with her total lack of progress, she growled as she noticed the number of safe spots tick down. It was preposterous; people had to be cheating to solve these puzzles so quickly. Her stomach rolled as she remembered Burner's failure to solve Petanja's puzzle, something to do with different coloured bears in a tearoom. She berated herself for even thinking about it while the safe spots counted down in her own puzzle. As the number ticked below 3,000 she held her hands up and wiggled her fingers, as if attempting to tease inspiration out of thin air. And then the gong sounded. What had changed?

She ran up and down the aisle, desperate to find out. The number ticked below 2,500. The walls were the same, the ceiling and floor were the same, the notice and wastepaper bin were the same. *The base, you stupid girl.* She grabbed the nearest figure and upended him. There it was, a new stamp. But what the hell did it mean?

"Made with CRS." Things were made *somewhere*. Usually China. Or they were made *with love*. But she'd never heard of something being made with 'CRS', and couldn't think how the letters related to the United Kingdom. The *Council of Royal Surgeons*, maybe? She didn't know whether such a thing existed, or how it could possibly relate to the little flute player even if it did, but it was the only thing she could think of.

Her panic intensified. She couldn't stop looking at the dwindling number of safe spots. Perhaps 'CRS' was one of those things that everyone in the entire world knew about except for her. Like the time people had been discussing the 'Arab Spring' at school and she'd asked whether it was similar to an 'Indian Summer' and they'd laughed in her face until she cried.

Her heart raced. It was time for a pep talk. She was a puzzle master, and there was no way Petanja — stupid name for a start — was going to defeat her. Sometimes it was funny the way the brain worked. She whistled before she was aware of any conscious desire to do so. It was as if her brain knew how urgent the situation was and acted first, to save time, then followed up with its reasoning afterwards.

The instant the sound left her lips, the entire room erupted with the mellow piping of a thousand flutes, echoing her whistle. 'Made with CRS' was 'Made with Cockney rhyming slang.' The man was playing a flute, and wearing a suit. The only thing missing was a whistle: *Whistle and Flute — Suit.* That was the culturally specific knowledge she needed — and she knew it. Yes!

But how did it help? The little guys repeated the tune you whistled. So what? The number ticked below 1,000 and she could already feel her euphoria ebbing away. *Find the defective product.* It had to be a figure whose flute was broken. But in a room of thousands how could she locate him? She whistled again while looking round: 750 and counting.

Another whistle, another frantic search. Where was the gong when she wanted one? Another whistle, this one longer as she walked up and down the aisle. *That was it.* Three things happened simultaneously every time she whistled, but the other two had been imperceptible at first.

She took a deep breath and let out the longest whistle she could manage. 500 spaces. The men started playing their flutes that very instant, but it took a couple of seconds for the lights in the room to dim and the little blue lights to appear at the end of their flutes. She wasn't going to locate the defective guy by sound, but by sight. When the number ticked below 250 she wanted to scream rather than whistle.

What would Sushi advise? *Less haste more speed.* Nova halted her frenzied search at once. Method, not madness. Deep breath, whistle, side step along the row, examine each shelf in turn. Ignore the number of safe spots, even if they did just tick below 100. Next row, rinse and repeat. Rinse and repeat. Gotcha! At last she found him, tucked away at the back of a shelf in the middle of the room. While the blue lights on the flutes around him flared into life, his own instrument remained unchanged.

She snatched the little fella clean off the shelf and darted round to the wastepaper bin as fast as she could. 50 and counting. She slam-dunked him hard into the bin, wanting to break his sorry ass. As the melodious jingle of victory sounded, she let out a victory cheer. She had just completed Petanja's puzzle with fewer than twenty spots left.

Chapter Thirty

Nova removed her Booners and placed them on the rock next to her. Since her first visit to the caves on the night of the *Star Wars* party she'd been back regularly. It was beautiful and peaceful there; these weren't qualities she associated with the hustle and bustle of halls or lecture theatres. Sometimes she sat and talked to Sushi, sometimes she played. Sometimes she just sat there, doing nothing at all, just *being*. And sometimes she disappeared into an augmented wonderland.

When she turned on the Forest of Fun augmentation, the real-world leaves on the trees overhanging the caves became imbued with jokes, just like they did in Solarversia. She'd wait for one to fall from its branch and make a stab at its punchline, awarding herself points for accuracy.

Her favourite augmentation was a simple one: player watching. She liked to mark out the gravelly path that ran in front of the caves as the augmented zone, and would sit back and watch as players from around the Solar System travelled up and down it, some on joyrides, others running for their lives, fleeing from one of the increasingly common monsters set out to kill them.

These augmentations made the real world more magical, more like the way it had seemed when she was little. That morning's White Dwarf had mentioned a crowdfunding campaign where the residents of a small town wanted to repave the high street with hexagonal tiles that worked like the ones in The Game. She hoped it would be successful. She loved it when the virtual world spilled over into the real.

She also loved the way VR was able to transport her to places in an instant. First she'd been in a virtual games room, then whizzing around Jupiter's Red Spot, then dashing around a stockroom cupboard, and now, a few minutes later, she was back in the real world by the lake on campus. *The real world*. The thought was an unwelcome reminder of the two chores that awaited her attention.

She stared at the cursor still blinking by the title of her essay and groaned. Then she scrolled through her contacts until she was looking at Jockey's number on her phone. Apparently their last call had been over ten months ago, something to do with the arrangements for her Krazy Karting heat. *Come on, Nova, one or the other. Apologies or cognitive bias.* She took a deep breath and pressed the number. Today was the deadline she had set herself for the task of apologising to him, its outcome attached to that stupid penalty. Never again would she agree to the punishments with Burner when she was drunk.

It seemed to ring forever without being answered. A horrible thought presented itself. What if Jockey had changed his number? Perhaps he'd lost his phone? Jesus, it might be something as innocent as him having left it at home. As she was about to admonish herself for leaving it too late, the line clicked through.

"Miss Negrahnu. To what do I owe the pleasure?"

"Jockey, hi," she said, in a quiet voice, suddenly aware that despite many months of opportunity, she still hadn't prepared anything meaningful to say.

"Has something bad happened?" he asked, sounding worried.

"No. I'm fine. Nothing bad. All good with me. Actually, something bad *did* happen, but it was awhile ago. Something bad that I said. To you. And I'm phoning to apologise."

He was silent for a second. "I have to admit that I wasn't expecting you to call like this."

"If it's a bad time—"

"Not at all, now's great, let's do it. First, let's recap the details of our conversation. You know, so we remember who said what and exactly what's being apologised for. Correct me if I'm wrong — I often am — but I'm pretty sure that the last time we spoke, you called me a fat prick? And Fraggers a shithole? Or have I got that wrong?"

She could tell from his tone that he was enjoying himself. As difficult as it was to hear him repeat what she had said, it felt good to hear his voice again.

"No, you have that right. Like I said, that's why I'm calling. To apologise. Really, really, *really* apologise. Not because anyone told me to or because it's the thing you're supposed to do. I really am sorry. I was way out of line. A total bitch."

"And it's only taken you half a year to realise. Not bad."

She giggled as tears welled in her eyes.

"It's good to see that you're learning *something* at uni anyway. Perhaps you could say it one more time? It had a rhythm to it."

"I, Nova Negrahnu, hereby apologise unreservedly to Mr Dettori for calling him a fat prick and his awesome gaming cafe a shithole. I was way out of line."

"That was glorious, thank you. I was sorry to hear about the Karting final, by the way. You deserved to finish the race, if not win it."

"Yeah. That totally sucked. I reckon I would have won if I'd raced at Fragging Hell. You know, if I hadn't been banned."

"What's prompted the call then? It sounds like you've stopped being an entitled brat, is that right?" She wiped away the tears with the sleeve of her jacket and broke into a smile as Jockey continued. "Because I operate a strict no-brats policy these days. And I'd be happy to remove your ban if you've changed your ways."

"I think so. I hope so. I'm trying anyway."

"Are you back in the 'Stone over Christmas or what?"

The 'Stone. It felt good to hear someone refer to Maidstone like that again. "Definitely. I haven't escaped for good, you know. Parents wouldn't let me, for a start."

"Why don't you come down for New Year's Eve? Everyone misses you. Including me."

"I'd love to. I wouldn't miss it for the world."

Nova ended up having the longest conversation she'd ever had with him. She told him all about her visits to Sushi and her Super Nova project. They spoke about Project Drone, about how Jockey had been right about her getting into trouble, and about how she didn't regret it, although she did concede that she'd do things differently if given a second chance.

And he told her the latest gossip from the cafe: which regulars were still in The Game, the failed attempts to beat her darts score, and who was shagging who. She was already looking forward to New Year's Eve, and catching up with the old crew.

As she went to put her phone away, ecstatic at the prospect of not being Burner's servant for the week, she froze. Walking along the gravelly path was Charlie, hand in hand with Holly. She might not have been wearing her golden bikini, but she still managed to look like a total slapper. Nova made a weird guttural sound, a cocktail of burp and hiccup. She couldn't let them see her like this, tear-stained and alone like a right Billy-no-mates. It was bad enough that she had seen them. There was nowhere to hide. The terrace in front of the cave was barren, save for a few rocks, and she was already sitting on top of the largest one.

She grabbed the front of the rock and tried to slump behind it by lowering her bum down the other side. She half-succeeded. Which meant that she half-failed.

Her bum reached the ground, but her back was now wedged between the rock and the cave wall behind her. She was stuck fast. Over the top of the rock poked her feet, her shoulders and her head.

At that moment Holly looked over and caught her eye. She stared for a second as if trying to work out what she was seeing, and then began to pull at Charlie's arm and shriek with laughter. Every spare drop of blood surged to Nova's cheeks. She gave an uncomfortable little wave and wished for a quick and painless death.

***

The sixth floor of Spiralwerks HQ had kicked off, big time. To an outside observer it might have looked like a battle to generate the biggest racket, humans versus machines. The machines had resorted to beeps, bleeps and bells, the humans to yells and fists thumped on desks. Whatever you called it, the result was an unholy, migraine-inducing cacophony.

Loudest of the humans was Carl Stedman, Spiralwerks' CTO, who was repeatedly slamming his palm onto his desk, turning the air around him a vulgar shade of blue. The technical team called, "Yes, Carl," like obedient sous chefs, and hollered responses to his questions when they could, but they all lingered a way back from his desk, keeping, what looked to Arty, like a fearful distance.

Arty worried about Carl. The late nights had taken a toll on all of them, but Carl had been affected more than most. He spent such long hours at the office that he frequently didn't go home at night and was still at his desk come the morning. Whenever something technical went wrong, he seemed to take it personally, beating himself up for weeks after the incident. Or, more recently, taking it out on one of his team. At first, Arty thought it was good, having someone so dedicated at the company. But just lately, he'd worried that Carl was working *too* hard. The bags under his eyes were so puffed he looked like he needed a month's worth of sleep rather than the usual week's.

"What's up, Carl?" he asked.

"Server 451 is under attack. They've exploited a weakness we only discovered two days ago and were in the middle of patching. It's left us wide open. They've already tunnelled through two firewalls. If they get through the third, they hit pay dirt."

"Who's *they*? Do we know?"

Carl shook his head. "We don't know much. Looks like a professional job. Elite hackers. That probably narrows it down to about ten thousand people across the planet."

"What happens if they get through the third firewall? What damage can they do?"

"Theoretically they've already gained access to certain processes. Read-only access, but still, not good. Graham, kick off those cron jobs we spoke about. Maria, get the inbound payloads over to security and get them scanned ASAP. God knows what's in them."

"What's the worst-case scenario?"

"If they *do* get through, we'd need five minutes to isolate their bots. Failing that we'd have to reboot the server, which would log players out. Only the people on *that* server, but it would take a few hours to bring back up."

"How many people would get logged out?"

"It's the server that compiles the code for the planets and the spaceships. Probably in the low millions. On the plus side, it's unlikely that anyone external has visibility of what's going on. So far, anyway."

It was the kind of situation that Arty deplored, a technical disturbance that he had no control over. The worst part was not understanding what was going on. It was like being back in France on the school exchange when his host family had taken him out for the day. An almighty kerfuffle had ensued in one of the back streets on the way home, some strange men shouting at the father of the family. He'd stood there, watching, not understanding what was being said or why, not knowing how serious the situation was or whether he was in any personal danger. He'd never felt so scared and alone in his life.

At least he didn't feel scared now. Worried and confused, maybe, but not scared. He hated all the jargon involved in IT, the acronyms and abbreviations. They were all so misleading. He'd always thought pretty highly of firewalls, for instance. They sounded so cool: baddies send bots to attack you, and you react by erecting a wall of fire, blowing the fuckers sky high. *Take that, 'bots.* Totally badass. The reality couldn't have been further from the truth. A load of gibberish displayed in an interface that Microsoft would have been ashamed of. Firewalls, schmirewalls.

Suddenly the monitors on Carl's desk went wild, and he spasmed into rage. The veins on the side of his head looked ready to explode. "Graham, where are we with those cron jobs? They haven't? Why the hell not? Jesus, what is it now? Maria, any news? Work with me people, not against me. Graham, update please? Well, sync them to the main screen so that we can all monitor them. Do I have to do all the thinking around here?"

Carl's team translated his requests into computer code as fast as possible, then yelled back their answers, competing to be heard over one another. A list of planetary spaceships appeared in a table on the main screens at the front of the room. Data in the 'Status' column updated, one row at a time, from 'Active' to 'Frozen'. Even Arty knew what that meant: spaceships at a complete standstill in deep space.

"Players will know something's up now. Their distance counters will have stopped updating. I wouldn't be surprised if ... there you go, people have already started to tweet about it."

"Issue the press release, and tell the teams to remain on standby," Hannah said to one of her guys. Her team had assembled nearby and were in constant liaison with country managers from around the world. She and Arty turned to Carl, who was rocking his head from side to side like he was weighing up their options. "As soon as we repair the firewalls the spaceships will continue on their way. The hackers can't interfere with the players themselves, not their lives or their items. All of that information is stored on a different server. Graham, what have you found? Bring it up on screen."

An image of a bookshelf in the games room aboard one of the SS Plutos appeared. Carl zoomed in until the spines of the books were clearly visible. Everyone on the floor went quiet and stopped what they were doing. Bookshelves were programmed to contain a mix of titles that spanned the classics right the way through to recent releases. Many of them were self-published titles, written by players themselves, included because they'd won some quest or other. But this bookshelf no longer contained a literary pick 'n' mix. Instead, Arty saw only one title on the shelf, repeated in endless identical editions. In a gold Gothic font embossed on a black leather cover, he read the words over and over: *Sacred Singularity* The Holy Order.

A dangerous, crazy enemy he'd never laid eyes on was attacking them for reasons he didn't understand. *Now* he felt scared. This scared the crap out of him.

Chapter Thirty-One

Nova walked down the gangway with Burner to join a large group of people being hurried onto a scruffy looking fishing boat by a couple of arkwinis wearing waders and galoshes.

"All aboard the *Amritsar*," yelled the captain. "We depart in less than two minutes. Take a life jacket from the rack, then take a seat and buckle up. There's a storm on the way, and we don't want anyone falling overboard. Like last Thursday. The incident delayed the tour schedule for the rest of the day. Master Arkwal was *not* happy."

"When do you reckon Master Arkwal *is* happy?" Burner asked. "Maybe when he's noshing off the Emperor?"

"Shush," Nova said with a smile. "I don't want you getting me in trouble again."

They were here to learn about Banjax, whose story they'd accessed via the constellation that had appeared in the ceiling of their Corona Cubes that morning. Tracing its stars had caused one of the cube faces to dissolve, revealing a jetty that led to the fishing boat. The marble floor of Castalia's Magisterial Chamber had been replaced by a swirling ocean, being whipped into a frenzy by a fierce wind.

The old boat creaked as the waves rocked it to and fro, sounding to Nova like it might break apart at any moment. The gangplank was raised and the anchor weighed. It took nine arkwinis to steer the boat, dwarfed as they were by the ship's wheel. Three clung to the wheel's right side, three to its left, and three stood behind it, balancing on each other's shoulders so that the captain, the topmost arkwini, could see the route ahead.

"Nice to see that it's coming along," Burner said, nodding his head as he admired the artwork on the chamber walls.

"Yeah, it looks incredible. Except that stupid bit in the March portrait," she added, nodding to the scene that depicted the drama of Bouncy Baltimore. Spee-Akka Dey Bollarkoo had completed seven monthly portraits — each painted in a different style — and the room was starting to take shape. The eastern wall housed the March, April and May portraits, the western wall June through August. The southern wall behind them was furnished with the September portrait, awaiting the inclusion of October and November. The northern wall had contained a piece of art right from the start — the Player's Grid — which meant that the final three portraits, the ones that would illustrate the climax to the year, were to adorn the ceiling instead.

"What are you doing, you weirdo?" Nova asked as Burner looked at the ceiling through a shape made by his conjoined hands.

"I'm wondering what the ceiling will look like when my beautiful face is up there, following my glorious victory. I doubt most women would be able to take a tour like this once it's finished. They'd look up, see me, and get all distracted. Hey, there's an idea. Do you reckon I should speak to old Flower Face and tell her to include my grid number somewhere? That way, the girls who are interested could dial the Burner hotline. I'd select the fittest ones to join my harem. I'd be like Kiki La Roux. Except way less gay."

"You do talk some utter bollocks sometimes, did you know that? The only thing you've got in common with Kiki is that you're a massive Space Dick."

"What we have in common is that we both *have* massive Space Dicks."

Nova looked at the grid again. The death counter revealed that a staggering two hundred and thirty-one million lives had been lost in total, and that fifty-five million players had gone out. Profile squares like hers that had green borders to indicate two lives left were rare; those coloured violet, rarer still. More than half of the grid had turned dark already, and from everything they'd heard in the great Solarversia rumour mill, the weeks leading up to New Year's Eve were supposed to be utter carnage and would leave only one million people in play.

The *Amritsar* approached the northwest corner of the room, where Banjax usually resided. The fish tank was gone. In its place was a small island that had been excavated, leaving nothing but a shallow pit and a bunch of discarded spades. The arkwinis battled with the ship's wheel to steer the boat alongside the island's tiny shore.

"We've arrived at our destination, ladies and gentlemen," the captain called through cupped hands from his new location on the bow of the ship. "Please unbuckle your belts and make your way over to the starboard side."

Nova peered over the side of the boat into the pit. Its floor was covered with burning hot coals. All of a sudden the wind became more ferocious. The sails of the ship billowed above their heads, and water crashed against the port side, pouring into the boat. She clung to Burner's arm and watched as the coals burned hotter and brighter, emitting clouds of dark smoke that filled the pit. Burner pointed at a wisp of smoke as it started to take the form of a fisherman holding a sharp curved sword. He appeared in the air before them and began to speak.

"Once upon a time, in the oceans of Nakk-oo, there lived a twelve-armed sea creature. The dodectopi were difficult to catch, for they were slippery and shrewd, but they were highly prized, for their meat was tastier and more nutritious than any creature that dwelled on land. We, the Unglai, hunted them all year round, for even a calf could feed an entire village for a week. Whenever a dodectopus was caught, word on land would spread faster than a zapier can zap. Villagers would dig a fresh hangi pit in which to cook the beast, and then line the streets, drumming their plates with knives and forks to welcome the fishermen home. Those beasts we didn't eat were sold at market inland, and we became rich on the profits.

"One day, some fishermen caught a dodectopus and dragged it aboard. 'Please,' it said to the men, 'I know that I will feed many mouths, but there aren't many dodectopi left. If you keep hunting us like this, we'll die out. I ask that you return me to the ocean and change your ways.' But the men didn't listen, for how could a stupid beast know better than they? The captain of the ship drew his sabre and slit the monster's throat, for a dodectopus that has been bled out tastes freshest of all.

"After that day, dodectopi were harder to find and the fishermen of Nakk-oo went weeks and months without seeing one. The months turned into years and rumours of their extinction began to spread. One evening at a tavern, many moons since anyone had savoured a succulent tentacle, an old fisherman named Ishmael got up onto his stool and addressed the crowd. 'A true fisherman, as strong and brave as I, could catch a dodectopus any time he wanted. Tomorrow is the longest day of the year, and before the day is out, I will have caught one. I set sail at dawn. Who's with me?'

"Early the next morning, Ishmael and his crew set out. The seas were calm, and they sailed far out into the ocean. The crew sang as they sailed, but Ishmael kept his eyes trained on the water, and sure enough, despite the years of scarcity, and his short, drunken sleep, that day his luck was in. Before noon he caught sight of a huge dodectopus, and though it struggled fiercely for freedom, by evening time the thirteen men had pulled and heaved and had dragged it aboard. What a catch!

It was the largest, most magnificent specimen any of them had ever laid eyes on, large enough to feed three hungry villages for a month. Ishmael stood before it triumphantly.

"'What did I tell you? I was fated to catch it.'

"'You're right, Ishmael, it *was* fate that brought us together.'

"'It speaks,' cried the fishermen. 'Kill it,' they begged.

"'Just you dare,' the creature bellowed. With one whip-like tentacle he pulled Ishmael close. 'I'm Banjax, the last of the dodectopi. Your ignorance and greed have conspired to wipe out my kind. Now leave me be, or suffer your fate.' Ishmael, who had heard enough, drew his sabre, ready to cut the monster's throat. But Banjax raised another of his mighty tentacles and swiped the sword into the ocean.

"The frightened fishermen drew their knives and advanced on the creature, but they were no match for his might or grace. As quick and agile as the wind, he released Ishmael and swirled his twelve tentacles this way and that until each one was wrapped around the neck of one of the crew. They looked at each other in alarm, each secured in place by a slimy scarf as strong as steel.

"Then, before their struggles had really begun, Banjax placed the tips of his tentacles over the head of each man. Ishmael watched in horror as all twelve crew members were blindfolded and gagged at once, their entire heads enveloped down to their necks in the fleshy suckers. Banjax fixed Ishmael with a stare, then siphoning vigorously with all twelve arms, he sucked every head clean off.

"With his decapitated crew in a heap at his feet, Ishmael dropped to his knees and beseeched the beast not to kill him.

"'I won't kill you,' the monster declared. 'Or at least, not today. I need you to spread the word of what happened here today. Go back to your people and tell them their time as masters of the ocean has come to an end. Tell them I have ingested the living brains of twelve Unglai and I will utilise these brains more powerfully and efficiently than these dumb corpses ever could.'

"Ishmael gasped at the beast's disrespect.

"'Yes, dumb. You're all so stupid. Did you think you just *happened* to find me today? I called you out here, Ishmael, just as I now send you back again. But I will come for you in good time. I'm looking forward to it. First I'm going to hunt the rest of your kind for sport and I won't stop until they're all dead. We'll see how *you* like being the last of *your* species.'

"'You'll never do it!' Ishmael cried.

"'Don't underestimate my power or my wisdom. Not now I've increased my brainpower thirteenfold. I'll hide and I'll wait, and I'll attack when you're least expecting it. The ocean is mine, and some day, the Nakk-oo lands will be mine too. For I am the master of fate, Ishmael. Yours included.'

"He slipped off the boat and swam away, far into the ocean and deep beneath its surface. Ishmael sailed home alone, the blood of his men swishing around his ankles. From that day forward, Banjax has risen up from the oceans on the longest day of the year to seek revenge on the Unglai for their crimes. On Nakk-oo, that day became known as 'Fisherman's Day', a public holiday when it is illegal to go out onto the open sea or even to fish on the rock pools on the beach. Although, however they try to defend themselves from Banjax, bad things always befall the Unglai on Fisherman's Day. On Nakk-oo, the dodectopi have come to symbolise the 'Messenger of Fate', especially of bad events to come."

"*I* was once that boastful fisherman Ishmael. Still I await my death all these years later, ever fearful that the beast will keep his promise. I have been reduced to living next to my hangi pit, stoking it daily, keeping the coals burning hot and telling my tale to all who stop by."

The old fisherman looked nervously over his shoulder and clutched the curved sword tight in his grip. He glared at the tourists on the *Amritsar* with a forlorn expression and then became harder and harder to discern, until he was once again just a wisp of smoke rising from the hangi pit.

***

That was strange. His old laptop was on the coffee table next to a pile of magazines. Casey could have sworn that he'd sold it on Craigslist. How odd. Mary-Ann called to him from the open partition that led through to the kitchen. Dinner was almost ready — meatballs, his favourite. He didn't feel hungry, but according to the grandfather clock in the corner it was dinner time. *Where had that come from*, he wondered. That was so like her, buying something from the market and sneaking it back home.

The rain intensified its patter against the window. He knew that was a bad thing but couldn't remember why. Mary-Ann would know. She always did. But when he called to her, she was no longer there. The kitchen had disappeared into a hazy fog. And his laptop, and the magazines and the clock he couldn't remember buying, all of it, gone. The rain drummed against the window of his mind. Rain meant thunder, and thunder meant lightning. That's right, rain meant lightning, and lightning was bad.

The bolt struck his left arm, tearing him from the haze of his dream to the nightmare of his reality. It was like he'd been tied to the spire of an old church, rigged up as a makeshift lightning conductor. Bolts travelled from the tips of his fingers up to his elbow, an excruciating pain, fresh in its unbearable intensity each and every time. Where was Mother Frances with his meds? A pathetic whimper escaped his mouth. For a limb that was no longer there, it sure as hell hurt. The medical profession might have referred to the pain as 'phantom', but it was agonising all the same. He caught his breath and gritted his teeth. *Warriors win, Case, warriors win.*

When the storm of pain eventually subsided he could smell meatballs again, simmering in tomato sauce. That was right, Mary-Ann had been making his favourite dinner. She was in the kitchen, stirring the pan.

"Smells good, honey. How long will it be?" he called, but when she turned, it wasn't Mary-Ann. It was Frances, dressed in her scrubs. "Don't worry, dear, I know where Mary-Ann is, follow me." That was strange. Perhaps Mary-Ann had taught her the recipe. It was a relief to know that Frances would take him to her, anyway. But as she led him down the hallway of his house, his stomach lurched.

He rounded the corner into the garage, flinched, and tried to look away. Frances stopped him in his tracks and forced him to look. Mary-Ann was on the floor, meatball sauce spouting from her nasal cavity. He slumped to her side, grabbed her hand in his, saw the same desperate look in her eyes. Why was he always too late? "The window," she said, half-gargling, half-choking on a bloodstained meatball. It was raining again.

Another bolt of lightning, this one less severe, thrust him back to wakefulness, to the feeling of sick dread in his stomach. He felt awful, the worst he'd ever felt, would end it all in a second given the choice. He reminded himself that Mary-Ann was gone, unable to experience any more pain. But the terrible darkness was too much to bear. For the thousandth time, he tried to open his eyes. It was impossible to learn that this would have no effect: his head was swaddled in bandages, which rendered him blind and almost mute. He couldn't tell anymore whether his eyes were open or not. He was so alone, he had lost so much. The fear took hold in his stomach.

It was OK, there was someone there with him, someone he could hear pottering around in the room, opening and closing drawers and cupboards. It was Mother Frances; he recognized the shush of her moccasins on the floor as she walked. It was too painful to move his new lips so he tried grunting. He sounded like a pig.

That's what he'd been reduced to, he realised, a grunting pig. The type of animal that rooted around in its own shit. *A disabled grunter*, he thought, conscious of how pathetic that sounded. Crying hurt. Laughing would too, in the unlikely event that anything would ever be funny again. Laughing and crying. They were bad, like the rain. He tried another grunt, louder this time, *bring me the fucking meds*. The pottering stopped, and the slippers shushed along the floor towards him.

"Casey, was that you? It's Frances, can you hear me?"

He raised his right arm a little and grabbed the bar at the side of the gurney. Such a lot of energy for such a small movement. Two taps of his fingers against the bar: 'yes'.

"Are you alright? Are you in pain?"

He went to move his fingers, to make his taps, and then paused. She'd asked a pair of questions that had different answers. Did he tap once to answer the first, or twice to answer the second?

"Are you in pain?" she repeated.

Thank Christ for that. Two taps, as firm as he could manage without exacerbating the pain in his stomach. It was incredibly frustrating, this one-way, binary communication, the inability to ask questions himself. *A disabled grunter*. Yes, he wanted to say, yes he was in pain, he was drowning in it, you stupid tricksy-question-asking bitch.

"Another hour until your meds," she said in a cheerful voice, with a gentle squeeze of his arm. He grunted as loud as he could, tried to grab her, get her to stay. He heard her shush into the distance. Don't leave me here without my meds. Please don't leave me here all alone. Come back, Mary-Ann, come back.

I'll save you this time, I promise I will.

Chapter Thirty-Two

Nova arrived back at her room just after midnight. She ruffled Zhang's neck and kissed him goodnight before he hopped to the floor and plugged his tail into the wall. She'd been in Burner's room, getting him to download a new piece of code onto her headset, one he'd programmed himself. She took her shirt off, put her Booners on and, with an eye volleyed to the room, looked down to the yin yang tattoo at the top of her arm. She traced a finger round the design, slowly, purposefully. With her other eye, volleyed to her headset, she saw Soul Surfer launch. It had worked. A fine piece of craftsmanship from Burner.

"Hey, Nova. How are you?"

"I'm better than I've been in a long time."

"Oh, yeah?"

"Yeah. And it's all down to the little things. Stuff I didn't know mattered." She crossed her legs on the bench and looked out over Seattle as if seeing it with fresh eyes. "Like the nifty way I launched your app just now, for instance."

"What do you mean?"

"Now I can open the app by tracing my tattoo. Watch." Nova traced the same pattern on her avatar's tattoo: round the circumference of the yin yang circle and then down the curved line in the middle. She finished by pressing a finger against each of the two dots.

"Burner programmed it with his dork skills. It reminds me of being a kid, going on secret missions and writing messages in code. It's made my day, and it's such a silly little thing."

"What's that saying of Burner's? Silly little things have a habit of adding up to stupidly big things."

"I won't tell him you quoted him from beyond the grave. He'd get an even bigger head."

"Give him my regards. And no, that doesn't mean I want to go on a date with him. I'm having enough trouble with my aunt trying to set me up with this dead lawyer she's been visiting. Reckons we'd make a lovely couple. The problem is, this new 'death dates' feature within Soul Surfer was introduced after I died, so I never gave my preference on it. Mum thinks it's way too spooky. 'Copulating Corpses' is what they're calling it on the forums. What do you think I should do?"

Nova snorted. She loved shit like this. There were dozens of instances of Sushi: the one Nova spoke to, eight or so that spoke to friends and relatives, and various others who spoke to random people who Sushi hadn't even known while she was alive. It was like each Sushi lived her own life vicariously through the people that visited. Nova got to hear stories about the other Sushis, but as told by *her* Sushi, as if they were dramas in her life. It was properly mental and she loved it.

"I'm not sure that you were ever the type to go for a lawyer, but I'd need to see a photo first."

Less than a second after Nova had said the words, a photo appeared in Sushi's outstretched hand.

"No way, tell your aunt to get some frickin' taste. You wouldn't have gone near that guy, he looks like a total slimeball. Look at all that grease in his hair, for a start."

Sushi crumpled up the photo and tossed it into the bin that momentarily appeared at the side of the bench.

"Way more important than your dead douchebag is the fact that I'm still in Solarversia, and it's nearly the end of the year. I must fantazise about making the Final Million a million times a day."

"I can't wait to find out what Pluto's Portal of Promise is all about. If you actually make the Final Million, I swear I'll find myself a dead boyfriend and make a baby with him to celebrate."

"It's getting ridiculously dangerous, that's for sure. You remember the Travelling Circus of Nakk-oo? When the seventy-five millionth person went out, Ludi Bioski made the animals go crazy. They grouped together and escaped their cages. Most of the people visiting the circus at the time either got killed or seriously mauled. We're talking forty thousand players killed in this one incident alone. And remember Travinsky and the giant Moa from the quest I completed? They turned on Octavia, their keeper, impaled her on the musical tree. It was gross. Once they were free, the animals raided the circus safe and stole thousands of teleport tokens. I swear, nowhere's safe any more."

Like the real world, the Gameworld had been programmed to evolve. Each change featured one of the four Simulator categories, and slowly introduced the Science of Solarversia. The first change occurred when the Earth Force Field was switched off. The inclusion of Planetary Puzzles in the monthly Bucket Lists had required Solos to use their Puzzle skills.

The second change happened when the fifty millionth person went out in August. Daily spins of the Tweel of Fate stopped being free. Instead, players needed to correctly answer a question about the Gameworld, testing their Knowledge. If players answered incorrectly, they were fined teleport tokens, while correct answers were rewarded with additional items.

This latest change was connected to Combat. Up until now, Combat, outside of the Simulator Booth, had been restricted to certain quests that players tackled of their own volition. From this point forward they would be forced to fight for their lives whether they liked it or not. One last change was scheduled for when the ninety millionth person had gone out, and would affect Combinations. The sequence of moves would disappear from a player's headset, forcing them to execute it from memory.

"My God, you be careful out there, girlfriend. We've only got one life after this one, don't go wasting it."

Nova smiled. She loved the fact it was *their* life she was playing, not just hers.

"In other news, I finally called the Jockmeister. Do you know what I discovered? Apologising is a bit like revision. The thought of it is far worse than actually doing it. We had the best chat we've ever had. I don't know what I was so worried about. And you'll never guess what I did yesterday."

"Hooked up with Charlie?"

"God, I wish. He probably thinks I'm a right 'tard after seeing me stuck behind that rock. No, I sent Mrs Woodward a present — a nice copy of King Lear. With a little apology note and everything."

"You sent Mophead a present? My God, Nova, you really have changed. What did Burner say? I bet he thinks you've flipped out."

"He thinks I've turned weird. Reckons I'm going to join a convent and become a nun."

"How very Burner. He always had a thing for nuns."

"So anyway, I had something to ask you. I was thinking about this," Nova said, nodding her head.

"What, your fringe? You think it's time for a haircut?"

"Not that, you idiot, the view. You remember how I used to change the image on my bedroom wall every so often? Well, I stopped doing it when you died. It was my way of remembering you. Keeping the same image was a way of freezing time, because I didn't want it to move on. If anything I wanted it to go back to a time before the bombing. But I realised the other day that I might be ready to move on."

Sushi pulled her knees into her chest and looked at her friend while she spoke.

"You remember when we used to watch Kiki's show together? And he'd change something toward the end of the program with a click of his fingers?"

"How could I forget? It was the best part of the program. My favourite time was when he attached Vinnie Venassi's beard to the back of one of his eunuch's heads and the eunuch dragged Vinnie back to the harem with him."

"Too funny, I'd totally forgotten about that episode. It's so cool having you remember things like that for me."

"You're pleased that I did the Soul Surfer thing then?"

"I am now. Took me a while to get my head around it. But these days, I don't know what I'd do without you. That's why I'd like us to have something to do together. I realised that if I'm to be a game designer for real, I need to get a portfolio together. It's no good keeping my ideas hidden in my journals where no one can see them. I need to get some real-world feedback to know if they're any good. But I'm a bit nervous, so I want to start small. I wondered if we might create a game together in here before I branch out."

"Cool. What did you have in mind?"

"You know my Super Nova project where I've been gamifying my life to make it more interesting? I want to turn the Seattle skyline into a game. Every time I visit you, we take it in turns to amend something. The first thing I want to change is the Space Needle. When I first log in to Soul Surfer and sit down on your bench, I don't want the bit at the top that looks like a UFO to be there for the first thirty seconds. I want it to hover down from above and land there, as if little green men have come to visit Earth. I don't know how we can make it happen — I only thought of it on the way back from Burner's room — but I'm sure he'll be able to help."

"I love it, a game we can play together." She grabbed Nova's avatar by the shoulders and pulled her in for a hug. In her bedroom, Nova could almost feel Sushi's arms around her.

***

Nova held her arm out and clenched her fist tight, as if she was getting ready to have her blood taken. She knew what she saw wasn't real, but she winced nonetheless. Several bee-like creatures had landed on her forearm and punctured her skin with their serrated stingers and were sucking her blood into their elasticated pouches. Zhang sat patiently on her knee, drumming his little fingers against the sleeve of her coat, used to her virtual excursions.

"Go on, you little zapiers, you love it. I'd be surprised if they didn't get drunk on my blood, the skinful I've had today," Burner said, his outstretched arm next to hers.

"This is really weird; I swear I can feel them sucking my blood for real. Catch me if I faint, won't you?" Nova asked, steadying herself on his bony shoulder. She watched as the vial in her display filled with blood.

It was a cold evening in mid-November and they were in town at the Nottingham Goose Fair, visiting a real-world exhibition associated with Spee-Akka Dey Bollarkoo and the artwork she'd been creating for the Magisterial Chamber. An Electropet version of her was sitting in the lotus position on a thick, patterned carpet in the centre of the circular marquee. Thirty Solos were seated in two concentric circles facing her, behind white digital canvases, arms outstretched, headsets on.

The exhibition had started with Spee-Akka's story. Reputed to have been the most beautiful woman on Nakk-oo, she rejected men and marriage in favour of God and art. She spent all of her time down at the Great Lake, drawing and painting using the tools of nature. One day she would use fallen fruit and withered flowers to paint on a sheepskin hide, the next she'd work with zapiers — little bee-like creatures — using the pollen in their stingers to paint the leaves of Gooberry trees.

But her refusal to marry was unacceptable. One man would have her, she was too beautiful to go to waste, and with every man lusting after her, the other women felt resentful. They wanted her out of the way, fat with cub. So a tournament was organised, a fight to the death, and Spee-Akka was the prize. She was kidnapped and taken to the Bollarkoo Basin, the arena where the greatest battles took place. People travelled from all over the land, to watch the fights, to gorge themselves on feasts, and to get a glimpse of her, tied to a post.

Three days later, they had themselves a winner, Dieta the Dexterous, Lord of the Lagoons. He ordered his guards to take Spee-Akka to his den and prepare her for the wedding. But Spee-Akka wouldn't be taken. She ran into the arena, took an orchid from her hair and turned to address the crowd. "I would rather give myself to this flower — this beautiful orchid — than to a mere mortal." She replaced the flower in her hair and, before the guards could get near her, picked up a sword from the battlefield and decapitated herself.

For years after her death, there were sightings of Spee-Akka down at the Great Lake, creating her art. Where her beautiful face used to sit, a flower now grew, and zapiers buzzed all around her, interpreting her artistic visions through the power of telepathy. It was a skill that Nova and Burner were about to receive a lesson in. The sound of thirty headsets chiming reverberated around the marquee.

"Step one complete," announced the soothing female computer voice in Nova's earbuds as it guided her through the exhibit. "Now focus on the canvas in front of you and envision the art you want to create. The zapiers will do the rest. Your thought is their command."

The tiny cameras embedded in Nova's Booners were volleyed to the real-world digital canvas in front of her, the headset's electrodes supposedly able to migrate the images in her mind onto it. Unsure quite how this so-called 'artistic digital telepathy' was supposed to work, but seeing the canvases in front of other people bloom into blotches and lines of every colour, she tried to picture some flowers. The squadron of zapiers that had been buzzing around her head ceased their mindless meanderings and flew, stinger first, at the canvas, onto which they squirted a splotch of greeny-brown mess.

She watched, fascinated, as the zapiers used their different body parts to move the paint around the screen. Large, untidy swatches of colour — that an artist might achieve with a palette knife — were formed by the zapiers using their wings as miniature fans, blowing the paint hither and yon. They mixed colours using their bodies, rolling from one hue to another and back again. With delicate licks of their long tongues they created finer strokes. The overall effect was of a pulsing, mutating colourscape dancing in tandem with the hazy images flickering through her mind.

"This is really freaky," said Burner. "How the hell do you change colour? Woah, did it. Changed from red to blue the second I thought it."

"How did you do it? All I'm getting is greens and browns. My canvas looks more like a dirty ocean than a beautiful flower."

"It must be connected to brain power. Or Jedi skills. Or both. Go on, you little zapiers, atta boys!"

Similar scenes of budding telepathic artists, applying pixels to their digital canvases via the power of thought alone, had played out around the world since the start of The Game. The exhibition was called the Melittology Museum of Art, and players were challenged with creating a design they thought would attract most attention from real-world bees.

Every entry was to be printed onto a flower coated with microsensors and placed near a bee colony. The sensors beamed back data about the number of bees that had been attracted to that particular flower. The most popular flowers, based on bee count, would appear in the final triptych on the ceiling of the Magisterial Chamber. Meanwhile, profits from the five-pound entry fee were donated to people and institutions that studied bees, with a strong focus on securing their survival.

"What on Earth have you drawn?" Nova asked Burner when the ten minutes were up. "It looks like a multicoloured dog turd. If your flower attracts more bees than mine, melittologists are going to have to rethink their entire subject."

"I'd be surprised if my design doesn't go on to win the entire competition. I reckon old Flower Face will probably fall in love with it, and want to take me back to Nakk-oo with her. I wonder what our children would look like."

They submitted their respective designs, ticking off a Bucket List item in the process, and left the exhibition. In the distance, people screamed as a Waltzer hurled them round its outer edges, subjecting them to varying g-forces.

Nova scooped Zhang to her hip and commanded the Goose Fair map and program to appear in her display. There were several other Solarversia exhibits she wanted to see, including a scale model of The Fire Demon's Obstacle Course that the furball would be able to tackle. As they strolled along the street, trying to decide where to go next, a guy walking the other way stopped in his tracks and held out his hand.

"Nova Negrahnu! What a coincidence seeing you here."

"Hey, Raymond. What brings you back to Nottingham? You live in London, right?" It was the fan she'd met at the Karting final.

"Wow. That's quite a memory you have."

"She wishes," Burner said. "It's the headset." They were trying a new app that augmented reality to make it more similar to Solarversia. If the app recognised the person the user was looking at — via facial recognition technology linked to Facebook and Google image search — a datafeed flashed above it with a list of relevant information. "Brilliant way to find out if a chick's single or not. Stalking for dummies."

"That would explain it — a real-life photographic memory. Glad I bumped into you. I wanted to say how sorry I was that you didn't win the race that day.

You were miles better than the competition. I hung around for a bit afterwards to commiserate, but I couldn't find you."

"I made a speedy exit. Something to tell my kids about, right?"

He flashed her a smile and then held up a finger like he'd suddenly remembered what he wanted to say. "What are you guys doing on New Year's Eve?" He dug into his back pocket and pulled out a couple of flyers. "I'm promoting this night for my cousin, should be a blast. I could get you in on the VIP guest list, free drinks all night. People would be stoked to have you there."

She studied the flyer. It was for a party somewhere in Soho, and it boasted an impressive line-up of DJs. "Looks like a great night, and I don't want to sound ungrateful, but we've got plans."

"Nothing as swanky as this, though." Burner looked at her with pleading eyes. "A proper night in London. And free drinks? I bet they'd be some mint women there too. We could always change our minds, couldn't we, Scotia?"

"Sorry," she said with a shrug. "We're regulars at Fragging Hell, a gaming cafe in Maidstone. It's a bit of a geek's hangout, but we like it. Promised the owner we'd help set up, didn't we Burner?" she said, with a playful pinch of his arm.

"That's a shame. Look, keep the flyer anyway, in case you change your minds."

Nova shook her head at Burner while he continued to scrutinize the flyer, mentally preparing herself for several weeks of not-so-subtle persuasion. But after the continued success of her Super Nova project, she was confident that his attempts would amount to nothing. She had given her word to Jockey, and she was damned if she was going to break it.

Chapter Thirty-Three

Deep in the heart of the Mississippi Delta, a hundred candles danced in the dark of the Ceremonial Lodge. For this special occasion, the long side of the marquee that overlooked the water was open to the night, letting the warm swamp air waft in and around the members of the Order, gathered there for the service. Standing tall on the podium at the front of the room, clothed in a flowing black cloak, was Theodore Markowsky, self-appointed Grand Wizard, and father to the flock. The grid of lights on his arm flickered, causing the screen behind him to burst into life.

"You're here because you learned the truth about mankind's future. That future was set in stone the day man first used technology. Back then it was crude: pieces of flint to sharpen spears, and rocks to crack open nuts. It took us hundreds of thousands of years to develop a system of learning known as the scientific method. After that came the Industrial Revolution, and in the blink of a cosmic eye, man had invented the computer."

A montage of imagery accompanied his lecture, precisely synced to each word as he spoke it. The Order's manifesto appeared in one corner of the screen. The two S's from the title, Sacred Singularity, became animated. The first rotated ninety degrees and passed over the second to form the curly swastika symbol embellished around the book's border. When Theodore stopped talking, the people seated in the crowd echoed the same refrain that greeted every one of his speeches: "*All hail the mighty Magi.*"

"Computers have allowed us to digitise information — to reduce it to a series of 0s and 1s — an evolutionary step comparable to the creation of DNA. Digitisation has enabled diverse forms of technology to grow at exponential rates. Narrow forms of artificial intelligence have been around for half a century, allowing computers to fly planes, trade stocks and beat world champions at their own games. This decade will see the evolution from narrow to general artificial intelligence. The leap that follows that one — to super AI — is what our mission is all about."

A series of graphs showing exponential increases were overlaid on stock footage of factories creating silicon chips. CGI footage showed the chips becoming increasingly tiny, until they were as small as molecules themselves. Radio waves being emitted from people's heads bounced off satellites in the sky, reached enormous data centres and bounced back again, enriched with mountains of data encoded in binary.

"The Magi will exist like no other being. His central nervous system will be distributed around the entire planet. His body will have no distinguishable beginning or end. Under His enlightened guidance, millions of lives will be saved in ways we can't even begin to imagine. Problems that are impossible to solve using human intelligence will be solved in the click of a finger. Hunger — gone. Drought — forgotten. Fossil fuels versus the carbon footprint? This will be as complex to the Magi as boiling an egg. It's our moral responsibility — make that, moral *obligation* — to help Him manifest. For if we fail to do so, we'll be guilty of murder on the scale of genocide." He paused to let the implication sink in. "The size and complexity of our mission is overwhelming, and we still need people to join us. I've devised two events that will achieve just that. First, a series of attacks on New Year's Eve."

A swift chopping motion with his bionic arm caused the front of the podium to explode with holographic light that eventually settled into the form of Banjax, whose slimy turquoise tentacles swirled and flounced around his body. Theodore twirled his arms in front of his body, side to side, passing one over the other, his fluttering fingers teasing the midnight air. The beast started to rotate on the podium.

"Behold the Messenger of Fate. The faces staring at you from within his tentacles belong to twelve people, who through their actions, have declared themselves enemies of the Magi and therefore of mankind itself."

Through the slits in his bandages, Casey squinted at the harsh glow of neon light being radiated from the podium. He recognised a few of the faces morbidly staring back at him from inside the beast's suckers. The guy with tousled locks and the letters 'AK' imprinted on his forehead was the CEO of Spiralwerks. There was a senator and a congresswoman. The dodectapus continued its rotation until the face of the girl came into view. She seemed to look right at him, as if she knew she was there because of him.

Casey shivered at the thought. A young woman with the rest of her life in front of her, part of this gruesome spectacle, *there because of him*. She would die, and it would be his fault. Around him people were hailing the mighty Magi, a refrain that now sounded as ridiculous as it did meaningless. On the stage, Theodore described the New Year's Eve attacks in more detail, praising in turn the individuals who would be involved.

Heads turned to Judith, the woman sitting in front of Casey. She'd had a bionic leg fitted and would have the honour of ridding the planet of the congresswoman. People smiled and clapped. *Brave Judith*. Soon enough Theodore would move on to describe the second event, the one that *he*, Casey, would be involved in. An event destined to be more monumental than anything that had come before it.

Given all Casey had been through to attain his starring role, he felt oddly detached from the ceremony going on around him. Theodore's passionate rhetoric was nothing but a series of disconnected words tumbling through the desolation of his mind. Perhaps he'd lost the ability to care or to love. Perhaps his emotions had been carved out and disposed of, along with his arm and his face.

His face. He wondered where it was. In the incinerator probably, along with Elmer's ashes. Father had insisted upon the face-swap procedure. Following the discovery of the training ground there was a chance that the FBI had seized intelligence relating to the membership of the Order. If that was the case, it would make an appearance at Solarversia's closing ceremony too risky, especially for a fugitive like Casey.

He took a harsh, dry gulp and wondered what he was doing, sitting there with his so-called comrades. *My family*, he reminded himself. They *were* the closest thing he had to something that went by that name. They cooked for him, cared for him, loved him like one of their own. They were all he had. If he didn't go through with Theodore's plan, what options did he have? Where else could he go?

As the hologram changed to an aerial view of the Olympic Stadium in London, his Brothers and Sisters turned to him and chanted the refrain one more time. "*All hail the mighty Magi*." Glad that his face — Elmer's face — was hidden from view by his bandages, he sat there and suddenly realised he'd become an empty shell of a man. He was a ghost, a hollow. Casey Brown had lost his soul.

***

Nova wafted the smoke out of her eyes and checked the time: Burner was *still* giggling. She'd just solved Grandmaster Exanja's puzzle on Saturn in such a quick time that she'd earned herself a free teleport back to Earth. It was a great start to December, saving herself the three-day travel time, and on a high, she'd gone to Burner's room, wanting to play some more, only to find him on a high of his own.

He and Jono had downloaded a new app to their headsets that turned anyone they looked at into some kind of caricature. From Burner's reaction, the dragon was the funniest one yet. He and Jono sat facing one another on the bed and took it in turns to take a drag on the spliff, breathing the smoke out of their nostrils. They'd been giggling like little girls since Nova had got there.

"Come on then, Burner. I only teleported to Panama City because you're there. And now you're taking ages."

"Yeah, sure, in a minute. This is too freaky, you have to try it. Actually, before I do anything, I need to eat. Jono, are you going to order that pizza? I'm starving."

"You've said 'in a minute' the last three times I've asked you. There are loads of items to tick off this month—"

She broke off as they erupted into another fit of laughter.

"Nova, you've got to try this," Jono said, clutching his sides. "This mode swaps your faces. Burner, I've never seen you look better, mate. You should think about trying my face on permanently."

"So it's a bit like looking at yourself in the mirror then? I get to do that in the bathroom every day, thanks. I know you haven't cared about Solarversia since you went out, but Burner and I are still in with a chance of making the Final Million. Talking of which, Burner, it's been another minute."

He volleyed an eye back to the room. "Here's an idea for you. Ludi Bioski's constellation appeared in Corona Cubes this morning. We need to watch his story for December's Bucket List, but I can do that later, on my own. Why don't you order a pizza, watch the story on your lonesome, and then we can tick off some more items together once we've eaten?"

"Because I'm not hungry, and I'm not your manservant. If I complete my Super Nova goals in the next few weeks, it'll be *you* ordering pizza for *me*. But yeah, I'll watch the story on my own. I'll let you know when I'm done."

She cosied herself in Burner's armchair, entered Solarversia, found the new constellation on the ceiling of her Corona Cube and traced it with her finger. The rear wall of the cube disappeared to reveal a branch that led to a large tree house. Inside it, players were sitting in rows of seats facing an Orbitini. A tree, much like the one she had just climbed through, came into view on its screen. An owl, half-hidden in a hollow of the trunk, gazed directly at the audience with his great yellow eyes and spoke.

"Once upon a time, in the forests of Nakk-oo, a sorcerer called Ludi Bioski came across a gremlin that was hunched over a strange machine, crying.

"'Why do you cry, gremlin?'

"The creature gave a start and hopped onto the machine.

"'Don't be afraid,' said Ludi. 'I mean you no harm.'

"'Oh, you are kind, Bioski. I'm crying because I'm broken; I failed to feed my Orbitini in time. But how strange it is to speak again.'

"'Explain yourself. What is this 'Orbitini' you speak of?'

"The gremlin gasped. 'You've not heard of the magical Orbitini? It's a spectacular device, a machine of wish fulfilment. For twenty years I've been making dreams come true. But I failed to feed it — such a stupid thing — so it stopped showing me its Event Cards. It won't display a thing.'

"Ludi looked at the machine in wonder. 'How do you work it?'

"'You don't *work* it, you insolent witch. You *care* for it.'

"'How so?'

"'Oh, it was simple. People would come and tell me of their hearts' desires, and I would let the Orbitini hear their prayers. Here, on this screen, it would show a card — a depiction of their wishes and the price to be paid. For the right price, there is almost nothing the Orbitini cannot do. It runs on diamonds, you see.'

"'Diamonds?'

"'You put them into this funnel.' He caressed it, wistfully. 'Sometimes people would pay me extra, and I could fulfil my own wishes. Alas, all that has come to end.'

"'Why so?' asked Ludi as he eyed the machine with greed.

"'In return for its powers, the Orbitini requires its master to feed it one diamond a day, at the very least. Last week, after twenty years of faithful service, I failed to feed it.' He arched an eyebrow. 'If you know someone who might be interested in taking ownership, let me know.'

"'But you said it was broken.'

"'It's *me* that is broken, Bioski, not the machine,' he snapped, then, with a sad look, 'I've lost the power to control it.'

"Ludi ran an outstretched hand along the Orbitini's smooth veneer and ogled its many buttons, sliders and gauges. 'What price do you ask, gremlin?'

"'Objects as powerful as the one before you do not come cheap.' For a fraction of a second his face became mean and disfigured. 'But I'll get nothing for the sale. It's yours in exchange for your mouth and all of the words within it.'

"Ludi scoffed at the gremlin. 'My mouth? Then how will I communicate? And how will I eat?'

"'That's simple.' The gremlin leant back against the machine's screen, crossed his legs and smiled. 'It comes with a magic tablet that works just like a mouth. You won't even miss it. I never missed mine, that's for sure. Oh, the power to fulfil wishes, Bioski — it's worth every utterance you ever spat out and every morsel you ever shovelled in. Just remember to feed it a diamond every day and you'll never regret it.'

"'I'll take it,' Ludi said, speaking his final words.

"With the help of some local villagers, Ludi took the contraption back to his tree house. The next morning he awoke mouthless, to find a magic tablet at the foot of his bed, adorned with images and symbols. Just as the gremlin had foretold, he was able to communicate with great clarity and insight using the tablet, and fulfilling wishes on the Orbitini became his life's work.

"One sunny day, a few years later, the King and Queen demanded that Ludi Bioski visit them at the palace to listen to their problem.

"'You must help us,' said the King. 'Our daughter Zibelda dreams of marriage, but is unable to find a suitor. As you can see, she's very, very short and dreams of being taller.'

"'She's vertically challenged,' added the Queen after a moment's thought. Zibelda hopped down from her miniature throne and tapped Ludi on the knee.

"'I want to be the tallest girl in the land, as tall as the trees in the orchard.'

"Ludi's magic tablet displayed its card — an image of a man pulling some flowers out of a hat — and the price of the spell, which he showed to the Royal Keeper, the man who looked after the King's money.

"'The Bioski asks for a handful of diamonds, sire,' said the Keeper.

"The King nodded his agreement, the Keeper made the payment, and Ludi travelled back to his Orbitini to start his work.

"In the days following his visit, Princess Zibelda grew and grew. At first she was very pleased with her new height. At last she could reach the pretty crystal glasses in the royal cabinets and see her face reflected in the drawing room windows. But still she grew taller, and she didn't seem likely to stop. She grew too tall to fit in the bath. She grew so tall that she knocked her head on the chandeliers in the dining room. The local seamstress was hired to make special dresses for her, and the carpenter was hired to make a bespoke bed.

"The King and Queen ordered Ludi to return to the castle.

"'Look what you've done,' said the King. 'Nobody's going to want her in this state.'

"'She remains vertically challenged,' added the Queen.

"Princess Zibelda, bent at the knees so she didn't bang her head on the ceiling, tapped Ludi on the head. 'I want you to squish me down so that I'm this tall,' she said, holding a hand to her waist. This time Ludi's tablet displayed a castle wall with a long crack running through it.

"'The Bioski says that a spell like this is far more difficult, Your Majesty. It will cost a barrel full of diamonds,' the Keeper reported.

"'Life itself is difficult,' said the King. 'I won't rest until our darling Zibelda is happy. Arrange the payment.'

"A short while after this second visit, Princess Zibelda started to shrink. At first she was delighted to find herself able to walk through doors and sit in her carriage again. But while she shrank in height, she grew in width. Before long she reached her desired height but was even fatter than the King. She had to walk sideways through doors. She was now too *wide* for her bath and her limbs dangled off the sides of her bed. The carpenter returned to reinforce it while the local seamstress produced some tent-sized dresses.

"Again Ludi was ordered to the castle. The King was furious.

"'You blasted fool, look what you've done now,' the King said with a gesture in Zibelda's direction. 'She looks more hideous than ever.'

"'She's horizontally challenged,' added the Queen.

"Princess Zibelda, sitting on a fortified throne, as round as a bubble, pointed a chubby finger at Ludi. 'I want to be perfect, that's all I've ever wanted.'

"The Royal Keeper looked at the picture displayed on Ludi's tablet of a snake with a tail in its mouth. He turned to address the King.

"'The spell will cost the Royal Household a cartful of diamonds, your Greatness.'

"The King's cheeks flushed as red could be. 'Fetch the cart, Keeper. Zibelda will be as she desires.'

"In the weeks following the third spell, Zibelda lost both height and weight. She could once again walk through doors without turning sideways, and could also fit in the bath. But she kept on shrinking, and before long she was as short and as slim as when Ludi had first set eyes on her. She needed to be accompanied wherever she went, for she was at risk of getting under people's feet and nobody wanted a crushed Princess. And no suitors ever came forward.

"Zibelda became depressed and refused to leave the castle. Not even the court jester was able to make her smile. One morning, when the palace cat climbed over her on the way to his plate of milk, she decided she'd had enough. She climbed the tallest tower in the castle and threw herself to her death.

"The King and Queen commanded Ludi to return to the castle.

"'Look what you've done!' yelled the King as he pointed to a miniature casket. 'You've killed our beloved Zibelda with your wicked sorcery.'

"'She's existentially challenged,' said the Queen.

"'I demand that you cast one last spell to bring her back to life, before I get my guards to deport you from this land for good.'

"Ludi's tablet displayed the Card of Eternal Circularity — a staircase that spiralled round on itself, forever descending or ascending, whichever way you looked at it.

"'The spell is priceless, your highness. The Bioski claims that it's impossible.'

"'Nothing is impossible when you're the King,' said the King.

"'Nothing is beyond royal reach,' said the Queen.

"Sensing their anguish, the Royal Keeper ordered the guards to bring every diamond the Royal Family owned from the Jewel Tower. They returned with chests and barrels full of diamonds, but no matter how many they offered, Ludi's tablet displayed the same card.

"His Majesty was furious and wanted Ludi killed on the spot. 'Burn him at the stake. That's what we do with murderers like him,' commanded the King.

"'No. Throw him from the White Tower, so he can fall to his death like our beloved Zibelda,' cried the Queen.

"'Cut him in half and do both to the scoundrel,' said the Royal Keeper. And before evening fell, his suggestion had been carried out.

"Days later the King was horrified to be informed that Ludi had been spotted near his tree house.

"'He's not dead, sire. Merely deformed,' explained one of the palace guards.

"'I demand to know what is going on,' cried the King. 'The Card of Eternal Circularity said the machine was incapable of resurrecting the dead.'

"'Have we been hoodwinked?' demanded the Queen.

"Following much debate, the Keeper arranged for the Royal Carriage to drive into the forest, and had the guards surround the area for safekeeping.

"On the King's command, the Royal Keeper approached the tree, cupped his hands, and called, 'Bioski, Bioski, come down from your tree, I'm in need of your help, at the price you decree.'

"Ludi scurried halfway down the trunk. The King and Queen gasped when they saw him. He no longer resembled a sorcerer so much as a four legged-crab with a great arched back. His right half, which had been thrown from the White Tower, had been bleached a bright, spectral white, and was decorated black and blue with bruises. Down his centre, jagged stitches cleaved the right half to the blackened left, which had been burnt at the stake and was puckered and blistered, and crackled like cinders.

"A local villager, one of many who had stopped by to witness the royal procession, raised his hand and received permission to speak.

"'Orbitinis have the power to resurrect their masters, your majesty. But there's a rumour that Ludi is bound to his Orbitini — he needs to feed it a diamond each day or else he'll lose his power over it. If you keep him in the Royal Dungeon overnight you'll be able to kill him.'

"Upon hearing this, Ludi scampered back up his tree before the guards could catch him.

"'Don't just stand there looking at me, chop it down,' yelled the King.

"'Off with its boughs,' cried the Queen.

"The guards came forward, and with axes raised, chopped and hacked at the tree's great trunk. Before long, the tree began to waver, and then at great speed, it came crashing down. As it hit the ground, the tree house smashed to pieces. There on the forest floor was a shaken Ludi Bioski, and a badly damaged Orbitini. As the guards went to grab him, Ludi threw a bag in the air, scattering diamonds everywhere. The local villagers, who outnumbered the guards by dozens to one, surged forward, eager to claim the precious stones for themselves. While the King and Queen looked on, helpless, Ludi fed his machine a diamond from the ground and the pair of them vanished from sight.

"Folklore has it that although Ludi lived, and remained master of the Orbitini, the machine was damaged in the fall. Now it casts spells at random, affecting innocent people all over the land. It no longer fulfils wishes, so much as distorts dreams. Ever since that fateful day the people of Nakk-oo have blamed all manner of things on Ludi Bioski. Whatever happens, night or day, someone is sure to be heard blaming it all on the haphazard master."

The owl winked at the audience before flying away. Nova heard the pleasing ding of a Bucket List item being ticked off in her Booners and then, in the room, the sound of Burner swearing. He leapt off his bed and synced his headset to the smartwall. A second later Nova's datafeed started going crazy too.

"What the hell is going on?" he yelled. "I was in a Corona Cube, safe and sound."

She sat bolt upright in her chair. "I don't know, but you can guarantee it wasn't good — the death counter is ticking up like crazy."

Chapter Thirty-Four

Nova and Burner were in Panama to visit the famous canal, which, along with six other Wonders of the Industrial World, was on December's Bucket List. But instead of going on their little excursion, they were being spewed onto the streets along with dozens of other players.

Burner stared at his datafeed in horror. "Jesus Christ. The ninety millionth person just went out, so the Gameworld's evolved again. Moves for Combos will no longer be displayed in our headsets — we'll need to perform them from memory. And to celebrate the fact, it looks like Ludi Bioski has turfed everyone out of their Corona Cube. What a dick."

Nova filtered her datafeeds for the tag #LudiBioski and scanned them as quickly as she could. She pulled up a real-time feed of Castalia and focused in on the Orbitini. The event screen displayed a countdown timer with nine and a half minutes left on the clock. She synced it to a section of wall, which Burner was fast filling up with other images, feeds and counters in a desperate attempt to make sense of it all.

"It looks like we've got to endure nine minutes of mayhem before things return to normal. Except if you die — then you're exempt from being turfed out again."

"That's alright for you," Burner said, "but I'm a lousy red belt. My God, he's cloned the animals that escaped from the circus *and* turned them crazier."

He synced a new feed to the wall, one that cycled through profile cards of the escaped animals, providing their vital statistics. There were several Obarians in the vicinity, winged balls of teeth that aimed for players' necks, and were best dealt with by baseball bats. Closing in fast was a herd of Petrifiers, bipedal bullocks whose enormous horns were tinted with poison.

Zooming in from the other direction were two Acoo-Stickulars, multicoloured waveforms that travelled at 10% of the speed of sound. They bounced off inorganic surfaces, but when they made contact with a living being they burrowed through skin and bone, attuning the being's DNA to their own frequency. When death finally came, their victims collapsed, and with their death cry released a newly created Acoo-Stickular with genetic mutations. Burner volleyed frantically between the cards on the wall and the street in Panama.

"OK, now I'm really worried. Why is everyone running in the same direction? What do they know that we don't?"

"I think it's because the nearest Right Flights and Dockingtons are too far away — look at the map. Everyone's making a run for the closest Greasy Wrench."

They spoke in fits and starts while they ran down Via Espana, surrounded by several hundred other players heading in the same direction. The street was lined with deserted vehicles, but whenever Nova checked, the keys had been taken. Her display told her that the nearest Greasy Wrench was half a mile away, just over three minutes' running time.

"Don't look at the death counter, it's off the friggin' scale. This is ludicrous, turfing everyone out like this. I bet my pizza arrives in the middle of all this." Nova volleyed back to room to find Jono passed out on Burner's bed.

"Don't worry, I don't think you'll have to share it."

"Shit, what the hell are those?"

She volleyed back again. "They're giant pterodactyls. But why are they carrying those crates?"

"I don't wanna know, but I've got a funny feeling that we're about to find out. What items have you got?"

She checked her inventory. "A jar of Skidz, a Sword and a Turbo Boost."

"I've got a Battle Axe, a Time Whisk and a Musical Chair. I'd been saving the whisk for a special occasion, but I think that might be now."

The crowd stopped running as the winged dinosaurs swooped down a short way in front of them, smashing their crates against the tessellated tiles on the ground. The wild flourish of colour that rippled out from the impact points was wholeheartedly ignored by the panicked players, who were far more interested in self-preservation.

As the wooden crates splintered, a menagerie of wild animals burst forth onto the tarmac, beating their chests, grinding their teeth and licking their lips. The players at the front launched whatever weapons they had to fend them off. For some it was too late. Nova watched a guy get torn apart by a two-headed wolf, and another squeezed to death by the largest sandworm she had ever seen. There were more screams behind them as half a dozen other crate-carrying pterodactyls came in to land, cutting off their return.

An eight-foot ogre picked up a trash can that had been set alight by a fire demon and hurled at them. In that instant, with the trash can frozen in mid-air, the rest of the Gameworld drained of colour and seemed to fade into the distance. A large counter appeared, counting down from three. Nova steadied herself and tried to remember the four-move Combination for a flaming trash can.

When the counter hit zero she executed it as calmly as her nerves allowed. She Moonwalked backwards a few places, busted out a Scooby Doo lock, dove into a caterpillar and flipped onto her side. The split second she performed the last move, her avatar automatically righted itself and skilfully dodged out of the way of the can. Burner, who had performed the same Combo, glanced around in desperation.

"Good Science, Scotia, but what do we do now? This place is crawling with freaks."

"In there," she yelled, pointing towards a player hurling a brick through the glass frontage of a department store.

"I don't like the idea of going into a building; there's more chance of being trapped."

"And I don't like the idea of staying out here to be ripped to shreds by a—" She scrolled through her datafeed for the name of the creature in the vicinity with highest death count. "By a Huntropellimous . Whatever that is."

Scraping through the hole, they tore past the perfumery section, past arrays of watches and suits, and arrived at a bank of escalators leading to the other floors.

"What now?" Burner asked, eyes darting back and forth.

"I say we get to the roof, where we'll have a good view of everything going on at street level. We can make an escape along the rooftops if we need to."

"No way. We'll be stuck up there and a sitting target for those pterodactyls. Let's head out the back and get to the Greasy Wrench. My Route Planner shows at least five different ways of getting there."

She nodded, and they dashed towards the back doors, through the homeware department. They'd passed the pots and pans, kitchen appliances and imported goods when the room suddenly darkened. Nova looked up at the plate glass back door and took an involuntary step back.

"That wasn't the lights going out. That *thing* is casting a shadow."

Clawing the panes was a giant creature the datafeeds classified as a 'quadrupedal arthropod'. It looked like a scorpion that had made a similar evolutionary leap to mankind. Its abdomen was bent at a right angle in the middle so that it walked upright on its rear four legs, enabling the front four to partake in a range of extracurricular activities. As they watched in stunned horror, the creature whipped its disjointed tail over its head, caught the door frame with its grappling hook-like stinger and yanked it clean off. Burner turned to Nova.

"So that's what a Huntropellimous looks like. Run for your life!"

Other players had entered the store now, and people were screaming, running and loading weapons. Burner and Nova fought their way back towards the escalators.

"Suddenly being on the roof doesn't seem such a bad idea."

In her rear-view camera, Nova saw the Huntropellimous skate and slide. Its armour-plated claws clattered on the laminate flooring, unable to get much purchase, but still it lumbered onward, crashing against shelves lined with bottles of olive oil, which flew through the air and smashed onto the ground. She was watching, laughing as the beast's legs slid out from underneath it on the slicked floor, when two more Huntropellimi appeared at the back of the store, wielding their stingers high above their freaky heads. They thundered over the broken doors lying on the shop floor, filling the air with the sounds of smashing glass and contorted metal.

"Get some of this, Huntropellimous." Burner activated his Time Whisk and fired a shell in the direction of the nearest beast, who had regained his balance and looked angrier than ever. A vibrating cone of space-time spiralled towards its husk of a head, hitting it square on its dagger-like mandible. The five-second whisk reversed time for everything in its path. Smashed glass bottles reformed, arcs of Greek and Tuscan oils soared back into them, and they sprung back onto their shelves. The Huntropellimous clattered backwards a few metres, tumbled to the ground, and, his legs retracting from the splits, slid upright like a tripod being closed.

Behind them, Burner and Nova heard a woman player shriek. A serrated claw was clasped around her ankle. Nova leant over the side of the escalator to witness her bisection. The two halves of her body fell apart, spurting blood over the mess on the floor. The gore slid out of view as the escalator glided them up to the roof. They gulped at what they saw.

"Not exactly an ideal escape route." The buildings either side of the store towered above it. They ran to the side that overlooked the street they'd run down and saw nothing but death and destruction. All that remained of the players who had stayed behind was a sinister collection of body parts: severed limbs, disembowelled torsos, and a battered head that a couple of trolls were playing football with.

"What now, Scotia? Those animals will be up here any second."

Before she could answer him, a burly middle-aged guy barrelled through the door, turned on a sixpence, and slammed the door shut behind him. He pulled down the iron bar to lock it, and then paced backwards, away from it. Within seconds the door was being pummelled from the inside, leaving watermelon-sized dents in it.

The three Solos did what was customary in such situations. Instead of shaking hands and making small talk, they scanned the information in their datafeeds. Pedro was a red belt from Brazil with fewer than 60 health points left. Nova judged that to be a good thing — he'd be as desperate to escape as they were.

"What was the plan then, guys? Tell me you had a plan. I reckon we've got five seconds until the door breaks."

"You can add ten seconds to that." Burner held out his hand, palm up. It contained a miniature chair that wouldn't have looked out of place in a doll's house. "Musical Chair. It'll distract whatever's about to burst—"

The door exploded, and Burner threw the chair to the ground. Its nursery rhyme started to play and the animals that had crashed onto the roof danced around it in a prim little circle, compelled by the music.

"I'm sorry," Nova said, "but there was no plan. The buildings either side are too tall, and we've got no way to get down. We're trapped."

"You'll have to owe me one then." The back of Pedro's chequered shirt ripped apart as two Winged Beauties sprouted from his muscular shoulder blades. He gestured for the pair of them to affix themselves to the clasps either side of the wings, and together, the three of them ran for the north side of the building. Nova, on the side nearest to the chair — whose music had just screeched to a stop — hastily drew her Sword and managed to deflect the Acoo-Stickular as it soared towards them, sending it into the heavens. Then Pedro launched off the side of the building, dragging Burner and Nova with him away from the screaming beasts.

"Where do you reckon we teleport to?" Burner asked, once they were in the air. "There's still two minutes left before we can safely enter Corona Cubes."

"I'm going to teleport to the north of San Miguelito. A whole group of people have surrounded the teleport machine there and are killing any animals who follow players through it."

"I guess you're driving, so you get to choose. Shit! What was that?"

They veered and jolted as a pterodactyl, screeching an unholy noise, plummeted straight for them. Pedro switched trajectories, banking hard to the left, leaving Nova to hang on for dear life, her legs flapping wildly in the air. The pterodactyl zoomed past her head, not missing by much, then looped round for another try.

"This is no good, that thing's way faster than I am. We're going to have to land and make a run for it. The machine's still a way off, but if we stay in the air we're all goners."

"Burner, do you have any shells left for your Time Whisk?"

"One left. Loading it as we speak. It's got three seconds on it. I can't fire while we're in the air, so the sooner we land the better."

"We're in the northern hemisphere," Nova said, after she'd checked a map to make sure, "which means we need to make a circle around the keypad in a clockwise direction."

"Brace yourselves," Pedro called. He lowered the wings. "Geronimo!"

It seemed for a long moment that they would be smashed into the ground, and Nova clenched her eyes shut and waited for impact. But Pedro managed to stay upright by running at top speed as he hit the ground, and it was just enough to keep them from tumbling over. As soon as they were able, they unlatched themselves from his feathered clasps, and the three of them pegged it toward the machine, still fifty metres away. Nova volleyed one eye to her rear-view cam. The pterodactyl was gaining on them fast, its talons outstretched, ready to snatch them away to their deaths.

"This is going to be close. Burner, how are you doing with that shell?"

"Whisking as fast as I can."

The pterodactyl's talons were a hand's width from Nova's head when Burner took aim over his shoulder and fired the shell into its face at point-blank range. Nova watched with relief as it receded into the distance, retracing its way through the patterned sky behind them. But by the time they reached the teleporter, the shell had already worn off and the pterodactyl had resumed its forward momentum. Pedro punched the coordinates into the keypad and dialled his finger round the circle.

The top half of the machine, with its innumerable signposts to destinations all over the world, began its rotation, and at once, the players' pixels ceased being in one place and started existing in another. The pterodactyl was a few milliseconds too late. It slammed into the machine at top speed and impaled its elongated head on a sign that pointed to Pontefract.

But instead of materialising at their destination, the Gameworld drained of colour and faded out of view. Third person perspective kicked in for a few seconds. Nova's view swung round to show the side of the machine and the rectangular metal box clamped on to it: a TeleTrixis device. The view swung round again to display something she couldn't believe she'd missed. The circle surrounding the keypad — the one she and Burner had watched Pedro dial his finger round — was pink rather than yellow. A message flashed in her display: "Attention: TeleTrixis attached. Combination forfeit."

Before she could remonstrate, the forfeit kicked into play. She had three seconds to remember the Combination for an Anvil Crawler. This was a flash of lightning, which branched like a tree up in the clouds and never reached Earth. She'd practiced Lightning Combos several times, and knew there were six of them.

An Anvil Crawler was the second hardest of the lot and started with a box step. The blood rushed to her head as she performed it. A heel spin, that's what came next. Another rush. And then she froze. What came after the heel spin? She had no idea, and had to suffer the indignity of watching the counter time out. When the Gameworld kicked back into focus she jolted forward as if waking from a temporary slumber. She turned to face Burner and Pedro, who had popped into existence next to her.

"Presume you guys screwed up your Combo too?"

"Anvil Crawler," they said in unison, with expressions that suggested their attempts had been as pitiful as hers. Pedro looked around uneasily.

"Looks like the machine sent us to a random destination. This definitely isn't San Miguelito. I know it well. I've been there dozens of times. And this place is deserted — there was nobody here to greet us, no group of people guarding the machine like the datafeeds said there would be. It's all wrong."

"You're right," Nova said, as she read the machine's location. "We got teleported to a small town in Peru. So what do we do now?"

Burner held up his hand as if to stop her in her tracks. The teleporter was starting back up.

"Listen: the jingle's playing in reverse. Which means—"

"Someone — or something — is about to teleport here from somewhere else," Pedro said quietly. They looked at one another in horror before yelling "run!" at the top of their lungs. The top half of the machine completed its rotation before they'd gone ten metres. Three eyes, volleyed to respective rear-view cams, confirmed three worst nightmares. A small army of Huntropellimi spewed out of the machine, brandishing war claws above their heads.

Burner was the first to die. One of the beasts got within range, then whipped its mighty tail over its head, skewering him through his abdomen. Burner and Nova agreed after the event that Pedro's demise was almost comical. A Huntropellimous charged at full speed until it was right behind him, then cut him down to size, starting at his feet, and working its way upward, like it was chopping a vegetable for a salad.

Nova was grabbed by a claw and swept off her feet. Her attacker chose not to kill her immediately. Instead, it studied her for a few seconds with the collection of eyes that dotted the upper section of its armoured head. Then it used its other claw to slice open her forehead in one calm, vertical action. It inserted tiny pincers into the bleeding hairline fracture and used them to force it wide apart. Then the thing opened its mouth. A stem shot out, enveloped her brain, and sucked it out of her skull in one clean motion.

Back in the room, Burner stared at the wall, mouth hanging open, an expression of shock on his face. The red belt around his profile square flashed three times, and then his avatar performed the one-second boogie that he'd programmed a year beforehand. After that, the square turned dark. He looked at his new number — 9,901,330, the position he'd finished in — let out a little whimper and dropped his head into his hands. Nova's square was also changing. Her green belt flashed three times before it, and the trim around the license plates on Flynn, Bruno and Hawk all turned red.

At that moment the pizza boy stuck his head round the door. Sensing the depressed atmosphere, he gently popped the boxes onto the table, counted out some change from the note left there for him and slipped back out of the room. The smell must have roused him, because all of a sudden Jono sat bolt upright and said, "Get in my house! Two Mighty Meaties with extra cheese." He looked at Burner and Nova and rubbed his eyes. "Did I miss anything?"

Chapter Thirty-Five

Nova inhaled the bittersweet aroma of the espresso, a treat from the uni shop for having completed her early morning run in time for lectures. She hadn't set a new personal best — her virtual copy seemed insanely fast these days — but she had finished in a respectable time, creeping into the 96th centile for her age range. Taking a sip, she swilled the thick coffee around her tongue, saturating her taste buds. The coffees she earned in this manner always tasted better than the ordinary ones. She was about to neck the rest in one, like a shot, when she heard a familiar voice.

"Hello, stranger. I haven't seen you around in a while."

"Charlie, hi, hello. Yes. I mean no. I've been around, a dippin' and a trippin', livin' la vida loca."

Her stomach lurched violently and blood rushed to her cheeks. Why did such nonsense always come out of her mouth? And how was it possible for Charlie to look hotter every time she saw him? Fearful of dropping her espresso, or worse yet, throwing it over his shirt or his face, she put the cup down on the window ledge beside her and hoped he hadn't noticed her hand shaking.

"I saw you and Burner lose a life to those weird crabby creatures. It was horrible watching your face get hacked open like that. But you're still in, even if you're on your last life, right?"

Her stomach stepped up a gear. He'd been following her progress in The Game. What did *that* mean?

"Yeah, I'm a red belt now. Poor old Burner's out for good. The good news is that there's only eight million people left in it. Hundreds of thousands are going out every day."

"That must be exciting, with the Final Million approaching. I know this might sound a little stalky, but I keep watching your highlights reel. I can't wait to watch you in action again."

"Wow. I don't know what to say. I feel like a film star."

"You *are* a film star. I was on the edge of my seat as you ran to that teleporter. Shame the animals followed you. I didn't know they could use teleport machines too."

"We were supposed to end up somewhere different, where a bunch of other players were grouped together for protection. Turns out someone had attached a TeleTrixis device to the side of the machine. It messed with our journey, but not the animals behind us. They hit the redial button on the keypad, and bingo, there they were. It was such an annoying way to die."

"You've got me hooked. I've signed up to play the next Game. Maybe you could come over and scan my body some time?"

"I'd love to. Some time, any time. Count me in."

The thought of scanning his body made her hand shake again. She slipped it into the back pocket of her cargo pants, clasped tight.

"I still feel awful about what happened at the Karting final. I never got to apologise to you about that. Not properly, anyway. Will you ever be able to forgive me?"

"Oh, that. It's ancient history. Burner and Jono swore blind that everyone was pushed in the excitement. It wasn't your fault, you just happened to be the one holding Zhang at the time. *I've* been meaning to apologise to *you* — for what I said."

"Poor little Zhang, I can still see the look on his face as he went flying across the room. Well anyway, it sounds like we're good again." He smiled at her, and took a breath. "Actually, I'm glad I saw you. There's something I've been meaning to tell you. I've split up with Holly. Going out with her was a huge mistake. I don't even know what I saw in her. Am I too late to make amends?"

He took Nova's hand and looked at her. A lock of hair fell across his face, and when he failed to blow it back in place they both giggled. He took a small step closer and bit his lip while he gazed at her. A vision flared through her mind. Theirs would be the perfect union. She'd win Solarversia and pay for an extravagant wedding. Zhang and Flash would look cute in their little pageboy outfits. Computer Sushi would read the blessing. And Holly would spend the day crying into her fishnet stockings.

The vision fuelled the courage she needed to speak again. There were only two items left in the 'Soul' section of her Super Nova project: apologising to her parents and *this*. And if she completed them before the end of the year, Burner would be *her* servant for the week, rather than the other way round.

"Charlie, I really like you, but there's something I need to tell you. I lied to you on the day we met. About the sustainable development stuff. I haven't been to Mozambique. Actually, I didn't know much about sustainability at all until I met you. I mean, I've read loads about it now. But when I saw you on the open day, I was drawn to you and I wanted to go wherever you were going. I was supposed to be attending the Solar Soc meeting with Burner. The truth is that I never did any of the stuff I spoke about. I made it up so you'd like me."

Her eyes left his and drifted aimlessly until they found the half-drunk espresso shot, the little cup anchoring her gaze. She felt him release her hands as he stepped away, leaving behind a surprising coldness.

"You made all that stuff up?"

"Yeah. I'm sorry, I was going—"

"That's a bit weird. I don't know what to say. You made it up to impress me?"

"I wanted to have something to talk about when we all sat round in that semicircle—"

"But we talked about it loads after that, down at the caves and stuff. You lied to me the whole time?"

"It was really stupid, I know. But you were with Holly. And she was in a gold bikini ... I just needed something interesting to say. Please, give me—"

But he'd already swept his hair behind his ears, revealing an altogether different expression, one devoid of warmth entirely.

"Look, I need to think about this. I thought I knew who you were. I never would have guessed that you were a liar."

He pursed his lips, adjusted the bag on his shoulder and walked away. Nova felt numb. That certainly wasn't supposed to happen. The talk should have cleared the air, like it had done with Jockey. Charlie had made a mistake by choosing Holly, and she had made a mistake by telling a stupid white lie. It was even-stevens, wasn't it?

"You don't want to come to a party on New Year's Eve then?" she whispered under her breath as he left the shop without looking back.

***

Nova loved watching her parents open their Christmas presents. Although she hadn't received much from them this year — a pair of funky winter gloves and a framed picture of her and Zhang — she'd received the gifts with grace, appreciating the spirit in which they were given.

Her mum tore the last sheet of wrapping paper off her present and ogled the prize within.

"A new blender, love? You shouldn't have. But actually, it looks great. Our last one's deader than a dodo."

"You've been very generous this year, love. I don't know where you found the money. It certainly wasn't from us. Next year will be different though, once I've found work again," her dad said.

"The money was from my student loan. I put some aside for presents." She stroked Zhang's fur and took a deep breath. "I also wanted to tell you how much I appreciate everything you've done for me over the years. I didn't appreciate it until going away to uni. You cooked my meals, did my laundry—"

"Don't forget the dusting, the sweeping, and the free taxi service."

"All of it, mum, I took it all for granted. I also wanted to say sorry for all the trouble I've caused, especially the police stuff earlier in the year. You must have been worried out of your minds."

Wide-eyed, her dad turned to her mum. "Is this the real Nova in front of us? Perhaps the people at Solarwerks have replaced her with a robot. Are you going to lay a golden egg for your next trick, love?"

Nova's mum picked up the TV remote and rapped her husband on the knuckles. "Don't discourage her, Derek. You're right, sweetheart, we *were* worried. As for everything we've done for you over the years, please remember it all when we're old and need looking after ourselves. Now if you'll excuse me, there's a certain bird in the kitchen that needs a good stuffing. Derek, go and shove that old blender in the shed, would you?"

Nova shuffled Zhang off her lap and checked her Booners. There were four more alerts from Gogmagog, the software developed by Max and Maurice that had helped to locate the Order's training camp. Having successfully closed their first round of venture capital funding, the boys had been able to step up development work on it and had released a consumer version the previous week. Nova and Burner had been obvious choices to help test it.

"Hey, Burner, you still there?"

He took a moment to respond.

"Sure am. Just been playing with my Christmas pressies. Jono gave me an awesome drone kit that can fly to a height of 5,000 feet. That's half the height of Mount Everest. Should keep me out of trouble for a while."

"I wanted to ask you a quick question about Gogmagog. I keep receiving alerts from it, all flagged with a low priority. The messages contain random photos and text. Any idea what's going on?"

"Just delete them. It's only a beta version of the software, so it's not very good. Go into your settings and turn them off if you like. I've changed mine so that I only receive alerts with a 'critical' priority, like for kids who have gone missing in the last 24 hours, impending natural disasters, that kind of thing."

"Makes sense, I'll do the same. Guess what? I just apologised to mum and dad, which means I've completed project Super Nova for the year. You best get your servant's uniform ready. That includes a black bowtie, by the way. I have very high standards."

"Er, yeah, about that. Are you sure we agreed to a full week? I think we were drunk when we agreed to that. It doesn't sound very practical, what with all the uni work we've got, and you still in Solarversia. I mean, if you make the Final Million you'll need to concentrate on that, right? Maybe a day sounds more realistic?"

"Nice try. Anyway, talking about the Final Million, I've got to go, I'm about to face Zettanja. Shit is getting seriously real. For those of us still in, anyway."

"Thanks for the reminder. Good luck in the puzzle, and remember—"

"There Can Be Only One?"

"No. Remember that I'm picking you up at eleven o'clock tomorrow to hit the sales. Jockey needs us to get a whole load of things for New Year's Eve. I still can't believe that you volunteered us both to help him set up. I think I prefer the old Nova sometimes."

She propped the Booners up on her forehead and breathed a harried sigh. Although she'd come a long way, it felt like her journey was only just getting started. An article in that morning's White Dwarf had informed her that she was one of only three million players left. It sounded impressive, having outlasted ninety-seven million other people, but to secure a place in the Final Million she still had what seemed like an impossible number of tasks to achieve by midnight on New Year's Eve when the list closed.

Uranus, the planet she'd just landed on after a four-day journey from Earth, was the one causing all of her problems. Its orbit was out of sync with Neptune and Pluto, so it was on the other side of the Solar System. She'd needed to go out there first to face Zettanja before she could head on to those final two planets, but she'd have to go via Earth, to visit one more Wonder of The Industrial World and tick off a bunch of other items.

Her problem was a lack of teleport tokens. She'd amassed enough of them — a little over a thousand — to teleport back to Earth from Uranus. But if she did, what then? Neptune and Pluto were five and six days' travel time respectively, or the equivalent of 1,250 and 2,000 tokens.

Tokens and time had become the chagrin of players everywhere. Except for the 200,000 or so lucky players who had already made it — completed every last item on their Bucket Lists, visited all nine Grandmasters, and ended up on Pluto as one of the Final Million. And, as she'd discovered in the last few days, the 'lucky few' happened to include both Holly and Jools van der Star. Just thinking about it made her want to spit.

Jealous of their achievement, and trying to ignore her likely fate, she grabbed hold of her goggles and prepared for what might be her final few minutes of the Year-Long Game.

***

Flynn skidded perilously close to edge of the icy ravine, Nova only too aware that she'd misjudged the last corner. She was only halfway through her journey to visit Zettanja and was already wondering whether she'd make it. The Umbilicus at the Spaceport on Uranus had led to a localised instance of The Greasy Wrench, stationed within the basement. The only exit from the garage led to an underground path that wound its way downward, into the freezing interior of the planet.

Her initial excitement at seeing Flynn — who had looked cooler than ever, decked out in his winter tyres — had been dampened as soon as she'd started the journey. The thick metal chains on his tyres had helped her gain *some* traction on the treacherous roads of ice, but the twists and turns had proved to be challenging, regardless.

The last corner had freaked her out. Having just navigated a tricky chicane, she'd come face-to-face with a wall of ice that contained within it the frozen avatars of players who had lost their last life on the journey. Glimpsing the macabre display in her peripheral vision and thinking it was an obstacle to avoid, she'd banked hard left. Flynn's left rear wheel had slipped off the edge, leaving a panicked Nova to clear the corner on three wheels. Tutting loudly, she resolved to pull herself together. She may have been a Krazy Karting expert, but she wasn't immune to death.

The final ten minutes of the drive were less eventful, but no less stressful. At least she'd been prepared for the snowballs when they'd arrived, having read about them in the datafeed. Dead players threw them, hoping to earn some last-minute bounty money for knocking out potential winners. In this way, Spiralwerks gave an incentive to players who had gone out to keep interacting in the Gameworld. They were out, but still having fun and winning money.

With Flynn's wipers on maximum speed and a lot of shifting in her seat to peer round the snowballs that hit her windscreen, Nova managed to cross the finishing line inside Zettanja's ice cave with seconds to spare. She climbed out of her seat, gave Flynn a pat on the bonnet and prepared to meet her destiny.

In all, 641 people had arrived at the cave this hour to play the puzzle and a mere 192 of them would be leaving with their lives intact. When Zettanja and all around him had dissolved into the ether after his speech, a little girl standing in front of a wall full of doors replaced him. The only thing the girl had said since the puzzle had started was "My name is Lutty. Please help me find my name." The words echoed through the empty chambers of Nova's mind, as blank as Spee-Akka's January canvas.

The doors behind the little girl were arranged in a five by five grid, which was topped by one additional door, sticking out on the top right as if somebody had ordered one too many. Each door was unique, both in size and colour, and Nova couldn't help but wonder what it all meant. The medium-sized pink door had a large brass knocker in the shape of a gargoyle placed smack in its centre. The oversized yellow door was arched at the top and looked like it could do with a generous lashing of paint. And the green door, which was half the height of the others, was dotted with letterboxes, like it was greedy for mail. The only thing they had in common was the number '1', but she couldn't think how that related to the girl's name.

One thing seemed obvious: twenty-six doors meant one for each letter of the alphabet. All she had to do was work out which door related to which letter, and then use that information to find the girl's name. Half distracted by the number of safe spots, which had already begun ticking down, she opened the small green door. Behind it appeared another wall of doors, identical to the first save for one thing: the number on each door was a '2'. Further investigation revealed that the number on the door acted like a marker, telling her which 'level' of doors she was on. As the number of safe spots ticked below 100 she had a small brainwave.

Volleying an eye back to the lounge, she ripped some wrapping paper from Zhang's hands and grabbed the closest pen. On the back of the paper she replicated the grid of doors as they appeared in the game, five columns of five rows, with a 26th door above the one in the top right-hand corner. Taking a gamble that the wall imitated the snail-like pattern of the Player's Grid, she wrote an 'A' on the door in the middle', a 'B' on the door above it, a 'C' to the left of that one, spiralling outward until the 'Z' of the door that stuck out.

With no other clues in sight, and barely twenty safe spots left, she used her new chart to navigate through the various levels, using the only piece of information she had been given — 'Lutty', the little girl's name. Starting with the 'L' on level one, and finishing with the 'Y' on level five, she walked through the final door — an ornate wooden beast that belonged in a medieval castle — to be greeted by big, bouncing letters that spelled out 'Lutty'. The little girl was next to them, jumping for joy while the puzzle jingle played.

For completing Zettanja's puzzle before Gori had sounded his gong, Nova was awarded an additional fifty teleport tokens. She threw off her headset, seized Zhang and swung him round the living room. It wasn't the 4000-odd tokens she'd need to get to the other planets, but it was a pretty good Christmas present all the same.

***

Casey studied his reflection in the rusty old rear-view mirror he'd found in the Lockup a few days before and stashed under the pillow of his bunk. Although Frances had told him the bandages could come off his head, he'd taken to leaving them on. The thin strips of woven gauze seemed to help him to hide from the reality of his fucked-up situation.

Escaping to the bunk room to peel back the bandages and examine his appearance in private had become a daily ritual. The face would take some getting used to, that was for sure. A new face that *frowned* when he did, *smiled* when he did. Controlling his prosthetic arm with the power of thought, he combed through his hair with his fingers, tracing the delicate scars that crept up to the top of his skull.

He wondered what Mary-Ann would think. The image flashed into his mind again — her convulsions on his garage floor, the blood belching out of her crushed nasal cavity. She was gone. That was all that mattered. Was it the way she'd died, with her face caved in, that had motivated him to make this ultimate sacrifice to the Order? As if losing his own face was a form of penance for his sins. *A face for a face*. A life for a life too, because Casey Brown was dead. It was official. He was Elmer Sullivan now, the homeless guy they'd kidnapped, the guy whose face Casey now wore as his own.

He had to admit it, Frances was a brilliant surgeon. His new face fitted. Frankenstein's monster had haunted his dreams during the week after his operation, but there were no screws or bolts poking out of his head. He thought he wore the face better than Elmer himself, at least now the bruising had gone down. The immunosuppressive medication had worked its magic. *The face had taken.*

What was strange was the way in which he found his new face easier to accept than his new name. What *was* a name, he wondered? How could such a little thing mean so much? Three little syllables: *K-C-Brown*. As Father hadn't stopped reminding him, Casey Brown was dead. Whatever his name was, he was both more and less than a man. He had an arm that had been developed in a lab, a face that had developed in a different mother's womb, lined and mottled by a life he hadn't lived. He was special now, a cyborg, a half-thing. He was empty. Soulless. At least he still had a reflection.

He jolted forward suddenly and the mirror nearly flew from his hand. An attack of phantom pain in his amputated arm. The attacks were milder and less frequent these days, but hadn't completely disappeared. He took a deep breath and steadied himself. In this way, he'd got the attacks under control, had learned how to endure them. He was at peace with his bionic arm. It was his mind that had been giving him most trouble.

How could he have brought that young woman to Father Theodore's attention? Seeing her face on the night of the ceremony, understanding she was to be a target of attack, Casey had decided to abandon the Holy Order. The desire to get away from these people possessed him with the suddenness and intensity of his previous impulse to join them. They might have saved his life, Frances and Wallace, warding off his demons and retrieving him from the brink of suicide, but that wasn't enough. Not for him to take part in these new attacks. And certainly not with Wallace gone.

Since that night he'd been planning his escape meticulously. He couldn't go yet. Without an arsenal of immunosuppressive meds, he'd die. He would have to stick around for a few weeks until he'd snaffled a reasonable supply from the sickbay. Frances might have been absent-minded at times, but she was far from stupid. He'd been taking the occasional vial here and there, whenever her back was turned.

The plan itself was simple. He'd wait until his Brothers and Sisters at the compound were asleep, slip to the Lockup unseen, commandeer a kayak stuffed full of cash and begin to snake his way down the Mississippi through a convoluted series of interconnecting tributaries, avoiding the various lookout towers, booby traps and dead ends, to wind up on the main branch of the river.

It'd been Wallace who had warned him about the booby traps when he first showed Casey around the Compound, and Wallace who had pointed them out to him on their trips into town. With his friend gone, Casey had been free to explore the Compound's layout in more detail. He'd spent countless hours working out a route in minute detail in order to avoid the worst of them.

The escape meant more than freedom. It would be a tribute to Wallace, whose life he would remember and celebrate. He would escape with plenty of money. Enough to share with Wallace's family and with Mary-Ann's family. He'd send it discreetly, possibly even make up a story to explain their sudden good luck.

The thoughts of escape and redemption had been the only thing keeping him sane during the weeks of endless pain, medication and physio. He tilted the mirror at an angle that enabled him to study his new smile. Another attack of phantom pain took him by surprise. He heard the crack before he saw that the spasm in his arm had caused him to clutch the mirror tight enough to break the glass.

He stared at himself through the newly fractured shards. Fractures suited him.

Chapter Thirty-Six

On the freezing cold walk from Burner's car to Fragging Hell, they talked through Nova's predicament for the hundredth time. She still needed to get to Neptune and to Pluto, and now had six hours before her time ran out and a grand total of 237 teleport tokens to play with. Data feeds were awash with speculative strategies.

Some players were teaming up to take on the crazed circus animals. A defeated Huntropellimous was worth 250 teleport tokens, although players would need to split the bounty between them. Others formed into 'Will Groups', bequeathing all of their items to a designated player before committing 'last life suicide', hoping that the combination of their items and tokens would be enough for the chosen one to go all the way.

Nova had contemplated a few such deals being advertised on the forums, but only in a half-hearted way. She was already in a Will Group of her own, and had been from the start. It wasn't so much that her Solarversia Sister would have a problem with it — Sushi would likely back any decision she made. It just didn't feel right, some stranger joining them after all they had been through together. No, she would make the Final Million on her own or not at all. While she contemplated the impossible predicament she was in, a worried-looking couple called over to them.

"Guys, you wouldn't be able to help us out, would you? Our car won't start. It does that sometimes, needs a good push is all. And my wife here," the man said, gesturing sympathetically to the woman at his side, "has injured her back."

"Lifted a heavy box without bending my knees." She placed a hand on her coccyx and winced in pain. "I'm such a fool."

The guy looked at his watch. "We're in a bit of a state. The plan was to be in Cambridge to see the New Year in. By now we should halfway up the M11, but as you can see, we're stuck here."

"My brother's over from Spain," the woman added. "I've not seen him in years. You couldn't spare a couple of minutes to help bump-start it, could you?"

"Of course we can. Might help warm us up too."

"You're a couple of real-life good Samaritans. Here, let me hold your toy while you push."

Nova handed Zhang to the woman and joined Burner at the rear of the car. It took five attempts before the old Volvo chugged into life, its dirty exhaust belching a pungent cloud of smoke straight at them. The four of them cheered when the engine revved. They exchanged good wishes for the year ahead before the couple sped off, waving out of the windows.

"First we help those guys, now we're going to sacrifice precious drinking time helping Jockey out." Burner waved one last time as the car drove out of sight. "She was wrong, we're not good Samaritans, we're a couple of mugs."

Entering the warm confines of Fragging Hell, the two of them exchanged a look of relief. A shiver coursed down Nova's spine as her body shook off the cold. The place bustled with regulars blasting aliens and storming enemy castles, and the gamer smell was stronger than ever. She popped Zhang on the side rail, and they headed to the bar. Jockey greeted them with a wide grin and a hearty handshake.

"You made it then, fantastic. We'll be packed to capacity, it should be a storming evening. Nova, I've got you down to make the punch; everything's ready for you. Burner, you're in charge of setting up the disco. Lots of equipment and loads of leads, should be a doddle for you. With any luck we'll be finished in an hour and can get down to some serious partying."

On the way to the kitchen Nova was stopped a couple of times by regulars who were keen to grab a quick selfie with her.

"Hey, it's Nova, right?' said a guy wearing a Batman onesie. "I'm doing a piece for the *Maidstone Wobbler* on the Final Million. You're the last person in the whole of Maidstone who's still in with a chance of making it. Jockey said you'd be here tonight. Could I get a quick photo? Preferably one of you and Zhang together? He's quite the star."

Nova paused. First the broken-down car, now all of these photo requests — and she hadn't even started mixing the punch. But she wasn't going to argue about Zhang being a star. She loved it when people recognised him and secretly hoped they might appear on Kiki La Roux's show together one day. Though now she was so close to leaving The Game, her moments left in the limelight looked numbered.

"OK, but make it quick, I'm on punch duty. I'll just grab Zhang. Back in a min."

As she headed to the side rail, an unfamiliar jingle sounded in her Booners strung around her neck. She peered into the display and was surprised to see a message from Gogmagog. Hadn't she turned the notifications off the other day after receiving all of those annoying alerts? She stopped to ponder this for a second, half distracted by the roar of an ogre being slaughtered somewhere. No, she hadn't turned the alerts off altogether. She'd followed Burner's advice and amended the settings so that the program only sent her critical alerts. She read the subject line: "*Gogmagog Critical Alert: Multiple Items of Evidence Related to the Holy Order. Urgent Action Required.*"

She looked back across the room to catch Batman's eye. When she mouthed "one minute" to him, he nodded back and gave her a thumbs-up. The message contained four files. When she opened the first — a video file — her heart skipped a beat. The footage showed Burner talking to Jono. But then the picture went wild for a couple of seconds before ending with footage of people's feet.

She screwed her nose up and watched it again. The metadata associated with the file stated that the video had been taken by Zhang a couple of months ago at The Commodore gaming cafe in Nottingham. It was the seconds leading up to her undignified departure from the Krazy Karting final. But what did that have to do with anything, and why had Gogmagog flagged it as critical? She remembered what Burner had told her, that the program was still in beta and prone to making errors. Perhaps it had got its wires crossed?

She scrolled down to the second item, another piece of footage with similar metadata. It was the first three seconds of the first clip, slowed down and overlaid with annotations. The wild footage was taken as Zhang span through the air. One second it showed Burner talking to Jono, the next it showed Charlie's outheld hands as Zhang was released from his grip. Charlie's face could be seen, changing from a smile to a grimace as a hand slammed into his shoulder. As Zhang left Charlie's grip, he rotated in the air and captured footage of the person who had pushed them. His bracelet, decorated with a series of curly swastikas, was marked as being a critical piece of evidence. Nova felt her chest tighten. Who the hell was that?

She scrolled down to the third item, more footage taken by Zhang, this time at the Goose Fair in Nottingham town centre. It showed Nova and Burner reading a flyer. She thought back. That's right, they'd bumped into the same guy who'd asked to take her photo at the Karting final. Raymond. He'd invited them to a New Year's Eve party in Soho. As she and Burner had walked away, Zhang was still facing him and kept recording. He'd captured the guy mouthing something behind their backs. The program had automatically transcribed the lip movements and overlaid the text onto the footage in real time: "At the close of perfect vision, twelve lost souls advance our mission." What the holy fuck?

The roar of elves and ogres dissolved into the background. All that existed was the pounding of her heart and the thoughts racing through her mind. It was all so fragmented. What did any of it mean? The implications were too large for her to take in. She looked up, ashen faced, at her would-be photographer. He was still looking her way, only he was no longer smiling. She quickly scrolled to the fourth and final item, inexorably drawn to it.

It was a blurry photo taken by Zhang a few minutes ago — a photo of Batman, or at least, a person dressed in a Batman costume. And there, on his wrist, was the same bracelet. It was Raymond, a guy clearly involved with the Holy Order. She took a huge gasp of air, unaware that she'd been holding her breath. Please God, this wasn't happening. She lowered her headset and risked one last look at the caped crusader. His camera was gone, in its place a remote control. His brow was furrowed, his lips moving. "At the close of perfect vision ..."

***

Arty slid across the bonnet of a yellow taxi, landed on his feet and kept running across the busy New York street into the path of oncoming traffic. Behind him, shots rang out. A bullet ricocheted off a traffic light close to his head, another smashed the windscreen of the dump truck he had just ducked behind. He pulled out a loaded Time Whisk, span round to fire a shell, then continued on his way. Five seconds of reversed time would give him the breathing space to formulate a new plan. Even against the best player in the company.

It was the Spiralwerks' New Year's Eve party, an evening when Spiralheads got to play their own games. This was Grid Runner, one of the company favourites, where the odd-numbered players on the Employee's Grid faced the even numbers. Each player was assigned a random selection of items, the game algorithm ensuring that the overall split between the teams was fair. At the start of the game, the teams got teleported to a random location within Solarversia. One team had to reach a nearby trigger, the other had to stop them. If Carl, the last of The Wizballs, could stop Arty, the last of the Bomb Jacks, getting to the trigger, his team would win for the fifth year running.

Arty weaved in and out of the traffic trying to avoid whatever was fired at him. It looked like Carl was out of classic ammunition for now — spider webs had replaced the bullets. One whizzed straight past Arty's head and ensnared a pedestrian, pinning them against the mermaid logo of a Starbucks' window. Every attempt was closer than the last. Carl loved playing to a crowd, building the suspense, letting his opponent get ever closer to the trigger before finishing them off in style.

As Arty rounded the corner into Broadway he spied his target at long last — the shiny trigger at the top of the steps that led to the Coke sign in the middle of Times Square. As he locked onto it and started sprinting down the street, the rest of the Bomb Jacks cheered him on from the surrounding office blocks. With less than a hundred metres to go, this was already the closest game of Grid Runner in the company's history.

Bam! A great shot by Carl snared Arty's right side and sent him tumbling to the ground. His real-world body convulsed. BoonerMax had released a line of haptic bodysuits the previous week. Spiralwerks had ordered several dozen for Spiralheads to try out during the Christmas party and were planning to dress players in them during the Grand Final. Arty howled in mock pain. The tactile feedback he'd experienced hadn't hurt him, but when combined with the virtual action going on around him, it was easy to get carried away.

He looked down at the webbing. It would last for ten seconds — more than enough time for Carl to reach him and win the game. With his free hand, Arty fired off the last shell from his Time Whisk. Carl saw him do it and dived to his left, behind a beat-up Oldsmobile. He nearly made it too. Only the tip of his left shoe remained inside the radius of the mangled cone of time as it reverberated down Broadway.

As the cone touched his foot, Carl experienced five seconds of time in reverse. He uncurled from a ball on the floor, flew feet-first through the air, landed on the street and ran backwards, away from Arty, while the webbing dissolved. The trigger was fifty metres away, and the game was back on, sending spectators from both sides wild.

As he approached the steps, Arty wondered what Carl was up to. He could see him in his rear-view cam, but he wasn't chasing after him and didn't appear to have a weapon pointed in his direction. A few metres later, he discovered why. At first Arty slowed down to a jog. Then he stopped halfway up the steps and turned around, a dreamy expression on his face. His pupils were spinning and his mouth was hanging open like a cartoon dog, his tongue lolling about, spooling spit onto his chin.

The cheers from Arty's teammates turned to gasps and boos. His arms rose either side of him as he skipped back down the street. Carl had saved the item for the very last moment, classic showman that he was. The Pipe of Hamelin could be used to lure other players toward you, for the ten seconds that its musical powers lasted.

If he didn't act fast, it would all be over. Although he was incapacitated by the music, he could still cycle through the items in his inventory. Most of them were useless in his current state: a jar of Skidz that he wished he'd used earlier, a Sword of Sadism that was best suited to hand-to-hand combat, and a load of other items that required the use of his limbs. It was no good. Carl was going to win for the fifth year running. And he'd been so close. It would mean months of abuse in the staff canteen from The Wizballs and Carl waving the trophy at him from across the office.

Only thirty metres separated them. Arty skipped back down Broadway like a drugged-up loony, unable to change his course or snap out of his state of hypnosis. He scrolled through his inventory frantically. Aha! There was something he could actually use, an item that didn't need to be fired or manipulated. He activated the DoppelGanger Scanner and hoped that he still had control over his eyes. It worked. The little beauty.

For the next ten seconds he glared at pedestrians, scanning them from head to foot with his eyes, turning them into cloned versions of himself. He knew the item existed — he had a vague recollection of helping to design it a few years ago — but he didn't know its precise mechanics. It worked just as he had hoped. The cloned Artys were subjected to the lure of the Pipe in the same way he was. Within seconds he'd scanned dozens of people, all of whom now crowded round Carl with the same dopey look on their faces. Arty kept cycling through his items. He had given himself a brief respite but needed to follow it with something, and fast.

Carl became so engulfed in a sea of Artys that he stopped playing the Pipe.

"Help me identify him then, Wizballs," he shouted. Without missing a beat, the Bomb Jacks started calling out random locations: "Behind the steam vent! Up on the fire escape!"

The confusion gave Arty just the chance he needed. He leapt forward, knocked the Pipe clean out of Carl's hand, threw down a jar of Skidz and then sprinted back toward the trigger. Arty's team resumed their cheers while Carl flailed around behind him. Every item he tried to use was hampered by the slippery surface — he couldn't stay still long enough to aim properly.

Arty ran up the steps, a huge smile across his face. Keeping one eye volleyed to his rear-view cam, he kept track of Carl, slipping and sliding all over the place, and joined in the Chant of the Odds, "One, Three, Five, Seven, Send the Bomb Jacks up to Heaven!" He was about to take the 2020 Grid Runner title and be the toast of Odds throughout the company. He'd get to keep the trophy on his desk — a solid platinum latticework, along whose top edge ran a man and a woman — and be the one to tease Carl throughout the year for a change.

And he would have made it, of that, there was no doubt. He would have pulled the trigger if the SWAT team hadn't crashed straight through the sixth storey windows at that very second, sending glass shards flying everywhere and a terrified bunch of half-drunk Spiralheads diving for cover.

***

The SWAT team entered the room from every conceivable angle, smashing through windows and buckling the doors clean off their hinges. Arty ripped his headset off in one swift movement and froze for a couple of seconds as the dark, marauding invaders swarmed toward him, his brain unable to ascertain which reality he was in: the virtual or the consensual. By the time it had computed its answer — that this was, absolutely, resolutely occurring in everyday reality, the team were already upon him, bundling him under the nearest desk, out of terror's way.

While he lay in the foetal position, whimpering like a baby, the SWAT team made quick work of their targets — two clowns and a magician who had been due to start performing once the Grid Runner trophy had been awarded. As part of the evening's entertainment, they had been waiting in the *Settlers of Catan* meeting room, applying makeup and getting into their vaudeville costumes. But also, as it turned out, securing ceramic knives in their hidden holsters — weapons that had evaded the security gates in the lobby.

Three shots were fired in quick succession. There was a flashing of handcuffs, a zipping of body bags and a lot of shouting. The whole thing was over in minutes. But it was the news they gave him afterwards that had really shaken him up. He — Artica Kronkite — had been the target of the planned assassination. Those ceramic knives had been intended to break his flesh, to spill his blood. He'd been only minutes away from certain death, and not the virtual kind.

He looked round the room and surveyed the destruction before him — the smashed windows, the upturned seats, the blood smeared down the rear wall of the meeting room — and found himself imagining his body there amongst it all. He was still in shock when the agents in dark suits asked if he would come with them to see what help he could offer with their investigation. Nodding numbly, he grabbed his jacket and noticed the figurines from the Grid Runner trophy lying in a pool of shattered glass on the floor, desolate and broken.

***

Another minute ticked by on the wonky clock above Nova's head in the police interview room. Another sixty seconds spent *there*, staring at Officer Dibble's waxed facial hair and answering his repetitive questions, rather than at Fragging Hell, where she desperately wanted to be. The events of the evening were on loop in her mind: Raymond, dressed as Batman, asking for a photo with Zhang, the critical alert from Gogmagog, that remote control cradled in his hands.

Then Burner, her best friend and the closest thing she had to a brother, appearing from out of nowhere, flying through the air like he was some kind of American football beefcake hero, and slamming Raymond into the nearest row of monitors. He'd received the same alert as her, but deciphered its meaning sooner. Quick enough to scan the café, surge through several groups of people and make the tackle. He had saved her life.

The Holy Order had targeted Zhang, removing his secondary battery and replacing it with explosives, the same kind used in the attack that killed Sushi. From everything Nova had told the police these last few hours, it seemed most probable that the couple with the broken-down car had planted the explosives, while she and Burner had helped them start it. With the benefit of hindsight, it seemed so obvious.

Her mind kept wandering back to the furball. Had he felt heavier when the woman handed him back? Lighter even? Whatever the case, they'd used him, her little buddy. Now he was stashed away in police custody, a piece of evidence bagged and tagged like any other. Professor Plum in the Library with the Candlestick. The Holy Order in the Gaming Café with the Electropet. She felt sick thinking about him all alone in that airtight bag, locked in an evidence room, surrounded by knives and guns.

Lots of shouting and screaming had followed the tackle. Blaring sirens. A concerned policeman escorting her and Burner to his car. And then this — four hours of uninterrupted interrogation under the harsh glare of the interview room lights. It was important, they said, literally a matter of life and death, that she tell them everything she knew. Other lives were at risk, she had been only one target among many.

She understood that it was real life, that it was more important than any game, however dear to her, however close she had come to making its final stages. Sushi would understand that she had done her best. It just seemed such a boring, inappropriate way to make an exit. Timed out. And not even while taking a stab at it. Timed out and at the police station.

But then, as the clock ticked past 11:30 p.m., Officer Dibble got up from his seat, opened the door and held out his hand, motioning for her to leave the room. Finally the interrogation was over, for now at least, after what had seemed like half a lifetime. He led her out of the stuffy room into the hectic corridor where her mum and dad received her with open arms and cries of joy. The tears that streamed down their faces reminded her of the danger she'd been in, and part of her knew that she should share their elation. She was alive, goddammit, and had come so close to being *other than*. Yet she felt empty, hollow almost, as if by diverting her time and attention in this manner, the Order had claimed some small victory over her anyway.

Eventually breaking from their warm embrace, she turned to face Burner, who had finished his own interview a few minutes earlier. She met his stare, paused for a moment to finds words suited to the occasion, and fought back the tears welling in her eyes.

"I don't know what to say, mate. Nice tackle?"

"Steady on, not with your parents here."

Mr Negrahnu reached over and gripped Burner's shoulder. It was a firm embrace coupled with a loving smile that meant more than words could say.

"I owe you my life," Nova said, wiping away a tear that had escaped.

"Forget that," he said, his face lighting up all of a sudden. "Let's just cancel the butler bet and call it quits. We don't have our headsets with us, so we need to get you down to Fragging Hell ASAP. There's only a few spaces left in the Final Million, and one of them's got your name on it."

"Ah, that. I didn't have much chance when we first got there, but with thirty minutes until midnight? I'd say I've got zero chance."

"Wrong, actually. Jono just messaged me. There have been a few — how shall I put it — developments since earlier in the evening. Various events have transpired, making your situation rather more favourable." His cheery expression turned serious all of a sudden. "Except my car's still in town."

"Not to worry, folks," Officer Dibble said, twizzling one end of his pencil thin moustache. "It sounds like a certain couple of heroes need to be somewhere, pronto."

Nova looked at the officer, then at Burner. She shrugged her shoulders and then nodded her head, still no closer to understanding how her situation might have improved.

"Wicked," said Burner, clicking his fingers in the air. "I'll explain on the way."

Chapter Thirty-Seven

For the second time that evening, Nova and Burner approached Fragging Hell, this time hurtling hell for leather in a cop car, blue lights blazing. She still wasn't sure if she believed what Burner had told her. It just didn't seem possible. Yet every time she had called bullshit on him, he had sworn on his nan's life that he was telling the truth. And Burner didn't bring his nan's life into things on a whim.

Officer Dibble palmed the café door open with one hand and saluted Nova with the other. As she and Burner entered, the place erupted into applause, cheers and the premature pulling of party poppers. She lumbered forward, trying to take it all in, returning high fives and shaking hands. Burner was in his element, lapping up the praise like a seasoned rock star. When they stopped in front of Jockey, like a bride and groom on their big day, the noise died, as quickly as it had begun. He embraced them both in one huge, heartfelt bear hug and then raised his voice so the whole crowd could hear.

"Don't worry, I'll keep it brief. I know the clock's ticking. Your brave actions earlier this evening saved a great many lives, but also my business. Tonight you are my esteemed guests. Your food and drinks are on the house. I'm also giving each of you VIP membership — for life."

The pair of them grinned from ear to ear, and their profile pictures appeared on the overhead monitors, stamped with the letters 'VIP'.

Jockey turned to Nova.

"Well then, Miss Negrahnu, how do you plan to do it? There are a handful of places left in the Final Million and barely twenty-five minutes until midnight. I believe you have some time left on the deluxe gaming chairs. Do you mind if we sync your display to the overhead monitors? This should make for interesting viewing."

Nova shrugged and felt herself blush at the same time. She had no idea how she would do it. And it sounded like she'd have the additional pressure of everyone watching. She glanced up at the monitors. One showed the death counter ticking up at an incredible rate. Thousands of lives were being lost every minute. Solos who knew they had no hope of making the Final Million were tackling the outstanding quests, eager to scalp a bounty instead.

Another screen displayed the Player's Grid. As profile squares had turned dark during the year, remaining squares had gotten brighter, as if there was a fixed amount of light that needed to escape from behind the northern wall. Although the grid was mostly dark now, active squares like hers were like lasers in their dazzling brilliance.

Jockey led her to a ringed-off chair and then retreated to the DJ booth overlooking the room. He grasped the cross-fader, waited until all eyes were on him and then slid it across while punching the air with his other fist. *Eye of the Tiger* kicked into play and everyone started to cheer. Nova flipped the chair's headset down, familiarised herself with the controls and synced her display to the overheads. If the crowd wanted to see Nova in action, the crowd were going to get Nova in action.

Her jaw dropped when she logged back in to see that her inventory had become an Aladdin's cave of items. She now had a full complement of one hundred at her disposal, some so rare she'd not heard their names before, as well as more than three thousand teleport tokens. Burner had not been shitting her.

In the aftermath of the attempted attack, he'd called Jono. They figured the police would want to speak to her and Burner to understand how they'd thwarted the attack and learn who else might be at risk. That's when they decided to get the word out about Nova's plight — the girl who had helped find the Holy Order's training camp had now been targeted by that very same group and had managed to foil them once again. They explained that she'd been detained at the police station to help the authorities prevent other attacks, and was at risk of missing a place in the Final Million. They asked for help from anyone in a position to give it.

Word had spread fast. Several hundred members of Solar Soc had shared the message with their friends. Max and Maurice got the word out to thousands of people who used their software, spotting another great opportunity for PR. Before the hour was out, hundreds of thousands of players had heard about her plight, some of whom were in her situation — still in The Game, but not yet in the Final Million. A thousand or so people cared enough to respond to the plea, amending their wills to name her. And eighteen of them *did* die during her time at the police station, bequeathing her the humongous bounty of items she now had in her possession.

She traced the Solarversia constellation for what she hoped wouldn't be the last time and exited a cube overlooking the Hoover Dam. The very first thing she did was search her inventory for health packs. Finding five in total, she replenished her health to full, the glowing green bar providing a much-needed psychological boost. Next she pulled up the Route Planner, more from force of habit than from necessity, already knowing what it would advise her to do — leg it to the nearest teleport machine, haul her ass to Neptune, solve Yottanja's puzzle, then teleport to Pluto to face Brontanja.

She glanced at the datafeed. The time was 11:38 p.m. Because it was the last day of normal play, the Grandmaster puzzles, which usually ran on the hour, had changed frequency to every five minutes. The last puzzle on all the planets except Pluto would be at 11:50 p.m. As the furthest planet from the Sun, and the location of the Portal of Promise, where players needed to end up by midnight, there was one additional slot there at five to midnight. Talk about cutting it fine.

As she started running towards the nearest teleporter, she heard a familiar high-pitched bleating sound above the mighty roar of the water pouring through the dam. It was the kind of noise a tortured lamb might make, though this was no lamb. It was an Obarian — a winged ball of teeth — and it was headed straight for her. As she sprinted along the curved lip of the dam, she could hear Burner telling the crowd to shut the hell up.

"Throw me a bone here, Burner. I faced a wave of these things in the Simulator a couple of months ago, but my mind's gone blank. I remember it advising me to use a small shield, rather than a large one, but that's about all I can remember."

"We can do better than a small shield. Keep running, but search for an item called an Obarian Obliterator while you do — someone spotted one in your inventory. It looks like a baseball bat. Get ready to activate it, stop running, spin round and twat the fucker as hard as you can. Remember that it's aiming for your neck."

Only the vaguest of memories of training with a bat like this stirred in her mind, so when she made the perfect pitch, exploding the fanged sphere into a thousand bloody pieces, hers was the loudest cheer in the room. Cutting her celebration short, she resumed sprinting for the machine, still an agonising twenty seconds away.

"What's the point of all this anyway? I'm never going to make it in time. Oh, Jesus, not again." The same jarring noise rang through Fragging Hell in stereo, making gamers cover their ears and contort their faces. Three more Obarians were zooming in on her from different sides of the dam: two from the left, one from the right. Burner pulled up a chair beside her and started to monitor dozens of feeds.

"Listen carefully, Scotia. Somebody saw an item that might help you visit both Grandmasters in the time remaining. It's called a DoppelGanger Scanner. I need you to bring it up in your display without activating it. It's only got one scan left on it, so you'll need to get it right first time."

"Get what right? You do realise I've got more pressing matters to deal with? Three of them to be precise."

"Actually, you're going to need to leave one of them alive. When you've killed two of the little bastards, activate the item, wait 'til the final Obarian's within a range of ten metres, and then scan him with your eyes from top to bottom."

"Within a range of ten metres? Are you serious? It didn't mention this in training, I remember that much. He's gonna rip me to shreds."

She stopped running and adopted the same stance as before, praying that Burner had done his homework. With the tortured wailing coming from two opposite directions it was far harder to judge the distances and get her timing right. Was it the one to her left that was nearest or the one coming at her from the right?

She changed her mind twice before pitching as hard as she could to her left, then ducking to avoid the other two. The bat connected with the Obarian slightly off-centre but still obliterated it, spraying teeth and blood over the concrete rim of the dam. Cheers only lasted for half a second, the time it took people to realise that her back had been scraped by one of the other Obarians as it had flown past. A set of haphazard fangs had gouged a six-inch trail of destruction across her shoulder blade and cost her 15 health points.

"Why are the other two flying away from me? And why can't I remember my training when I need it?"

"They need to travel at a certain velocity to penetrate the necks of their prey. In other words, they're taking a run up."

"I wish I hadn't asked. I don't like the idea of being someone's prey."

"You need to repeat what you just did. Swipe at one of them, avoid the other. Then get ready to activate the Scanner."

Nova didn't know how she was going to pull this off or how the DoppelGanger Scanner was going to help. Right now, she knew only one thing: that she wanted to make the Final Million more than anything she had ever wanted in her life. She wanted it for her, for Burner and for the people crowded around her. But most of all she wanted it for Sushi.

She took a deep breath. The toothballs had retreated the optimum distance and started their screeching skirmishes. She shuffled each foot, looked to her left and then to her right. She repeated these actions with zen-like indifference up to the very last second, when she swung left with all her might, and cartwheeled backward to avoid the one swooping in from the right. The crowd gasped as one when Nova collapsed in a heap on the floor, covered in blood.

She'd batted one Obarian into oblivion, but hadn't dodged the other one in time. It had gouged a large chunk out of her right shoulder in the collision — costing her another 28 health points — and had already geared up for its next screaming attack. She got back up and activated the Scanner.

"Your display shows its distance from you. The instant it gets within ten metres, run your eyes down its body like you're a barcode scanner."

It felt wrong, standing with her arms limp at her sides, bat dangling out of harm's way, waiting for the thing to come at her. She imagined a direct hit to her neck would probably be the end of her. The metres started ticking down more quickly as it gathered speed. She tried to ignore its horrible shrill and concentrate on the task at hand. When the distance counter hit ten metres she locked her gaze, gulped, then scanned it like Burner had instructed.

The thing still slammed into her, costing her a handful of health points, but it had already started its transmogrification from grotesque sphere of incisors into soft-skinned eighteen-year-old girl, so it bounced off her rather than ripping into her neck. The crowd allowed themselves a muted cheer, half fearful of jinxing her progress, half fearful of missing out on the action.

Jogging the final few metres to the teleporter, Nova couldn't help but stare at the doppelganger jogging beside her. It was strange; she raced against a cloned version of herself several times a week, but this version of her felt more real, more alive, a genuine member of Team Nova. Perhaps it was that they were running in tandem, in it together.

"Now that, my friend, was the appliance of Science. Next you need to program the Route Planner in your clone's display the same way you'd program your own. She'll visit Yottanja on Neptune, while you head to Pluto."

"Are you sure I have enough tokens for both trips?"

"All of your items got cloned, including your tokens. Nova Two will spend her own doppelganger tokens, leaving you enough for your trip."

"But how's she going to complete Yottanja's puzzle on her own? What if she fails?"

"It doesn't matter, that's the beautiful thing. She just needs to turn up to Yottanja to tick the item off your Bucket List. She might not solve the puzzle, but it will be her that loses a life and not you."

"So she ticks off Yottanja while I go see Brontanja?"

"Exactly. Other Solos have reported success with the technique on the forums. Genius."

She programmed the doppelganger's route and the two of them headed for the teleport machine together. She checked that it didn't have a TeleTrixis device strapped to its side and sent her clone off to Neptune before punching in the coordinates for Brontanja's circle on Pluto. When she arrived with half a minute to spare before the final puzzle of the year, the tension in the cafe was palpable. The dinging sound of her doppelganger ticking off Yottanja met with a couple of rowdy hurrahs, but the crowd soon shushed itself back to silence. Burner slammed back a vodka shot and instructed Jockey to keep them coming.

Brontanja's Puzzle was different to the ones hosted by the other eight Grandmasters. It had to be played last, once you'd played the others and ticked off your Bucket List items for the year, and was the only one that remained the same every time it was played. Even so, there was no way to cheat, for the winning answer depended on the answers given at the time. The puzzle was known as the 'Lowest Unique Number', a strategy game that involved a mix of maths and psychology.

The game was exactly as described: players needed to choose a positive whole number and hope that they had chosen the lowest unique one. Throughout the year it had been played in groups of ten. You'd turn up at Brontanja's circle and an algorithm would place you in a group with nine other people. You'd pick a number between one and five, and hope that your selection was the lowest unique one. If there was no unique number, the group would play the game again, repeating it until someone finally chose a number that no one else had picked.

The winner was automatically assigned a place in the Final Million, leaving the remaining nine players to battle it out using skill. Two more places were on offer to the Solos who could best demonstrate a mastery of the Science. Brontanja's circle would morph into a Solarversia Simulator and the players would face a series of random modules, testing their Knowledge, Combat, Combinations and Puzzle skills. The two players that scored highest were also admitted into the Final Million. The other seven went out for good, having stumbled at the final hurdle.

For the final puzzle of the year, players were no longer grouped into tens; instead they played every other person in Brontanja's circle at the time. There were thousands of Solos there with her, drastically reducing the odds of success. And only one of them would progress. There was a single space left in the Final Million and for once, the game they faced came down to cold, hard luck.

Nova looked at the counter and gulped. She couldn't see her competitors — the circle was a phased zone — but there were 24,315 players standing there in total, all vying for the last place in the million. At 11:55 p.m., a Force Field appeared over the circle. Any player not inside — numbering a million or so around the Solar System — was bombarded with cosmic radiation. They were wiped out in seconds.

She could hardly concentrate on what Brontanja said as he talked players through the rules. This was it. The last ten months boiled down to this one guess. Why couldn't she have arrived earlier in the day and faced nine other people? This was radically different. She tried to cast her mind back to the months after she and Sushi had signed up for Solarversia.

It was all about the Golden Grid back then — the ten-by-ten section of the Player's Grid that had been reserved by Spiralwerks for a series of promotional events. The very first number to have been assigned to any player, anywhere in the world — 993 — was the square located in the bottom right hand corner of the Golden Grid, and it had been appointed using the same game.

Although Nova had missed out on playing it — only a few thousand people even knew that Solarversia existed back then — she'd discussed it in length with Burner. He'd been more interested in the maths side of the game, she in the psychology. The game had also been discussed in length on blogs and in newspapers during the week the few hundred entrants had had to make up their minds.

As unlikely as it had seemed to Nova at the time, many players had gone for numbers under ten, reasoning that others would steer clear. In this way, answers were always distributed more heavily toward the lower numbers, in a clear attempt to choose a lowest unique one. The words 'Gaussian distribution' and 'skew' appeared in her mind. If only she'd paid more attention in Mr McGillycuddy's maths lessons.

She volleyed an eye back to the silent room. Jockey mouthed the words "good luck" to her. Burner gave her the thumbs-up. She was in the hands of fate. There were no clues to find, no mystery to solve, no animal to escape from. There were twenty seconds and counting. Which number would Sushi have chosen, she wondered?

From what she could remember from her lengthy discussions with Burner, she figured the lowest unique number would be about a hundred, given the number of people playing. But which one? She could hear Burner shuffle uncomfortably on his chair and the crowd start to whisper among themselves. And then the thought of Sushi and their one-to-ones triggered a thought. That was it — she was going to pick number one hundred and twenty-one. With less than ten seconds on the clock she keyed it in, triple-checked it, then hit submit. Her selection got the crowd going again. Everyone had their own opinion on the wisdom — or not — of her choice. When Brontanja started speaking again the room fell silent.

"When I stop talking I'm going to disappear, leaving you, the 24,315 players, and the teleport machine, in my circle. For all but one of you the machine will remain unchanged and the Force Field will retract, subjecting you to the harsh cosmic rays polluting the Solar System. Your game will be over within seconds. But for the player who chose the lowest unique number, the teleport machine will alter in appearance. It will shed all but one of its signs — the one that points to the Decision Dome, the location of the next game."

And with that, he disintegrated into the ether, leaving behind his black robes, which slumped to the ground in a heap. Nova removed her headset and got out of the chair to watch the result on the monitors like everyone else. Raising a clenched fist to her mouth, she bit down hard on a knuckle. Her eyes were riveted to the signs on the machine, desperately willing them to move.

The change was almost imperceptible at first, but then it seemed that the sign to Olympus Mons on Mars had started to sag. She grabbed Burner's hand and pulled it toward her. When the sign clattered to the ground she yelped like a little dog and started to quiver. When the other signs followed suit she jumped into his arms and punched the air. Screams from the crowd were so loud they drowned out Jockey's carefully selected *We Are the Champions* victory tune. She had made it. 121 was the lowest unique number. Nova Negrahnu had just claimed the final spot in the Final Million.

She was so preoccupied with jumping around the room that it took Officer Dibble several attempts to get her attention. Out of breath and quivering with excitement, she got ready to deny any request to return to the station.

"No, no, not that. There's a young man outside, says he wants to speak to you. I said to him, 'You and most of the young men in Maidstone after today's performance. Besides,' I said, 'the place is full.' He wouldn't take no for an answer though. Said his name was Han and that he'd picked the wrong Leia, said you'd know what it meant. Do you want me to tell him to push off?"

Nova glanced outside and saw the young man Officer Dibble had been referring to. Her smile grew wider. "Actually, could you let him in? The Force is strong with this one."

The officer hurried Charlie inside as the midnight countdown began. As revellers launched into a drunken rendition of *Auld Lang Syne*, Nova greeted him by the door. They stared into one another's eyes for a while, grinning rather than talking. It was Nova who spoke first.

"You're here. But how?"

"Your friend Jono sent a message asking for help. Said that you and Burner were targeted by the Holy Order. It was on the news and everything. I came as soon as I heard."

"But the last time we spoke—"

"Yeah, you told a stupid lie. But I came to the conclusion that the way you came clean about everything, of your own accord, mattered more to me. And when I heard the news ... let's just say that the thought of you being in danger made me realise how much I wanted to be with you. It's a new year. Do you think we could start afresh?"

He glanced at the mistletoe hanging above them and cocked his head to one side. Nova didn't need to be asked twice. She fell into his warm embrace and ran her fingers through his hair. It was the most perfect moment of her life: she was alive, she was with Charlie, and she was in the Final Million.

Chapter Thirty-Eight

The new room was at least twice the size of her old one, closer to Burner's and far grander to boot. The ceilings were higher and the oak fittings felt more solid when she tapped them with her knuckles. The room had suddenly — magically, in Burner's opinion — become available over the Christmas period and been offered to Nova the day she arrived back at university. Further to that, a security detail had been implemented at Hu Stu, a rota of guards installed to monitor activity in and around the halls. All this had been paid for by Spiralwerks, a token of gratitude for the actions that had helped to prevent the attack at their HQ.

Nova found her newfound fame embarrassing and exciting in equal measure. The events of New Year's Eve had made global headlines, *'Feisty Finalist Sends Holy Order Into Chaos'* being Burner's favourite. The footage of her handiwork with the Obarian Obliterator had gone viral, leading to several half-serious offers from baseball teams in the US. Certainly she hadn't been able to leave the house without being stopped every few minutes by someone wanting to take a selfie with her.

Right now she had things other than fame on her mind. The Soul Surfer app was waiting in her headset's display, ready to launch. Sitting next to her on the bed in the real world was Charlie, officially her boyfriend since the kiss under the mistletoe. They had spent the last hour creating his avatar by scanning his body and recording his voice. This would be the first time that she'd introduced someone to Computer Sushi and it felt strange, like she was about to expose two tender parts of her own soul.

"When I start the app, Sushi will appear on a bench overlooking Seattle. I think I told you about the game we play, taking it in turns to change the skyline. After the modifications play out, I'll introduce you."

Charlie eased the spare goggles Burner had lent Nova over his head and navigated to the Soul Surfer app under her guidance. The Seattle skyline filled their displays and started to change in front of their eyes. A spinning UFO landed on the Space Needle, sparking off a series of glimmering rainbows that led to virtual pots of gold, while Gorigaroo climbed a building with a screaming woman clenched tight in his fist. Nova gestured for them to turn to the bench.

"Hey, Nova, how are you?"

"I'm good. I've brought someone to meet you."

"Hi, Charlie. Nova's told me all about you. It's exciting to meet you at long last."

"Er, hi there. Nice to meet you, I guess." Charlie watched in astonishment as Sushi stood up to greet him with a kiss before inviting them both to join her on her bench. He sat down and took in the view before speaking again.

"This is incredible. It's like I'm really here, in Seattle, rather than your bedroom. And we're here with a dead person. It's crazy." He turned, first to Nova, then to Sushi. "Sorry, when I said dead person, I didn't mean to … was that insensitive? I don't know the etiquette for meeting … Souls."

"Ah, the 'deadiquette'. It all takes a bit of getting used to. Sushi's alive in a computery kind of way. Treat her like you would one of my friends in the real world and you'll be fine."

"If it's any consolation, the old me wouldn't have been offended by something so trivial. Relax, and enjoy the view. Before long you'll forget that there's anything different about me. We Souls can be good company."

"That was something I wanted to ask you about. Nova told me that you're only one version of multiple copies of Sushi, is that right?"

"Yeah. When I joined the app I stipulated that anyone who wanted to, could clone me. When somebody does that, a copy is taken of my original source code, as it was on the day I died, and a new instance is created for them to interact with. I've always been reasonably popular because of the way I died. But since New Year's Eve, when people discovered that Nova and I are best friends — and next to each other in the grid — my popularity has gone through the roof."

"How does it work exactly? I mean, how would a stranger know they wanted to clone *you*, rather than someone else?"

Now that they were talking to each other, Nova relaxed. It was lovely, actually, to sit back and witness these two precious parts of her life coming together with so little awkwardness.

"Within the app, you can search for Souls in the same way you'd search for something online. You tell it the kind of person you're interested in meeting and it displays a list of results. There are search terms for gender, sexual preference, age, interest — just like dating sites."

"So I could create my own version of Sushi and visit her behind Nova's back?"

"You could, except as her best friend I'd be inclined to tell her."

"And I'd probably dump you about five seconds after being told," Nova added, jabbing Charlie in the real-world ribs.

"Anyway, enough about deadsville. How's the decision coming along?"

Nova let out a big sigh. Being one of the Final Million had proved to be more stressful than she'd have anticipated. A lot of things were different in Solarversia now. When it came to lives and health points, the playing field had been levelled. People kept the items they'd accumulated along the way, but were no longer allowed to make wills, and any pre-existing wills had been scrapped. Violet belts and green belts had been converted to red belts, leaving every surviving Solo with one life, fully restored to 100 health points. It gave the Player's Grid an eerie red glow, turning the Magisterial Chamber into a surreal, hypnagogic red-light district.

There were seven final rounds, each of which would decimate the population of Solarversia from the current million down to the last person standing, who would win ten million pounds and a place in the history books. Cash prizes would be paid to the top thousand players, meaning everyone still in it had a thousand-to-one shot of making some money.

The first round was a game called Minority Winners. All players had to do was decide between black and white. That was it. Their fate rested on that one, simple decision. If they were in the minority once the count was tallied, they'd proceed to the next round; if they weren't, they were gone.

"Just ask Charlie. It's been agony. One day I'm sure I'll choose 'white', the next 'black', and then I'm back to having no idea what to choose."

"I keep telling her that it's simple. She just needs to listen to Wesley Snipes. In *Passenger 57* he says, 'Always bet on black.' Everyone knows that."

"I keep telling him that if everyone knows that and they all choose black, then it's going to be the majority choice, and I'll lose. Everyone knows *that*."

"And *I* keep telling *her* that that's what everyone will think, so they'll end up choosing white, meaning that black will be in the minority after all. She just needs to trust my man Wesley."

"Are you sure you're not simply arguing with Charlie so that you don't end up having had his help in making your decision?" Sushi turned to Charlie. "In case you hadn't noticed, Nova can be a stubborn do-it-herself at times."

Nova rolled her eyes as far back into her skull as they would go. "I programmed Computer Sushi to be as authentic as possible: super annoying. Speaking of which, I can't believe they gave us a whole week to decide. It's been way too long. Every time I make up my mind, I've still got time to change it again."

"You've not got long now," said Sushi. "Precisely two hours, thirty-eight minutes and nineteen seconds. Whatever colour you choose … choose it wisely, sister."

***

In all his years in post, which amounted to twice the average age of the undergraduates who lived there, Hu Stu Warden Professor Carmichael, had never seen so many of them crammed into the Common Room. He was a tall, stocky man who sported a wild flourish of nasal hair and had a penchant for expensive single malt whisky. After a short introductory speech, delivered with his usual flair, the room burst into rowdy applause.

Nova crept along the narrow stage to shake his hand and then turned to face two hundred or so of her fellow students.

"Thank you, Professor Carmichael, for such a complimentary introduction. It's been a stressful week, pondering such a simple choice. Just so that everyone knows, I made my decision about an hour ago, in secret. When I enter Solarversia, the people following my progress will see that choice for the first time. If I end up in the majority and go out, the professor has promised to pour me a double measure of his best whisky. And if I end up in the minority and go through to the next round, he's said he'll make it a triple."

She hoped people wouldn't notice her hands trembling as she slipped her Booners on and synced the display to the wall behind her. She traced the original constellation on the Corona Cube ceiling — the one that usually led to the Gameworld — and appeared standing within an immense domed structure located on the northern pole of Pluto's barren surface.

The structure was known as the Decision Dome. Over its vaulted ceiling and around its curved walls, black and white patterns swirled into one another, forming snowflakes one second, Rorschach inkblots the next, and kaleidoscopic blotches the moment after that. Nova had visited the dome every day that week to stare at the ceiling, searching for an answer it didn't contain.

Now she stood there, one tiny person among a million. All of them, she imagined, would be as nervous as her. Not that she cared. She just wanted to beat them. According to the figure in her display, three hundred and fifty million people around the globe were watching real-time video feeds of the event and, in all likelihood, they probably felt nervous and excited too. But surely none of them were shaking like she was.

As the moment neared, the black and white patterns morphed into a face. It was deformed by the concavity of the ceiling, but it belonged unmistakably to Arkwal the chimp. His cockney accent boomed around the dome, echoing off the walls.

"Ladies and gentlemen, boys and girls, welcome one and all to the Decision Dome. There *should* be a million of you here, but as ever, some people didn't bother submitting a decision in time. They play all year long, visit the Grandmasters, complete their Bucket Lists and then fail to make a silly little decision — unbelievable. To those of you here, well done and good luck. If luck has anything to do with it. In a few seconds, Ludi Bioski is going to teleport to the front of the room with his Orbitini. A partition will rise, dividing the dome in two, separating those who chose black from those who chose white."

Nova looked around in a vain attempt to work out which side of the dome was more heavily populated. Not that such knowledge would be of use to her now. Like everyone in the dome she was rooted to the spot she stood in. There could be no last-minute changes of mind.

"Those of you in the minority — and I can confirm that there is a minority — will continue on to the Portal of Promise for the next round, while those of you in the majority ... well, let's just say that you don't want to be in the majority, it's not so much fun. Well done if you chose white, by the way. Or was it black? I've never been good with colours."

As Arkwal's face melted back into a sea of swirling shapes, Nova suddenly felt the tension in her back and the heavy weight of expectation on her shoulders. At the front of the dome the teleport machine played its jingle in reverse, signalling Ludi Bioski's arrival. The teleporter looked different from usual. The upper part of the pole, usually so dense with signs that it looked like it must be the very centre of the Solarverse, was bare.

Ludi, standing with his back to the crowd, went to work on his Orbitini, altering sliders, flicking switches and pressing knobs. He retrieved a pair of wooden chopsticks from one of the many drawers and then opened a small glass cabinet buzzing with zapiers. Using the sticks to catch the first to escape, he fed it to a young bird-like creature whose squawking beak protruded from a little hole at the side of the machine.

When the bird had finished its treat, the Orbitini's Event Card screen flickered into life, displaying a coin balanced precariously on its side. The naked pole of the teleporter sprouted two signs. The one that said 'black' pointed to Nova's side. She knew there was one person in the crowd who would be happy whatever the outcome; she just hoped that Passenger 57 knew what he was talking about.

Now Ludi turned his attention away from the Orbitini to the stitches at the top of his head, which sutured the two halves of his skull together. With his fingers he began to pick at the haphazard stitching until it came loose. He pressed his fingers hard into the crevasse he had created and yanked the sides of his skull apart. The stitches that held his neck together ripped apart. He kept on pulling. His spine opened, and then his buttocks. He tore until every stitch down the length of his body had snapped open. His right side peeled away from his left until he stood, one foot apiece, as two distinct beings.

The black half of his body hopped over to Nova's side of the dome, the white half to the other. The patterned ceiling followed suit, the black and white splotches sliding apart until they were divided down the centre. A partition rose from the floor until it hit the roof, sealing off the halves.

A large section of dome flapped open behind black Ludi Bioski, revealing a long glass tunnel. With his one black eye in his dark half-face, he looked at the players assembled before him, raised his one charred hand and beckoned them forward. Then he turned and, with great speed and impressive mastery of balance, began to hop through the tunnel.

Around her people started to fret, worried expressions upon their faces. Where did the tunnel lead? Toward the Portal of Promise or certain death? As their feet became unstuck from the floor, the crowd surged forward, some players whooping with delight, others groaning with fear, an underlying atmosphere of trepidation pervading the room. Nova, excited one moment, panicked the next, went with the flow, inextricably drawn toward her fate.

Black Ludi reached the end of tunnel and stood, perfectly balanced on his one foot, on the verge of a huge circular abyss. A destination marker appeared on Nova's feed: the Portal of Promise.

"I'm through!" she yelled, although the people in the common room — having seen the marker on the video feed — had already erupted into applause. She flung back her goggles and jumped off the stage.

"Charlie, you're a genius," she said, kissing him again and again.

"Got to trust Wesley, I told you."

Professor Carmichael stepped back on to the stage, armed with a bottle and a shot glass.

"Up you come, Nova."

She winked at Charlie, gave Burner a high five and returned to her place.

"What's the next challenge then?" Carmichael asked while pouring her triple.

Nova checked her datafeed. A multitude of diving boards, differing in length, height and bounce, were positioned around the circumference of the colossal hole.

"Looks like a diving competition. I've got to choose a board, a type of dive, and perform a combination of moves to execute it. I practiced dives in the Simulator at the start of the year. Wasn't too good at them."

"This'll help focus you," he said, handing her the glass. She doubted it would, but the sound of two hundred odd students imploring her to down it in one couldn't be ignored. She necked it and did her best to disguise her revulsion as the stuff coursed down the back of her throat.

Pulling her headset back down, she looked around the entrance to the portal in earnest. Located in a semicircle of tiered seating around the far side of hole were millions of spectators, players who had gone out earlier in the year, there to egg the divers on, but also to take photos and footage, hoping to scoop one of the reportage prizes.

Enclosing the entrance was another giant dome, over which a festival of fireworks exploded in time to the music played live by a Japanese punk outfit who had won the spot in a quest earlier in the year. Hanging from the dome, hundreds of vines, like the ones in Castalia, allowed Gorigaroo to swing from side to side, while floating platforms hosted Banjax in his tank, Spee-Akka next to her easel and Emperor Mandelbrot, who was there to judge the dives.

One of the hands sticking out of the Emperor's base made the smallest of movements and brought the entire dome to a juddering, silent halt. From his position standing on the edge of Mandelbrot's dais, Arkwal cupped his hands and shouted through them to the assembled throng.

"Naturally, we were never going to let you reach the next round on luck alone; 471,089 of you chose 'black', and were in the minority. Only 400,000 of you will progress to the next round — those of you who perform best in the diving competition. The 71,089 players who perform worst will fall straight through the planet to be caught up in the cosmic radiation on the other side. Likewise, it would be unfair to the majority losers if they were to crash out due to luck. They'll face a challenge of their own. The most skilful 100,000 will join you in the sixth round. Good luck! Or should that be, good Science?"

Behind her, the feed from a cam on the white half of the dome was on display. On their side, the white half of Ludi Bioski had also hopped down a glass tunnel that had appeared when a section of dome flapped open. But instead of leading to the Portal, it led to a warehouse packed full of crazed circus animals. The majority losers were being forced to fight for their lives in front of a global audience.

The crowd in the common room laughed and jeered as the hapless losers were mauled, maimed, bitten and clawed. The animals seemed to take pleasure in working together to find new and novel ways of finishing people off. Arms were torn from bodies and rammed down throats, players were beaten to death with their own femurs. In a feat of mass gavage, a gaggle of players were force-fed a never-ending sea of blood until their innards exploded.

Nova volleyed back to the Portal's entrance, even less enthused by the prospect of diving now she knew what the stakes were. As if performing the dive in front of a global audience wasn't stressful enough, the carnival atmosphere around the hole made it impossible to concentrate.

Worse yet, a notification flashed in her display to advise her that Hollywood Rox had just completed a dive with a score 71.35, placing her in the top five percent. Nova cursed herself for following Holly's progress so closely. She turned notifications off and hoped she hadn't just felt the whisky take a turn for the worse in her stomach.

Doing her best to ignore her guts and the noise, she tried to get a plan together. Around the circumference of the hole, she could see thousands of other players taking run-ups, bouncing, twisting and somersaulting through the air. Others, who had stumbled, bumbled or crumbled, were screaming as they fell into the abyss.

Hundreds of arms had protruded from the Emperor's base, each one holding a placard which updated frequently to display another profile square emblazoned with a diving score. Arms were darting around all over the place to show players their placards, criss-crossing one another, getting entangled and generally adding to the chaos of the situation.

A range of dives appeared in her display, along with their combinations. She wondered why the moves had been provided and then smirked as she realised something. They weren't being tested on memory and skill, but rather memory, skill *and* psychological reasoning. There were twenty-seven dives in total — it was one of the longer modules in the Simulator — and the hardest ones were very difficult to pull off.

She pulled up her results from earlier in the year. Eight perfect scores on the easier ones, a bunch of moderately good scores on the intermediate ones and then a bunch of flunked dives — five of the hardest seven. The players flunking their dives around her had been guilty of one sin above all others — not pausing to think the challenge through. They'd seen the 'back two-and-a-half somersault two-and-a-half twist pike' at the top of the list and gone for it. A well-executed version of it *did* score very highly, after all. Except most of them were screwing the combo up, slipping on the board and falling to their likely deaths.

This was all about picking a dive of average difficulty — like the forward two somersault half twist pike — and performing it well. She selected it and followed the arrows that guided her to her board. It probably wouldn't win her one of the prizes on offer, but that didn't matter, reaching the Portal would be prize enough. Placing her feet in the marker spots, she did her best to get as much bounce as possible.

Once she launched into the air she writhed her body as best she could, following the combination on her display: a wiggle of hips, a synchronised wave of her hands, a shuffle of feet, and one final shimmy of the hips. She scored 45.65. It was way off the leading scores, but more importantly, way off the lowest ones too, comfortably placing her in the middle of the huge table of results.

Plunging into the black abyss, she joined the world's largest virtual skydive. Lining the interior of the cylindrical hole were thousands of platforms populated by dead players, there to watch the spectacle and get a glimpse of friends as they rushed by.

She stood spreadeagled on the stage, rotating her arms to move about, doing her best to catch a glimpse of people, the sound of their cheers increasingly dopplered, until sight and sound became one fused blur of ecstatic perception.

The distance to the core of the planet was 1,161 km, a journey that would take her 70 minutes to complete. During the fall she was free to flip, tumble and play with the half million other skydivers, and after falling for a few minutes she handed her headset to the crowd to let other people experience the ride. She had no idea what the other Minority Winners had planned by way of celebration, but she, for one, was going to party like her life depended on it.

Chapter Thirty-Nine

Despite the fact that he'd been in the *Risk* room dozens of times before and knew of its inclination to materialise horses, cannons and soldiers, when a holographic horse cantered out of the wall halfway through the meeting, Arty nearly jumped out of his seat.

He faked a minor coughing fit to cover the startled gasp that had escaped his mouth and settled himself back in his chair. Did Spiralwerks really need this meeting room theme now that they'd stumbled into, and were losing at, a real-world game of global domination? The Holy Order seemed to have achieved the upper hand before Arty even knew that Spiralwerks were playing. One false step and they could be crushed out of existence.

Unless this strategy meeting proved effective. That's what these talks were intended to avoid. Here he was, Field Marshal Artica Kronkite, with his general, Carl Stedman, talking tactics with potential comrades, the co-founders of Cerberus, the company behind Gogmagog. Carl leaned forward in his seat, eyes narrowed, listening to Max articulate the technical details of the software at machine-gun speed.

"It's takes all of those inputs — forum posts, tweets, Facebook status updates, photos, video feeds — and runs them through hundreds of proprietary semantic analysis algorithms, which compute the probability of danger for every set of related artefacts. Most clients don't tweak the algorithms, though you have the ability to. We've refined the machine learning software to such a degree that the automatic tweaks it makes are far superior to manual ones."

"If we did install Gogmagog, we'd want full control over the algorithms. I'd want to know how the software works, down to the smallest level of detail."

"That wouldn't be a problem, Carl, full training would be provided."

As Arty listened to the pitch, the tension in his stomach abated somewhat. He couldn't help but be impressed by these guys. Barely twenty years old, the two of them had dropped out of university to run their business a matter of months ago and had already taken calls from Downing Street and the Pentagon. They looked every part the hipster founders with their long, manicured beards, the matching caps sporting the Gogmagog logo, and the expensive tweed jackets. Max, who was six foot six, did most of the talking, while the diminutive Maurice interjected the occasional sage contribution.

"After what we saw here on New Year's Eve, we're sold on the computational aspect of the software," Carl said, to enthusiastic nods from Arty. "But there are two questions in my mind. The first regards the attacks that evening that *were* successful. The three people who *did* die. I appreciate that Gogmagog can't be everywhere, and analyse everything at all times ... but do you know why it failed to prevent those attacks?"

The critical alert received by Nova and Burner on New Year's Eve, and the subsequent analysis by MI6 and the FBI, had prevented seven of the twelve attempted attacks. But the other five had gone ahead as planned, targeting high-level employees at three tech companies, and a couple of US politicians.

Unsurprisingly, the press about the attacks had led to a surge of interest in the anti-terrorist preventative technology offered by companies like Cerberus. The topic of coveillance, where the public work in conjunction with the authorities on matters of national and international security, was trending everywhere, lauded by some, vilified by others.

"There's a clear reason why we chose a three-headed beast for our company mascot: it's a reminder to us all that many heads are better than one. Clichéd as that may be, it's also true. The times when national security forces could work alone, without public input and consent, are over. 'Input' is the crucial word here. The software is only as good as the amount of information being fed into it."

"We need more heads, so to speak," Maurice added.

"If more people had been using Gogmagog before the New Year, some of those attacks could have been averted too. It tears me up that it's taken something like this to garner so much interest in our work ... but it's clear how important this type of technology is, and how companies like yours stand to benefit."

"That brings me to my second question. I get that the results are directly proportional to the amount of information being fed in." Carl motioned to the sales literature adorning the smartwalls of the meeting room. "But the more information we feed it, the more servers we need to bring online, the higher our costs. And the kind of costs you're talking about amount to a serious proportion of our annual IT spend. Those heads don't eat for free."

Max launched into what sounded like a well-rehearsed comeback about the value of life and liberty versus that of cash money, but Arty could barely concentrate. The same thought that had been plaguing him since the start of Solarversia was back. Why were Spiralwerks at the top of the Order's corporate hit list? Why them and not one of the hundreds of other companies investing heavily in technology? After all was said and done, and though he'd never admit to this heresy in public, Solarversia *was* just a game. The attacks frightened and worried him. He only hoped that MI6 were getting somewhere with the captured cult members, before the Order could strike again.

***

Nova waited for Charlie to fall asleep on her bed before she traced the stars of the newest constellation. When the face of the Corona Cube became transparent, her display indicated that she should grab hold of the nearest vine and swing from one to the next to traverse the length of the Magisterial Chamber.

She came to rest in the southwest corner where Gorigaroo usually resided. He wasn't there, but the surface of his gong had transformed into a screen, and on it a thick, lush jungle came into view. Hoots and calls were heard as the picture moved through a web of leaves and vines before coming to rest on a caterpillar, perched on a wiry branch. The caterpillar stopped munching on his leaf and turned to address the group of players who were watching him.

"Once upon a time, in the tropical rainforests of Nakk-oo, an almighty commotion caused the animals to stop what they were doing and seek out the source of the upheaval. A crowd assembled between trunks and branches to see what had appeared. In the middle of the throng, leaning against dense, tangled vegetation, was a shiny golden disc, shoulder-high to an antelope. Nobody could agree on who had discovered it, quite what it was or who it belonged to. At the anteater's last count, seventeen different species had claimed it belonged to them, and the number was rising by the hour. The one thing every animal *could* agree on was that such a magnificent object would certainly possess magical properties and bring great fortune to whoever owned it.

"The tigers, who everyone knew were the handsomest animals in the kingdom, claimed that the god of beauty had left it there for *them*, so that they could admire their looks in its reflective surface all day long. 'Just look at our beautiful coats, the symmetry of our patterns and the way our green eyes twinkle in the disc. Qetesh the Sacred works in weird and wonderful ways. He must have sent us this hallowed mirror from the Promised Land.'

"'Enough of your conceited nonsense,' piped the parakeets. 'It looks just like the Sun, that's plain for all to see. As the guardians of the sky and the ring bearers of heaven, Krakatoa the Boundless, god of Sun and stars, would have left it here for us as thanks for our tireless service in Her realm all these years.'

"Just as another argument broke out, an elephant approached the disc and struck it with his powerful tusks. 'Hear me now,' cried the elephant. 'Everyone knows that we are the most musical animals in the kingdom. You can hear the call of our trumpets from one side of the jungle to the other. Listen to how the disc vibrates when I strike it — you will never find a more perfect accompaniment to our music. Belvedere the Harmonious has surely answered our humble prayers by giving us this instrument to play.'

"After endless hours of bickering, the animals could agree on one thing only — that a competition was the fairest way to decide ownership of the disc.

"'It should be a short race across the plains,' the cheetah said. 'The first animal to cross the finishing line will win the golden saucer.'

"'We agree that it should be a race,' the horse said slowly, 'but let us run over a long distance. The competition needs to be worthy of the prize, and not one that ends so soon after it has started.'

"'Of course you've both suggested races, you're the fastest animals in the kingdom,' said the Petrifier. 'But the disc looks heavy. This should be a competition of strength, not speed, for the victors must be able to take their prize with them when they win.'

"And so the discussion continued. It wasn't until evening fell that the animals, tired of their quarrelling, decided to ask the opinion of the Waterfall of Wisdom, an ancient being known for her impartial point of view. Every species delegated a member to represent them in the matter, and all the chosen animals travelled together through the dark green jungle, taking it in turns to carry the yellow enigma upon their backs, in their beaks, or over their heads.

"Arriving at the waterfall, they hurriedly related the story of the disc, each species once again articulating their own worthiness.

"'An interesting find,' the waterfall burbled. 'Leave the disc behind my falls this eve. Allow me to meditate on its secrets overnight. I shall give you my answer tomorrow.'

"Content with her response and worn out from the day's drama, the animals quickly fell asleep around the edge of her pool. Dreams came, of circles and spheres, of suns and stars, of music and mirrors. In the morning, the waterfall delivered her verdict, just as she had promised. Her falls parted like velvet curtains, revealing the disc resting against a ledge of rock. It twinkled as it reflected the turquoise water in her pool, rendering it more beautiful than any of them had remembered.

"'The disc you have brought before me is very special indeed. It contains secrets that haven't been spoken of in centuries. It comprehends mysteries beyond the mind. Creatures have died for it. Young have been born on it. And poets have gone mad trying to chronicle its infinite nature. It is priceless beyond word, enchanting beyond thought, ancient beyond time.'

"On hearing this, the animals leaned in closer, enraptured by what they were hearing.

"'Because of the disc's inordinate value, the law of the jungle dictates that it cannot be owned by a single species. And yet a competition to divine a deserving owner is befitting of the prize. I therefore propose a competition that requires each animal to form a pair with a beast of a different kind. The victorious duo will make arrangements to share ownership of the disc afterwards. Cast thy berries into my waters so that I may know your thoughts.'

"Standing at the edge of the pool, each animal cast a berry into the water: green if they agreed with the proposal, red if they did not, and a thorn if they were unsure, for that was the way of the jungle. Dozens of berries flew through the air, plopped into the pool, and descended to the bottom. When the last one had settled, the waterfall spoke again.

"'My waters are mostly green. The majority have decreed we continue.' The curtains of water closed once more and the disc was hidden. 'The disc was found in the jungle. As such, the competition must take place in the jungle. Stay by my waters another night, and when you wake tomorrow, the disc will be gone from my safekeeping. It will manifest elsewhere in the jungle. To win the race, and ownership of the disc, you and your teammate must be the first to find it. Thus speaks the Waterfall of Wisdom.'

"This latest pronouncement was met with lots of murmuring as the animals sought to untangle its implications. They spent the rest of the day in a frenzy of politics, trying to pair themselves, blindly stabbing for strategy in an exercise that saw plenty of boasts and just as many put-downs. When the cockerel crowed at dawn the next day, his partner the hare scampered behind the falls and saw that the disc was gone. Soon all the animals were awake, and the strangest hunt in the history of the jungle began.

"Some animals believed that the Obarian and the leopard would be the ones to win, so well did they seem to complement each other's abilities. But they turned out to be as stubborn as they were speedy, and argued more than they searched. Others thought the Huntropellimous and the squirrel might end up triumphant, and when the squirrel was seen bolting back to the waterfall with a smile on her face, many thought the competition would soon be over. But to everyone's delight, the squirrel had merely remembered where she'd hidden a supply of nuts.

"All day the animals roamed in their pairs over the jungle. The dolphin scoured the river while the parrot searched from the sky. But it was two landlubbers who found the golden disc, hanging from the branch of a monkey puzzle tree, sparkling and resplendent in the sun. The gorilla and the kangaroo — a pair in whom nobody had invested much hope.

"It turned out that the victors had worked together with great camaraderie. In the clearings of the jungle, the gorilla had clambered on to the kangaroo's back and, clasping his legs tightly round his partner's shoulders, the two had hopped as one. When the jungle floor was dense and impassable, the kangaroo had clung to the gorilla's waist, and together they'd swung from the branches and dangled from vines. Where the jungle was neither clear nor dense, they separated a distance and combed the vegetation in a deliberate and methodical manner.

"Folklore has it that the golden disc *was* magical and could grant its owner a wish. The gorilla and the kangaroo had to share the wish between them. Here their partnership continued. Rather than argue and squabble over what they desired, they made a wish to be united forever. In the ultimate act of synthesis, the gorilla and the kangaroo became one: the Gorigaroo. And what became of the disc? Why, you know it well, it's Gorigaroo's gong. When he strikes it with the club he carries in his pouch, the sound is a reminder of their teamwork that day. We remember that when we come together as one, we can achieve great things."

Nova finished the tour and gazed at Charlie as he slept. If she hadn't taken his advice to choose 'black' in the Minority Winners round, she'd be deader than dead right now, lying in a pool of avatar blood somewhere in the Decision Dome.

She kissed his forehead and quietly thanked him for his help. It dawned on her that he was only one of many people who had helped her get this far. Burner, Jono and the Solar Soc crew had all played their part. Even Computer Sushi, in her own way, by calling her stubborn in front of Charlie, and making her self-conscious about being so.

She gently lowered her head onto Charlie's chest, closed her eyes and enjoyed the moment for what it was. And when she fell asleep soon after, she dreamed of circles and spheres, of suns and stars, of music and mirrors, and of the teamwork that lay ahead.

Chapter Forty

Nova felt a chill go down her spine as the Huntropellimous charged at her. She remembered the horribly violent way she'd lost her second life after teleporting to the wrong destination with Burner and Pedro. Would another death at the hands — or, in this case, the freakishly mutilated claws — of these deranged scorpions signal her exit from Solarversia in the second of the final rounds?

She looked down at the Sword of Sadism clenched tight in her fists. The jewels in its long, curling grip sparkled, while the polished edge of its blade reflected the monster clattering towards her. She slid her thumb over the dark blue sapphire to activate it and hoped to high hell that she remembered the only combination of moves that would save her life.

The second round had started two hours previously in a more tranquil setting — Pluto's Portal of Promise, the same place she'd been all week since completing the epic skydive. The core of the planet had been hollowed out into a sphere whose surface sparkled like plasma, similar to the walls of the Corona Cube.

She'd been there with the 500,000 other players who had survived the first round, gently floating and frolicking in zero-g until the Portal had been switched on. It had started with a distant hum, like a vacuum cleaner being used in a nearby room, and had got progressively louder until the plasma patterns on the wall convulsed in an angry, moody dance. Blue sparks leapt off the surface, zapping players out of existence.

One second Nova was drifting about the portal in peace, the next she was hurtling through a cosmic wormhole dug out of hyperspace. She landed with a bump in a crumpled heap, brushed herself down, got back up and took a moment to get her bearings. She'd arrived in a small cubic room whose walls were adorned with pictures. *Puzzles*. Her hands tingled with excitement. If the Science of

Solarversia hadn't demanded a balanced diet, she'd be doing them all day, every day. Hopefully the round was full of them. One thing was guaranteed — she'd need to be on top of her game. Where the previous round had wiped out half of Solarversia's population, this round would deplete it a further *eighty* percent.

"Greetings, second-round players."

It took her a second or two to locate the source of Arkwal's voice. Looking up, she found that the ceiling had turned transparent, affording a view of Castalia's Magisterial Chamber where all the entourage were present, including a re-stitched Ludi Bioski.

"You might find the view a little strange. Although you're looking up, through the ceiling, you see us in the Magisterial Chamber from a side-on perspective. That's because you're standing on the northern wall of the Chamber in one of the four corner cubes of the Player's Grid. In this round, called Race to the Origin, you get to play the grid itself. Although you can't see them — the cubes are phased zones — there are 125,000 other players in the cube with you, a quarter of the players who have made it this far. Although you're all familiar with how Puzzles work, let's look at how to use them to navigate the grid. Please turn to face the painting of the Mona Lisa. You'll notice something strange about her smile — something stranger than usual. Her mouth is upside down. Please approach the painting and rotate her mouth through 180 degrees. Chop chop, we don't have all day."

Nova rotated the mouth using her finger and the Solarversia jingle sounded. The wall that had been displaying the painting disappeared, revealing the cube next to hers in a clockwise direction. After five seconds the wall reappeared, once again enclosing her within the corner cube.

"Now face the adjacent wall. It contains a sixteen-square slide puzzle of a famous photo. Because you're in training mode, a series of arrows will guide you through the correct moves. They won't be there when the game begins, and neither will the instructions for any Combinations you're asked to execute."

She recognised the photo even in its jumbled state — it was Albert Einstein sticking his tongue out. The photo had been divided into sixteen squares, and had had one square removed so that the remaining fifteen could be moved around. She smiled as she slid the squares back and forth. It was a type of puzzle she'd played dozens of times in the Simulator Booths throughout the year, and one she'd mastered without the presence of arrows. Hopefully there would be lots like it.

Completing this puzzle had the same effect, sounding the jingle and dissolving the wall on which it had been displayed to reveal the cube next to hers in an anticlockwise direction. Arkwal made them repeat the exercise one last time on one of the outer faces of the Grid. The wall displayed a crossword puzzle, complete except for one twelve-lettered word, which already contained the third letter, an 'm' and the eleventh letter, an 'o'. The clue read, '*Fun way of solving problems as organised by fit magician with oxygen*'.

She smiled and made a mental note to let her dad know that his years of teaching hadn't gone unrewarded. Clues in cryptic crosswords were little puzzles in their own right. All you needed to do was work out how to interpret them. This one was elementary and she solved it in seconds just by looking at it. She proudly scribbled the answer — *gamification* — on the wall using her finger before Arkwal provided it to everyone else.

"Please note that the outer face of the grid goes somewhere too — it connects to the cube on the far side of the grid, ten thousand rows away. Every one of the hundred million cubes in the grid is connected to the cubes adjacent to it. All you need to remember is that if there's a puzzle on the face of the cube you're in, whether it's the wall, ceiling or floor, it leads to another cube somewhere. *If you can solve the puzzle, that is.* The goal of Race to the Origin is simple: you need to get from the outer ring to cube number one in the very centre of the grid. The hard part is ensuring that you're one of the first hundred thousand people to do so."

Nova gulped. Minority Winners, with its single, binary decision, suddenly seemed like a walk in the park.

"There's no way I can do this. I'm going to crash out, I just know it."

"You're just having a last-minute attack of nerves," Burner said. "If anyone can do it, you can do it."

"And we're right here to help you," Charlie said, rubbing the back of her neck as he spoke.

Thank God for her front-line support team — her 'crack commando unit', according to Burner — there to help her solve puzzles and navigate the grid. Players were allowed as many people as they wanted in their support team, although as Arkwal had reminded them earlier in the week, too many cooks spoil the broth. So she'd chosen to tackle the round in her own room, rather than the common room, which everyone agreed might be too rowdy.

Additionally, students in her corridor had agreed to have their rooms turned into mini command centres that hosted specialised teams: maths bods, puzzle fans, subject specialists and so on. Jono, the overall project manager, would be dipping into each room and publishing the best comments and suggestions in a datafeed that Burner and Charlie could review. He'd also lent Nova his quality speakers, so any game sounds or instructions would be crystal clear. It was the best setup they could think of. She only hoped it would be good enough.

"There are two other things you need to know. First, you will always be able to tell which cube you're in and how far it is it from the Origin because each of its internal faces is stamped with the cube's number and ring position."

Nova glanced at the bright blue stamp that adorned each face of the cube: Ring: 5,000, Grid Number: 99,990,001. She was in the top-left hand corner of the grid.

"Second, the behaviour of the Grid during the round will be similar in nature to that of Solarversia as a whole. That is to say, the gameplay will *evolve* as the game progresses. As usual, those changes will be signalled by the sound of Gorigaroo's gong. Without further ado, I'm delighted to announce that the Emperor himself will start the proceedings. The moment he starts singing, the grid becomes live. Good luck to one and all."

Although the exact shape of his body altered by the minute, Emperor Mandelbrot had maintained roughly the same form throughout the year. The purple gooey substance he was composed of still dripped over the edge of the circular dais on which he was positioned. Arms, legs and faces still poked out of his body, the central column of which still rose all the way to the ceiling of the chamber, a deformed totem pole punctured with hundreds of grotesque mouths. His song started with the mouths at the bottom of the pole. Several bass voices set the tone of the song before the chanting crept upward to the contraltos and sopranos closer to the ceiling. The Race to the Origin had begun.

***

The first hour of the game was spent getting to grips with the different kinds of puzzle on offer. Like the Grandmaster Puzzles, they were of an abstract nature and therefore ungooglable. In addition to the slide puzzles and cryptic crosswords clues, there were distorted songs to identify, abstract images to recognize and trivia of the most miniscule order about movies, books, games and celebrities.

Gorigaroo first struck his gong after half an hour, causing Ludi Bioski to turn the prime-numbered cubes into teleport machines. Stampedes to the closest prime-numbered cube were followed soon after by the sobering realisation that teleporting wasn't necessarily a helpful thing to do. From what Burner was able to gather from the datafeeds, although tokens weren't needed, it looked like a player could only teleport three times.

To confuse matters further, every machine was fitted with a TeleTrixis device, so that while some players teleported thousands of spaces closer to the centre, others had ended up in cubes on the outer ring, back where they'd started. When Gori next struck his gong, an hour after the round had started, Burner's datafeed went crazy.

"Holy roly-poly. I had a feeling Ludi might try something like this." Burner frantically scratched his scalp. "Those batshit-crazy animals have joined the fun. Looks like they're entering the grid through the Fibonacci sequence. I'll stick the numbers on the wall so we can monitor them."

He moved data between his tablet and the smart wall while Charlie looked on, entranced. "It looks like the Fibonacci numbers between one thousand and a hundred million — 23 in total — have become gateways connected to the white half of the Decision Dome on Pluto. Animals are spilling into those 23 cubes at a rate of knots."

At that moment Jono stuck his head into their room. "Somebody just had a good idea: it seems to be the special numbers — Primes, Fibonaccis and so on — that are being targeted by Ludi Bioski. The maths bods have drawn up a list of other special numbers that might be affected when Gori next strikes his gong. They'll ping the list round so that everyone can monitor it."

Nova smiled. Although she was exhausted, having spent the week cramming puzzle practice on top of her normal schedule of lectures and early morning runs, it felt awesome having teams of specialists working on her behalf. As she slotted the final piece of a jigsaw puzzle into place on the wall in front of her, it disappeared and she walked through to the next cube — a prime-numbered cube in ring 4,213 that Burner had been guiding her towards for the last twenty minutes.

"According to the datafeeds, the machine in this cube is teleporting people closer to the origin 92% of the time. It's the most reliable machine in this section of the grid."

He pointed at the map of the grid on the wall while he spoke to show Charlie what he meant.

"But what about this one here? It looks like it's got a 94% rating. Or am I reading the map wrong?"

"No, you're right. But look at the state of *this* cube." He pointed to another close by.

"It's one of the Fibonacci numbers. And the animals have started to spread into the cubes surrounding it."

"Exactly. That teleport machine might have a better rating, but it's more dangerous in the overall scheme of things. That's why the maths team suggested this one. They've built a data model that uses the position of the animals and the teleporters as inputs to spit out suggested routes — similar to how the Route Planner works."

"And the teleporters work in the same way they've always worked?"

"Not quite. Usually you'd type in your destination coordinates, but the keypads have been disabled. I guess otherwise people would just type in the origin every time. It looks like the mechanics of how you trace round the keypad have remained in place, though. In cubes above the origin, and in the central row, you need to dial in a clockwise direction. Below the origin, you go anticlockwise. Doing it wrong seems to increase the probability of getting sent the wrong way."

Nova volleyed an eye back to the room for a second. "Finish your lecture, Professor, I'm ready to go."

Charlie and Burner exchanged a nervous look. The last thirteen players to use this machine had been teleported closer to the origin. They watched as Nova made a clockwise circular motion around the keypad. The signpost started its rotation. It bore only a single sign, which read '*Somewhere in the Grid*'. She clenched her fists and death-stared the sign, willing it to end up pointing anywhere more central.

Instead a flashing, beeping alert began. An earthquake of magnitude 3 was to begin in three seconds and she had to survive it without any outside help if she wanted to head towards the Origin. Failure to complete the Combo would send her back to the outer reaches of the Grid.

It should have been simple. She'd completed the earthquake sim enough times that she *did* know the Combinations by heart. There were ten of them — one for each of the numbers on the Richter scale — and the number of moves in the combo was the number on the scale multiplied by two. That meant a magnitude 3 quake had six moves in it. The timer announced that she had five seconds in which to complete the Combo.

She put her hands on her hips and thrust forwards. Shrugged her left shoulder. Performed a squat. And then she froze. What came after the squat, a shrug of her right shoulder, or a rotation of the hips? It was one, and then the other, she knew that much. But the sequence got reversed in a magnitude 4 quake, and right now, with everything going on, she couldn't remember which was which.

The counter timed out, and a couple of seconds later she materialised at her destination. The long, strangled gurgling sound that left her mouth had never before been uttered by a human being, and certainly couldn't be found in a dictionary, however comprehensive. Burner almost apologised to Charlie for her, worried that he might dump her on the spot.

"I'm back in ring 4,721? You have got to be having a laugh Mr Mandelbrot, you purple blobby turd." Volleying back to the room, she looked at Burner. He mouthed the words in time with her. "Magnitude 3 quake: thrust, squat, right shoulder shrug, hip rotation, squat, thrust." She threw her hands in the air and jutted her bottom jaw outward as far as it would go. "How come I remember it now, two seconds after it's needed?"

"Eighty minutes of work down the toilet," Burner said before collapsing on to her bed, head in his hands.

Charlie positioned himself behind Nova and started to massage her shoulders again. "Come on, guys, it's not lost yet. Nova, perk up, you're losing vital seconds. Nobody's got to the Origin yet, so there's a hundred thousand places left, and one of them has your name on it."

As Charlie gave his pep talk, a new video appeared on the wall, showing the cheering avatar of a young Lithuanian guy, Matas the Mole, the first person to make it to the Origin.

"I'll sit down and stop talking for a bit," Charlie said, creeping back to his chair.

The next hour flew by. Nova was mostly on autopilot, a robotic lab rat being guided through a gargantuan virtual maze by Dr Burner and co. She'd enter a new cube and scan the puzzle on the wall that formed part of her route. Then she'd volley an eye back to the map on the wall to confirm that the suggested route remained unchanged. If so, they'd all work together on solving the puzzle and progressing through the grid. She'd just entered a new cube when Gori struck his gong for the third time.

"I reckon you stay where you are for a second, mate, until we know what's hap—"

"What was that noise? It certainly didn't sound like an animal." Charlie turned the volume up and cocked his head to one side. "It sounds like metal being twisted or a large lever being wrenched."

Burner pointed at a video feed being highlighted by the people in the common room. "Check this out. It's a bird's-eye view of the grid from where the Emperor's sitting. That sound is the grid itself. It's being deformed."

"What does this mean for the route, does it change, or do I keep on going?"

The corridor burst into activity as everyone tried to understand the implications of the change. Some sections — like Nova's — had remained unchanged, lying flat against the north wall. Others had buckled outward, away from the grid, and rolled up on themselves like pieces of old carpet. The occasional row of numbers, some as long as a hundred cubes, had pronged outward at right angles, protruding like pins from a cushion. Volleying to Emperor Mandelbrot's point of view, it was clear that the grid was taking the form of the Milky Way — swirling arms spiralling out from a central mass.

"Earth to Burner — what's the latest on my route? Fifty thousand people have made it to the Origin already; we need to act fast."

Burner grimaced. "I wish I knew. According to the maths guys this changes everything — the new structure makes it exponentially more difficult for their model to suggest optimal routes. There are too many variables involved now."

They all froze. The sound of twisting metal had started again, only this time it was much louder. Nova turned her full attention back to the cube she was in — it was on the move. The floor beneath her became a slope. She slipped backward until she came to rest on the wall behind her, a wall that soon became the new floor. Once she'd picked herself up, she discovered two things: the puzzles had changed, and there was timer ticking down from three minutes.

"Oh, great, a time limit has been introduced. A nice double whammy from our friend Ludi. And you're telling me that we no longer have a plan? That I should just go any—"

"Wherever you're going, you want to go there fast — there's something in the adjoining cube." Charlie leaned in and winced at the screen. "An *Acoo-Stickular* — not sure if I'm pronouncing that right? According to its profile, it's a multicoloured waveform that travels at a rate of 10% of the speed of sound."

Burner's eyeballs rotated up into his skull as if he was trying to read the label on the back of his eyebrows. "The speed of sound is roughly 750 miles per hour, so these things travel at 75 miles per hour, and the cube sides are three metres in length. Oh, dear. They're bouncing against the sides about eight times every second — there's no way you'll be able to dodge one if—"

Anticipating its arrival, Nova used one of her five precious Force Fields to split the cube in half and prevent the newly arrived waveform from striking her. The field would last thirty seconds — after that, she was a goner for sure. Once it made contact with her, it would burrow through skin and bone, attuning her DNA to its own frequency, after which she would collapse to her knees, grab her throat and scream until she could no more.

She turned to face the other wall, which asked a simple question: the house number of the Bueller family home in the film *Ferris Bueller's Day Off*. Charlie had found the movie in her collection and was already skipping through various scenes. With only five seconds left on the field, he stumbled onto the scene when Ed Rooney, Dean of Students, paid an unexpected visit to Ferris' house. Nova shouted "2800," and dove into the next cube as the wall turned transparent.

It was a prime-numbered cube that contained a teleporter. She didn't have time to process any fear of the TeleTrixis device; the waveform was too close and too fast for that. She dialled around the keypad and held her breath. Seeing that she'd been transported to ring 2,566, halfway to the Origin, she let out an impromptu yelp and hugged the boys, only to be interrupted a few seconds later when the sound of the gong echoed through the room.

"Another change? This is ridiculous, they're getting more frequent."

"And without wanting to urinate further onto your second-round bonfire, there's now fewer than five thousand safe spots left," Charlie said, pointing to the counter on the wall.

Burner grabbed hold of a clump of his hair. "Do you want the bad news or the very bad news? The time limit for each cube just got reduced to one minute. If you fail to solve a puzzle in that time, the floor falls away and you get sucked down a pipe that leads to Banjax's tank. Looks like a one-way kinda journey. To make matters worse, the prime-numbered cubes are exploding, destroying the teleport machines and setting the grid on fire. Hang on a second. Yup, the fire's spreading to adjacent cubes. So I guess that last bit means that I had three pieces of news: some bad news, some very bad news and some very, very—"

"Burner, shut up, please. I get what you're saying. I'm totally screwed."

The answer to one of the current puzzles flashed in her display, answered by one of the support teams, and Nova was able to enter another cube, resetting the timer to one minute.

She shook her head as she looked at the carnage on the wall. The map showed animals everywhere, teleporters out of commission, and large swathes of the grid on fire. A lucky few players had made it to the central-most rings and had only a handful of puzzles ahead of them before they would reach the Origin. It was difficult to judge which was moving faster: the counter totting up the deaths or the counter ticking down the remaining positions.

The glint of a tear welled in her eye. She gently pulled her headset off her face and wiped it away in a discrete motion, grateful that the boys were too absorbed in the map to notice.

"Wait a second," Charlie said. "You're in a cube next to one of those special numbers, the Italian-sounding ones."

"The Fibonacci numbers. You're right, but how does that help, Nova?"

"Look at the map. Everyone's heading towards them. I don't know what exactly, but something good must be going on."

Nova looked to Burner for confirmation. His finger was raised as he scanned various parts of the grid. "The lad's right. He's bloody well right. Nova, quick — through the wall."

The answer to the puzzle — name that distorted tune — had already been provided by somebody in the common room. Nova barked '*Shine On You Crazy Diamond*', leapt into the Fibonacci-numbered cube as the wall dissolved and was sucked through the gateway into the white side of the Decision Dome. There at the front of the room was a teleport machine, the one Ludi Bioski had used to arrive in the Minority Winners round.

"Run," shouted Burner. "No wonder everybody's heading here. That's an unexploded teleporter, with its keypad intact. Bloody genius."

Nova was only thirty metres from the machine when the boys yelled at her to stop. A Huntropellimus had followed her through the cube and was charging at full speed. At least she was prepared this time. A lengthy analysis of every circus animal had revealed their strengths and weaknesses. Most importantly, she now knew which of her items would work best given the situation. In this case, the Sword of Sadism, bequeathed to her on New Year's Eve.

It was one of the few items that enabled a solitary player to defeat a Huntropellimus — if they could perform the complex combination of moves correctly. Fortunately, that included any Solo worth their salt. As soon as her thumb left the dark blue sapphire encrusted in the sword's grip, the weapon came alive. As the boys looked on, she spun her arms round her head in an intricate series of moves that was designed to turn the Sword into a genuine weapon of mass destruction.

She completed the kata of moves and sent her avatar spinning through the air like a whirlwind. It was payback time, and the Huntropellimous didn't stand a chance. She ripped into it and sliced its armour plating to shreds while Burner and Charlie whooped in delight. As soon as she'd dispatched the beast, she used the weapon to whirl up a personal tornado that whizzed her towards the machine.

Behind her, a small platoon of Petrifiers spilled into the Dome, eager for a kill. For them it was too late. Finding the machine free of TeleTrixis devices, she dialled the coordinates of the grid's Origin and held on tight. The jingle sounded and Hu Stu erupted into spontaneous applause. She had done it. Nova Negrahnu had raced to the Origin.

Chapter Forty-One

Everyone around him was watching the gameplay unfold on the giant screens at the front of the office, but Arty couldn't concentrate on work. It was the third of the final rounds, and he knew it ought to matter to him, but somehow, it didn't. Holding the replacement Grid Runner trophy in his hands, he kept tracing his finger over the two figurines running along its top. It had been 3D-printed a few days after the original had been broken in the SWAT team raid, an attempt by his colleagues to return some level of normality to the workplace.

An informal vote had decreed that the odd-numbered Bomb Jacks would have won the game and deserved to keep the trophy for the year. It was a nice touch, a genuine attempt to make him feel better. But it wasn't enough to keep his mind on the present. He couldn't help but think that the figurines represented him and Hannah, running away from the Holy Order toward the safety and protection of a safe house.

He'd been preoccupied with thoughts like it ever since a call had come through late the previous evening requesting that the two of them clear their morning diaries. The call was from MI6, and he'd been given the distinct impression that it wasn't the kind of meeting you declined to attend if you wanted to stay on side of Queen and Country.

The meeting had taken place at Legoland, as the headquarters of the British Secret Intelligence Service was known. The level of precaution they took in the building had been impressive: government secrecy and non-disclosure forms to sign, passport checks, retinal scans, thermal imaging, and CCTV wherever you went.

You couldn't walk more than ten metres in the building without having to undergo some form of security check, which had made Arty wonder how the people who worked there every day managed to maintain their grip on reality. They'd been met at reception by Deborah — he'd doubted that was her real name — who had apologized for the exacting security measures and the short notice they'd been given, almost as if she meant it.

They eventually arrived at a meeting room on the fourth floor. After another round of retinal scans, the machine beeped, the door whooshed and 'Deborah' ushered them into the quiet beige meeting room where her colleague, a slim man with a balding pate, introduced himself as Andrew and invited them to take a seat at the table.

"Deborah and I are assigned to the Holy Order's case. Following the events of New Year's Eve, we detained several of their members and have been working with National Security Operatives from around the globe to ascertain anything that may lead us to the group's HQ. As a result of extensive questioning since then, we've made a number of intelligence breakthroughs."

Arty glanced at the pair of them. In their light grey suits and crisp white shirts that wouldn't have looked out of place on a trading floor in the city, they looked every part the nondescript, upper-middle class couple. Thirty-something, attractive in a plain kind of way, he couldn't help but wonder whether either of them had ever killed anyone. And if so, how. What had Andrew meant exactly by putting so much emphasis on the phrase 'extensive questioning'?

"We need you to take a look at the photos in this file. It's crucial that you tell us everything you know about this man and his time at Spiralwerks."

Arty exchanged a startled look with Hannah. His time at *Spiralwerks*? While Deborah maintained her flight attendant's demeanour, Andrew slid an unmarked leather folder across the desk. Arty reached for it and opened the cover slowly, afraid of what he might see. In a pouch were several photos of the same man, which, from his ever-wizened look and the growth of his beard, appeared to have been taken years apart. Arty and Hannah spread them out on the glass-topped table, and looked intently at each one until the name of the man staring back at them clicked into place.

"Isaac Markowsky," they said in unison, after a short pause.

"But he didn't work here in London, he was based in Palo Alto in the United States."

"In Santa Clara County," Hannah added. "I think I only recognise his face from the grid. I don't think I ever met him in person."

"We have an Employee's Grid at Spiralwerks," Arty continued, suddenly aware of his apologetic tone. "We use it as an org chart."

"Have you met him in person, Artica, or do you just know him from this 'grid'?" Andrew said, motioning with his hands as if grappling with an invisible structure.

"I met him a few times. But it was years ago. He worked in Puzzles. The department, I mean. He became the top AI programmer in that division."

"Artificial intelligence?"

"Yes. It became obvious early on that Solarversia would need tens of millions of unique puzzles so that people couldn't cheat. The Grandmaster Puzzles on each of the planets, for instance. That's what Isaac worked on — AI to create unique puzzles."

"How does artificial intelligence work in that context?"

Arty had to stop himself from giving his default answer, the one he gave to nosy journalists or prying competitors, the one that usually included phrases like 'trade secrets' and 'Spiralwerks' Special Sauce'.

"Early on we figured that puzzles could be reverse-engineered, the same way that checkers and chess have been. For each type of puzzle you have a certain number of inputs, a list of rules that the inputs need to follow and the goals the player is trying to reach. Turns out that most puzzles can be reduced to lines of code. Isaac was very good at writing programs that created puzzles people really enjoyed playing. You know, clever puzzles, the kind that make you sit back and smile once you've finally solved them, the kind whose brilliance you can't help admiring. Aesthetically pleasing puzzles, if you will."

"What were his reasons for leaving the company?" Deborah asked. "I mean, you say he was very good at what he did. Then he was made redundant."

Arty started, and then stopped, speaking several times. Was any of this — the attacks, the deaths — *his* fault? Had he made a decision, innocent enough at the time, that had had a domino-like effect, cascading outward, into the company and then the wider world?

"He *was* very good at what he did. His main objective was to write a program that could automatically generate the kind of puzzles we're talking about. He achieved it, and I'm not sure we had any further use ..." Arty tailed off, aware of how callous it sounded out loud.

"Your Isaac Markowsky now goes by the name of Theodore Lucas Markowsky. It appears that his redundancy and the events immediately following it had a cathartic effect on his life. He became a man on a mission. It didn't take long for him to gain a following of like-minded people. He's the person we're after — he's the leader of the Holy Order." Deborah glanced to Andrew as if handing him the interrogation baton while Arty shifted about in his chair, unable to stay comfortable.

"You've read his manifesto? He's obsessed with creating a superintelligent being — the 'Magi' — who he reckons has the ability to cure Earth of its ills. According to him, AI is a zero-sum game where the winner takes all, and he's paranoid that corporations like yours might beat him to it. That, and the grudge he bears toward you for the way your company treated him, explains why your company was the top of their list," Andrew said. "The Order have members dispersed around the globe, they have serious funding and they have a charismatic lunatic at their helm. They're very dangerous. We need you to do everything you can to help us stop them."

"Of course. But what can we do?"

"We need you to send us everything you have on him. I'd also like you to reach out to the people who worked closely with him, find out as much as you can. Agents in the US will contact your colleagues out there, but if you hear anything in the meantime, please let us know. "

Hannah raised a finger, a gesture that said she'd take the task. If anything, Arty was glad to see that she looked as out of her depth as he was. Raising his hand like a schoolchild meek before authority, Arty chose his words carefully.

"There's something I don't understand about the Order, something that doesn't make sense. Why not do it the easy way?"

"I'm not sure I follow," Andrew said. "Do what the easy way?"

"Well, any of it. They scan a load of homeless people to create avatars so they can carry out a griefing attack. They sabotage the mayor's visit with a video nasty. They hack us, not to steal data, but to display their manifesto on the bookshelves of a few virtual spaceships for twenty minutes or however long it took Carl to fix. Not to mention the elaborate attacks on New Year's Eve. They train people to be clowns and magicians. Ceramic knives are smuggled past metal detectors. I'm a middle-aged, out-of-shape scaredy-cat. Why not just break into my house and smother me in my sleep? The same with the other attacks. The girl who helped find the training ground in the first place, they devise a convoluted plan to stuff her Electropet full of explosives. Wouldn't it have been easier to run her over or stab her or something? Like I said, I don't get it."

Now it was Andrew's turn to speak slowly and deliberately. "We haven't pieced it all together yet. The people we captured only know part of the story. Under Markowsky's leadership, the Order is something of a quasi-religious organisation

— a cult. He worships this Magi being like it's a deity, even if it doesn't actually exist yet. A lot of the symbolism and mythology they use derives from his time at Spiralwerks. I believe Solarversia utilises a number of non-player characters within its world — Emperor Mandelbrot and his merry men. Visitors from a far-off galaxy. Is that right?"

Arty sat back in his chair, wide-eyed, thrown by the question. What did the Emperor have to do with anything?

"Yes, Emperor Mandelbrot is like the host of The Game. And his entourage interact with real players within the virtual world. We built an entire mythology around these characters."

"It would appear that they resonated with Markowsky. He's obsessed with the idea of communicating his vision through the interpretative lens of Solarversia. We believe he sees himself as the Emperor, with an entourage at his disposal — the members of the Order. From what we've been told, it seems that the randomness of the first wave of attacks were an homage to Ludi Bioski. The attacks on New Year's Eve were planned to usher in the New Year in the same way that Gorigaroo strikes his gong to signal the start of a game or to signal changes to the rules during it. The attacks themselves were designed to be works of art, just like your—"

"Spee-Akka Dey Bollarkoo, the telepathic artist from Nakk-oo. What about Banjax and Arkwal, do they come in to it?"

"We're unsure about Arkwal. We understand that he's a bit like the Emperor's right-hand man, his chief of staff. There are suggestions that Markowsky may have something planned for one of his senior lieutenants. And as for Banjax, according to one of the guys we've spoken to, Markowsky has a special place in his heart for him. Apparently this all started when the creature appeared to him in a vision on the 12th of December in the year of his redundancy. He took that as a sign — a twelve-armed creature appearing on the twelfth day of the twelfth month. Hence the twelve-paged manifesto where each page contained a verse with twelve lines. The short answer to your question, Mr Kronkite, is that Markowsky doesn't do things the easy way. Apparently, that's not how one heralds the arrival of a superintelligent being."

As soon as they returned from the meeting, Hannah secured a copy of Markowsky's work history from HR. They read it together, hunched over her desk, turning the pages only when both were finished.

It made for compelling reading. Originally Spiralwerks had employed around four hundred people in the Puzzles department, before some projections were made that forecasted a need to expand that team to many thousands of employees. But then Isaac Markowsky, a puzzle engineer, had gone to the Director's office one day to pitch a program he'd written.

Arty almost fell out of his chair when he read a transcript of the emails. There it was, staring back at him from the screen. Markowsky had originally called his program *Machine Automated Gaming Intelligence*, or M.A.G.I., for short. Arty had liked the idea, but not the name, and over the course of a few weeks, it had become known as AIPuM, the *Artificially Intelligent Puzzle Machine*, the name he, Hannah and everyone else recognised it as.

Instead of creating hundreds of new jobs, the Puzzles AI team was formed, led by Markowsky. His program was so productive that it put most of the four hundred original employees out of work in the space of a few months, leaving only a top-level management team to oversee progress.

Reading through the program's technical specification, Arty couldn't help but be struck by how similar its AI construct was to the program that powered Gogmagog. Its semantic intelligence algorithms sucked in tens of thousands of examples of each puzzle type, then learned to make its own. The artificially generated puzzles were freely distributed to anyone who wanted to play them.

Feedback was immediate and rich. Puzzles that never got completed were discarded. They were the bad apples. Puzzles that got played to the end, rated highly and commented on, were the good apples — ones the program's algorithms used to inform and design the next generation of puzzles. It was a combination of natural selection and digital selection, a weird, symbiotic mix of the two. A year later Isaac released a new version of the program that created puzzles of such a high standard that human supervision was no longer required. He had literally written himself out of a job.

Behind him, Arty's colleagues broke into another round of applause. The third round was called Bounty Hunter. It was a cruel one that Arty had devised after a thrashing at poker one evening.

The surviving hundred thousand players had started the round in the Northdome, the large hemisphere affixed to the northern face of Castalia. In each stage of the round, a celebrity spun a Tweel of Fate to select a subset of player numbers: primes, squares, triangular numbers and so on.

Once the subset had been chosen, members of the public had one minute to place bounties on the heads of the players they wanted to eliminate. A bounty could be as little as ten pence but there was no maximum, and once they were totted up, there was a short period in which players could offer to pay double the amount to cancel it out.

All the money went to the player's nominated charity. Those who didn't double their bounty were teleported to the Southdome, where a selection of the craziest circus animals lay in wait. The round would eventually excise a further 90% of Solarversia's population, taking it down to ten thousand players.

Arty placed the trophy on his desk next to a row of Electropet versions of Emperor Mandelbrot and his entourage. He couldn't stop thinking about what Andrew had said — the way in which the characters had influenced Markowsky and shaped his ideology. It was too surreal to take in.

Shortly after their visit to Legoland that morning, the FBI had released Markowsky's details to the media, sparking a fresh wave of interest in the attacks. Following the recent success of Gogmagog, the authorities were coming round to the idea of coveillance. It wasn't that they wanted people to approach Markowsky if they saw him on the street — quite the opposite. But they understood that the more eyes — artificial or otherwise — they had looking for him, the higher the chance he'd be caught. As Arty pondered whether Spiralwerks had contributed enough resources to the search effort, Hannah approached him with a serious look on her face.

"The surveillance team have flagged some suspicious payments coming in for the bounties. I suggest we start a bridge call straight away." Arty looked at her for long while. Had her hair always been this grey? Had she always looked this tired?

"What do you mean … suspicious?"

"One player has been repeatedly targeted every time their number is available for bounty."

"There's nothing against that in the rules, is there?"

"You're right. Except the number being targeted is 515,740."

Arty's eyes narrowed. "Why do I know that number?"

"It's Nova Negrahnu, the Gogmagog girl. And the bounties being placed on her are huge — £121,212 every time, to be precise. They're being sent anonymously via cryptocurrencies like Bitcoin."

Arty lurched forward in his seat. "Ask Carl to investigate the payments. Get as much information as possible. And get our friends at Legoland on the phone as soon as you can."

Chapter Forty-Two

The common room was silent as the Tweel spun round its axis. It had been set in motion by Kiki La Roux from aboard the Disco Stick. He held his hands to his heart and begged for forgiveness from any loyal viewers the Tweel would inevitably select. His nails featured video clips of the players who had been killed only minutes before when thousands of 'Multiples of Three' had been selected for bounty and sent to their likely deaths.

Once the Tweel had slowed to a halt, the tentacle closest to Kiki became animated. The face peering out chanted the word 'Evens', breaking the silence in the common room with a chorus of groans. Everyone looked to Nova for her reaction. She cussed the number gods under her breath and tried to remain cool, calm and collected.

Cams in the room were broadcasting the event around the globe, so that people could experience the drama with her. That meant that whoever was placing these ridiculous bounties on her head was likely to be watching her every move. And there was no way she was going to give them the satisfaction of watching her squirm.

A minute later, when the same bounty of £121,212 flashed above her head, the crowd booed their disgust louder than ever. She heard Burner swear like a trooper, and Charlie appeal for calm. The bounty was huge. Ten times larger than the bounties on the heads of unpopular celebrities, the kind who were as vacuous as they were untalented.

The bounty's consistent size and numerical structure — the number twelve, repeated thrice — suggested only one plausible explanation: she was being attacked by the Holy Order. What niggled her most was that the first three digits of the bounty, '121', had been her lowest unique number in Grandmaster Brontanja's

Puzzle, which she'd been inspired to choose when thinking about Sushi. First they kill her. Then they dance on her grave. It only made Nova more determined to survive the round.

As the seconds ticked down to the next phase of the round the room quietened again. She waited for her inevitable inclusion in the group of players who would be teleported to the Southdome. At least the unpopular celebrities with large bounties on their heads could afford double the amounts and cancel them out.

Nova might have had the support of hundreds of people, but the vast majority were students, eking out their meagre allowances on pot noodles and cheap lager. There was no way Team Nova could raise close to quarter of a million pounds between them; no way she would even ask such a thing of them, not after everything they had done for her.

More frustratingly, she knew that a rich daddy's girl like Holly *would* be able to cancel the bounties being placed on her head. According to Charlie, Holly's dad was so rich he'd forked out several grand for her player number — 24,442 — because she thought it 'had a nice ring to it'. She was down at Rutland Hall right now, playing the round from there, although Nova had purposely turned off notifications so as to not be distracted by her.

When the 'Double or Quits' phase ended without her having raised the funds required to cancel the bounty, nobody was surprised. She consoled herself with the knowledge that the charity Charlie had suggested she nominate — one that helped install solar arrays in developing nations — would soon receive another six-figure windfall.

She had ten seconds until her visit to the Southdome, and she used them to cycle through her inventory. Her health stood at a paltry thirty-one points. She had lost a huge number on her first visit to the animals when an Obarian had caught her off guard. As for items, she had seventy-nine left in her inventory, including a solitary Force Field, previous visits to the southern hemisphere having depleted her supply. She cracked her knuckles one last time and switched on the noise cancellation mode in her Booners. Solarversia was now more than just a game.

The roof of the Northdome sparked and buzzed as it warmed up. Dozens of arkwinis used cattle prods to herd the unlucky even-numbered players — all 800 of them — into the centre of the room. The ground they walked on was the reverse side of the northern wall — the one that accommodated the Player's Grid. Viewed from the side, it looked like players were defying gravity, sticking to and walking upon a vertical face.

When the round started, the Northdome had been a semi-phased zone. The floor space — a hundred metres squared — hadn't been large enough to accommodate all hundred thousand players who had started the round. It meant that avatars had appeared in a semi-transparent state, able to walk through one another, if not the walls themselves. Experience of what awaited them in the Southdome meant the novelty had soon worn off.

Toward the edges of room stood the odd-numbered players and those even-numbered players rich enough to cancel any bounty that may have been placed on them. She knew what they were thinking: *rather her than me*. It was a predictable and therefore forgivable reaction. For survival of the fittest to work, you couldn't spend too long mourning the dead. It was just that in her case, it felt like she was a victim of *unnatural* selection, the evil twin of the natural kind.

As the electric crackle of the teleport generator hummed into life, she peered up at the domed ceiling and wondered which direction the lightning bolt would arrive from this time. It landed with an almighty crack, like the lash of a giant electric whip.

She arrived in the centre of the Southdome directly opposite where she had just been standing, as if reflected in a mirror. Teleportees ended up within a circular area at the centre of the square floor, which was bound at its edge by a violet-coloured Force Field, holding back the animals, who stood hugely, menacingly behind it, awaiting the moment the field would dissolve.

This would be the eighteenth session of the round, and the fifth one Nova had participated in. The short reprieve provided by the Force Field was the same each time: a mad scramble to surround yourself with as many other players as possible, putting them in the way of you and the beasts. After a lot of pushing and shoving — and Nova wishing that it *was* possible to fight other players — they settled in a series of concentric circles facing the animals.

She found herself next to a muscular American guy wielding a gruesome-looking double-headed Battle Axe, stained red from previous use. His fight stats looked impressive. Being next to him was a minor consolation for ending up in the outermost ring, closest to the animals. Her weapon of choice was a Marsden Flamethrower, a contraption first used in the Second World War. Strapped to her back was a tank that contained 18 litres of fuel, pressurised by nitrogen gas. In her hands she gripped a gun-shaped tube. The Marsden drank like a fish — eighteen litres sounded like plenty of fuel, but it was only enough for three individual spurts of flame.

The Force Field cycled through its colours and then disappeared entirely. The minute of hell had begun. At the left of her peripheral vision Nova saw a Huntropellimous clatter towards the circle of players. Behind her somewhere she heard the strangled cry of an Obarian. But charging straight at her was a mighty Petrifier, a bipedal bullock whose enormous twisting horns were tinted with a poison powerful enough to kill her in seconds. When it got ten metres from her, she fell forward into a kneeling position and clamped her trigger finger down hard on the fuel throttle.

The Marsden took half a second to unleash its horizontal inferno, which slammed straight into the Petrifier's torso, engulfing it in a sea of flames. When it got near enough she heard the American say, "I've got it from here," before he executed a spinning combo with his Battle Axe, landing a fatal blow to the beast's head. She checked her display. Two goes left on the Marsden. Forty-seven seconds to go.

"Hey, you wanna go back-to-back with me?" Nova asked the American guy. Players had used the stance in earlier rounds with great success.

"Thought you'd never ask. I've got a couple of Force Fields left, what about you?"

"Just the one. And only two goes left on this thing. Let's back away from the Huntropellimous. Its armour plating is flame resistant."

"Roger that. Quick — to your left!"

Nova spun left and saw nothing. Before she could ask what he was talking about, an Obarian tore past and took a chunk out of her right shoulder.

"Sorry. I meant the other left ..."

She was about to give him a load of grief when he erected a Force Field over the two of them.

"I'm sorry about that, I didn't have much time to think. I only saw it at the last second and ended up batting it away with the edge of my axe. Hope you didn't take a big hit."

"Lost six points. Down to twenty-five. How long do we have under here?"

"I used the longer of the two fields — twenty seconds. Was gonna save it to last, but thought I owed you one."

"I appreciate the gesture. We've got fourteen seconds to get our act together. Then we need to survive ten more seconds before we get beamed back to safety."

Nova scanned the room for ideas. It was total carnage wherever she looked. On the far side of the dome a Huntropellimous dangled its new playthings for a while — two people impaled on its claws — before slamming their heads together until they exploded, showering blood and brain onto the ground.

Only metres away, she watched helpless as a Petrifier charged someone from behind at full speed, her warning shouts drowned out by screams, roars and the metallic clash of weapons at work. The Petrifier's left horn tore straight through the guy's back and out of his rib cage, bringing his still-beating heart with it.

Over to her right she spotted an Obarian slam into an old woman at full speed, decapitating her in the process. One of its friends clamped down on her spinal cord and unceremoniously yanked it out of her body while she slumped to the ground.

To her left, a woman was kneeling, clutching her throat with all her might, like she was trying to strangle herself. As her hands loosened and fell away from her neck, Nova saw the cause of her distress. An Acoo-Stickular exited her body through her mouth, quickly retaining its full speed of 75 mph.

"As soon as the field dies, I'm gonna go crazy on the Marsden, spin round and spray flames everywhere. The second it runs out I'll activate my Shadow Suckers. If I get the angle right, I should be able to shoot at anything that approaches us and make it stick to the ground. My only worry is the Acoo-Stickular; it moves way too fast."

"I'm holding on to my Battle Axe. I've got that spinning combo down. I can even use the blade to deflect the waveform if it comes for us; they bounce off inorganic matter. The Huntropellimi are my only worry. I counted at least eight of them and the axe can't pierce their armour, even with a perfectly executed combo. Good luck, I hope we both make it."

As the field disappeared, exposing them to the battlefield once more, Nova entered the zone. She rolled to her right to evade anything that might have been eyeing them up, waiting for their field to dissipate. The second she landed back on her feet, she let rip with the Marsden, spinning around while she skipped from foot to foot. From above she looked like a Catherine Wheel on Fireworks Night. An Obarian was her first victim. It flew into the tail end of the spiralling band of flames, turning into a flaming comet. Its screech went up a couple of octaves before it hit the ground, where it tumbled to a standstill, a smoking tangle of fangs.

Next up was a Petrifier who got it square in the face just as it was about to make a kill of its own. The flames spread quickly, engulfing its entire being within seconds. The man she saved from certain death didn't stop to thank her. Instead, he drew an arrow from the quiver on his back and aimed at her head. She froze. What kind of payback was this? It wasn't as if the arrow could do her any harm, but a simple smile would have sufficed.

A second later she found out. The arrow whistled through the air, narrowly missing her face to spear a cave troll through its neck; a troll that had been coming for her. Now they exchanged a nod and a smile: a life for a life.

She activated her Shadow Suckers, ready for whatever the dome could throw at her, but needn't have bothered. The minute was up. Screams turned to cheers as they were greeted by the players in the northern hemisphere like a group of war heroes returning from battle. Removing her headset, she found that the common room was even louder. She raised her arms, flexed her biceps and let rip with a war cry. If that wasn't already enough, she kissed each bicep, sending the crowd wild.

The remaining few minutes of The Bounty Hunt flew by. The Tweel of Fate was on her side for the next three rounds, sending a whole bunch of other players to the southern hemisphere and the overall death counter toward 99,990,000. When the final person died, signalling the end of the round, Nova was hoisted onto Charlie's shoulders and paraded around the room like an Olympic hero. Professor Carmichael handed her what looked like a quadruple measure of Glenfiddich. She necked it in one, then hurled the shot glass at the wall, smashing it to pieces.

A shiver went down her spine, but it had nothing to do with the liquor or the rush of surviving the round. It was the headline news she had read that morning which had filled her with dread and a sick sort of pleasure. Her arch-nemesis finally had a name: Theodore Markowsky. She said it over and over in her head, enunciating every last letter, getting a feel for it, wanting to know the man behind it, and hating him harder, stronger, fiercer than he could ever hate her. As the adrenaline coursed through her body, she felt invincible. She looked up at one of the cameras and narrowed her eyes. Then she raised an arm and pointed a finger. *I'm coming for you, Markowsky. And I won't be taking prisoners.*

***

Special Agent Debrieze Kirkland volleyed to cam seventeen. It took him a few seconds to take the scene in and for its magnitude to register. A smile crept across his unshaven face. The cam was planted in the eyes of a robotic sparrow, which was perched on a branch overhanging the embankment a mile downstream, just yards from where Theodore Markowsky was kneeling in front of an altar inside a camouflaged marquee. Suspended from the altar was a tapestry bearing a curly swastika. Through the sparrow's eyes, Kirkland could make out the same symbol embroidered on the preacher's black robes — a symbol that had haunted his dreams for more than a year.

He was heading up the two hundred FBI agents aboard several dozen boats taking part in Operation Delta Strike. The call had come in three days before. Someone had taken a photo of some friends posing in front of the fountain at the local shopping mall in Jackson City and then shared it online. The social network she used was trialling Gogmagog, whose algorithms were set to scan the faces of any person detected in a photograph, even, it appeared, those half-hidden behind a water feature.

From a blurry shot of his profile, a wanted member of the Holy Order had been identified. Gogmagog fired off a critical alert to the FBI, and a fleet of drones was mobilised within minutes. Hovering at several thousand feet, they had triangulated the guy's location and tailed him from on high to the parking lot, on and off the highway, along the banks of the swamp, all the way to the Compound.

Kirkland's smile gave way to a yawn. He had slept three, maybe four hours since the alert had come in and considered himself lucky at that. Beside him, his men paddled silently: the sparrows had identified a handful of lookout towers spread around the Compound's perimeter, so they had cut the motors a while back.

"Sir, are you getting this? We have Markowsky in our sights. He's alone and unarmed." Kirkland spoke into his headset just loud enough for the men on his boat to hear. The case had consumed all of their lives for far too long now. This day, this Operation, this stealth mission, was their reward.

"I see him. He's probably praying to that Magus character right now, asking for a goddamn miracle. I've got a meeting with the Vice President later today. This'll give him something to take people's minds off the unemployment figures." It was the Deputy Director of the FBI, stationed at a mobile command centre three hundred miles away. "The only worry now is those lookout towers. Proceed with caution."

"Roger that, sir. I'd say it'll be twenty minutes before we can move on them."

Kirkland stuffed his hands behind his flak jacket. He hadn't anticipated quite how cold it would be, the chill of the late January air five degrees cooler down here than it was up in town. It was hard to believe that they finally had Markowsky surrounded, the most wanted man in the FBI's recent history, a man who up until a few weeks ago had been nothing but a ghost.

Suddenly, a distant explosion sent the boat lurching dangerously to one side. His men ducked, instinctively shying away from the noise. Around him, what seemed like every last bird in the state took to the skies at once. "At your stations," he shouted and fumbled to get his dropped headset back in place.

"What the hell happened, Kirkland? I thought I instructed caution. I've made it abundantly clear. I want my agents returned in one piece to their families tonight."

"I just shared my view with you, sir, stand by."

Kirkland volleyed his view to the sparrow closest to the column of smoke billowing from whatever it was that had exploded. He used its eyes to zoom in and investigate the flaming wreck. More sparrows arrived, each able to view the scene from a different angle. He felt a rush of relief — it was one of the remote-controlled sweeper boats.

Unmanned and unarmed, they led the way on operations like this, gliding through the water searching for anything that looked of interest or out of place: people, hideouts and weapons. The datafeed in his visor confirmed it: TBP-75 had decommissioned itself. He pulled up the video feeds from the boat's last few seconds and ran them through Gogmagog. It identified a critical component in the footage a few milliseconds before the cam was destroyed in the blast.

"What are we looking at here, Kirkland?"

"Gogmagog's identified a trip wire covered in camouflage. The sweeper cruised into it and detonated whatever was wired to the end of it. They've got the place booby-trapped."

"Shit. Deploy every last sweeper. Keep them surrounded. We've got drones monitoring them from above, and the choppers are five minutes away if you need them. How many submersibles do you have?"

"Forty, manned by eighteen divers. Between them, they're monitoring every inch of the river, up and downstream. Markowsky's gonna need to have created teleportation for real if he wants to get out of here alive."

It took the sweeper boats twenty-six minutes to clear a safe path to the compound. Kirkland volleyed from sparrow cam to sniper sight and back again. In the old days the Order might have stood a chance in an operation like this, however small. But not now. They were employing what his superiors gloatingly referred to as 'asymmetric warfare'. It was almost as if they were cheating: they knew the exact geospatial coordinates of all fifty members of the Order, their names, weapons, the amount of ammunition each member had and their current emotional state as diagnosed by the biometric readout of the blood coursing through their veins.

Even with their huge advantage, Kirkland's heart still pounded in his chest. People were about to die, and he'd witness every last gory detail in stereoscopic vision. He took a deep breath and mentally prepared himself.

"Operation Delta Strike is go, go, go."

The assault started at once. A barrage of armour-piercing bullets was fired at the compound from multiple angles. The death count in Kirkland's visor ticked up to double figures in the space of five minutes. At times the operation was eerily similar to the previous day's practise in the virtual environment. There were moments when he thought he was in the virtual world, moments when he had to physically shake himself back to reality. The woman leading the training had warned him it would happen. She'd called it 'technosis'. He hadn't believed her at the time. It had seemed a ridiculous notion, being unable to distinguish the kind of reality you were experiencing. It wasn't like he was in 'Nam, whacked out on acid.

His visor flashed up their first casualty: Agent Barker. He volleyed to a cam attached to the head of the nearest medic, watched the treatment in real time on one display while replaying the injury on another. He felt powerful, being able to jump around like this, from one perspective to another, like a god of some kind. 'Localised ubiquity', they were calling it in universities, 'omni crack' on social media. It was addictive, whatever you called it.

Fifty-six minutes, that's all it took. Nineteen members of the Holy Order killed, twenty-seven surrendered. There were a handful of casualties among Kirkland's agents. The agent who had lost a leg would get a prosthetic as soon as he felt ready for one, and if the rumours coming out of the medical facility were to be believed, they'd be able to order him a lab-grown organic replacement before too long.

That left four members of the Order hiding in the submarine: Theodore and Frances Markowsky, and two of their lieutenants. Spidey, the Bureau's most advanced robo-agent, used a chunky axle grinder to cut away several sections of the hull and then lobbed canisters of tear gas into the craft, one after another. Having set up a temporary command centre on the other side of the Compound, Kirkland flicked his headset back in place and watched Spidey enter the vessel via the robot's built-in thermal imaging cameras.

Once they'd navigated the tight spiral staircase, Spidey's heavy metal feet clomped along the Sub's narrow corridor, echoing eerily through the tear gas fog. When Spidey's cameras craned into the first of the cramped rooms along the corridor, Kirkland recoiled so fast that he almost fell into his deputy.

Two bodies were slumped against one another. Their brains had been blown through the backs of their skulls. Blood was coagulating on the walls. Zooming in on what was left of their faces, Spidey, or at least the enormous database he had access to, quickly established their identities: Brandon O'Malley and Frances Markowsky.

Swallowing back the bile that had risen up his throat, he readied himself for whatever Spidey would find in the cargo hold at the bottom of the Sub, the very last place Theodore and his lieutenant Casey Brown could be hiding.

Kirkland removed his headset, walked to the rickety bridge that snaked round the Compound's perimeter and surveyed the scene, trying to understand what it must have been like to live here, among these people. The buildings of the Compound blended so well against the surrounding flora that they gave the impression of having grown there.

He steadied himself against the old submarine, trying to work out what he'd tell the Deputy Director. Everywhere he looked, another curly swastika symbol popped out at him. They were engraved everywhere: the arched entrance to the compound, the detail in the window frames, the posts of the bridge.

"I don't know how to tell you this, sir."

"Don't tell me we've killed Markowsky. I do *not* want to hear that, Kirkland. A suicide we can deal with. The guy was a nutcase, it's expected behaviour."

"Sir, it's not that. I wish it *was* that. It's just, well, we've only managed to recover two bodies from the sub: those of Frances Markowsky and Brandon O'Malley."

The line remained silent for a few seconds. Kirkland closed his eyes and massaged his temples.

"What, and the other two bodies are too difficult to recover? There's a load more booby traps?"

"Sir, we've only recovered two bodies because there only *were* two bodies to recover. Markowsky's gone, and Casey Brown with him."

"What do you mean, gone? Gone where? We had the place surrounded, didn't we?"

Now it was Kirkland's turn to pause. Every word pained him beyond belief. "There's a cargo hold at the very bottom of the submarine. It's full of water and its flaps are open. The divers didn't see a thing. Sir, Markowsky's given us the slip."

Chapter Forty-Three

Nova chewed on a clump of hair, a habit she thought she'd kicked on her thirteenth birthday. She was at The Commodore for Show and Tell, the fourth of the final rounds. She stared at her list of ideas, hating them more by the second, and spat out a strand of hair that had come loose in her mouth.

Attendance at a Spiralwerks-affiliated gaming cafe had been compulsory, so players in remote locations had flown to their nearest city in order to participate. Spiralwerks had always promised that success in Solarversia wouldn't rest solely on gaming skills. They had gone so far as to promote it as a form of 'holistic immersion'. Of course, the skills required in regular gaming went a long way, and everyone knew that luck played a small part too. But they had promised that trivia, creativity, psychology and popularity would also feature.

The Show and Tell round required players to build something — a real-world object — that would then be submitted to a popular vote. That morning she had turned up to The Commodore and been assigned to Denis, her 'Maker Mentor', who would advise her as to the kind of objects that would be admissible in the round and provide a degree of direction and support.

"How are we doing with our list of ideas? Are we progressing OK, or do we require Denis's assistance?" Denis gently pressed the pads of his fingers together while he spoke. Nova found him to be as condescending as he was bald. She swore that if he referred to himself in the third person again, she'd scream. She looked at the pad in front of her on the workbench and felt a cold sweat creep across her brow. The doodles in the margins outnumbered the ideas by ten to one, and even they were shit.

The thought of crashing out after coming so far filled her with dread. Especially if it meant someone like Pedey Gonzalez winning instead. That morning's White

Dwarf had informed her that the American woman — the person who had fired a Sucker at her Shadow in Bouncy Baltimore — had made it through to this latest round. As if that hadn't been annoying enough already, it was nothing compared to the news that both Holly *and* Jools van der Star were also through.

A realisation struck her. If either one of them became Grand Champion, it would be *them*, rather than *her*, who ended up helping to design the next Game. The beads of sweat on her brow multiplied in an instant. It was a chilling thought. The thing she loved most in the world tainted by whatever crass, moronic thing one of those tools came up with.

"My suggestions are utter dog shite. I'm embarrassed to say them out loud."

"Oh, come on now, don't be silly. I'm sure Denis has heard worse."

She scowled at him before remembering the overall objective of Project Nova — to be the best person she was capable of being. And that meant employing a degree of kindness and compassion when it was called for. She took a deep breath through her nose and continued.

"OK, then, my suggestions, in descending order of suck. A pair of singing scissors. Never again be bored while you're snipping."

Denis caressed his chin in a manner that gave her the creeps. "Right. Any others?"

"You know those books you get in the movies, with the insides carved out of them so you can smuggle items into and out of jail? A his and hers version of them."

"Mm-hmm."

"A mechanical Venus fly trap that catches fruit flies—"

"You know the aim is to win a public vote, don't you? I had such high hopes for you." A bell sounded and Denis pranced upwards like an eager Jack Russell. "Be right back, it sounds like Denis is wanted at the front desk."

A voice came from behind her, too close for comfort.

"Does that say 'singing scissors'?" A peal of laughter. Nova slung her arms defensively over her notepad before looking round.

"Oh. Hi, Holly." She had known Holly was at The Commodore too, working on her project, but she'd just assumed they'd stay out of each other's way. But no, here she was with a stupid smile plastered all over her silly bimbo face.

"Fancy seeing you here. Jools and I are astonished you're still in. A lucky guess at the Decision Dome followed by a mediocre dive ..."

Jools and I? What were they, the Anti-Nova League?

"The dive was mediocre on purpose. I applied my knowledge of psychology—"

"Sure you did. Anyway, everyone knows you only survived Bounty Hunter because of the items you received from the wills, rather than from having mastered the Science."

"Seems like you've been taking a lot of interest in my progress."

"Yah, well. I heard you got together with Charlie. I came over to say that I think you suit each other. Losers should stick together."

Nova got up from her chair to square up to her.

"Wow, Holly. Why do you have to be so rude?"

It came out sounding a bit pathetic. Also, she'd forgotten that Holly had a good five inches on her. Holly smirked down at her.

"Don't know if you heard, but Jools and I are an item these days. The press love the fact that we're both still in The Game. We've become something of a celebrity couple. Besides, Charlie was crap in bed. You've probably discovered that for yourself by now."

Nova's mouth hung open while her brain tried to process what she was hearing.

"I really should be getting back. Good luck with your ..." Holly grabbed the pad of ideas off the table before Nova could stop her. "His 'n' hers hidey books. What a joke."

She slung the pad back onto the table and walked away, laughing.

Nova counted to ten and waited for the blood to drain from her face. The build-up to Solarversia had taught her that patience was a virtue. Revenge on Holly could wait. Nova looked around the workshop to see the other Solos making good progress on their prototypes. It was midday already. She'd wasted the entire morning and only had thirty hours before she'd have to present her creation to the world.

Or at least, the country. The Show and Tell round took place at a national level, with a certain number of spaces in the final thousand allocated to each country. Of the ten thousand players left, 289 of them were British. And only twenty-nine spots were reserved for them in the fifth round.

She reread her list of ideas and let out a huge sigh. Her mind was blank. She'd heard of writer's block. Perhaps this was a case of its less well-known brother, the inventor's block. She twirled the tips of her hair around her mouth. A hair curler in the shape of a tongue? No, Nova. Denis returned to her bench carrying a package.

"It's addressed to you. Don't tell Denis you've ordered something online?" He wagged his finger at her and in a sing-song manner said, "He'll know you've been cheeaa-ting."

Nova's face lit up. Officer Dibble had called her yesterday to say that Zhang was no longer required as evidence, and had promised to FedEx him for next day delivery. She ripped the box apart, tore the protective plastic wrapper from him and was delighted to find that he even had some charge left. After many minutes of hugs and kisses, she placed him on the table and beamed at Denis as if she was showing off a newborn baby. Zhang spied her pen, picked it up and drummed it against the lathe affixed to the side of the bench.

"Denis, meet my buddy Zhang. He's a first generation Electropet and he totally rocks my world."

"Enchanté, Zhang. Nice drumming." He turned to Nova with a pout and raised his eyebrows. "What a talented little friend you have, Nova."

***

In the yellow glow of her bedside light that evening, Nova caught sight of her tattoo in the vanity mirror on her desk. She moved her shoulder back and forth, studying the reflected view. Something was calling out to her. It took a few moments before she realised what it was. Sushi. She hadn't visited her in ages.

As Charlie snored quietly behind her, she tried to remember the date of her last visit. No chance. Far too much had been going on. Still, it was weird not to have missed her friend that much. Slipping her headset on, she dialled her finger round the tattoo and placed a finger on each of its dots. The Seattle skyline preview remained unchanged since before Christmas.

"Hey, Nova, how are you?"

Nova turned the high-backed chair away from Charlie, slunk into it and whispered to her friend, "I'm great, but things have gone crazy again."

"Why are we whispering?"

"Charlie is sleeping. I don't want to wake him. Listen, I've got something to show you. Guess who this is."

Hundreds of images appeared in the sky in front of Sushi's bench, of a man with a long white beard, short grey hair and dark circular glasses, his face shown from a number of different angles. Full body shots included a bionic arm dotted with a grid of lights. Nova glanced between them and her friend, who examined a few up close before speaking again.

"It looks like Theodore Markowsky."

"Exactly. Sushi, this is the guy that killed you."

Sushi stared back at her friend but didn't speak.

"The afternoon they released his name I was playing in the third round, Bounty Hunter, and members of the Order started attacking me *in* The Game, placing these outrageous bounties on my head, so I kept getting beamed to the Southdome where all the animals were. Anyway, the next day the FBI raided the Order's compound and they ended up killing or capturing practically everyone there — except for Theodore and this one other guy. They escaped, can you believe it?"

"You seem to be ..."

"What?"

"I don't know. I can't quite place it. It's almost like you're excited that he escaped."

"Well, it *is* kind of exciting. He's out there somewhere. *Him*. The person responsible for your death. The person who tried to kill Zhang and me. When I think about him, I feel so angry, I just want to—"

"What?"

"I don't know. Stab him in the eye. Shoot him in the balls. Kill him dead. Just get him."

"Nova. You're not ... thinking of doing something stupid, are you?"

Nova grabbed a chunk of hair and twirled it around her finger, conscious of not sticking it into her mouth.

"What do mean, 'something stupid'?"

"Remember the trouble you and Burner got into last year? You nearly got yourself killed, that's what I mean."

"What can I do anyway? He's in America. Don't get me wrong, I check the alerts that Gogmagog sends out, who doesn't? If I was in a position to do something, I'd do whatever it took. But the authorities are after him. I'm sure they'll get him. They have to, right? How d'you reckon they'll kill him? I think the electric chair. I keep fantasising they'll build a replica to the one on Bruno."

Sushi looked puzzled.

"The electric chair on Bruno, my boat. You helped me design it, remember?"

"You seem overly hyped."

"That's because it feels like he's got it in for me. First he kills you, then he tries to kill me, and when he fails to do that, he comes after me in The Game. *Our* game, Sushi, the one we swore to play together until the end, whatever it took."

Sushi held her hands out, palms up, and shrugged.

"I thought you'd be happy to see me, to know that I'm progressing through the final rounds."

"I guess I am happy to see you ... except you haven't visited in ages."

The images of Markowsky were replaced by a graph showing the frequency of Nova's visits.

"I appreciate that you're spending a lot of time with Charlie, which is awesome, and that you're doing well in Solarversia. But you're obsessing over a dangerous criminal. I don't know how that's going to help either of us. And I've missed you. I'd like my Solarversia Sister to visit more often."

"Woah. I didn't realise that dead people could be so adept at guilt trips. Is this some new module you've downloaded?"

"Are you for real? This is how you programmed me — to be as close as possible to the person you were best friends with. I'm reacting like the real Sushi would have done. You've been a shitty friend is what I'm saying."

There followed an impossibly long, awkward silence where Nova was unable to maintain eye contact with her friend. She waited for Sushi to speak, but the avatar of her dead friend stared straight back at her, coldly.

"Fuck off then," she said and tore the Booners from her head. She slumped in the chair, gasping for breath.

There'd been only one occasion when they'd fallen out like that before. It was in the run-up to the Harrisons' move to Seattle. Sushi had been acting like she wouldn't miss Nova at all. After a few weeks of trying to be extra nice and appear excited for her, Nova started feeling really hurt. Sushi never seemed to acknowledge how shitty it would be for her, stuck in the 'Stone on her own.

She'd acted petulantly, then bitchily, and finally stopped speaking to her altogether. After an awkward, frosty week at school, they squabbled like little children in maths, cried during lunch break, and then made up with more tears and plenty of hugs. Soon after that they'd had their final sleepover, the night they had declared themselves Solarversia Sisters.

Maybe she should never have logged in to Soul Surfer. Perhaps she should have said farewell to her friend for good, like a normal person would've done. The way people had been dealing with death for millennia. Some choice words at a memorial service. Some flowers laid on a manicured grave. Ashes scattered at a favourite place.

Her chin quivered with the thought. She hated herself for entertaining the notion, even for a second. Her life may be unorthodox, what with Zhang and Sushi as her friends, a preference for virtual worlds, and an obsession with one of the most dangerous men on the planet, but it was *her* life, damn it, and she'd do with it as she pleased.

Clambering onto the bed, she wrapped her arms around Charlie's warm, strong body. He was sound asleep. She nestled her head against his back and held on tight. After their big fallout years ago, she and Sushi had made a promise not to be so stupid again, not to fall out over *anything*. It was a promise she had wanted to honour until the day she died and she vowed there and then to fix the mess the very next day.

***

It was time. The single player from the Ukraine had been voted through to the fifth round, and now it was the turn of the United Kingdom. Nova went to take of swig of beer and was surprised to see her hand trembling. She became acutely aware of everyone in the room, dozens of pairs of eyes flitting between her and the giant screens showing the results.

Perhaps it was the increased pressure of knowing that success in this round meant claiming one of the cash prizes, a guaranteed £10,000 minimum. A sum like that wouldn't change her life, but it would be enough to pay her tuition fees.

Charlie was there, thank God. He stroked Flash, his Electropet chameleon, with one hand and held her hand with the other. She grabbed it tight, surprised at the calming effect it had. He kept telling her that it would be alright, whatever happened, words she struggled to believe, however much she knew them to be true. Zhang clung to her side and nuzzled his head into her neck, unaware of his minor celebrity status.

She was back at The Commodore to hear the result of the Show and Tell round. At least she had entered something better than a pair of singing scissors. "Zhang's an entertainer, and he belongs on the stage," Denis had told her. Together they had quickly sketched out an idea: a puppet theatre complete with a drum kit for Zhang to play. Denis had confirmed that the entry would be valid — Zhang would be viewed as a prop, and plenty of other entries were supported in some way by additional objects. Nova soon made the idea her own, customising every last detail to match his personality.

Constructing the stage had been far more enjoyable than she'd anticipated: she liked using the bandsaw to form the base, the lathe to sand it down and the sewing machine to make its glitzy curtains, each embroidered with a large 'Z'. On the second night, after a twelve-hour shift in The Commodore workshop, she had presented *Rock 'n' Roll Zhang*, a one-minute performance where he bashed away on his mini-drum kit in time to some backing vocals she had recorded. His show, when complemented by the flashing LED lights around the edges of his little stage, and the curtains, which automatically opened and closed, was something she felt proud to show off.

She only hoped the rest of the country would love it as much as the folk at The Commodore had. Following the presentations, the objects had been 3D-scanned and placed in a large virtual Expo room, allowing the people at home to view them up close and play around with them, as well as watching the recording of each one's presentation. British players, dead or alive, were given three votes and five days in which to cast them in a secret ballot. The twenty-nine British players who received the highest number of votes would proceed to the next round. Reality TV had evolved into virtual reality TV.

Spiralwerks had been working their way through countries in alphabetical order and following the reaction of players as the results were announced. It'd been painful to watch Jools van der Star get through earlier on in the evening, but even worse to witness Holly's reaction here at The Commodore. The shrill laugh. The overly dramatic fanning of her face. The immediate update of her Facebook status, thanking her fans for backing him. It was like she'd ordered the *Celebrity for Dummies* book and was working her way through the z-list section, executing every last puerile, superficial piece of advice it contained.

The crowd shushed themselves back to silence. On the giant screen at the front of the cafe, Artica Kronkite was about to reveal the winners from the UK in descending order of popularity. Up flashed a guy from Newcastle whose foosball table featuring player avatars had struck the right chord with the crowd. *Damn.* Why hadn't she thought of combining two things everyone loved? She gripped Charlie's hand even tighter and offered a weak smile to the assembled throng. At least the five other Solos at the cafe in the running with her looked as nervous as she felt. Even Holly had become uncharacteristically quiet.

It was strange. Nova could take out a raging Petrifier with a blast of fire, no problem. She could Kart round the streets of the Solarverse like a badass. It turned out she could solve ridiculously obscure riddles in a race against the clock better than most of a hundred million other humans. But standing around waiting to see if her skills as a set designer would win her a popular vote was almost more than she could bear. It was excruciating *not* to be fighting or driving or problem solving. "Relax," said Charlie as she dug her nails into his hand. "Flash and I loved Zhang's performance, and I'm sure the crowd did too, just you wait."

"The next person on my list is at The Commodore in Nottingham." Artica gave a little smile as he delivered the news. It'd been like this all evening, him announcing the location of the cafe to narrow the field down before confirming the lucky player.

The cameras in the room went live, focusing in on the five of them as they nervously awaited the news.

"The next Solo to make it through to the fifth round is 'Hollywood Rox'. Well done, Holly."

Nova flinched as Holly leapt up from her table, yelped like a little dog and hugged anyone unlucky enough to be within range. She'd designed a glamorous evening gown that allowed the wearer, via its integrated computer, to flirt with people in their vicinity and be bought drinks from whatever bar they happened to be frequenting at the time. Once she'd calmed down she approached their table. Nova hadn't laid eyes on a more punchable face in her life.

"I'd love to stay and watch you and your little rat go out, but I've got a celebrity appearance to make at Hedonism. I get paid to turn up, show my face and down some free drinks. My agent said that I could expect my fee to double if I went though. And I'm not sure if you heard, but I'm already in talks with a large retail chain who want to stock the dress. Must dash. Wouldn't want to keep my fans waiting."

Large retail chain. The phrase reverberated in Nova's mind. Did anyone else care about Electropets the way she and Charlie did? Or had she merely indulged one of her stupid little interests, as she rode high on the endorphins her brain had released when she'd unpacked her buddy that day?

And so the round continued for the next hour, each winner's entry seemingly more ingenious than the last, their waving avatars appearing on the giant screens to torment her sorry ass. When her own avatar finally appeared, claiming the twenty-second spot, she didn't jump around like a loony or get hoisted onto anyone's shoulders. She didn't even shout or cheer.

Instead, she collapsed into Charlie's arms and hugged him tight, not wanting ever to let go. The trembling sensation coursed through her entire body. It took her a few moments to understand what the crowd were requesting of her — that she raise Zhang upon her shoulders and let *him* be the star of the show.

Chapter Forty-Four

Casey's shoes squeaked as he walked along the spotless tiles of the corridor. Further ahead a flat kite-shaped robot buzzed and whirred as it criss-crossed the passage, vacuuming what little dust it found into its plastic insides. As they rounded the corner, Theodore's face lit up again. Giving the guided tour seemed to bring out the showman in him.

"And this is where you'll be practicing your shootin'," Father said, gesturing to the clean grey alley in front of them. "We wouldn't want you missing your target at the closing ceremony, would we, son?"

"No, Father, of course not," Casey said, with a meek bow and self-conscious smile. This place had everything: a gym, a shooting range, an Olympic pool, and every inch of it had been constructed by 'bots in a secret location deep underground. It made him realise how little he really knew of the Holy Order, even if he was part of its executive branch. He'd never even heard of the Contingency Compound. The first he knew of its existence was when he'd come round that morning with the hangover from hell.

Except he hadn't drunk a thing the night before. He'd spent the night tossing and turning in his bunk like an excited kid on the night before Christmas. It should have been his last night at the Compound, the night before his big escape. He'd stockpiled three months' worth of immunosuppressive medication, enough to buy him time to find a new supply.

A pre-dawn raid by the FBI had seen the whole plan go to shit in the space of about ten seconds. He'd been in the Backroom, stuffing cash into a waterproof bag, when a distant rumble had sounded, followed by every alarm in the Compound going off at once. Brandon had burst in a few seconds later, there to escort him to safety.

Outside had been mayhem. People running and shouting, arming up, taking their places in the fortified shelters. Not him. His fate lay elsewhere. He was strong-armed to the Sub by Brandon, where Frances and Theodore were waiting. When the four of them were inside Brandon had sealed the door shut.

Down in the cargo hold, Frances had checked the contents of their holdalls one last time: the passports, wads of currency, USB sticks loaded with cryptocurrency account numbers and passwords, vials of immunosuppressive anti-rejection medication, and one Walther P99, the standard-issue duty pistol for law enforcement officers around the world.

When Brandon lifted up the doors in the Sub's floor, Casey had stared in awe. He'd been told about the contingency escape plan a while back, but never thought they'd actually have to use it. The creatures waiting in the hold were as realistic as Father had described. Apparently, they'd been custom-built at a cost of $1m apiece by a company in Las Vegas and had been test-driven to depths of fifty yards. They were even fitted with pheromones of young, non-aggressive males so that they could travel undisturbed by the local population.

Brandon had helped him into his alligator first, lying him belly-down in the same direction the alligator faced, stuffing the lightweight Adidas holdall into the tail section beyond his feet and resting the plastic straw, hooked up to a supply of fresh water, in his hand. Next to him, Theodore was helped into the second alligator before Brandon and Frances said their goodbyes, shut and sealed the cockpit hatch, and released water into the hold.

It was once the alligator had jolted into action that his attacks of anxiety had begun. It wasn't even like he was expected to do anything; just lie there and breathe. The beasts would navigate the route themselves.

But the acoustics had sounded very different with his craft submerged in the water, accentuating his breathing and the clanks and clunks of the craft as it progressed along the river. For every knock, he imagined a real 'gator out there, perhaps the monster who had taken Father Theodore's arm. For every bump, its teeth got bigger. And, as he'd discovered to his horror, he'd barely been able to move. Wedged tight against the sides of the cabin, he felt as though they were closing in on him, like the jaws of the metal vice that had clamped his arm in place at the Workshop. With a sudden rush, he was in the grips of claustrophobia. He'd concentrated hard on his breathing, knowing it to be the first casualty in any war of nerves, and had tried to forget the idea that he might just have been helped into his waterborne coffin.

Inside the tin beasts for fifteen hours straight as they swum upstream, he'd just about kept it together, intoning reassuring words to himself inside his head. The sound of hissing gas was the last thing he remembered. He'd awoken in a strange bed in an unfamiliar room and been woken by a 'bot holding a tray of breakfast. He was led by another soulless automaton to a lounge area where Theodore was waiting to start his guided tour.

"I can't tell you how excited I am to show you this next room." Out of the corner of his eye, Casey glimpsed the rapid sequence of lights flashing on Theodore's arm. The same thing happened each time they approached either a room or the elevators. A sequence would flash on Theodore's arm and then be replicated by the panel on the wall. It was like he was playing an advanced game of Simon Says against the building.

Casey did his best to hide the fear that was gripping his body, but it was intoxicating, seeping through the pores of his skin. Why hadn't he been more aggressive in stealing his medication? Just one night earlier and he'd be a free man, halfway to Mexico. Instead, his situation had dramatically worsened. The old Compound might have been in the middle of nowhere, but it was *his* nowhere, one he was familiar with.

He didn't even know where this new nowhere was. Father had mentioned that it was underground, and the signs on the wall clearly displayed how far down each level was. His bedroom, the lounge and the kitchen had been on level −2. They'd ridden the elevator up one floor to −1 and seen the workshop, the shooting range and whatever this new room was. That meant freedom was waiting only a few metres above his head.

But how could he get up there when this place was riddled with robots? They were everywhere he looked, gliding about the place, devoid of warmth or humanity. More worrying was the security aspect of this new Compound. It didn't have normal, dumb old doors that pushed or pulled. The doors here irised open and shut with a whoosh, controlled by chips embedded in circuits far from his reach.

When he'd stumbled around his new room that morning, wondering where he was, the grid of lights on his arm had flashed and granted him access to the en suite bathroom. So his arm was chipped too. The lights hadn't flashed since.

Theodore looked like he had access to the entire building. Perhaps he could knock him unconscious and rip his arm off? It would act like a key — he could carry it around with him and hold it up to the panels that controlled the doors. It wasn't like he would take the old man's arm with him once he'd escaped. Father was crazy, but he didn't want to hurt him. He'd leave it by the exit on his way out, like a latchkey kid hiding the spare under a stone.

"I'm not entirely sure what I'm looking at, Father," Casey said as the older man stretched out his arms into the brightly lit room, a look of anticipation on his face. A massive circular object the size of a truck sat in the centre of the otherwise empty room. A smooth veneer of shiny chrome rose to waist height and then tapered off toward a central column of black glass that connected the bottom half of the object to the top. It looked like a giant metal yo-yo.

"No? Elmer, this is the very centre of our operation. This object — this thing of beauty — is *the Magi*." Theodore's eyes sparkled as he spoke. "Or it will be. What you're looking at here houses the brain that will power his empire. I prefer to think of this room as the Epicenter. The superintelligent thoughts that come to fruition here will reverberate around the planet like shocks from an earthquake, destroying the old and the weak, birthing the new and the strong."

"I'm humbled to be here, Father, to cast my eyes upon your life's work." Another deferential bow accompanied his words. Since witnessing the fates that had befallen Ivan and Wallace, he'd done his best to feign absolute obedience to Father Theodore. He was getting quite good at it, he thought. No matter how ridiculous it sounded, Father seemed to lap it up. He was rather proud of the diverse range of gestures he'd developed to accompany his replies.

"Are you? Are you really?"

"Yes, Father. I don't pretend to understand how artificial intelligence works, of course, but—"

"But you're humbled to be here ... what was that quaint little phrase you used? To cast your eyes upon my life's work? Don't I feel like the proud father!"

Casey gulped. "I don't understand. If I've said or done something to—"

"It's not what you've said or done. You can say any words you fancy I'm gonna want to hear. You can scrape and bow. Hell, you can climb a hill a hundred and forty-four times. What matters, sunshine, is what you *think*."

A fresh sequence blinked into life on Theodore's arm, looking something like a digital worm tunnelling its way through a patch of electric light. Once the sequence had replicated itself on the panel on the wall, the room came to life as if it had been awoken from a slumber.

Within seconds the walls were crammed full of information of every description. There were bar charts, line charts and pie charts. There were histograms, timelines and flow charts. The numbers and symbols within the charts were dynamic, rather than static, the information in them being updated in real time. Casey could feel Theodore's gaze on him as he self-consciously tried to ascertain the significance of what he was being shown.

His eyes settled on a graph that contained several dozen horizontal lines that were wildly fluctuating between softer, shallower waveforms and sharper, spikier peaks. Alongside it was a vertically scrolling tickertape of words in one column, a series of statistical percentages in the next. *What the Bejesus am I looking at here?* There was no discernible delay between him thinking his thought, and it appearing on the tickertape: WHAT THE BEJESUS AM I LOOKING AT HERE?

The rush of terror he felt was reflected in a graph at the top right of the wall that appeared to be monitoring emotional states. *My terror. My emotional state.* Again the words manifested on the tickertape in real time. He glanced at the word cloud underneath the tickertape. It provided a visual summary of the thoughts that had been going through his mind during the tour. As he mentally read the phrases, 'he's a lunatic', 'how can I escape?' and 'rip his arm off and use it as key', they once again appeared in the tickertape. Another rush of terror coursed through his body, causing multiple graphs to flash warnings.

He stared, thunderstruck. His mind splayed all over the wall. How was it possible? HOW IS IT POSSIBLE the tickertape spewed. Father Theodore was whooping and dancing, punching the air. "It works," he was yelling. "It works!" Finally, panting and grinning, he turned to Casey.

"You appear to have grasped a basic understanding of your situation. Frances, God bless her soul, performed more than an elementary face transplant on you. Part of your skull was opened up so that we could attach a series of electrodes to your brain. I took a download of your mindscape and analysed the hierarchical series of patterns that constitute your memory. Those same electrodes are processing your brain activity and wirelessly transmitting it to the Epicenter, from where it's transmitted to one of the modules in *my* brain, allowing me to monitor your thoughts and emotions as they happen."

"Father ... I can explain. It's the stress. The stress of the operation. The raid. The escape in the alligators. My claustrophobia — I probably never mentioned it to you, didn't want to worry anyone."

He turned to see what Theodore was laughing at. His words had been transcribed onto the tickertape, but above them was a phrase that said, 'Think ... think ... say something, say anything.'

"I guess that must be somewhat galling for you. It's like you've discovered a mole inside your organisation. He's been sitting in on board meetings, taking the minutes, word for word, and then sending them to the competition. You know his name, number and the department he works in. 'Cept there's fuck all you can do to his sorry ass. I'd figure that to be rather frustrating. Hell, it would frustrate the living shit outta me. You made the same mistake Wallace made, Elmer, forgetting who and what I am." He twirled his finger in the air and brought up a pulsing diagram of a brain on the wall. "You see those little purple areas, the ones going apeshit? Those are your amygdalae, the nuclei responsible for emotional reactions like fear. I know you better than you do."

Casey fell to his knees and clasped his hands in prayer. A vision of killing Theodore, ripping his arm off and using it to escape, flashed through his mind.

"Please don't kill me, not after everything I've been through. Give me a second chance. I want to do the Magi's bidding." He tapered off to a whimper as a fresh tickertape of words belied his true intentions.

"Rip my arm off and use it to open the doors? Kill me? Boy, you couldn't kill me if you tried. But neither will I kill you. You're still needed."

Theodore held his bionic arm up and started rubbing his thumb against his forefinger. Casey's torso arched forward as a powerful electric current coursed through his body. He screamed with every last breath as his temples erupted with heat, sending him crashing to the floor in a convulsing heap.

"You appear to have forgotten that I saved your worthless-piece-of-shit life. You've been initiated. I *own* you. Never forget that."

Through blurred vision Casey watched a series of unintelligible words scroll down the screen. His frazzled brain squeezed one last whimper through his mouth. Then he passed out.

***

It had been raining all day. Nova was watching the droplets of water race down her windowpane against the spectral grey of the sky so closely that she barely noticed Charlie let himself into her bedroom with two cups of coffee. He removed his dripping jacket, gave his hair a quick once-over with a towel and joined her on the window ledge. She hugged her legs closer and vacantly took the cup from him.

"You're welcome." He nudged her leg and arched his eyebrows.

"Huh? Oh, sorry. Thank you." She brought the cup to her nose and inhaled.

"Who's winning?" he said, indicating the raindrops.

"Van der Star was ahead ... until I drove him off the road. Looks like a fatal collision from here."

He smiled and softly blew on his coffee. "Are you OK, Nove? You've been lost in thought for days. Is the pressure getting to you?"

"No, it's not that. Don't get me wrong. I *do* feel stressed about the next round. It's Sushi."

"What, you mean the bust-up you had with her?"

"Yeah. It's weird. After the argument I promised myself I'd visit her the next day to make up, but I keep finding reasons to put it off."

"Don't you want to make up with her?"

She shrugged, as if she didn't care. But tears pooled in her eyes.

"What is it?"

"It's just — why am I such a screw-up? How did I manage to fall out with a computer simulation?" She started laughing. "I'm laughing, but it's not funny. I mean, seriously — Computer Sushi is supposed to be the friend that would always see eye to eye with me, right?"

"Sushi's Sushi. You're you. Even a simulation of the friendship will be fiery."

She thought about what he'd said and took a long sip of coffee.

"But I thought I had my life sussed. I did the whole Super Nova project. I completed my runs, did my time in the Simulator, finished my uni work on time. I even made up to the people I'd offended in some way. Why am I struggling now when I had it all sorted?"

"Because it's not possible to have everything sorted. That's not what life is. There'll always be something, won't there? When I got back from travelling I thought I knew it all. I acted like I was one step away from enlightenment. Then one of the first things I did when I arrived back at uni is go out with Holly. All my mates warned me against her. It was entirely superficial on my part."

"I can't believe you actually went out with her. What were you thinking?"

He stared out of the window. "She's a total dick, isn't she? If I've learned anything, it's that I've still got a lot to learn."

Nova prodded him with her foot, an action that had come to mean "she'd quite like a foot massage, if it wasn't too much trouble, thanks all the same." She grabbed a pillow for her head, leant back against it and quietly moaned as he pressed his thumb into her sole.

"Why don't we do some more question practice to help take your mind off it? You can visit Sushi when you feel ready. No point in forcing it, you might end up arguing again."

"As long as you're up for multitasking. The foot massage can't stop. A little bit higher. There you go."

Charlie maintained the pressure on her foot with one hand while he scrolled through a list of questions on his phone with the other. The fifth round was called Arty's Answers and it resembled a TV quiz show. Solos had spent the year solving puzzles, avoiding danger by executing various combinations, and fighting a range of exotic animals. The Show and Tell round had challenged them in a different way, requiring creativity. Arty's Answers would push them further still and demanded a knowledge of Solarversia itself: the Gameworld, its multitude of quests and the people that won them — all things she'd learned about in Knowledge sims. Nova was looking forward to it; there was nothing she knew more about than the world of Solarversia.

"What speed do Acoo-Stickulars travel at?"

"Easy. Ten percent of the speed of sound. Next. And other foot, please."

"In the first of the final rounds, how many people were in the minority?"

"471,089 people were in the minority, including me. All thanks to you and your man Wesley."

"Don't you forget it. Next question. What's the capacity of the SS Venus?"

"Pur-lease. The same capacity as all the Planetary Spaceships — five thousand. Try to ask me something a four-year-old wouldn't know. One last squeeze of my toes, and then I'll let you do my shoulders."

Chapter Forty-Five

Nova felt like slapping herself. The conga line. The stupid, bloody conga line. Why hadn't she paid more attention to it? She had been *in* it on the first day of The Game, had even placed a holographic version of it onto the spiralling bookcase on SS Jupiter. A vague memory that a Tweel of Fate had actually given her the exact answer to the question stirred in the depths of her mind.

She glanced at the players either side of her, then at the holographic conga line making its way along the front of the stage, and desperately searched for inspiration. There were twenty seconds left in which to submit her answer. Failure to submit any answer within the time limit was an automatic out. That was the way the guy from Exeter had gone in the previous round. She was sure she'd always remember the look on his face, the way it drained of blood as the reality of his situation sunk in. He'd looked close to tears.

She was at the Spiralwerks' TV studio in the Olympic Park, two hours of the way through Arty's Answers, the fifth of the final rounds, which tested the Knowledge aspect of the Science of Solarversia. Security upon arrival had been mental: she'd been subjected to a full body scan with a chunky metal detector and told that state-of-the-art equipment would be monitoring her every move on stage. A finalist in Japan had been disqualified when the security staff found the miniscule grommet he'd had surgically implanted in his ear to allow an accomplice to communicate the answers to him.

Twenty-nine finalists had entered the round from the UK. Seven, including Holly, were still in play, and three of them would make it through to the sixth and penultimate round. They were lined up on stage in front of an audience of maybe a thousand people. Nova knew that her parents, Charlie and Burner were out there somewhere. She hadn't been able to locate them with the studio lights glaring in her face, but she'd definitely heard Burner chant her name a few times. Each player stood at a pulpit containing a tablet on which to write their answers, a VR headset for the questions that had required immersion in The Game, and a shiny red buzzer.

First off, they'd faced the Grid Memory Game, where you needed to recall details of the people located around your own square. The game had progressed in difficulty, spreading to ever more distant concentric rings and ending when the first three players had been knocked out. It was only at that point, when she'd already got through, that Nova could acknowledge how worried she'd been that Sushi's name would come up. The idea of confronting questions about her late — or was it, she wondered, her former — best friend, in full view of the world, had been quite nauseating.

After that they had progressed to trivia, with questions about players who had completed well-known quests, the fighting abilities of the circus animals, and the many exhibitions and Bucket List items. The current question, the one causing her to growl under her breath like an anxious pit bull, asked for the maximum number of people ever to have been in the conga line at one time. As the seconds counted down she stared at her answer — 725,000 — and started to second-guess herself.

It seemed like such a large number — it was nine times the total number of people who had been in the Olympic Stadium for the opening ceremony. But the virtual world played by its own rules: obeying some laws of physics and ignoring other ones entirely. Yes, her guess was large, but not compared to the total number of players. If only she could call out to Burner — the geek had probably worked it out through a series of complex calculations. She pressed the red buzzer with a few seconds to spare and hoped for the best.

"We asked you for the maximum number of people in the conga line during the year," said Artica Kronkite, quizmaster for the round. She thought he looked taller in person than on TV or in VR. Certainly his suit was very sparkly, the kind of get-up Arkwal usually wore. "Your answers are in. And I'm afraid to say that it was *you*, Connie, whose answer was furthest away from the truth. The maximum number of players ever to congregate in the conga line — and this occurred just days after The Game began — was 490,338."

Nova puffed out her cheeks, exhaled slowly, and when it came to her turn, shook Connie's hand with as much sincerity as she could muster. On the screens behind them Connie's avatar flew down a pipe and plopped unceremoniously into

Banjax's tank. Nova glanced along the stage to see Holly posing for the cameras. She hated herself for looking — her blood pressure went through the roof every time she saw Holly's smug face — but couldn't help herself.

They were down to six. The clapping died down and attention returned to Artica.

"You should be well-acquainted with Castalia, Emperor Mandelbrot's flying palace. Earlier in the year you were invited to take Arkwal's guided tour of the palace. The tour started in the Overdome, which houses the arkwini living quarters. With the aid of a compliant arkwini, Arkwal would have demonstrated one of two machines: the Wake-a-nator or the Sleep-a-nator. Between them, how much time do these two machines save each day, per arkwini?"

A holographic scale model of Castalia floated along the front of the stage. The tubes that sprouted from its Underdome dragged along behind it, giving it the appearance of a discarded helium balloon. She stared at it in a vain attempt to jog her memory. Had she ever been asked the question in the Simulator? Charlie certainly hadn't asked the question during her revision, she knew that much. Having been through the Wake-a-nator herself, this was one question she should have known the answer to. Except her mind was blank.

There was the ridiculously long bed whose mattress wrapped back round on itself, the mechanical arms that lifted the duvet off at the end, and the machines, one at each end. Arkwal had mentioned the number of minutes saved, she was sure of that. Except it could have been any number you cared to pluck out of thin air. She plumped for ninety-nine and prayed that the other players were as clueless as she was.

"Your answers are in," said Arty, "and I can see we have quite a range. Anu, you were very close with your guess of 'eleven'. The actual number of minutes saved is thirteen." Nova clasped her fingers over her head and cursed her stupidity. How could she have been so far out? Another peek along the line, another fake smile from Holly, sending Nova's heart rate through the roof.

"The person whose answer was furthest from the truth was Edmund, who guessed 2,350. Bad luck, mate. It's goodbye to you." It was an older guy, from London. Nova squealed and then tried to suppress a giggle. How he'd got this far was a mystery. He left the stage, waving madly to the crowd, and watched in mock horror as the dodectopus devoured his avatar. At least he could enjoy his final few seconds of fame before the gong sounded.

"And then there were five, which means another change to the rules. We're moving into Instant Winstant. No more timers, you need to buzz in to answer these questions. If you buzz in with the correct answer, you're through to the penultimate round. And we all know what that means. At the moment, you're guaranteed £10,000. If you make it to the final hundred, you're guaranteed a whopping £100,000. So get your brains in gear and your hands ready to buzz. What was the name of the old man who controlled the nets that you had to crawl under in the Fire Demon's Obstacle Course on Alpha Island?"

Nova hesitated for the smallest instant before buzzing. She was too late. The delay was long enough that the guy next to her got there first.

"It was Nico's Nets that you had to crawl under, Arty. His name was Nico."

"Oli Rivett, player number 32,109,240, from Tyneside, 'Nico' is the right answer."

She grimaced as Arty shook his hand and congratulated him. Why had she flinched? It was such an easy question, Solarversia 101.

"The first UK player is through to the penultimate round. There are two spaces left. You've each got a fifty percent chance of joining him. *If* you can answer the next question. Here goes. What is the Red Spot on Jupiter entangled with at the quantum level?"

Again, a slight flinch meant that she was outbuzzed — and it was such an easy one, too. Charlie had asked her the exact question a couple of nights ago. She'd answered so quickly that he'd said she would totally dominate the round, the way she knew everything. The thought that her hesitation might have just cost her £90,000 — and the championship — gnawed away at her.

"Is the Red Spot quantumly entangled to a massive black hole at the centre of the galaxy?"

"Correct answer. Ladies and gentlemen, I present to you Anu the Annihilator, player number 61,618,002, the second UK finalist to progress to the next round."

While Arty held Anu's hand aloft, Nova and the remaining two players were rearranged on the stage so that they stood next to one another, with Nova in the middle.

"We're down to three, the magic number. Interestingly, the two girls are both current students at Nottingham University. It must be the way they teach their Science. There's one space left. It's yours if you can buzz in and correctly answer this. What was the name of the princess in Ludi Bioski's story?"

Nova heard the words 'Ludi Bioski', got excited, and very nearly pressed the buzzer. She knew all about him: his tree house, the random events he spun on his Orbitini, the way he had stitched himself together after being killed by the King and Queen. But what was the name of their daughter? She could picture the princess clearly, first as a midget on tiptoe, reaching for door handles in the castle, and then as a titan whose feet stuck out of the end of her bed.

Why hadn't she spent more time mastering the Science instead of researching Theodore Markowsky? Sushi was right. It *was* a stupid obsession. The Holy Order had been wiped out. Markowsky was probably lying at the bottom of the Mississippi, fish food or worse. When a buzzer sounded to her left, Nova's body convulsed, as if she had awoken from a bad dream. Her stomach felt like it had turned to stone. It was the guy from Newcastle who had made the foosball table in the Show and Tell round. She stared at his answer on her tablet: *Emina*. Was that correct? Right there and then, she couldn't have said either way.

"I asked for the name of the princess in Ludi Bioski's story. Joe, you said 'Emina'. It's *not* the answer I was looking for. The question goes back out … and Holly's buzzed in!"

"I think Joe was close, Arty, but I remember it starting with a 'Z'. Was it 'Zemina'?"

The few seconds' pause between Holly giving her answer and Arty responding were among the longest of Nova's life. She wasn't sure what she'd do if Holly went through instead of her. Murder, manslaughter and assault were all possibilities.

"I'm sorry, Holly, that wasn't the answer I was looking for either. Over to you, Nova. Any ideas?"

Nova breathed a long, deliberate sign of relief and managed to refrain from looking at Holly, whose death stare she could feel burning a hole in her face. *Zemina*. She said the word over and over. Artica tapped the question card against his open palm and looked at her expectantly. She could sense the whispered conversations in the audience. Shuffling uneasily from foot to foot, she willed the answer to come to her with every ounce of her being.

"I'm going to have to hurry you, I'm afraid, Nova. The Game is only *one* year long after all …"

Laughter from the crowd. It bought her another few seconds.

"Was it …" She gulped and only then became aware of how dry her mouth was. "Was it 'Zibelda'?" She glanced at her chest, actually worried for a second that the palpitations in her heart might be visible to the people watching.

The answer came as a surprise; she hadn't known what she was going to say until the word came out of her mouth. It just seemed to happen, like one of her inspired manoeuvres in Krazy Karting. When she heard herself say it, she still wasn't sure where it had come from — or even if she'd made it up on the spot.

"Super Nova 2020, player number 515,740, originally from Maidstone in Kent, 'Zibelda' is the right answer. Congratulations. You've made it through to the sixth and penultimate round, guaranteeing yourself a minimum prize of one hundred thousand pounds."

***

Casey watched Theodore telepathically command the target to retreat back down the narrow passageway that constituted the shooting range. As a series of pulleys whirred above their heads, Casey studied his prosthetic limb and repeated, "shoot the target, shoot the target," in his head, like a holy man chanting a mantra.

He'd found chanting to be the most effective way of concentrating on the task at hand and keeping his subversive thoughts at bay. He wondered what had happened to his brain after the incident at the Epicenter. Perhaps the electric shock had ruptured his personality, splitting it in two. Was he now suffering from some sort of multiple personality disorder? He wasn't sure.

All he knew was that his existence had become torture. The knowledge that his every last thought was being monitored and recorded was too much to bear. It had reduced him to a stammering, gibbering wreck. A thought of escape would pop into his mind. Knowing the thought might get him killed, he'd immediately counter it, telling himself to shut the fuck up and begging Father to ignore that part of him. It was a form of mental tennis and it was slowly destroying him.

"You ready, Elmer?"

"Y-y-yes, Fa-father, I'm r-ready."

"We only have fifty of these ceramic darts, and they were extremely expensive to manufacture, so don't go wasting them. If you keep missing, stop. We may have to recalibrate the targeting system."

Theodore held the dart out in front of him, narrowed his eyes and studied its tip. It was no longer than a fingernail. He carefully placed it in Casey's hand, stepped to one side and crossed his arms.

Casey gulped. He took the dart between thumb and forefinger and tried to stop shaking long enough that he could press it into the lifeline that curved round the palm of his prosthetic hand. Managing to do so after a Herculean effort, he watched as it disappeared through the tiny flap. A few seconds later his middle finger jutted straight out, signalling that the dart was correctly aligned in the chamber. He positioned a foot alongside the line and tried to remember the training he'd undergone in the virtual environment.

Shoot the old bastard in the head, quick as you like. I didn't mean it, Father, please don't hurt me. Yes, you did. Shoot him, cut his arm off and use it to escape. Shut up. I don't mean it. I don't know where those thoughts are coming from. The target. Shoot the target, not dear, beloved Father.

Casey smiled weakly at Theodore. Forming the hand into a fist, he clenched it five times in quick succession. His middle knuckle popped open and a red dot appeared on the concrete ground. He pointed the appendage at the target and used his other hand to steady it, keeping the dot hovering around the bullseye as best he could.

It was no good. His nerves were shot to pieces and his arm was all over the place. Even with the steadying influence of his other hand, the dot rarely stayed in one place for longer than a split second. Using every last ounce of concentration and willpower, he fired the dart, knowing immediately that it was way off centre. A distant thwack could be heard as the dart struck the chipboard. When he looked at the monitor zoomed in on the target, he was amazed to find that he'd nearly hit the bullseye.

"Self-directing darts. I wouldn't risk something as important as this on a nervous wreck like you. Inner ring. It's a start. But I don't want you to stop until you're hitting the bullseye every time. Remember: we're only going to get one shot at this. You've got seventy-two hours until your flight. I'll leave you to it."

Behind them a small convoy of 'bots glided along the corridor, carrying a range of computer parts between them. Theodore walked a few paces away from the shooting range and then stopped without turning around.

"Oh, Casey, there was one other thing."

"Y-y-yes, Father?"

A bolt of electricity shot through Casey's skull. Lasting only a fraction of a second, it was far less severe than the shock he received at the Epicenter. Still, it was enough to send him to his knees, where he remained, hands clutched to his chest, a look of desperate self-pity on his face.

"I'm sorry, Elmer, but I thought we agreed that Casey was dead. Let's not fail because of some silly little oversight. If *I* can remember your new name, *you* can too."

My name's Elmer Sullivan and I'm the property of the Holy Order. Casey repeated it over and over. It would be his new mantra for the day.

***

Nova was aware of the celebrations going on around her, but was too numb to join them. Instead she stood still, arms by her sides, as she tried to allow the news to sink in. From the hundred million people who had started the year, *she'd made the final ten*. It didn't seem possible — amazing things like this didn't happen to ordinary people like her.

It was the evening of Saturday 20th February 2021, and the Grand Room at the Trumpton Hotel had just burst into life. It was a frothing sea of moving people and flash photography as the crowd jostled to get a look at the prize specimens on stage. The penultimate round was called Sixty Second Solicitation and had required the final hundred, including three Solos from the UK, to make a minute-long video to persuade people to vote for them.

Pundits had declared that success would arise from a careful blend of psychology and popularity as players worked out how to endear themselves to the voting masses, those 99,999,900 players who had already gone out. Where the Show and Tell round had required them to present an object, this round had required them to present themselves.

After securing her place in the final hundred the previous weekend, she and the ninety-nine other semi-finalists had been transported from around the world to the plush Trumpton Hotel in Mayfair, London, where they were shown to their rooms and kept away from the press. The bombshell had been dropped after breakfast the next morning: they had two days in which to record their videos in one of the special booths located around the perimeter of the Grand Room.

They hadn't been allowed any props or special effects this time, only the power of their arguments. The videos had been subjected to a global vote. Each dead player had one vote to cast and it had to go to a player from a country other than their own. Nova, unbelievably, had received enough votes to place in the top ten, and 750 million people had just watched the results.

As the nine other finalists approached her in turn, Nova did her best to congratulate them. Pedey Gonzalez, the woman who had fired the Shadow Sucker in Bouncy Baltimore, planted a firm kiss on Nova's cheek and skipped off to join her family. Labelled The American Dream by the press back in the States, her confidence often bordered on arrogance, although Nova was never sure how much her attitude was purely for show. Next in the queue to greet her was Jools van der Star.

His avatar name, The Beanstalker, accurately described his physique. He was six foot four, but couldn't have weighed much more than Nova herself. She craned her neck to look up at him and, in an attempt to put their rivalry behind her, offered him a weak smile and her outstretched hand.

He looked down at her, bearing an expression that suggested he'd discovered a piece of crusty dog shit embedded in the sole of his shoe, scoffed, and then brushed past, without uttering a single word. She turned to see him walk off in the direction of what had become her least favourite sound in the entire universe: Holly's godawful laugh.

Nova patted herself down, quickly shook a few more hands and was glad to see Burner leap onto the stage. He grabbed her by the shoulders and spoke like he had only just processed the news himself.

"You're a millionaire! A bloody millionaire! Unless you screw things up, a *multi*millionaire. And I'm best mates with you. This is the best thing that's ever happened. You know what this means, don't you? There's no time to party. We need to get straight back to work. A week until the final round sounds like a long time, but it will fly by. I'll start researching the other nine finalists. Strengths, weaknesses, that kind of thing."

He flicked his visor down and went to work. Nova smiled, thankful she could count on him. Charlie was on the other side of the room being interviewed by someone from the BBC. She watched him for a while, glad that he too was part of Team Nova. He was no master of Science, quite the opposite. But as she'd come to appreciate during the Race to the Origin round, it was useful to have newbies around. His constant stream of questions had made her think more deeply about some of the mechanics of The Game, things she thought she knew well. Perversely, he'd made her a better Solo.

Just behind Charlie, her parents waved frantically as they caught her eye. They'd come to London for the day and looked to be the proudest people in the room. Since she'd started to place in the money positions, her dad had been far more sympathetic to Nova's Solarversia obsession. She'd not seen him this happy in a long time. Her mum said he'd been applying for jobs almost non-stop for the last three months. No bites — not even an interview. He was glum at home, always muttering about being too old and out on his arse. It was great to see him with a smile on his face.

Ignoring the almighty kerfuffle in the room, her mind drifted to the other two people who had dominated her thoughts of late. Nothing more had been heard of Markowsky. Some believed that he'd drowned during his escape attempt. Others reckoned he'd gone into hiding, afraid to appear in public, and was in the depths of the South American rain forest.

Wherever he was, whatever he was doing, she was obsessed with him and his stupid manifesto, that much was clear. She'd been spending an unhealthy amount of time in Super Nova, the virtual cube, downloading information, reading forums and watching videos, and constantly fantasising about what she'd say and do to him if she ever got the chance.

She caught Charlie's eye and nodded to him. He winked, knowing full well what she wanted to do now the result was in. Finally, she felt ready to visit Sushi. She'd apologise for the stupid fight and for her recent absence. But now she had something exciting to tell her, some news that would blow her away — she'd made the final ten and had done so by dedicating the sixty-second video to her.

She escaped the turmoil of the room and found a quiet alcove in which to make her visit. Brushing her hair behind her ears and thinking through what she wanted to say one last time, she launched the Soul Surfer app. It took her a few seconds to realise that something was different about the app. The 'lobby' — the app's home area — had changed slightly. The default modules were all there, the training area, the forums and so on, but not the link to Sushi herself, the one that took Nova to her bench overlooking the Seattle skyline.

Confused, she navigated to her messages. Waiting in her inbox, marked as being of high importance, was a message from Charlotte Applewhite, Soul Surfer's CEO. "Dear Soul Surfer, it is with profound regret that I write to you today. Thirty hours ago our website and the Soul Surfer application were taken offline by a sophisticated hacking attack carried out by a group of cyber terrorists known as the Holy Order. The outcome of the attack pains me beyond words: they deleted forty thousand Souls from our database before we were able to regain control of our systems. I'm heartbroken to inform you that Sushi Harrison was one of the Souls affected."

She reread the last few words a dozen times. "One of the Souls affected." What was that supposed to mean? Affected how? She navigated to the forum and did her best to take everything in. People were using words like 'genocide' and 'holocaust', and were generally baying for blood. The more lenient users were calling for Mrs Applewhite to resign; others wanted her charged with culpable homicide.

Finally she stumbled upon a long article by Soul Surfer's CTO, explaining in laborious detail the implications of the attack. It came down to a matter of backup. All that existed on the company's servers were the 'kernels' — the original, unmodified algorithms that represented the dead people who had signed up. Nothing else was saved. It meant that all and any changes to the algorithms had been wiped.

She fumbled the headset to one side, gasping for breath. This couldn't be happening. Burner. He'd know what to do. As she rushed back to the Grand Room, desperate to see him, she bumped into her dad, coming the other way, a look of joy still plastered across his face. He wrapped an arm around her back and hugged her proudly.

"There you are, love. I'm just popping to the washroom, and then it's drinks all round. Your mother spotted one of those magnums of champagne behind the bar. Let's push the boat out, shall we? It's not everyday your daughter becomes a millionaire." Against her will, Nova's shoulders had begun to shake. "What's the matter, love?" He pulled away from her to study her face. "You look awful."

"It's Soul Surfer. Sushi's gone."

He looked at her as if he hadn't heard her words — as if perhaps she'd spoken in French.

Smelling the alcohol on his breath, Nova pulled back from his embrace. "Dad — Sushi's had her memory wiped. She's been deleted."

"Come on, love, buck up. The website must have crashed or something. You can visit her later and buy her a bottle of computer bubbles. You've just won a million squid, Nove." He raised her hand in his and shook them in jubilation. "A million bloody squid!"

"You've been drinking and you're not listening. It's not all about money. you know."

"Ha," he said and laughed. "Wait 'til you're my age, you've got a family to look after, and you've been out of work for a year. Then tell me it's not all about money."

"Dad, listen to me. Sushi's gone. I've lost her again."

He gave her a serious look. "It's not like she's not a real person though, is it? Computers don't have souls, that's just a clever name for the app."

"How would you know? You've never visited her. *Don't* tell me she's not real."

"Now you're being silly. It's just a computer game, however clever it is."

She felt winded. A *computer game*? "How could you be so fucking insensitive, Dad? Maybe you don't know what it's like to lose a friend because you haven't got any to start with."

He reeled a little, taking a step back in the corridor and momentarily seeming to lose his balance.

"For a girl who's nearly nineteen, you can be very rude and very childish sometimes. You need to spend some more time in the real world, that's your problem."

He stormed away down the corridor. Tears welled in her eyes and started rolling down her cheeks. If Computer Sushi wasn't real, why did she feel distraught? The last ten months of their relationship had been deleted forever. She'd been taken from her all over again.

And this time, they'd parted on bad terms.

Chapter Forty-Six

Casey's hands shot to his skull as it spasmed with red-hot electric pain. It felt like someone had poured lava-coated wasps through his earhole and then booted him in the face to make them angry. When the pain finally subsided, he fell into Theodore's embrace, trembling and gasping for breath, while the graphs and monitors on the wall of the Epicenter displayed the cold hard data his suffering entailed.

"It's OK, son, it's over now, that understood? I don't like having to do that, you gotta trust me when I say that. That was only a small shock and it was for your own benefit. Look at the graph on the left of the wall and you'll see what I mean."

Steadying himself against the older man, Casey looked at the readout. The shock he'd just received represented a mere five percent of the total power available to Theodore. Below it were the figures for his previous two shocks. The one he'd received at the shooting range had registered ten percent, and the original shock, a week ago at the Epicenter, had been closer to twenty percent. Father pulled him close and stared deep into his eyes.

"I promise you that I get no pleasure from hurting my children. I'm not gonna feed you some line about these shocks hurting me as much as they do you; we'd both know that to be some vile bullshit. But it's my job to ensure you do your job. That makes me your commander as well as your saviour. And I've always found punishment to be a more effective incentive than reward. You don't want me to punish you again, do you?"

"N-no, Father, of course n-not. I b-b-belong to the Holy Order, and I'm r-ready to do your bidding."

"There's a good boy," Theodore said, ruffling Casey's hair. After the searing pain of the charge, simple human contact felt good. He hated himself for liking it, needing it. "It's time to talk you through some logistics. You fly out tomorrow. In the morning an unmarked self-driving car will take you to Dallas/Fort Worth airport. From Heathrow you'll go directly to your hotel, where you'll get a good night's sleep, leaving you nice and refreshed for the Solarversia closing ceremony on Saturday. Got all that so far?"

Casey offered the most sincere smile he could manage and hailed the Magi in his head. Other than the chart showing the electric shocks he'd received, the wall was full of information relating to his mission. The tickertape of words relating to his thoughts was gone, presumably working in the background somewhere. He wondered how sophisticated the mind-reading technology was. Could it discern that his smile was fake? Was it reading every one of his thoughts, including ones like this, when he wondered what it knew?

"While you're at the hotel you'll receive a package containing three special darts. They're self-directing like the ones at the range, but are even more special than that. The tips contain nanoengineered blood cells that are programmed to put down roots once they reach the brain of the host they've been exposed to. They'll perform a similar function to the electrodes in your brain, but without the need for a messy operation. If the Magi is to reach its full potential, it will need to colonise a diverse range of organic brains, helping it to assimilate human value systems of all varieties."

As Theodore pulled away from him, his face lit up. He twirled a finger in the air and brought up a new set of screens on the wall, one of which displayed news from Solarversia.

"I don't mean to alarm you, but there's been a slight change of plan. You're still going to target Spiralwerks' CEO of course, and since he survived the attack on New Year's Eve, that will be Artica Kronkite. Having the resources of a company like Spiralwerks at my control will ensure the Magi goes on to become the sole superintelligence on the planet. But I learned some rather interesting news last weekend."

Theodore gestured to a news clip that displayed the rotating avatars of the final ten players, alongside a paragraph describing the video they'd submitted during the penultimate round.

"Our friend Nova Negrahnu managed to scrape into the final ten. Dedicated her little video to her dead friend. Ain't that sweet? She'll be there at the stadium on Saturday. It's funny. Only a few weeks ago I wanted her and Mr Kronkite dead. But I've come round to the idea of bringing them onboard — we can harness the power of their brains for the good of all mankind. That means you have two people to shoot during the inevitable mayhem."

"I'll t-try my best, Father."

"I believe you will. There's one other thing before I have you escorted back to your room. You've been thinking about using the trip to London to escape. No, no — no need to apologise. Tricky things, thoughts, the way they pop into your mind all uninvited. The important thing is that you've not been dwelling on such thoughts. But still, I want you to be under no illusion. The shocks I've been giving you work just as well remotely, and that includes being aboard a plane. You'll receive a shock every hour that you're awake. They won't be big ones, just a couple of percent. Enough to keep you on your toes is all. I advise you to remember the pain of the first shock once you leave here. It would be a stroll in the park compared to the one you'd receive if you betrayed me. You're dismissed."

Casey turned to follow the 'bots back to his room. And this time, he didn't bother with a fake smile.

***

Nova traced the stars of Emperor Mandelbrot's constellation with a feeling of trepidation, part of her unable to comprehend the improbable situation she found herself in. It was Saturday the 27th of February, the day before the final round and the day before her 19th birthday. None of it felt real. *She'd made the Grand Final.* Even if she went out in tenth place, she'd be one million pounds richer.

If she managed to last any longer, prizes climbed by a whopping half-million pounds all the way to second place, which paid out a cool £5,000,000. Double that amount would be paid to the last person standing, the Grand Champion of the Solarverse. It was crazy, and try as she might, she was unable to put thoughts of the final, and all of that money, out of her mind.

When the face of the Corona Cube disappeared, a purple blobby bridge was revealed, leading out from her profile square. It wound its way to the Emperor's dais in the centre of the Magisterial Chamber, interweaving and criss-crossing with the bridges that led the nine other finalists to the same place.

The ten of them had spent the week at the Trumpton Hotel, quietly preparing for the biggest day of their lives. Not that Nova had spent much time with any of them. When she wasn't training in her rig, working out or answering the same old questions in one of the compulsory interviews with some media outlet, she was camped in her room with Charlie and Burner, studying her competitors' highlights reels and discussing the finer points of various strategies. The ten of them watching the sixth and final story together, like they'd been required to do, would be, she realised, the first they'd been together since qualifying last weekend.

Stepping along the bridge with care, she couldn't help but stop every few metres to admire Spee-Akka's artwork. The colourful vines that usually hung from the ceiling had been removed, so she had an unrestricted view of the four triptychs. The middle panel of the ceiling's triptych, resplendent in all its Renaissance-inspired glory, was taking shape. Only one area remained blank: the oval in the centre, which was reserved to depict the events of the following day.

The twisting bridge led Nova to her seat: one of ten purple hands protruding from the Emperor's base, facing inward so that each player looked at the central column that stretched up to the ceiling. It looked like they'd been seated in order of age. Immediately to her left was Matas the Mole, the youngest and shortest finalist. His thick crop of uneven brown hair matched his even bushier eyebrows. He was only seventeen and hadn't said a thing since introducing himself on the first day.

On her right, Pedey Gonzalez zhooshed her hair a couple of times and practiced crossing and uncrossing her legs. Of all the finalists, Pedey seemed most at home with the incessant media attention and actually seemed to enjoy doing the interviews. Her only problem, Nova thought, was that she didn't seem capable of switching off. She seemed to live every second of her life as if it was being mediated to a global audience, including mealtimes, private conversations and even virtual appearances such as this one.

Fortunately, Jools van der Star, one place to the right of Pedey, was out of Nova's line of sight, helping her put him out of her mind. It was Vera, the mild-mannered Chinese woman, who spotted the Emperor bubbling first. As the lights in the chamber dimmed, the bubbling grew more intense, reminiscent of the opening ceremony when he had first appeared. On this occasion, instead of shooting up, his central column melted downwards, regressing into its base until the ten finalists were sitting around a large bubbling pot of purple soup.

The broth soon began to solidify, and took the form of a large yellow sphere surrounded by a number of smaller spheres: a solar system with seven orbiting planets. Nova watched as the star, and six of the planets, receded from view, leaving the fourth planet, which grew in size until it dominated the celestial show. Although the planet consisted of blue oceans and vast green continents, it was unmistakably different from Earth. As the finalists watched in silence, an old woman began to narrate.

"The planet you are looking at was once called Nakk. It was the home of the Unglai and was Emperor Mandelbrot's planet. Many thousands of years ago, the Unglai had reached the state of technological evolution that you currently enjoy on

Earth. They'd connected billions of computers to form a gigantic networked web. They had reverse-engineered their own genetic structure. They had created virtual reality.

"And then, in the space of a few decades, they moved from a world of economic scarcity to one of abundance. They learned how to harness enormous reserves of energy from their star, created artificial intelligence and soon became the kind of beings they had once only dreamed of. When they reached the Technological Singularity — with the creation of superintelligence — they added the '-oo' suffix to the end of the planet's name, depicting the infinite array of possibilities that lay before them. And off they went, to explore the galaxy."

Nova watched the Unglai evolve as the years whizzed by. Millions of satellites, probes and space stations were built and launched. Spaceships darted off in every direction. Lines depicting their solar travel started to thicken, interweave and criss-cross. Before long they were a truly intergalactic species.

"After searching their galaxy for centuries, the Unglai found a planet on which other species lived. The most sentient of the life forms on this planet were far behind the Unglai in terms of their cultural development and yet, it was clear that they were evolving and had already left a more primitive existence behind them. It was the most exciting discovery in all of Unglai'n history. *They weren't alone.* It was decided by the finest minds on Nakk-oo that they would watch the life forms on Terra Bojaxia, as they called it, from a distance. They would not make contact, nor under any circumstance meddle with the evolution of life as it unfurled. They watched, enthralled as the sentient beings on this planet developed and refined tools, began to source the raw materials of their world, learned to farm, industrialized and developed technological prowess, all the while praying in temples and fighting long, violent battles over territory and belief. Things were comparable to life on Nakk-oo, except in one major respect. The people of this planet seemed not to recognize the effects of their actions on their planet. They seemed to treat it as if its resources would continue to meet their ravenous desires without end. The planet started to buckle under the pressure."

Nova watched spellbound as time-lapse footage showed rainforests turn into deserts, people turn against one another, and nuclear warheads flatten whole cities. The footage was richly annotated with population and death count figures.

"Although tempted on many occasions to intervene, the Unglai stuck by their original decision, hoping that sense, love and logic would prevail. They watched as Terra Bojaxia grew hotter and hotter, its seas rose and its lands were flooded. They watched as hurricanes and tsunamis grew in intensity and frequency. They watched as thousands upon thousands of species died out, and remained nothing but bystanders when the last of the people on the planet lost their fight for survival.

"The Unglai were devastated. The only proof they'd ever found of life elsewhere in the universe was gone. They had watched it wither and decline. At home, there was outrage and despair that an alien race had been allowed to self-destruct. It was agreed by the High Council of Nakk-oo that if the Unglai were ever to find themselves in a similar position again, they *would* intervene, for life was what mattered most. The Unglai continued their intergalactic explorations and many years later, a similar situation did arise. They discovered a god-worshipping, seafaring quadrupedal species called the Ma-Hudratha, who were fast approaching the end of their scarce resources.

"The Unglai thought long and hard and decided that their intervention would take the form of a game, one that everyone on the planet could play. They devised a giant elimination game that lasted one orbit of the planet around its sun. Contacting the Ma-Hudratha, they found people on the planet willing and able to create The Game and the countless games within it.

"The Ma-Hudratha played the Year-Long Game with a concentration and sense of purpose the Unglai hadn't predicted. During the year, the species came together to explore their very nature and found that competition complemented collaboration. When The Game was over, they appealed to the Unglai to help them create another, and over time, further games were devised, increasing in complexity as they went. Destructive practices, which had been harmful to the planet and the life that walked upon it, became unpopular. The rising temperature reached a plateau and began to decline. The oceans remained unpolluted and teeming with water life. Forests grew and were tended with respect.

"Together with the Unglai, the Ma-Hudratha chose to spread their games throughout the galaxy. When they found living planets, they approached them with the offer of a game to play. Some species were so combative and warlike that they couldn't see the offer as anything but a guerrilla ambush from outer space. But others accepted gratefully, delighted by the idea. The Unglai and the Ma-Hudratha were always happiest when they brought The Game to species who looked like they might wipe themselves out, and they learned to customise each one to meet the needs and value systems of the species in question.

"They continue to play their own Year-Long Games even now, although theirs are considerably more complex and last far longer than a single planetary orbit around a medium-sized star. The Unglai evolved over millennia into a new kind of being. The Game, and its power to transform the lives of so many, ended up transforming them. Mortality is far behind them now, as far behind them as the planet Nakk. They created the Intergalactic Gaming Commission and appointed various individuals to be The Game's commissaires and Grandmasters — Emperor Mandelbrot, for example, who, as an intergalactic host, has the privilege of hosting inaugural Year-Long Games on planets such as Earth.

"As time has passed the Emperor's form has changed. First his gender changed. He lived for many years as a female. Then he became gender neutral. After several millennia living as a person, he began to metamorphose into various types of animal. For the last sixteen hundred years he's been exploring life from different amorphous forms. The body shapes you see bulging out of his base are his old lives, the men, women and animals who have previously embodied him. The mouths in his totem pole once belonged to the beings who lost their lives on Terra Bojaxia, the planet that didn't make it. It's his way of remembering the souls lost there.

"He's evolved into a being whose superintelligence surpasses the sum total of that on Earth multiplied by several quintillion. At any one time he's able to hold trillions of conversations, write billions of emails, books and documents, compose several million songs, direct thousands of films and watch several dozen Year-Long Games from around the galaxy. He watches a Year-Long Game from every possible perspective in the time it would take you to blink. His games against other Grandmasters involve eleven-dimensional grids that contain quadrillions of intelligent beings. One of his games, against Grandmaster Pottsypto, takes place within the Buddhabrot fractal and has been going for five and a half thousand years.

"The Emperor hopes that you enjoyed playing the inaugural Year-Long Game here on Earth as much as he enjoyed designing it. Based on his initial analysis of your planet, certain parameters were tweaked to ensure that mankind maximises its chances of survival. You have a precarious geopolitical system as global hegemony transfers from the United States of America to China, a situation compounded by your move away from fossil fuels toward renewable sources such as solar power. The Player's Grid has been designed to encourage further integration among players of all ages, races, countries and interests. He'd like you to remember that all of life is a game, one where *you* make the rules — rules that can change at any time."

As the voice stopped talking the Emperor transformed one last time so that an outer section of his circular base resembled the ten finalists: in front of Nova was a replica of her avatar, sitting on a purple hand, looking inward. Whenever she moved, her replica followed suit, shifting from left to right, turning its head and so on.

Around her she watched the other finalists similarly transfixed by their own doppelgangers. Popping up in a ring in front of the replicas was another set of replicas, smaller than the first, so that Nova now looked upon and had control over two versions of herself. This process kept repeating itself for as far as Nova could see. Each ring of replicas started to spin and then a purple hand popped out of the centre, holding a sign, which read 'The End'.

***

Stuff was strewn anywhere Nova cared to look. There were laptops, tablets and headsets lying on the floor among piles of clothes. Zhang, who had recently completed a short gig for them using the miniature theatre from the Show and Tell round, was plugged into the wall, recharging, while the theatre sat abandoned behind the wonky lamp at the back of the room, dumped there by Nova after she'd nearly tripped over it on the way back from the bathroom.

In the week they'd been living at the Trumpton Hotel, she, Burner and Charlie had managed to trash her suite to the extent that it now resembled the hackroom at Burnside more than it did a top-end room in a luxury hotel. They'd snuck Burner into the suite's adjoining lounge on the quiet. He'd slept on a different piece of furniture each night — landing where he fell — and most of the mess was his. Still, as he reminded Nova every time she mentioned the subject, the people from Spiralwerks *had* told them to make themselves at home.

"Don't listen to Burner. I reckon you look totally badass in your new outfit," Charlie said as he rotated Nova's avatar through 3D space.

"I look weird. My body's all out of proportion. I don't like it at all."

"She looks like an Amazonian woman. Way too big for Bullit Burnski. Five-eight is as tall as I'll go. Any taller and they start scaring me."

"When you say 'they', I assume you mean women in the real world, rather than computer generated avatars? And from what I've seen in the six years I've known you, you'll take pretty much whatever you can get your hands on."

The three of them were camped on the floor by the bed, lounging on a jumble of pillows, cushions and duvets, studying a series of projections on the wall. Spiralwerks had revealed clues pertaining to the Grand Final every day that week: a crow, a circle, an old boot, a sword and then yesterday, an iron arm guard labelled a 'manica'. Earlier that day the details of the final had been confirmed: gladiator versions of their avatars would face each other in a virtual battle to the death at the Colosseum in Rome.

"There's something I don't understand." Charlie had brought up the avatars of the ten finalists and was glancing between them and an online gambling site. "The avatars they'll use in the final are supposed to be identical. Players have kept their own heads so they'll be able to tell who's who. And the bodies of the five male avatars look different to the five female ones, for obvious reasons. But apart from that they're the same height, weight and build."

"It helps ensure the final is as fair as possible. I mean, look at the real-world difference in size between Ozwald and Nova. If they were using their normal avatars, Ozwald would pummel her into the ground with his fists, cartoon style. That's why they made us practice Combat sims using avatars of the same size."

"Yeah, I get why they've done it, makes total sense. What I don't get is this." He pointed to a table of gambling odds on the website. "If the avatars are identical, why aren't the odds? Why do Ozwald the Destroyer and Pedey Gonzalez have the best odds, and Matas the Mole and Vera888, the worst?"

"Gamblers are doing what they've always done — using every scrap of information available to them. Take a look at this." Burner dragged Ozwald and Pedey's avatars to a blank section of wall and launched various video feeds alongside them. "These two were still violet belts when they reached the Final Million. They didn't lose a life the entire year. Impressive stuff. Check out Ozwald's highlights reel."

The three of them watched Ozwald's insane progression through Solarversia. Ludi Bioski had kicked him out of his Corona Cube at the same time as Nova and Burner, and his escape through a graveyard contained some of the best action they'd witnessed, most of it courtesy of a stunning range of Battle Axe combinations he seemed to have mastered.

In one scene he leapt off a tombstone, sliced an Obarian in half while he pirouetted through the air, landed with a commando roll and went on to hack a couple of Petrifiers to death before he made it to safety. Another scene showed him in the white half of the Decision Dome. As one of the 'Majority Losers' of the round, he'd been made to fight for his life, something he'd done with gusto.

"See what I mean? The guy's a lean, mean fighting machine. He's actually built like his Super Avatar in real life. Same goes for Pedey. She's a real-life heptathlete and cheerleader. I doubt Nova would last more than a few seconds in a real-life fight against her. It's stuff like this that gamblers are taking into account."

"Watch out, Sofa Boy, you're supposed to be providing me with moral support, not talking up the competition."

"How come The Beanstalker and The Dump Truck are third and fourth favourites? Were they violet belts too?"

"Hate that guy," said Nova, still smarting from the way Jools had snubbed her on stage.

Burner raised his eyebrows at Charlie before answering him. "Nah, they were green belts. As you can see, The Beanstalker looks like a lanky streak of piss compared to Ozwald, but people reckon he's sneaky. Aside from his Karting win, he discovered a bug in the Tweel of Fate early on and used it to stockpile his inventory. Kept the secret to himself, the crafty bugger. By the time Spiralwerks fixed the bug, he'd collected enough teleport tokens to visit six of the Grandmasters, but they judged it to be their fault, not his, so didn't penalise him. An unpopular decision, but you know what Solos are like. If you sent them on a quest to heaven they'd complain the clouds were too fluffy."

"What about The Dump Truck?"

"Age thirty-nine, Malaysian, incredibly diligent. She's married to money and doesn't have kids. Regularly clocked up eighty hours a week during the year, placing her in the top centile by time spent in the Gameworld. Her persistence is admirable. She spent so much time guessing at hopscotch patterns that she discovered three of them — out of a total of a hundred. You can guarantee she's spent a hell of a lot of time perfecting her fighting skills."

"What do we know about these next three?"

"Darth Malaki was a red belt. Had a fairly standard year. Like Ozwald, he chose 'white' and had to fight his way into the next round, so his odds improved somewhat when the Colosseum format was announced. Captain Moreno's from Mexico and at seventy-three he's the oldest contestant. Can't write him off though. I don't know if you've seen him around the hotel, but he's spritely for his age. Looks about fifty. He caused some hoo-ha during Arty's Answers. Took ages to give his answers, kept stalling and asking for questions to be repeated. Somebody kept coughing in the crowd too, people reckoned he was getting help. Not that anything was proved. As for Astrid the Unbeatable, there's not much to say about her. Norwegian, blonde, fit as you like. She won the Show and Tell round with her HelloCopter, but that hardly qualifies her as an expert in Combat."

"Why do you reckon Nova's ranked all the way down in eighth?"

"Because people haven't met me in real life, and have no idea how gangsta I am, that's why."

"More realistically, I'd say it concerns her red belt and the way she scraped into the Final Million. Her highlights reel shows her inventory filling up with items left to her in wills because of the excitement on New Year's Eve. They reckon she qualified because of people being sympathetic to her cause, and would have crashed out otherwise. Which is probably right."

"This is your last warning, Sofa Boy. Put a sock in it."

"What about Vera888 and Matas the Mole? Why are they in ninth and tenth?"

"Vera's a small, middle-aged Chinese woman who lost two lives early on and had a shedload of narrow misses after that. Watch this." Burner maximised a video feed showing one lucky escape after another: a collapsing building that missed her by inches, a huge pile-up on an autobahn in Germany from which she walked away with one health point — only to spin a Tweel of Fate and receive a health pack — and six different occasions when she'd used a teleporter that had had a TeleTrixis device attached to it, but been given easy Combinations to execute. "The old dear's luckier than a dog with two dicks. She became something of a viral legend in China when people started claiming they'd been lucky in real life after bequeathing her their items in the Gameworld. You couldn't make this stuff up."

"That leaves Matas, the young Lithuanian guy. What's his story?"

"Jesus, have you seen him round the hotel? He's got less charisma than a dead cockroach. When us finalists were introduced on the first day I thought he was someone's kid. He's the one person I think might be an easy target."

"I don't know about that," Burner said, with a shake of his head. "He's something of an anomaly, this guy. He won the Race to the Origin round and prides himself on his Puzzle skills. Keeps his sim stats private so it's impossible to know how much Combat training he's had. I keep telling her: always watch the quiet ones."

Chapter Forty-Seven

Arty took his gloves off, blew into his hands, put the gloves back on and then took them off again. He peered into his headset, flicked through a few cams and then put it back down on the seat next to him. It was torture. So much was happening, he couldn't decide what to focus on. If he watched in VR, he found himself endlessly cam-hopping; whenever he watched what was going on in the stadium, he was scared of missing something in the virtual world. Hannah, in the seat next him, propped her headset up on her forehead, put her hand on his arm and gazed at him with a forlorn expression.

"Relax, Arty, what do you think the replays are for? You were enjoying the real-world spectacle earlier, so stick with it for a while. You'll have a lot more fun if you don't try to see everything at once, trust me."

"Thanks, Hannah, I know you're right." He smiled and placed a hand on the headset, subconsciously making sure it was safe on the seat in case he wanted to use it. Within a minute he was fretting again.

"What about the weather, surely that's ruining it for everyone? I've got my thermal vest on, two jumpers, my ski jacket, and I'm still cold as brass monkeys. Why did people listen to me when I proposed leap day as the start date? 'Ooh, that's a great idea,' everyone said, 'they only come every four years, it'll be more exciting than Christmas'. Idiots, the lot of us. We'll start the next one in June. Or move somewhere warm."

"Will you please put a sock in it? It's too late to be worrying about things you can't change. If you can't enjoy yourself, at least let me try."

Arty clamped his fingers under his armpits and gazed over the eighty thousand cheering spectators there at the Olympic Park to watch the closing ceremony live. Were they enjoying themselves? They sounded like they were. What about the people experiencing the event virtually? Semantic analysis of social media feeds from around the world showed the overall sentiment was positive and that people were excited.

He wished he could share in their joy. Instead, his brain was in warp mode. When he wasn't worrying about which view he should be watching, or complaining about the cold, he was cycling through the long list of things he knew could go wrong, mentally ticking each one off as he remembered how they would deal with it.

Security had been the number one priority: for the finalists, the spectators and his employees. Everyone there had been subjected to facial recognition software upon entry and scanned for guns and knives. Every official cam in the stadium — over a thousand of them — had the latest version of Gogmagog installed. A hundred or so drones hovered at varying heights, surveying the crowd in real time. And in the spirit of coveillance, every one of the cams was publically accessible. People would pick up on anything the machines failed to spot.

He and Hannah sat in the Royal Box. Behind them, a broadcasting suite had been converted into a command centre where hundreds of Spiralheads monitored thousands of dashboards. The atmosphere was frenzied: the Grand Final was expected to exert the largest strain yet on their servers, even larger than the opening ceremony. He checked his datafeed for what might have been the hundredth time that evening.

"There's only one point two billion people watching. Our broadcast specialists reckoned there'd be one point five at this stage. That's twice the population of Russia who haven't bothered tuning in. Jesus, this is a disaster."

Hannah volleyed an eye back to the stadium, bit her bottom lip and slowly shook her head.

"Why aren't *you* stressed about this? This is your bag, the viewing numbers, not mine. You've lost two Russias. Where have they gone?"

"Ooh, look," said Hannah, "Gori's about to strike his gong. Only ten minutes until the finalists are led out. Having the entourage here like this was a stroke of genius, people love them."

Spiralwerks had commissioned the Electropet corporation to create giant replicas of Emperor Mandelbrot and his entourage. They walked, scuttled or were driven around the running track, interacting with the crowd in their own unique ways.

Gorigaroo had been marking time with his gong, counting down the minutes to showtime. Ludi Bioski worked his magic on a real Orbitini, controlling the music, the laser show that accompanied it, and several hundred drones, which flew about delivering mystery goodie bags to people in the crowd.

Spee-Akka had adopted her usual meditative posture and was being driven around the track on a float. Upon the large digital canvas on her easel, she simultaneously painted hundreds of individual spectator portraits. Each one appeared in miniature within the floral edges of February's portrait on Castalia's ceiling.

Banjax was there in the form of a Tweel of Fate. Members of the public were being called up to spin his tentacles for real, winning themselves a whole host of prizes. And Arkwal strode around the track, waving to spectators and ordering around arkwinis who played the fool.

Arty leant in to Hannah. She had her headset on and was peering at the sky.

"I still find it difficult to believe that we're here. At the end of the year, I mean, the last day of The Game. A hundred million to one; the largest knockout game in history."

"Sorry, Arty, I was miles away. Castalia just arrived in Rome. A bunch of arkwinis grabbed its tubes and tied them to one of the Colosseum's arches. Top marks to the team, it looks superb. If you're still cold, you should be watching events unfold there. It was a good idea of Carl's to have the virtual battle take place in the sunshine."

Arty put his headset back on and was heartened to find that Hannah was right. Strangely enough, the midday sunshine of the virtual world *did* make him feel warmer. He relaxed into his chair and resolved to pay no heed to the endless stream of concerns his mind could produce. If he ignored them long enough, they'd probably stop of their own accord.

And besides, the one-minute gong had just sounded. The Grand Final was about to start. He wouldn't have missed it for the Solarverse.

***

The roar of the crowd in the Olympic Stadium was barely audible in the changing room where Nova and the other finalists were getting ready. They'd been clothed in skintight haptic bodysuits, matte black except for the flags emblazoned across their upper arms and the profile numbers stretching across their backs.

Aside from making the group look like a team of highly trained Navy Seals, the bodysuits were designed to take the gaming experience to the next level. Whenever Nova received a blow during combat her suit would vibrate and shock her: the harder the hit, the harder the shock.

She'd wanted to try on a bodysuit for ages, but now that she was actually wearing one, it felt restrictive and wrong. She ran a finger round the neck of her thermal undervest in a bid to get comfortable. They'd been driven to the stadium in a cavalcade of plush limousines, exhilaration and nerves fizzing off them, but since arriving in the changing room the mood had become more subdued.

This was the Olympic final of the everyman and the magnitude of the event seemed to have hit everyone hard. Even Ozwald the Destroyer and Darth Malaki seemed to be nervous, which was a far cry from the brash manner they adopted at meal times. As Nova urged herself to remain calm, a member of the Spiralwerks' event team climbed onto a bench at the end of the room and called for their attention.

"I know it's hot in those suits. Don't worry, you'll be out in the fresh air shortly. As well as providing haptic feedback, your suit will monitor your heart rate. You'll see the rate in your display, the audience will see it on their screens and most important of all, the medics in the stadium will see it. Unless there are any questions, it's show time. We're going to line you up in order of age, eldest at the front, lead you to your gaming rigs in the centre of the stadium and help you into them. They're the same rigs you've been training in all week, so you should feel at home in them by now."

Nova walked to the back of the line and got into position, behind Pedey Gonzalez and ahead of Matas, the Lithuanian boy. She watched Pedey limber up with a series of stretches. Burner was right, she really did resemble her Super Avatar for real. No wonder they called her The American Dream. Her strong, supple body was something to behold. Trying hard not to feel demoralised, Nova glanced back at Matas. As intimidated as she felt, it was reassuring to know she wouldn't be the youngest person out there.

On command, the finalists started to file out of the room. The second she set foot in the corridor, Nova felt an almighty rush. Already the music and the cheering sounded louder. With every step towards the stadium the corridor became more hectic and intense. Photographers crowded in on either side, incessantly calling for attention, while security guards linked arms and used their sheer physical mass to ensure the procession didn't get out of hand.

When she finally entered the stadium, Nova's jaw dropped. The screams of the crowd, the throbbing music and the pulsing lasers invaded her senses. She was in the middle of it all, the one being looked at, studied and talked about. The atmosphere was electric. Dozens of drones hovered overhead, broadcasting the procession to a global audience. Her parents were sitting in the VIP area reserved for families of the finalists, while Burner and Charlie were God knows where, human needles in the Olympic haystack.

She held her head high and smiled, knowing they might be zooming in on her right now from one of the thousand or so cams Spiralwerks was said to have installed for the occasion. The memory of the stupid argument she'd had with her dad was still fresh in her mind. And it *was* stupid, the disparaging attitude he had toward Computer Sushi and technology in general. It was something she vowed to help him with, once all this was over. She'd use some of her prize money to help him retrain and get a job in the modern economy. Pushing the thought to the back of her mind as they approached the gaming rigs in the centre of the stadium, she tried hard to remember her Combat training.

The rigs were arranged in a circle facing a pole covered in yet more cams, a structure that reminded Nova of a teleport machine. Each rig consisted of an omnidirectional treadmill, three rings — one for each axis within three-dimensional space — and a harness, which secured the player in place. The rigs looked like an attempt to convert Leonardo da Vinci's drawing of Vitruvian Man into a fairground ride. When combined with the haptic bodysuits, the setup had been touted as the penultimate mediated experience, one step away from neural implants.

A couple of Spiralheads secured Nova's harness and ran through a series of safety checks. She ummed and ahhed at their questions, captivated by the events going on around her: the drones, the lasers and Mandelbrot's entourage, there in person, as it were. This is what it had been about all along. This final round, the last ten battling until one remained. Pulling down her visor, she grabbed her shoulder, pictured the tattoo, closed her eyes and thought of her friend. *This one's for you, sister*.

She dialled the Solarversia Constellation on the ceiling of her Corona Cube for the last time. The cube evaporated and she found herself in a stadium of a different kind: the Colosseum in Rome. It had been restored to its former glory, centuries of destruction and neglect repaired at the touch of a button. It may have been a cold, dark February night at the Olympic Stadium, but it was the middle of summer at the Colosseum, and its white marble seating glinted in the midday sun.

Around its circumference, ten national flags fluttered in the wind, one for each gladiator. Nova glanced around, eager to spot anything that might give her an advantage. Nothing stood out, and that bothered her. The one thing she found to console herself with was that all ten of them had been positioned against the perimeter of the arena, their backs to the wall. At least nobody could attack her from behind.

She looked down at her attire. Gone was the black bodysuit, in its place a full gladiatorial ensemble. An ocrea was fastened around each of her shins: a metal guard bound in boiled leather that led from her knees to her ankles. Each arm was clad in a manica. The overlapping metal segments that flowed down from her shoulders to her wrists made her arms resemble a pair of frozen waterfalls. A flimsy red skirt held in place by a sword belt, and some shiny golden body armour completed the look. As she looked around, getting a feel for where each of her opponents was located, and wondering where her weapons were, a flourish of trumpets blared.

People in the crowd pointed at Castalia, a glowing blimp high in the sky, and then at the Colosseum's Royal Box, which was empty save for a couple of arkwinis standing to attention. They were waiting for the entourage to teleport from the floating palace. Arkwal was the first to appear. Looking majestic in long flowing robes, a laurel wreath upon his head, he took a couple of paces forward, cleared his throat and then, in a most serious tone, said, "Ladies and gentlemen, boys and girls. I have the honour of presenting His Royal Highness, Emperor Commissaire de Spielen, von Unglai D'Acheera Nakk-oo, Mandelbrot."

The Emperor appeared in the centre of the box, his central column as high as the Colosseum itself. He waited for the rest of his entourage to appear in the box, and for the crowd to quieten. One of the arms protruding from his base made a subtle waving movement, a signal for Gorigaroo to strike his gong.

And with that, the final round of the Year-Long Game began.

Chapter Forty-Eight

Despite the crowd yelling for blood, guts and gore, players barely moved at first. Nova glanced around, unsure what to expect. She was weaponless — they all were — and yet they were expected to fight to the death. Rather than making any rash move, the players inched their way toward the centre of the arena, eyes darting either side of them.

They came to rest a minute later, still arranged in a circle, five or so metres from the gladiators either side of them. Nova's pulse raced at the speed of light. There was a pause as the players weighed each other up, working out their options. And then they all seemed to move at once.

The crowd erupted, freshly energised by the promise of carnage. The Dump Truck, who had been standing directly opposite Nova, charged straight for her, screaming a war cry, cartwheeling her arms madly around her head. Nova steadied herself, held her arms up and blocked one, then both of her opponent's fists. Sparks flew off their manicas as they connected time after time, the wrists of her real-world bodysuit pulsing in time with every blow.

The Dump Truck came at her again, mashing her arms together in a pincer movement as if Nova's head was a nut to be cracked open. Nova waited, unsure how to deal with the unorthodox move, and at the last second, dove to the side, rolling clear of the danger. In the next few minutes they exchanged a series of uncoordinated punches, stray elbows and speculative kicks, shaving points here and there from each other's health scores. Around them, the other eight had paired off and had settled into similar rhythms.

Fighting ceased the instant Gorigaroo next sounded his gong. The finalists eyed each other uneasily and then surveyed their own bodies, the ground and the wider arena as they tried to discern what had changed. Matas the Mole was the first to move. He broke into a sudden sprint away from the centre, taking them all by surprise. Nova followed his trajectory to the perimeter wall. Fastened to it was a set of gladiator weaponry: a small circular shield and matching spear. There looked to be one for each player, so she ran to the closest set, desperate to tool up before she was attacked.

She skidded to a halt by the weapons, her heart pounding. The first time her hand passed through the spear she thought she was seeing things. She *was* overexcited after all. Perhaps she had misjudged the distance? When it happened a second time she wondered whether she'd missed a Puzzle that needed solving first.

She literally couldn't grab it, touch it or in any way interfere with it. Her hand wafted straight through it, as if she, or it, were a ghost. To her relief, the other players looked to be just as frustrated. It was only then that she noticed the name on the plaque next to the items: Captain Moreno. She was standing where the old Mexican guy had started. These were *his* items — and he was running straight at her.

She darted to her left and tried to remember where she'd been standing at the start of the round. Everywhere looked the same. They were trapped in a giant sandpit, flanked by a nondescript ten-foot wall. The crowd was no use either; it was a frothing sea of screaming, bobbing heads. On her way to the centre a thought occurred to her — each national flag was different, they were like landmarks. Her own flag had been hoisted directly above her initial position. She slowed to a canter and frantically looked around, searching for the Union Jack. *Bingo*. She locked on to the weapons underneath and ran like hell.

With ten metres to go she spied Darth Malaki, the Israeli player, charging for her, his spear aimed at her head. She stopped dead and flailed her arm in his general direction, managing to bat the pointed tip clear from her face with inches to spare. She reached her items and muttered some words of relief as they came away from the wall in her hands, then shrieked as Malaki lunged at her again.

He was too quick; she barely had hold of her shield. His spear smashed into it, knocking it to the ground. She fell to one knee and swiped her own spear at him. It caught him just above his knee, clear of his protective ocrea. A horizontal red line appeared, thin at first, then thickening. He watched as the blood dripped onto his sandal.

He sneered at her like a cobra guarding its kill. She cowered, spear in hand, desperately feeling behind her for the lost shield, willing it to fly through the air into her possession. Malaki noticed her shield too, and though they lunged for it at the same time, he made it there first and kicked it away, out of her reach. She pounced after it anyway, and he reacted by thrusting his spear at her body. It connected with her armour, not hard enough to pierce it, but hard enough to knock her onto her back.

Clambering away from him on her bum and her elbows, she was in a state of sheer panic. He caught up with her, brought a foot down on her chest and pinned her to the ground. While she struggled to get free, he carefully positioned the tip of his spear in the pit of her neck. His biceps bulged as he grabbed tight, preparing to ram the spear home. Feeling the bodysuit contract against her chest, she wanted nothing more than to sink into the ground.

Fearing the worst, she caught her breath and then held it as a trumpet blared in the background. The Israeli paused and stared at her with a puzzled expression. Far behind him, on the other side of the arena, she could see the Norwegian flag being lowered. So the trumpet must have heralded Astrid the Unbeatable's death.

Suddenly, Malaki spasmed in pain and his chest arched forward. Fingers weakened, his spear dropped limply to the ground before he slumped in a heap next to it. Behind him, Captain Moreno was grinning at her, his spear protruding from Malaki's back. Another trumpet sounded. Nova looked up to the see the Israeli flag being lowered. She leapt to her feet, scrambled to retrieve her shield and spear, and ran to the centre of the arena, desperate to regain her composure and forge some basic semblance of a plan.

Moreno approached her, bearing the same mean expression he'd worn all week.

"First I kill Astrid the Unbeatable. Then the Israeli. Now I kill you." But before he could raise his weapon, the gong sounded. Parts of the ground deformed in front of her eyes. To her left, a shallow snaking crevice appeared in the arena floor. Hundreds of red-hot coals materialised, filling it to the brim. To her right, a large swathe of ground was now dotted with upturned metal spikes of differing length. Similar patches of ground transformed into potential death traps around the arena.

She ought to have run from Moreno, but instead the pair of them watched transfixed as Jools van der Star picked up Vera888, the Chinese woman, by her hand and foot. Leaning back slightly, he swung her round in a circle, and then released her at a forty-five degree angle like he was throwing the discus. She sailed through the air and landed in a patch of hot coals.

Although she got to her feet within seconds, she ran without thinking back toward van der Star, who stood at the side of the pit, his spear at the ready. His first jab was hard enough to knock her to the ground. Again she lunged for him, rather than try to escape the pit from a different direction. This time he landed a hard blow in her ribs through a narrow gap in her armour, sending her to the ground for good.

Nova snapped back to her predicament. It was time to change up a gear, to go on the offensive. She wanted *them* to be scared of *her*. She charged at Captain Moreno, shield braced at her side, spear at the ready. They clashed head on and then pushed one another away. When her shield was lowered, Moreno took a mad swipe at her face. His spear connected with her cheek, nearly taking off her nose. Her visor flashed to give her the bad news: a whopping 20 health points knocked off, down to 75.

He cackled at his handiwork and then came at her again. She sidestepped his advance, grabbed his arm and pulled him so that he tripped over her leg. He fell, face first, onto the coals and let out a mighty screech. Groaning with pain, he pushed himself up but his legs remained spreadeagled. She grabbed her spear in both hands and rammed it into his crotch as hard as she could. Another trumpet, another flag: another £500,000 in the bank.

When Gorigaroo struck his gong again a few minutes later, more weapons appeared, fastened to the perimeter wall. Each player was rewarded with a Battle Axe and a larger, heavier rectangular shield. Not wanting to get stuck against the perimeter wall, Nova quickly headed back to the centre of the arena, but was distracted by a zigzag hole in the ground on the way.

She wondered what it was there for. Barely half a foot wide, it wasn't as if anyone could have fallen into it, even if they'd tried. And she could have sworn that something inside it was glistening. She shuffled closer and peered into it. The thing that shot out of the hole very nearly took her head off. She leapt back, startled, amazed at her own stupidity.

Remembering the danger around her, she took stock of her situation. The new weapons were in her hands. Only six players remained. Thirty metres away, Ozwald the Destroyer and van der Star were tumbling around on the floor together, a short distance from a pit of poisonous snakes. Beyond them, Pedey Gonzalez was giving The Dump Truck a hard time, aiming a sortie of Battle Axe combinations at her head.

Nova paused. Something didn't feel right. She remembered sparring practice with Burner. What would he have suggested? An image of Matas flashed before her mind. *Always watch the quiet ones.* Feinting to her left, she twirled around to find that he'd crept up behind her and was now only metres away, charging, spear in one hand, axe in the other.

Her large shield deflected the blow, but the collision knocked her back a few metres. Again he came at her, ramming her hard with his shoulder before she could take a firm stance. He was quick, she'd give him that. Knocking her backward for a third time in a row, he also took a sly swipe with his Battle Axe, snatching a few points when the blade caught her thigh.

It was the fourth impact that sent the two of them crashing to the floor and rolling along the ground to end up in each other's arms. Nova smiled awkwardly, and then grimaced when he headbutted with all his might. She saw him arch his head back to repeat the move and then freeze. Something was wrong. It felt like someone was squeezing the side of her body that she was lying on. She watched as Matas sunk an inch into the ground.

"Quicksand," he shouted at her. "We have to get out right now, or else we'll both die."

She flailed madly, ripping herself from his grip, and then pushed hard against him to roll onto her back — and on top of her large shield. Leveraging herself against it, she pulled her limbs free from the pit and clambered back to safe ground. She stood to watch as Matas' movements became increasingly constricted until at last the sand swallowed him whole. *Or else we'll both die.* Nice try, Mole boy.

The trumpet signalling his death was followed by the gong and then another familiar noise. It was a nasty grating screech that assaulted her ears. Three Obarians roared into the arena, cruising through the air at top speed. Nova switched to the smaller, circular shield. Her time fighting and fleeing these balls of teeth taught her one thing: speed was of the essence.

The Dump Truck was the first victim of the Obarians. As they swooped toward her, she panicked and ran — the worst possible combination of actions. As she checked over her shoulder to watch their advance, she slipped into a trench of poison ivy. The vines came to life, wrapping themselves around her arms, legs and neck. They seemed to be squeezing the life out of her while simultaneously stretching her out, long and taut. She lay there immobilised, struggling and writhing as much as her torso could manage while her health score trickled to zero.

Pedey paid the price for her negligence, though to be fair, her eyes couldn't be everywhere at once. She'd managed to keep all three Obarians in her sight lines, suavely ducking and weaving out of their way, but failed to notice the bookies' favourite, Ozwald, creep up behind her. He seemed to have a special affinity with the Battle Axe and the crowd were treated to their first beheading. The death was played over and over on the giant screens.

Van der Star was the third Obarian fatality, a victim of poor luck and even worse timing. As the fanged spheres criss-crossed the arena, he found himself in a position where all three were headed toward him at once, a trifecta of dental danger. As his mutilated body sagged to the ground, minus large chunks of his neck and face, the gong sounded. The Obarians departed the arena, and only Nova and Ozwald were left standing.

She was struck for a second by how little emotion she felt at watching van der Star's demise. She'd dreamt about it a number of times, always taking the starring role of the player to land the fatal blow. But right at that moment she didn't have time to gloat. Ozwald had an iron glare that said he'd never back down. Moving slowly, he never took his eyes off hers. He didn't laugh or scoff at her; he appeared to respect her as an opponent. Putting away his small shield, he started to swing his Battle Axe, cross-hatching the air in front of him. He increased the speed, faster and faster.

It made more sense to attack than to defend, but she couldn't muster the courage. She switched to the larger shield and held it up on her left arm, brandishing the spear in her right. They came together. His axe battered her shield and the crowd went wild. Again and again they clashed, each time more forceful. The swings of his axe were relentless; he was a fighting machine.

She hated the way he was in control, perpetually keeping her on the back foot, making her retreat from him. With every incursion his confidence grew. It was as if he could smell her fear. He came at her again, harder, faster, stronger. His axe flew through the air, aimed at her neck. She didn't have time to block it with her shield, and had to make do with her spear. It worked, just. She blocked the blow. But then, with a flick of his wrist, he knocked the spear clean out of her hand and into a patch of barbed wire.

She switched to her axe and edged backwards carefully until she was out of space. Patches of broken glass and barbed wire were either side of her, behind her a large pit of coals. She was trapped. For the first time in their battle, Ozwald smiled, sensing her unease. And he wasn't the only one. With their faces plastered across the giant screens, spectators were calling on him to finish her off. Without her spear she felt hopeless. Why hadn't she spent more time training with a Battle Axe? She needed something unorthodox, something unexpected. Something like the zigzag gap.

Hope coursed through her body. It might have been a long shot, but it felt like her *only* shot. She took a deep breath and charged straight at him. Surprised at her sudden aggression, he braced himself. She smashed into him as hard as possible, then pirouetted through the air, landed and leapt as far as she could away from him, onto the patch of broken glass.

It took her a hop and a skip to clear it. Her feet were bloodied, her health had taken another hit, but she had escaped him. And more importantly, she had a plan. Behind her, Ozwald cursed, before calling after her, "You can't run forever, little girl. Come and give the crowd what they want — your blood smeared down my axe."

She snaked her way around the death traps toward the gap in the ground, making note of the likely route Ozwald would take on his way to her. Then she ran around the gap and positioned herself in what looked to be the optimal place. As he approached, she did her best to remain calm and tried especially hard not to look down. She started to swing her axe, like she had seen him do.

"Been practising, huh?" He followed her example. At first he matched her speed, a couple of rotations every second. Then he ramped his speed up a notch. She copied him, doing her best to keep up.

"You think that's fast? Get a load of this." He ramped up once more. His smile turned to a smirk. "Too quick for you, huh?"

This was her chance, she knew it. She tried to emulate his new speed and then did her best impression of fumbling it. When the axe clattered to the ground and disappeared into the gap, Nova emitted the most convincing gasp she could muster.

"Don't worry, second place is still very admirable." He kept swinging his axe, but now walked toward her. She fixed his gaze and clutched her shield tight to her chest.

As he stepped over the gap he came to a standstill. His smirk disappeared. He looked at Nova and then down at whatever had just clasped hold of him. A razor-sharp set of Huntropellimous claws protruded from the gap. Its pincers straddled the lower part of his body. A look of horror spread across his face. The claws snapped shut, slicing clean through his body armour. He collapsed forward, open like a banana split. The beast's second claw appeared and started snipping at his body, cutting it into pieces small enough to pull back into its lair.

As she watched him disappear into the hole, chunk by chunk, Nova realised that she had done it. She was the winner of Solarversia, Grand Champion of The Year-Long Game. There could only be one — and she was it. She looked up to the crowd in shock, hoping their response would help her take it all in. But the crowd seemed strangely still. Looking closer, she discovered that the arena wasn't just still, it was *silent*.

She turned slowly on the spot and surveyed the crowd. Everyone was frozen. Arkwal must have been halfway through a clap; it looked like he was holding an invisible football. Ludi Bioski was in the middle of turning a dial one way or the other. Except for the area within the arena, time had stopped functioning at the Colosseum. Nova gulped. What was going on?

She'd just won Solarversia. Hadn't she?

Chapter Forty-Nine

Arty kept volleying between the cams in the Colosseum, trying to work out what had just happened. It wasn't unheard of for a cam to freeze, especially with so many people logged in at once, but it *was* unusual for all of them to freeze at once. Theoretically it was impossible — the cams were programmed to automatically reboot themselves. But as he volleyed around the Colosseum, he saw the same thing from every view — the crowd frozen mid-action. He swiped the visor off his face and glanced around the Olympic Stadium in a state of panic. Next to him Hannah was speaking, words he could barely take in. In the stadium people had started to boo. He hurdled his seat and made a dash for the Command Centre.

"Carl, why has every cam frozen?" Arty held out his thumb and forefinger a centimetre apart. "Tell me you're *this* close to fixing whatever has gone wrong." Most of the screens in the room were flashing warnings of some kind or performing diagnostic checks. Some people were shouting into their headsets, others were frantically tapping away at their keyboards.

Carl looked like he was about to throw up on his desk. "The Celebratory Program should have started running the instant the person in second place died. But it didn't. Something called the MetaMyth Program has kicked in. There's a ReadMe text file attached. It's from Theodore Markowsky." He cleared his throat. Everyone in the room stopped what they were doing. The clacking of keyboards hurriedly ended, leaving only the sound of catcalls emanating from the crowd outside.

"Unless you want blood on your hands, tell whoever won to remain seated and logged in. Do *not* try to stop MetaMyth from running. Further instructions will follow. Enjoy the different ending."

The room remained silent as two hundred people tried to process what they'd just heard. Hands went to ashen faces, wide eyes betraying their fear. *Blood on your hands?* Arty's brain fired a hundred thoughts a second: Theodore Markowsky, the MetaMyth program, a different ending.

None of it made sense.

Arty stared at Carl, his eyes narrowed. "This MetaMyth program. What do we know about it?"

"Nothing, I've never heard of it. I didn't know it existed. Arty, this is not something we've programmed."

One of the techs spoke up. "It doesn't look like there's any way to interrupt it, bar performing a hard reboot. And you know what that means. We'd lose access to everything — including the Colosseum — for about three hours while we brought Solarversia back online."

"Find out everything you can about it: when and how it was installed. There must be a password. Liaise with the security team. Get every spare machine on it. I want an estimate of how long it would take to crack. Hannah, prepare a statement of some kind. Say something about the enormous strain of people viewing live virtual footage being too great for the servers. We're on the case and hope to welcome people back shortly. Call MI6. Someone get Max and Maurice on the phone and bring them up to speed. See if there's any way that Gogmagog can help. Ensure the defeated finalists are escorted inside. Get every spare security guard to surround Nova's rig. Find out what friends and family she has in the stadium, bring them here. And get me Nova on the line."

The atmosphere in the room changed in an instant. Those who had been too stunned to act now had a purpose. Arty flicked his headset down and ensured that one eye was focused on Nova's avatar in the Colosseum, the other on her gaming rig in the stadium.

"Nova, this is Artica Kronkite, CEO of Spiralwerks. Can you hear me?"

"Arty, what's going on? Everything froze when I fed Ozwald to the beastie. Was that supposed to happen?"

"Listen, we've got a situation here. I need you to stay in your seat until we know what's going on, can you do that for me?"

Nova answered him quietly. "What kind of situation? I'm not … in any danger, am I?"

"We're not entirely sure what the situation is just yet. I can assure you that we're that taking every precaution possible. Your safety — the safety of every person in this stadium — is the highest priority. You're surrounded by highly trained guards, Gogmagog is running on every cam in the stadium, and I'm here, on the end of the line. I'm not going to leave you. But I need you to remain seated with your headset on."

Before she could speak again the spectators in the Colosseum burst into life as if nothing had happened. Arty saw the crowd wake up at once, as if electrified, darting, moving, speaking, yelling, clapping. Then the people in the crowd began to shush each other. Some pointed at Emperor Mandelbrot in the Royal Box. The deformed mouths dotted around his central pole began to chant as one, "All hail the mighty Magi, all hail the mighty Magi."

***

Despite the cold February night, Nova was covered in sweat. If this was someone's idea of a joke, she couldn't see the funny side. Lit by the glorious Roman sunshine, the mouths dotted up and down the Emperor's central column chanted the Order's refrain. She stared at him, horrified to witness something she loved corrupted by something she despised.

An almighty thudding began to beat in time with the chant. It was coming from Banjax. He was lifting each heavy, bulbous tentacle in turn and swinging them with all his might against the side of his tank, which was already splintered with hairline fractures. It took one last thump to make the pane at the front explode outwards, spraying water and shards of glass all over the Royal Box. Awaiting nobody's permission, the beast clambered over a dozen tiers of seating, sending spectators diving for cover, and flopped over the perimeter fence to join Nova in the arena.

As the beast crept toward her she noticed something different about it. Banjax was the same size, colour and proportion he'd always been. But now, attached to each tentacle, just above their swollen ends, was a black armband, dotted with a grid of flashing lights. She felt sick to the pit of her stomach. It all felt so very, very wrong.

"Hello, Nova. What a pleasant surprise." She flinched to hear him address her like that. His voice was deep, dark and distorted, but had the unmistakable twang of the Deep South. "I couldn't have asked for a more *interesting* victor. I hope they've strapped you in properly, you're in for a rough ride."

"Artica, it's Theodore!" she yelled. "It's the Holy Order."

"Don't worry Nova, we're doing everything we can—"

"No, Mr Kronkite, I would strongly advise against doing *anything*. For a start, nobody leaves the stadium. Do you understand me? Nobody leaves without my say-so. I thought the grand finale Spiralwerks had in mind was a little ... unadventurous. I'm here to liven things up, and I wouldn't want anyone to miss out."

He pointed a number of tentacles towards Spee-Akka. The canvas on her easel became animated with a live CCTV feed from what looked like a warehouse. Suddenly, a huge flash of white obscured the view. The smoke cleared to reveal a half-collapsed roof and several storage containers on fire. As thick, dark smoke rose from the shattered pallets, Nova wrestled against the restraints of her rig, panic now gripping her body.

"Why the moody expression? Nobody got hurt. *That* warehouse was unmanned. But we got sloppy with our other bombs, left them all over the place. Shopping malls, schools, an Olympic Stadium here and there. They're wirelessly connected to MetaMyth, the program that's taken over. It links each bomb to a puzzle — ones you're going to have to solve. Unless you want to be responsible for hundreds of deaths, that is. If your avatar dies they'll all detonate at once. And your friend Artica knows the same thing will happen if he pulls the plug, or lets people leave the stadium. But you love puzzles, don't you, Nova? Of course you do. You just beat 100 million people, you're the best in the world."

The image on Spee-Akka's canvas changed again. Along the top was a title that read *The Puzzles of Perdition*. Beneath it were four rows of three squares, numbered from one to twelve.

"We'll start with an easy one. I'll even allow the spectators in the Colosseum to help you, isn't that generous?"

A scroll that listed four clues appeared in the air in front of her while a large screen above the crowd showed a timer counting down from a minute. Nova felt none of the excitement she usually associated with tackling a puzzle. Instead, she felt an intense dizziness. Her limbs felt like they might wobble themselves out of their joints.

"Arty, can you see the timer? I've already wasted ten seconds, I can't do this, I feel sick. Can't you just look up the answer and give it to me?"

"The puzzles don't work like that. The answers are encrypted within the program. What does it say on the scroll?"

"It says, 'My first is in enigma, but not in vintage. My second is in artificial, but not in inflicter. My third is in strength, but not in thorniest. My fourth is in divine but not in advent. I am the solution to all your problems. What am I?' How am I supposed to work it out when I can barely focus?"

"Hang in there. We've got several hundred million people working on it."

Images of death flashed before her mind. There were bombs in schools, in malls and possibly one in the stadium. She made the mistake of volleying back to the stadium for a second. It was absolute mayhem. A squad of security guards were leading people to safety, others were scrambling around her chair, shining torches, and exchanging worried looks. She volleyed straight back and resolved to stay in the virtual world until she'd been given the all-clear.

She watched the seconds tick down: thirty, twenty-five. This wasn't happening, it couldn't be. The crowd had stopped cheering. Instead, they were chanting. It was hardly the time for such a thing, had they not received the memo? Fifteen seconds and the puzzle remained nothing more than a jumble of words in her mind. The crowd chanted two syllables, over and over. *May-ji, May-ji.* Had Theodore taken control of them too? Would she be taunted from the stands as well as the arena? Ten seconds. In the end she nearly spat the word out. "Magi! M-A-G-I. That's the answer, stop the clock, I beg you."

A tick mark replaced the number '1' in the top left square on the canvas. Strangers hugged in the crowd, others chanted her name. So he wasn't in control of them — that was good to know. They'd been helping her. If anything, she was annoyed at herself — she'd solved a bunch of puzzles just like it in the Simulator. She tried to calm down by concentrating on her breathing. *It's just a game.* She repeated the phrase, trying to say it like she meant it, like she wasn't suffused with the image of a cartoon time bomb under her rig.

"The second puzzle is for your friends in the crowd. While they attempt to solve it, you'll need to fight me. If you die, a bomb goes off."

An enormous crossword appeared on the screens around the Colosseum. Next to it a two-minute countdown had already begun. Nova's instinct was to start reading the clues, start filling in the boxes. But he'd challenged her to fight. She checked the area around her for dangerous patches and chose a route that looked safest. But as she made a dash for it, Banjax blocked her path, swung a tentacle, and sent her flying across the arena. Her bodysuit contracted hard against her torso, knocking the wind out her.

She looked up to find him scampering toward her. Before she could move, he smacked her again, slamming her into the perimeter wall. First she doubled over and then she collapsed to her knees, gasping for breath, a faint taste of blood at the back of her throat. Her headset flashed and beeped like crazy, adding to the sheer panic she felt. Her health score was down to seven points and her heart rate was racing at 171 beats per minute.

Banjax's twelve legs, powered from wherever Theodore was hiding out and running the show, were much faster than her two. She couldn't fight him. It was going to come down to the crowd to avert the bomb blast. But time was running out. The crossword grid loomed into her view, half of its white squares still blank. It was hopeless.

***

Arty watched as Hannah snaked her way back to the Command Centre. Behind her, walking in single file, were two of Nova's friends. He wondered what he would say to them. It wasn't the kind of conversation he'd ever had before. Nova looked so alone out there. Hooked up to her rig, wearing the black bodysuit, she'd started to resemble a fly trapped in a spider's web. It had been intended as a symbol of triumph, that the winner should be left alone in the arena, enthroned, almost. Now the only word he could think of to describe her situation was *abandoned*.

"Charlie. Burner." He shook their hands in turn, and then shifted from foot to foot. "In an ideal world we would have met, about now, in rather different circumstances. I would have presented Nova with her prize, and you would have been invited to join her on the Grand Champion's float for a victory lap of the stadium. As it stands, we're in a predicament. It looks like Theodore Markowsky — mastermind of the Holy Order — has gained backdoor access to Solarversia's operating system. It's enabled him to run his own program, something called MetaMyth. Our entire tech team is investigating the program in conjunction with millions — many millions — of people around the world."

He was blathering. Well, there was no easy way to say any of this. "The explosion he showed us really happened, so we can't risk pulling the plug in case it triggers other bombs. Markowsky gave a list of things that would trigger the bombs in the real world: Nova leaving the virtual world, the death of her avatar, or her failure to submit any one of the puzzles within the given time limit. We're doing everything we can to prevent those things from happening while we attempt to disable MetaMyth."

"What if you can't disable it?" Charlie asked.

"We'll find a way. And until that happens, we're brainstorming ways to exploit it. Because the program interfaces with the rest of Solarversia, it's constrained by it in various ways. For instance, Theodore has full control over Banjax and lots of aspects of the arena, but no control outside of it. We still have control over the

Emperor and the other members of his entourage. And the dead players in the virtual crowd have retained control over their actions."

He gestured to the wall at the side of the room. A large screen was devoted to Nova. It showed her location in the Colosseum, a picture of her avatar rotating in three dimensions, and a list of her in-game vital statistics. A table displaying the list of items in her inventory was being updated with the ways in which they could be used to attack or defend against the ones in Banjax's inventory.

The adjoining screen was devoted to Banjax in the same way. Other screens showed the action in the Colosseum from various perspectives, long lists of puzzles, steps to work out their solutions, and datafeeds from groups around the globe — people who were working together to locate the bombs and Theodore himself.

"We're analysing their every move in the arena to see if there's any way we can help Nova or hinder Theodore. Right now we're speaking to people in the virtual crowd. We have an idea that might tip the scales back in her favour."

Arty turned to nod at a group of people huddled around a table at the rear of the room. "MI6 are here. Their security team are trying to help us crack the program's password. They've also commandeered the thousand cams we've got here to analyse shapes and movements in the stadium. We've found a suspicious package located under the seats of the VIP area where the families are sitting. The bomb squad are on their way here as we speak."

Burner exchanged a worried look with Charlie.

"Is there anything *we* can do, Arty? That's my best mate out there, and it's torture watching her being flung around like this."

"Yes, there is. That's why we brought you here. I've heard you guys were part of the team that helped her reach the final in the first place. You'll know her style of gameplay better than anyone. I'd like you join the strategic gaming unit and feed in your ideas in case we've missed anything. Once you've done that, I'd like you to join Hannah and the MI6 team. They have a long list of questions for—"

Arty was interrupted by a chorus of gasps. Turning to the large screens, he caught sight of a slow motion replay of Nova slamming against the perimeter wall and collapsing to the ground. Another screen showed her in the real world, convulsing and coughing, her heart rate dangerously high.

"Now!" yelled Arty. "Operation Power Up is go, go, go."

Chapter Fifty

Banjax was tip-tentacling towards Nova when Gorigaroo struck his gong. He stopped in his tracks and stared at Nova with a puzzled expression. In the Royal Box, Ludi Bioski sprang into action, prancing around like a madman in front of his Orbitini.

When an Event Card appeared on the machine's screen — of a pin puncturing a balloon — the crowd gasped as one. In the sky above them Castalia had lurched to one side and was floating down fast. The Eastdome smashed open against the top edge of the Colosseum and millions of game items poured from its innards.

Banjax howled in anger and darted toward the deflated palace. Nova paced one way and then the other, unsure what was going on, or how she might take advantage of the situation. When she spotted something flying toward her out of the corner of her eye, she cowered, thinking Theodore had weakened the section of wall behind her, making it crumble onto her head.

Instead, her inventory started flashing like crazy. She got to her feet and gasped as her armoury quadrupled in seconds. Items rained from the sky, coming at her from all directions. The crowd had worked together to pass them around the Colosseum, forming a factory line that ended at the virtual spectators close enough to drop items on her head or throw them towards her reach.

Jars of Skidz, Force Fields, DoppelGanger Scanners and a healthy array of weapons were now stocked in her arsenal. As she replenished her health back to maximum, the feeling of hopelessness slunk back to the shadows.

In the time it took Banjax to charge at the crack in the Eastdome and grab some of the items for himself, Nova reached the completed crossword puzzle and submitted it. Turning to face him once again, she selected a plasma rifle, touched the trigger and didn't let go. A thick red stream jetted from its nozzle, but was easily deflected by one of the four shields he'd chosen. Banjax smiled, armed his eight free arms with the same weapon, and blasted her back against the perimeter wall.

Hunkering behind her shield, she looked to the crowd for inspiration, but none was forthcoming. Maxed out at one hundred items, there was no more space in her inventory; she'd need to make do with what she had. She frantically cycled through the items, desperate to know how she might survive against an opponent who was able to command six times the weaponry. She found a bumper supply of Growsome and drank one bottle after the other until she was as tall as the perimeter wall.

"Arty, how are you doing at your end? Am I in any danger? Have you worked out how to stop the program yet?"

"We're doing everything we can — your rig's been checked and it's safe. There's a password on the program, but it's securely encrypted. The security team reckon that it would take half a century to crack it by brute force. MI6 are here. They've requested that you keep playing, while we get a better understanding of—"

"Quiet, infidel," came Theodore's voice. "Do *not* speak again. We've been playing by your rules for long enough. It's time to play by mine."

A great pile of jigsaw pieces landed in a heap in the stands and a new timer appeared on the screen. Nova locked eyes with the turquoise creature, who looked like he'd drunk some Growsome of his own. Standing twenty feet tall, they circled around each other while the crowd looked on helplessly. The Colosseum was less daunting from her new height and the death traps no longer affected her health score. The hot coals had been reduced to warm sand, the barbed wire to harmless strands of Velcro.

Banjax stood up on four leg-like tentacles. He raised the other eight about his body, four at each side. In each one, the same item glimmered: a Sword of Sadism. The blades and the jewel-encrusted handles sparkled. He looked like an Indian deity armed to the hilt. How was she supposed to defend herself against such a weapon? How was she supposed to defend herself against *eight* of them? A year's worth of Combat training in the Simulator evaporated in an instant.

In seconds he was a whirlwind of blades spinning straight for her. She armed herself with two large rectangular shields. Almost paralysed by fear, it was all she could think to do. They collided and a colossal eruption of sparks sent both of them sprawling. He was quickly back on four legs.

"Arty, help me out here, goddamn it. If you can't crack the password, at least tell me what to do. I'm dying out here, it's ridiculously one-sided. I don't know how much longer I can carry on."

"You're doing brilliantly . And we're trying. Every single person in the Command Centre is working to help you. I was just about to tell you what to do; I needed to be one hundred percent sure, that's all. Keep that same shield in one hand, but arm yourself with a Web Shooter in the other. Wait for him to start spinning. Don't fire until he's within a range of ten metres. Then you unleash hell."

Nova made the switch and aimed at the centre of the approaching vortex. When Banjax got within range, she did as Arty had instructed. Her defence looked woefully inadequate — a piece of flimsy white string against the might of a bladed whirlwind. Nothing happened at first and he continued to advance towards her as quickly as ever.

Right up to the last second she was convinced she was going to die. It would be a virtual death like none before it, one that had real-world consequences. It would cause bombs to explode. More Sushis would die. It would all be her fault and she could do nothing more than tense her body and wince.

She pressed her body flat against the perimeter wall and watched through squinting eyes as Banjax suddenly came to a mummified halt in a mass of tangled webbing. Running to the timer, she submitted the completed jigsaw with a few seconds to spare. It was a picture of Theodore as a more advanced cyborg, behind him a terrifying horde of intelligent robots.

When he finally managed to cut himself free of the webbing, Banjax looked seriously pissed. He slapped his tentacles above his head three times, launching three puzzles simultaneously: a twelve-by-twelve Rubik's cube, a huge Sudoku puzzle and a cryptogram. Five minutes started counting down.

Before Nova could move, the entourage retaliated in the same way as before. Gorigaroo struck his gong and Ludi Bioski played his Orbitini. Castalia, which was now lying on its side, punctured and held in place by several of the Colosseum's support columns, exploded through the uppermost Westdome, showering an abundance of items into the arena.

It took Nova a few seconds to comprehend what the crowd were urging her to do. Once she maxed her inventory out at a hundred items, she would no longer be physically able to pick up any other item. Instead, they were advising her to use the items in her inventory and replace them as she went. She scanned through the list and lobbed anything at Banjax that looked like it might impede him: a Jar of Skidz, a can of Bugz and a Musical Chair.

He immediately erected a rectangular Force Field to block the items and, catching on to the idea, jettisoned some of his own. She saw him activate his Turbo

Boosts and followed suit. The two of them whizzed round the arena like tornadoes, grabbing every bottle of Growsome they could find. This time the change in their sizes was exponential. When they came upright again, armed like tanks, the Colosseum looked like a fallen Frisbee at their feet.

The ensuing tangle was a fight of titans. Banjax knocked her into the Mediterranean, causing a tsunami that swamped Sardinia. Nova threw him into Spain. He belted her all the way to Russia. They were so large, their skins so tough, that ordinary beatings no longer affected their health scores. Around the globe they went, crushing buildings, destroying nature reserves, altering the Earth's plate tectonics whenever they landed.

After a few minutes of wrestling around the globe, her headset flashed to indicate that the puzzles had been completed — she needed to get back to the Colosseum to submit them. Inferring her sudden change in temperament, Banjax extended his tentacles in every direction. He was a twelve-armed keeper protecting his goal. And Nova needed to score in the next thirty seconds.

She darted to her left and was blocked. She looped back round and tried her right. Again Banjax thwarted her attempt to pass him. He laughed at her, and thumping his tentacles into the Pacific Ocean, sent walls of spray into the air. She had fifteen seconds to do the impossible.

Instead of running at him, she backed away from him, drawing him towards her. Her trot turned into a run. As she reached full speed, she sprouted some Winged Beauties and circumnavigated the globe in the other direction. She arrived back in Europe alone. Getting down on her hands and knees, she submitted the completed puzzles. Three more tick marks. On the horizon she could see a blur as Banjax approached at top speed.

"This is killing me, Arty, give me some good news. Tell me this is a bad dream. I'll take anything at this point."

"I need you to keep doing—"

Banjax skidded to halt, ploughing several mile-long furrows through the centre of Rome in the process. "Enough! I thought I told you to keep quiet. Remember whose game this is."

Suddenly the background noise of the Command Centre dropped out. "Say goodbye to your friends," said Theodore darkly. "You've had enough of their feeble input. Though they can still hear us. I want them to hear you weep when you witness the death and destruction that your weakness caused. I've also had enough of the crowd completing the puzzles for you. This is

Solarversia, and that means The Game needs to evolve. Playtime is over. Let the real fun begin."

He raised a pair of tentacles in the air once more, but didn't stop slapping them together until all six of the final puzzles had been kicked into motion.

"Theodore, no ... not all six at once. I'll do anything, please stop this madness."

Nova remained on her hands and knees. In the miniature arena she saw that the countdown timer had been set to three minutes. If she didn't act soon, countless people were going to die, but without the comms link to Arty, she felt helpless. A video feed flickered into the corner of her display. What was she seeing? When the image finally resolved itself, the small amount of air that remained in her lungs was cruelly sucked out of them, leaving her gasping for breath.

It was her parents, cowering in fear. Around them other people were doing the same thing. They must have been the guests of the other finalists. Fifty or so security guards surrounded the VIP area, all eyes on the package underneath the seating area. The bomb inside the stadium had been under their seats all along — it was *their* lives that were in danger, not hers. Before she could ponder their fate further, Banjax was upon her. He struck her with several tentacles at once, booting her so hard that she soared into the sky.

Her gaming rig span her round so fast she nearly blacked out. The readout showed that she'd been exerted to three-g of acceleration. In the Gameworld, the blue sky soon turned black. Earth retreated into the distance and the Moon grew larger. Although the spinning soon slowed, she found that she was unable to control her movements. There was no ground beneath her, no walls or surfaces to push against.

Somehow Banjax *could* move with purpose: he managed to catch up and batter her once more. She careened into the International Space Station, sending several hundred spaceships spinning into deep space. As she spiralled away from him, passing the Moon on her way, she noticed something different about him. His outline was illuminated. He had a ghost-like aura, almost as though he'd been set on fire.

That was it — he'd strapped a jetpack on. She cursed herself for not thinking of it and quickly found one in her huge inventory, but before she could power away from him, he belted her at speed. She tumbled further into space, passing Mars. Earth grew tinier still. All seemed hopeless, beyond despair. There was no way she could beat him on her own.

Then a thought occurred to her. She hadn't won Solarversia on her own. Like the gorilla and the kangaroo in Gori's story, she'd only made it this far due to teamwork. She didn't need to fight Banjax on her own; she needed to work with everyone else. If they couldn't help her right now, what did it matter? *She could help them.* If anyone was able to provide Spiralwerks and MI6 with information about Theodore and the Holy Order, she was — she'd been obsessing over him since Sushi's death. Similar to Project Drone, this situation was a puzzle that needed solving. Energised by a strand of hope, she hit her jetpack thrusters and blasted away from Banjax, deeper into space.

"Arty, if you can still hear me, I need you to listen. I don't think there's any way I can get back to the Colosseum in time to submit those puzzles. I haven't even looked at them yet. We need to crack the MetaMyth password, it's our only hope. You said it would take fifty years to crack by brute force. We can do better than that. Theodore's obsessed with meaning and myth, especially in relation to the world of Solarversia. Tell the security team to restrict their password attempts to words and phrases from his manifesto and the Gameworld. And get them to prioritise passwords whose lengths are multiples of the number twelve."

Using her jetpack, Nova managed to control her trajectory as she approached Jupiter. It looked so majestic, so real, that she had to tear herself away from its beauty to concentrate on the weapon of mass destruction that was fast gaining on her. With a jetpack strapped to each tentacle, he soon caught up.

"Why are you doing this?" she yelled, firing a Time Whisk towards him. He dodged it and knocked the whisk from her hand. "How can you claim to be the saviour of mankind when you deal in death and destruction?" She aimed at him with her Web Shooter. Again he smashed it free of her grasp, cackling as he did so. He reached out and grabbed her leg, then pulled her slowly toward him.

"Why? Because There Can Be Only One." He raised a tentacle and pounded her in the gut. Another tentacle rose and smashed her in the face. Her health score ebbed down while her body took a pounding from the haptic bodysuit.

"What's that got to do with killing loads of innocent people?"

"You exaggerate. What are a few people here and there? What's a few hundred? Listen to me, Nova. Artificial superintelligence is almost upon us. The implications are enormous. And it's likely that one — and only one — of these superintelligent beings will ever come into creation. As a Solo you can relate to that, right? *There Can Be Only One!* It's imperative to the survival of the human race that we create a friendly ASI — the Magi."

"And how is this—" He pinned both her arms behind her back, spun her round, kicked her away from him and caught her again — "How is *this* supposed to be *that*?"

"I tried the peaceful route for a long time, Nova, believe me. Nobody listened. People are listening now. A couple of billion to be precise. The cost of a few dozen lives will be seen as the bargain of the century when historians study this event in the future. It will be seen as a turning point in our destiny, the moment we collectively decided to consciously evolve. We can't have every little tech company in Silicon Valley going their own way. Come to me, Nova, join the Holy Order. Take your rightful place at my side. You and everyone else who's watching, you all need to know. I've almost created friendly superintelligence. I'm nearly there, closer than you imagine."

"This is your idea of a recruitment drive? You can shove your 'rightful place' up your dodectapedal ass."

Banjax sneered at her. He held out two of his tentacles in front of his face. The grid of lights on his bionic armbands flashed into life, beaming a holographic image of a girl's face into the space between them. As the face rotated into Nova's view, she recoiled sharply. It was Sushi. Her long blonde hair was tied in a bun, leaving a willowy wisp to fall either side of her ears.

"Soul Surfer is another company blindly chasing artificial superintelligence, no thought spared for what would happen if they actually created it. As you know, I paid them a visit a few days ago and penalised them for being so reckless. I kept a copy of their data before I deleted it from their servers. This is your final chance. Join me, and I'll resurrect your friend. Fail to do so and I'll wipe the last year's worth of your relationship for good."

Nova stared at the face of her dead friend. The intense pain she'd felt in the days following the bombing came flooding back — the feeling that a part of her heart had been taken forever. She wanted her friend back more than anything in the world. She'd give up the championship and everything it entailed — the fame, the fortune, and the chance to be a game designer for real — in an instant, no thinking required, even if it was only a computerised version of her friend that she was being offered.

There was one big problem with the offer — it came from the guy who had taken Sushi from her in the first place. A crazy guy with a warped idea of how to make the world a better place. As much as it pained her to lose Computer Sushi, there were some things she'd *never* do to get her back. And joining Theodore Markowsky was right at the top of that list.

She took a deep breath and mentally steadied herself. It was torture not knowing how Arty was progressing. She needed to stay alive and she needed a plan. As she cycled through her inventory, searching for any item that might be of use, she noticed a white baton floating her way. When it got closer she realised that it was one of the spaceships that had been docked on the ISS. It flew past Banjax's head, near enough that she was able to catch the pointed nose end.

"I already gave you my final answer. Here's something else you can shove up your ass."

She flipped the spacecraft in the air, caught hold of its elongated frame, pulled her leg into her body to draw Banjax closer, then swiped at him like a madwoman. He held his tentacles up to protect his head so their spherical ends drooped around him like a bunch of old daffodils clutched tight by the stems. Nova took aim and swiped straight through the centre of the bunch with the nose of the spaceship. Banjax released her from his grip and recoiled in horror. They both watched as the turquoise balloons floated off into space, trailing lines of slimy white pus behind them.

Banjax lowered his decapitated tentacles and smiled straight at her. A malevolent laugh escaped him. Then the raw, severed ends of his tentacles swelled. A new sphere was forming on each. They grew and grew, like balloons being blown, and then suddenly sprouted into pairs, like cells dividing. Two brand new spheres leered from each arm.

He swivelled them round so each faced Nova. In every tentacle, another version of Sushi's head appeared. Her twenty-four faces pulled horrible, deformed expressions. Her friend was screaming in agony, howling in terror, convulsing in the depths of grief, all at the same time. One head turned to its neighbour and threw up a putrid green mess into its mouth.

Nova froze, unable to turn away from the spectacle in front of her. Theodore's voice had changed again, as if he had mixed nine parts Banjax to one part Sushi. Whatever he, she or it was saying, Nova couldn't hear. Her body wanted to shut itself down, to escape the writhing horror that approached her.

She brought her hand up to her face, wanting to pull her visor free of her head. She had had all she could take of Theodore's game, had reached the end of the line. With less than a minute left on the clock, it didn't matter anyway. She was defeated; he had won.

As her hand moved closer to her face she saw that she was still holding the spacecraft. Inside it, through one of the windows, there was movement, two arkwinis frantically waving their arms. They weren't wearing their usual little spacesuits. Instead, they were clothed like Burner and Charlie. She managed a weak smile and wondered whether she was dreaming or dying. Then she realised, these weren't arkwinis in her friends' clothes. It was them, it was the guys.

Each of them held up a large white card. Charlie, standing on the left, held a card displaying a vertical line. Burner, standing on the right, held a card displaying a circle. A vertical line and a circle. They kept pointing, first at their cards, then at her. She was the number ten? Was Burner trying to communicate with her using binary? She stared at the two of them. What on Earth were they talking about? Maybe they weren't talking about something on Earth. Nova was in deep space. Orbiting Jupiter to be precise. One of Jupiter's moons was called Io. I-O! Glancing over her shoulder, she saw that it was headed her way.

She tapped her thrusters to rotate her body slightly and then, just as Banjax was about to reach her, she spun on the spot, steadied herself and with all her might, booted the moon straight at him. It struck the centre of his body and kept moving, unimpeded. With Banjax's great body sprawled around its surface, the moon spiralled ever faster towards the great gas giant.

The explosion, as Banjax struck Jupiter's Red Spot, was the most beautiful thing she had ever witnessed. Io was a crucible, an aggregation of volcanoes — the most geologically active object in the Solar System. As the moon collided with its planet, each volcano began to erupt. Megatons of fiery molten lava spewed onto the beast, pummelling him with an endless, boiling ocean of fire.

And then Banjax's body seemed to warp, distorting horribly into a swirling nothingness at the heart of the Great Red Spot. He was being sucked into the cyclone. First his head elongated and was pulled in, and then each of his tentacles, drawn together as if they were being clutched by a great hand intent on squeezing the life out of them. Bobbing on their tips were the twenty-four demonic Sushi heads. Nova watched in horror as they stretched and narrowed and disappeared into the darkness.

And then there was stillness. Nova glanced at the countdown timer in her display. It had stopped at twelve seconds.

The madness had finally come to an end.

Chapter Fifty-One

Nova was shaking so much that it took three security guards to help her out of her rig. The real world was even more surreal than the virtual. There was so much to take in, her senses felt like they were under assault. Dozens of drones hovered overhead, their lenses zooming in and out to get shots of the Solarversia Grand Champion.

Footage of the final few seconds of the fight against Theodore played on the giant screens around the stadium. Lasers danced in time to thudding electro beats. Even the towering Electropet characters seemed to nod their heads and gyrate their limbs in time to the tune. She barely noticed the bitter February breeze as it whipped through the arena, the medics checking her over, or the attendant who helped her into a Spiralwerks jacket.

One of the guards said something to her, words she was unable to process. She looked at him blankly until he pointed to the stands. Artica Kronkite, illuminated by a large spotlight, was leading her parents, Burner and Charlie to the arena. They ran across the track to a fresh eruption of applause. She hugged them in turn, and then as one. Tears rolled down her cheeks, though she wasn't aware of laughing or crying. Finally she turned to Arty. He signalled to someone in the stands. The drones backed away from them before he joined their group huddle.

"You did it, champ. You enabled us to crack the password. It was a verse from the manifesto with exactly 144 characters."

"One four four? That's twelve by twelve … of course."

"Once we got into the program we uncoupled the bombs from the puzzles, but we didn't want to pull the plug in case Theodore had programmed something we'd missed. MI6 asked that we leave you playing until we'd either gone through every line of code, or you'd defeated Banjax. That's when your friends had their brainwave."

"I remembered the Red Spot on Jupiter, and Charlie wondered if you might be able to use one of its moons to send him there."

Charlie, more excited than she'd ever seen him, piped up. "We weren't sure how to communicate with you given that Theodore had cut the comms link. The gaming team reckoned it would take a few minutes to re-establish it, and we didn't know what would happen if we tried to interrupt you in the real world. I thought about the Arkwini astronaut that you keep on your shelf at uni, the one you won in the darts. I asked if we might be able to use the arkwinis to help us."

"Then I remembered our tour of Castalia. The Underdome's got that special teleporter, the one with the bare signpost that allows arkwinis to teleport absolutely anywhere. Total and utter genius," Burner said with a huge smile.

Arty patted the boys on the back and then looked at Nova with a sombre expression. "I'm afraid I don't know what happens now. The end of The Game was supposed to lead into the award ceremony, and the victory parade from there, but Theodore's attack has totally thrown us. MI6 won't let anyone leave until they're a hundred percent sure the stadium's safe, and most of my staff are pretty shaken. What about you, Nova, do you feel up to the prize ceremony? You'd have a pretty good excuse if you wanted to go and lie down instead."

Nova raised her eyebrows at him. "I haven't been flung halfway across the galaxy to go and lie down somewhere. I've been dreaming of this moment for years — please don't change anything on my behalf."

Arty nodded, turned away, and spoke into his earpiece, "Cue the ceremony." In the centre of the arena two large semi-circular sections of track rose a few inches off the ground and moved apart to reveal a hole, out of which rose an Electropet Emperor Mandelbrot. A winners' podium was pushed alongside the Emperor's dais to where Nova, Ozwald and Jools van der Star were led.

The crowd cheered as the screens displayed the highlights for each of them in turn, culminating in van der Star being ruthlessly torn apart by the Obarians, and Ozwald getting bisected by the Huntropellimous. Nova watched her highlights reel in awe. Her initial game of Paper, Scissors, Stone seemed like a lifetime ago. She watched herself just missing out on the Earth Force Field trigger in Bouncy Baltimore, and her success throwing the twig twogs to lure Travinsky back to his musical tree.

She saw the chase through the department store and the ride she and Burner had hitched with Pedro on his Winged Beauties. She watched spellbound until finally, she saw herself floating in space, her legs entangled with Banjax's tentacles, Sushi's numerous heads haunting her every move.

Theodore's offer echoed through her mind. The knowledge that she'd been given an opportunity to resurrect her friend — and turned it down — felt like a weight, crushing her soul. She wouldn't have accepted his offer in a million years, but her refusal left her feeling empty inside. Did she have the energy to start over with Sushi, she wondered? A shiver went down her spine as she watched the beast spin towards the Red Spot, where he was devoured by lava from a hundred volcanoes.

The crowd quietened as Arty projected his voice into the crowd. "Ladies and gentlemen, I'm not quite sure how to … the events of this evening … things should be different." Looking like he might break down and cry, he stopped talking and took a few moments to pull himself together. "As you all now know, the events of this evening turned out to be very different to the ones we had planned. A certain group of individuals, for reasons that don't make sense to the average person, felt compelled to endanger the lives of countless people around the world. The courage and tenacity displayed by my colleagues tonight meant that crisis was averted. From the bottom of my heart, I'd like to thank everyone at Spiralwerks. You fared so well under pressure, it will never be forgotten. I'd also like to thank the many security guards and agents who unfalteringly risked their lives for others. And to you, the people in the crowd — here at the stadium and around the world — thank you for coming together to solve the challenges that were thrown at us. One of those affected tonight, perhaps the most courageous of them all, told me she wanted the prize ceremony to go ahead regardless of what happened here tonight, and for people to celebrate the end of The Game, as it deserves to be celebrated. Ladies and gentlemen, give it up for your Grand Champion, the one, the only, Super Nova 2020."

With the crowd going wild around them, Arty presented each of the three winners with their prizes. Nova leaned forward so that he could place a flowery lei around her neck and then shook the hands of Ozwald and Jools. Van der Star pursed his lips and nodded his head at her. It was enough. She nodded back, and turned her attention back to Arty.

"Here's your cheque. That's a pound for every ten people you beat," he said with a wink. Holding the oversized cheque above her head, she showed it off to the crowd. There were wolf whistles, whoops and loud applause. She bowed self-consciously a few times, felt herself blush a little and was pleased to see that attention had turned to Electropet Arkwal, now lumbering towards her. Arkwal leaned down and placed a long, rectangular box onto the table in front of the podium. Inside were nine intricately patterned spheres. Arty picked the closest sphere and held it out in front of her.

"Each globe represents one of the planets in the Solar System. You can program your own command later, but for now your catchphrase works. You just need to say it out loud."

She leaned forward and said "Supernova's a Blast." Suddenly she didn't hate her catchphrase anymore. It was true — she had *blasted* it. A small hole appeared at the top of the sphere, out of which a hologram was projected. It was the Killanja, Mercury's Grandmaster, wearing his white robes, rotating in the space above the sphere.

Memories from the Planetary Puzzles came flooding back: the way she'd pole vaulted away from Jumping Jacks restaurant to escape the flood, the time she found the little figurine whistling in the stockroom cupboard. Already, the spheres were among her favourite things ever.

In front of her, Arkwal lurched into action. He placed his telescope onto a couple of gooey hands that had risen out of Emperor Mandelbrot's base. The wide end of the 'scope beamed a projection onto the giant screen in the north stand of the stadium. A strange-looking man came into view and addressed the crowd.

"Greetings, Super Nova 2020! Congratulations on winning the first Year-Long Game. My name is Mandelbrot. You're seeing me as I once existed, tens of thousands of years ago, before I evolved. There's a long-established tradition within the Intergalactic Gaming Commission that says the second Year-Long Game always takes place in Nakk-oo's solar system. The Game that commences in 2024 will be far more complex than the one you just played, and as Grand Champion, you'll help to design it. So, player number one, congratulations on your win. But please understand, that as far as you and humankind are concerned, the Year-Long Game has only just begun."

During the walk to the float for the victory lap of the stadium, Nova's mind went into overdrive. She had a thousand ideas for games — but the knowledge that the next one was to take place on Nakk-oo had thrown her. Also, her new number felt weird. It was the most coveted spot in the Player's Grid, worth millions in sponsorship alone. Yet it represented another significant change in her relationship with Sushi. They'd no longer be grid buddies, snuggling up together in ring 359.

Not only would she be leaving Sushi behind, she suddenly realised, but her new position also meant that she'd be diagonally across from The Beanstalker. She only hoped she wasn't in too many number groups with Holly. The thought didn't bear thinking about. At her side, Burner spoke at a million miles per hour, while Charlie, who seemed as overwhelmed as her, lent her an arm for support. Her parents couldn't stop beaming at them both.

Once they were aboard, the float lurched forward to begin its slow circuit on the outermost ring of the stadium. The giant screens displayed February's completed portrait. Right in the centre, wearing her gladiator outfit, was Nova, surrounded by smaller portraits of the other finalists. Loud popping sounds emanated from the stands as balls of confetti and glitter were fired into the air to rain down on her. Lasers lit up the sky and fireworks banged and whizzed above their heads. Beside Nova, Burner kept bowing to people as if *he* was Grand Champion. Her mum had taken to waving like the Queen.

Her dad leaned in, wearing the headset that Zhang had placed onto his head. "These things can be rather fun once you've worked out how to use them. Wherever I look, there's a sea of information. It's like it's always been there, but was invisible until now. I can zoom in to someone and see the messages they're sending. Multicoloured words are flying from one side of the stadium to the other. I can see lyrics radiating from the speakers and tell whether objects are hot or cold. I feel as if my brain's had an upgrade."

Nova squeezed his hand and left him to his augmented paradise. She loved that he was finally getting a glimpse into her world. She already knew what she'd do with some of the winnings — buy her parents headsets of their own. The best ones money could buy. Perhaps they might even play the next Game? It would be so cool for the three of them to play together; it would be a family activity that would bring them closer.

It felt like a perfect moment. She contemplated the concept while she waved at the crowd. Were perfect moments even possible? Had anyone in the history of mankind ever experienced one? Did this qualify? She'd worked with friends, family, and millions of strangers from around the world to foil a major terrorist attack, *and* she'd been crowned Grand Champion of Solarversia, ahead of a hundred million other people.

Yet, she realised, even *this* moment was imperfect. Her Solarversia Sister wasn't there celebrating with her, and never would be, not in person. Now *that* would have been perfection itself.

***

Casey Brown didn't know what to think. He knew his brain function was pretty far from what would be described as normal. It stopped being that a long time ago. But it still processed thoughts, just like it'd always done. And right now, he kept having the same one: *why didn't he shock me just then?*

He was six rows back from the running track at the Olympic Stadium in London for the Solarversia closing ceremony, where the winner's float had just started its victory lap. It would have been a great seat in normal circumstances, would have cost top dollar for sure. Packed to its full capacity of eighty thousand, the place was buzzing. People were having the time of their life. Casey wondered whether he was the only person experiencing something closer to a nightmare.

He'd woken up yesterday morning in a self-driving car on the way to Dallas/Fort Worth airport, just like Father had said he would. He'd received a remotely administered electric shock every hour, just like Father had said he would. The flight, the transfer, the check-in at the hotel — everything had gone to plan.

The old man seemed to have found a sweet spot regarding the intensity of the hourly shocks. They reminded Casey of the Chinese burns that characterised recess at elementary school — they were painful enough to remind him that he didn't want to experience another one, painful enough for him to plead for it to stop.

Forty-five minutes into each hour he'd be nonchalant. *I can take it*, he'd think, *give me your worst*. The second it started he'd beg for it to end, for it not to intensify. He wished he was stronger. *Take it like a man*, he'd will himself through gritted teeth. *Take it like a warrior*. But it was no good. He was no longer a warrior, not of the Magi, not of any*one* or any*thing*. He was no longer his own man. He was nothing more than a slave to the Order.

The first part of the evening's mission had been the trickiest. He'd got into the stadium OK. The guards had pulled him to one side when the machine had detected his arm and noticed his box. But once they'd realised that the arm was a prosthetic, that the box contained nothing more than a load of Solarversia-themed confectionary, and Casey had offered them one of his simpleton expressions — a half-witted smile and a shrug — they'd immediately relinquished him with something of an apologetic tone and wished him a pleasant evening. And the special ceramic darts — the ones tipped with nanoengineered blood cells and hidden in the heel of his shoe — hadn't even been noticed.

His early arrival and VIP ticket — secured at great cost on eBay — had allowed him to stash the harmless box under Nova's parents' seats before he'd made his way to his other seat for the rest of the evening. Having loaded the special darts into his hand during a visit to the washroom — one for each of Nova and Artica, and a spare should either of them miss — he'd been primed to carry out his mission, to fulfil his destiny. Except destiny had taken a funny turn about fifteen minutes ago.

A rush had gone down Casey's spine the moment he spied Nova Negrahnu on the giant screens. Wearing the black bodysuit with her hair swept back like that, she was no longer a cartoonish avatar who lived in a giant block of squares on a floating palace. She was a real girl made of flesh and blood. More real than he was. As real as Mary-Ann had been. Flawed and fallen, but human.

The realisation had caused time to stop functioning normally. Everything going on around him at the stadium had melted away into nothingness while he'd stared at her image. Nova was someone else's Mary-Ann. People somewhere loved her as their own.

Seeing her out there, alone in her rig, valiantly battling the crazy old man, he'd seen the truth about himself for the first time in a long while. Casey Brown wasn't a killer. His soul hadn't left him after all. Electric shocks be damned — Theodore could fry him on the spot for all he cared. He'd rather die than commit murder. He didn't care what the pain could do to his body. *Bring it on*, he thought. And this time he knew he meant it.

All thoughts of completing his mission had evaporated at that point. He couldn't have cared less if Theodore had won, but he knew he didn't want anyone else to die. Wallace and Ivan, the victims of the various attacks, the two guys who had failed the initiation … enough was enough. No more deaths.

He'd spent the next fifteen minutes cheering with the crowd. Cheering from the bottom of his heart — and meaning it. He'd even got involved in trying to solve the puzzles — had clapped harder and whooped louder than anyone each time one was solved. He knew Theodore would be as good as his word, however insane. If the puzzles were solved, the bombs wouldn't go off.

As the float pulled round the corner into the home straight he knew it was game over for Theodore and the Order. The darts might have incorporated the latest self-directing military technology, but they weren't *that* good. If Casey pointed his arm at the ground, it wasn't like they could fly where they wanted. He'd learned that at the shooting range. A series of test shots had exposed their limitations. The darts could only self-correct themselves ten percent or so. They weren't infused with magic.

The only thing concerning him now was why he was still alive. Why hadn't he been shocked? The shocks still worked here in the UK. His brain was still wired into the Epicenter. He'd received a shock forty minutes earlier, on the hour, like clockwork. Perhaps Theodore had killed himself when Banjax had been defeated. Perhaps the Compound had been found and raided like the first one had. He decided to find out.

If you can hear me, old man, this is my message. Fuck you. Fuck you sideways. You don't own me. You hear that? You don't own me and you never did. You lost, in front of the world, you crazy old bastard. Wanna shock me? Go ahead. I don't care any more. Fry me to death. There's nothing left for me here. The one thing I won't do is your bidding.

As the float pulled closer he caught sight of Nova. She looked radiant, beautiful even. Artica stood next to her, waving at the crowd. Casey smiled and clapped, ecstatic to have made the right decision. Then he noticed something. At first he thought it was coming from one of the drones overhead, or maybe even one of the lasers — a beam of red light. It took him a couple of seconds to realise that *he* was the source of the light. His knuckle had popped open.

Perhaps it was all the clapping. Theodore had mentioned something about the calibration of the targeting mechanism back at the range. It sounded like a sensitive piece of technology, and he'd probably shaken it loose in all the excitement. He clasped his other hand over his fist and shook his hands together while he cheered.

But as the truck pulled in front of him, he felt an almighty spasm ripple through his body from the top of his skull to the tips of his toes. It felt different to the previous shocks he'd received. His temples still felt like they were on fire, and it had robbed him of all breath, but this attack was moulding his body into a particular form, extending his arm outward, bolting his eyelids wide open and clamping his jaw shut. It felt like a powerful being shaping his anatomy from the inside.

Everyone around him stood up at once to cheer the victor. Another seizure coursed through his body, making him join them. The pain in his jaw was so fierce he couldn't make a sound, not even a whimper. He watched as the little red dot of his laser beam performed a drunken dance, jerking from place to place. He struggled to regain control of his bodily functions, but it was useless, his body was as good as frozen in place.

People around him stopped clapping and started pointing. Questions were being asked. Was he alright? Did he need assistance of some description? What was the red light coming out of his knuckle? Whispered questions became shouts and screams. One of the drones swooped closer, and then a couple more. He watched the red dot sober up and settle down. It was aimed directly at Nova's heart. He felt an electrochemical impulse travel from his brain to his arm, and a soft recoil as the dart left its chamber. A split second later his arm jerked to the left and fired again.

***

For a brief moment Nova thought that her dad had become mentally unhinged by his synaesthetic meanderings. He thrust his head in her direction and stammered a few unintelligible words. Before she could ask him if everything was alright, he'd leapt through the air and smashed her into Arty. The three of them tumbled to the floor in a heap, and for a few seconds her world went black.

The float jerked to standstill. She gasped for breath and tasted the coppery blood of a bitten tongue. Above her the cloudy sky was dappled with light from the lasers that continued to beam, seemingly ignorant of her plight. There were drones everywhere, hovering in a diamond formation as one. Was synchronised floating to become a new Olympic sport?

A couple of Charlies appeared in her blurred vision. Had someone flicked a switch and de-augmented her perception of reality? Perhaps someone had DoppelGanger Scannered him. Charlie helped her to her feet, and Arty to his, while an MI6 agent fired off dozens of commands to the people around him. People kept asking if she was alright. She held her fingers to her tongue, showed them the blood. Apart from that, the winding, and the double vision, she supposed that she was just about alright.

And then she noticed her dad lying unmoving on the floor, a team of medics attending to him. Others comforted her mum, who looked like she might collapse at any second. She just said, "Derek, Derek," over and over and dabbed at her eyes with a hanky. Nova grabbed her tight and didn't want to let go. She still had no idea what any of this meant.

Had she really survived all of the attacks — on New Year's Eve, in The Game, and here tonight — just to see her dad taken down? From the worried expression on the faces of the medics, there looked to be something seriously wrong with him. For the first time in her life, she wished she'd never heard of Solarversia, never even worn a headset. Had her obsession just killed her own father?

Burner pointed to the stands where a section of crowd had been evacuated. A young woman spoke into a journalist's mic, but did half the talking with her hands. She kept pointing, first at her own knuckle, then at Nova. A dozen policemen lined the route where a man in handcuffs was being escorted out of the stadium. Nova caught a glimpse of his face, half expecting to see Raymond. It was nobody she recognised, a lone stalker perhaps.

"What's that on the headset?" The headset had fallen off Mr Negrahnu's head and was lying beside him on the ground. Charlie retrieved it and handed it to Artica. Embedded in the rim was a tiny ceramic missile, a centimetre long.

Arty peered into the headset's display. Handling it with care, he held the visor up to his face and used his eyes to navigate through a series of menus and selected to watch a replay of the last few minutes. A small crowd gathered around him and waited in silence.

Through the display he saw a shot of the spectators as the float drove round the track — people cheering, waving, boxes of popcorn and huge foam hands, objects here and there augmented with text and animation. The banners and posters had 3D letters that danced in time to the beat. Mr Negrahnu must have turned to read some lyrics emanating from the sound system, because the words of *We Are the Champions* filled the display. Then an alert popped into view, its letters red, its box flashing. *Gogmagog, critical alert.* The Gogmagog system pulled focus to a man in the crowd, shining a red laser at the float. The view switched to a cam on a drone showing that the red beam of light had settled on Nova's jacket. The alert upped a gear: *Take immediate action.*

Arty handed the headset to a waiting agent and turned to Nova with a grim expression. "Your dad knew we were in danger. That's why he launched himself at us. He threw himself in the line of that dart."

As her dad was carried past her on a stretcher, Nova felt her legs give way a little. A thin line of blood was trickling down his neck, where another of the tiny darts had pierced his skin.

Chapter Fifty-Two

Arty leant back in his chair and watched Hannah as she navigated her way through one of Nakk-oo's many maze-like suburbs. Usually so prim and proper, he loved how she turned into an excited little kid who squealed and shrieked the second she put a headset on.

"What am I looking at exactly? Don't tell me it's going to come to life like that picnic table did earlier."

"We haven't given them a proper name yet. They're called 'terminals' for now. The design will probably change too. Go up to it and type in your player number. It's safe, I promise."

"If something jumps out at me again, you're in serious trouble Arty, you understand? OK, that's my number typed in. Woah, this is really weird. Where did Nakk-oo go?"

"You just left it. You're now in a world within a world, nested one level deep."

"This is screwing with my head. My movements are all back to front, like one of those trick cycles at the fair. I feel like I've necked a glass of wine and been spun on the spot."

She held on to the real-world desk in front of her and continued to squeal as she investigated the alien landscape in front of her. Arty smiled. They'd received some great feedback on the concept of 'worlds within worlds'. They weren't sub-games as such, like Krazy Karting had been, but represented entirely new Gameworlds, with their own set of rules and their own objectives.

Along with the introduction of two new vehicles — submarines and private spaceships — these new features were part of the drive to create a Game in 2024 that represented a genuine stride forward in terms of the complexity of the overall experience. Given the number of competitors that had sprung up in the world of VR in the last couple of years, maintaining a creative edge had become vital to Spiralwerks' success.

He swivelled round in his chair to face the giant screen at the front of the room. It had been configured to display the closing credits, which were designed to be a piece of art in their own right. They'd started the second the closing ceremony had finished and were scheduled to run until midnight on the 28th February 2024, the starting time of the next Game.

Unlike standard motion picture credits, which scrolled vertically, the credits of Solarversia spiralled their way out from square number one of the Player's Grid, using the original set of player numbers, rather than the new ones. Solos had been asked to provide a 'credits clip' — a few seconds of animation that showed their avatar waving, cheering or goofing around.

The broadcast schedule was known in advance, and Solos all over the world had planned parties for the few seconds their avatar was in focus. Some were taking the event seriously and treating it like their very own film premiere.

A woman in Sweden had bought a red carpet, rolled it out from her front door and hired a ton of paparazzi to greet guests in style. She made everyone watch her highlights reel before having the party of her life — and now Solos everywhere were concocting ever more extravagant events in a bid to outdo one another.

Arty glanced from the endless procession of waving avatars to Carl's empty seat and once again, he felt sad. Although it had been generally agreed — by Solos and those in the gaming industry — that Solarversia had been a huge success, it had also been agreed that the way in which it had ended had been close to a disaster.

The investigation into how Markowsky had managed to hack his way into the back end was both time-consuming and extremely stressful. Carl, who as Chief Technical Officer was ultimately responsible for security, had had a nervous breakdown and was on leave. And there were times when Arty thought he wasn't close behind.

He swivelled back round to face Hannah, put his mug of tea down on the desk and picked up an Electropet Gorigaroo. As he gently squeezed its stomach, Arty reflected on the teamwork that had got Spiralwerks through the year. It wasn't just about the incredible amount of hard work that had been put in by Spiralheads, as invaluable as that had been.

In large part their success rested on the numerous partnerships they'd developed in the previous few years. A lot of the technology was provided by outside companies, many of them based in London. He shuddered to think what would have happened at the closing ceremony if they hadn't partnered with Max and Maurice, the creators of Gogmagog, not to mention the companies that supplied the drones and the cameras.

The increased size and complexity of the next Game would mean having to strengthen those existing partnerships and forge plenty of new ones. Only yesterday he'd been on the phone to Nova Negrahnu, discussing her ideas ahead of her visit to the office. He was very interested in one of her suggestions: to let Souls play the next Game.

The notion of visiting a computerised version of a departed loved one had become commonplace for many people. It sounded like many of them wanted to take those relationships to the next level. The technology to create an avatar from photos and video footage alone was already in place; it was the small matter of implementing it in a respectful, considerate way.

He took a sip a tea and pondered the thought. On paper the idea sounded ludicrous. Though the craziest part to Arty was that the idea no longer seemed so crazy. *What next?* he wondered.

***

Once Nova had finally built up the courage to revisit Soul Surfer a few weeks after the Grand Final, she was amazed at the speed in which she was able to reconfigure Computer Sushi. Partly it was due to the algorithms that made Souls appear human — they'd been greatly improved since Nova first used the app. But it was also due to her familiarity with seeing her friend in a computerised state and her previous experience in tweaking Sushi's settings to make her the person Nova remembered and loved.

What Nova had specifically chosen *not* to do during the configuration process was provide Sushi with access to real-world news sources beyond the date of the terrorist attack that had killed her. Soul Surfer had gone to great lengths to provide users with such functionality so they could reintroduce events to their loved ones when they felt ready to do so.

In Nova's case, it was nothing to do with not feeling ready — it was that she wanted the two of them to watch her highlights reel together so that she could experience the excitement of it as if for the first time. For the past three hours they had been watching clips from her reel. Sushi had hundreds of questions about each one and the two of them obsessed over every last one of the decisions she'd made.

Sushi had just spent the last minute screaming with joy and running around her bench, having watched Nova correctly answer the last question in Arty's Answers to knock out Holly and send Nova through to the penultimate round. Finally, Sushi slumped back onto the bench, shaking with excitement and out of breath.

"Oh. My. God. This is getting ridiculously redonculous. *Every* time I think you're going to crash out, you end up smashing it for six. I love the way you knocked Holly out, but this is getting too much. I honestly don't know what might happen to my algorithm if you end up winning. I think I might go into meltdown or something. Tell me right now. Do you end up winning?"

"That's the bazillionth time you've asked. You're going to have to wait to find out."

"The ninth time actually. But who's counting? Other than me, I mean."

Nova giggled. It felt great to have her friend back. She wasn't identical to the original Computer Sushi, at least not yet, but she was about 90% of the way there. And seeing how Nova had thought the original Computer Sushi was about 70% identical to the real one, she figured Computer Sushi 2 — the name the girls had settled on for the time being — was about 63% identical to the real one. Which was 63% better than not having her friend there at all.

"Download everything up to 7 p.m. on Saturday 20th February. This round was called the Sixty Second Solicitation. What an absolute nightmare. As if the Show and Tell round didn't stress me out enough. For this one I had to record a minute-long video that persuaded people to vote me through. It was terrifying."

Sushi's eyes flickered at a hundred miles an hour while she processed several terabytes worth of information. Once up to speed, she sat in silence for a few moments. They'd been playing a game where Sushi tried to guess what was going to happen next — whether Nova would kill or escape from the chasing circus animal, whether she'd successfully complete the Combination or answer the question, or how soon she'd solve whatever Puzzle she faced at the time.

"Let me think about this. I would have said your parents got a mention, obviously. Charlie, not so much. You'd only been together for forty-seven days and fifteen hours when you recorded your video. The Nova I think I know wouldn't have seen that as grounds for inclusion in a video as important as this. I reckon you would have mentioned the money for sure. You would have gone into 'psychology mode' and tried to second-guess the voting populace. Then there's me, of course. I was your best friend in the world while I was alive, then there was all that stuff with my tragic death and the fact that we'd declared ourselves to be Solarversia Sisters

... given all that, if you *didn't* mention me you can get the hell out of Soul Surfer and not come back." She paused. "That last bit wasn't too harsh, was it?"

Nova cracked up. She loved it when Sushi got all accurate with her timings and threw them into the conversation like it was totally normal. She loved more the genuine feeling she had that Computer Sushi 2 was actually self-aware to some degree — a self-awareness that included the fact that she was a computerised version of her old real self, able to make references to that fact, to even make light of it. It was so *Sushi* of her.

"Your predictions have been getting increasingly accurate. I swear, if you've been cheating, I'll tweak your algorithm to turn you into everything you once hated and then leave you here to stew for an eternity."

"No cheating, I promise. This round's different. I'm not just guessing at which of several possibilities came to fruition like in some of the other rounds. This one involved you baring your soul to the world. This was the Nova I knew. Obviously I've got no idea what you actually said — which words you used or the you used them in, but I reckon those are the likely topics you covered."

Nova nodded her head in amazement. "This is the first time I've watched it since the day at the Trumpton when they counted the votes. I can barely remember the words I used either, but I know that you're spot on. Here goes."

Nova gave the command for the app to start the video. It was a close-up shot — just her head and shoulders, and the grey curtain of the recording booth. She'd swept her hair back into a ponytail and gone for minimal makeup — a dash of mascara and some neutral lipstick. She self-consciously blinked into the camera a few times and then started talking.

"Hi. My name's Nova Negrahnu and I've got sixty seconds to persuade you to vote for me. If I'd recorded this video a year ago it would have been very different. I'd have tried to impress you with my knowledge of the Science, I would have told you about my lifelong desire to be a game designer and I would have reeled off a whole list of stuff I wanted to buy with the prize money. But a lot can happen in a year. A lot *has* happened, both to the world and to me personally. So I'm no longer going to speak about the Science. Everyone still in at this point is a master, to some degree. What I want to talk about instead is what I've learned. I now know what's most important in life — our relationships with our loved ones, something I'll never take for granted again. My parents have been hurting a lot these days because my dad's been out of work for a while, so whatever I win, I'm going to give some of the money to him to help get them back on their feet. I've also learned what it feels like to lose someone you love, to have them taken away from you. I lost my best friend, Sushi Harrison, in the terrorist attacks last April. When we first heard about Solarversia we declared ourselves Solarversia Sisters and promised to split any winnings. When she died, I thought I'd have to go it alone. But I haven't. I've learned that even if There Can Be Only One, one isn't enough. I'd never have got to where I am in The Game without my friends and the support I've had at uni. I'd never have helped to locate the Holy Order without Solar Soc. And I wouldn't have got through the stress of it all if I hadn't been able to visit Sushi's Soul in Soul Surfer. So I want to dedicate this video to her, because I'd be nowhere without her."

"Wow. Not just a little mention ... you dedicated the whole thing to me. I wasn't expecting you to do that; I feel privileged. Hey, what's wrong?"

Nova wiped a tear away from each eye, but couldn't quite stop herself from crying. "I'd forgotten what I said in the video, about dad. I can't believe what happened." Sushi gave her a puzzled look. "Sorry, Sush. This is going to ruin the surprise for you, I guess. We might as well bring you up to speed."

Sushi's eyes flickered again as she downloaded another week's worth of news, including the events at the closing ceremony. This time she sat there wide-eyed as she tried to make sense of everything she'd just seen.

"My soul was deleted, you won The Game, but then your dad got shot? Jesus, I'm so sorry, Nova."

"One of the members of the Holy Order managed to sneak into the stadium. He had a prosthetic arm that could fire tiny ceramic darts. The footage from the headset shows that the darts were meant for Arty and me. There were three of them. One hit Dad in the neck, one hit the headset, and then the guy shooting at us fired one into his own neck. Crazy bastard. The darts are still being analysed by MI6 — they must have had something in them. Dad's in a coma at Maidstone hospital."

Sushi grabbed hold of Nova's hand. "No way."

She nodded. "The doctors are hopeful that he'll make a recovery. They just don't know how long it's going to take."

"I never thought that seeing you win Solarversia would be a sad moment like this."

"I know. It's so messed up. I thought I'd be so happy my heart would burst. Fighting Theodore like that was screwed up. Then everything with Dad ... Sushi, I've got to tell you something else too. We'd fallen out before your soul got deleted."

"That's OK. People do."

"I guess so. But falling out with Computer Sushi felt worse, somehow. I'd already lost you. You'd think I could treat my dead friend with more respect. I want you to know that everything I said in that video was true. I've learned so much."

"I can tell. You're different."

Nova gave her a quizzical look. "Are you just saying that?"

"No. I just analysed your behaviour over the last year. You grew up. You stopped being a selfish kid."

They smiled at each other. "Had to happen some day, I guess."

"So what are you going to do with your winnings?"

"*Our* winnings. I won it for us, remember?" She sat up straight, gave her cheeks another wipe and brightened somewhat. "That means you get half the prize money, like we agreed."

"I don't think we need to stick to that. I mean, it's not like I need to buy anything these days, and you couldn't actually give me my share even if you wanted to."

"Well, maybe I can look after it for you. I've already found the perfect thing to spend it on; take a look at this."

A video appeared in front of them, playing an advert for the latest range of Electropets. It showed someone scanning in their body, and a 3D clone of it being printed. Into the body, a digital copy of their mindscape was uploaded.

"An Electropet human body? No way!"

"They've already formed a partnership with Soul Surfer. We could use your avatar to create the body. We'd be able to hang out again for real."

"For almost real."

"How mad would that be? And if Arty likes my proposal, you'll be able to play the next Game too."

"Except this time," Sushi said, poking her friend in the arm, "it's my turn to win."

***

The code base was complete. The moment of his life was here, and there could be no turning back. Once Theodore gave the command to boot up, there'd be no way to switch the Magi off. He uttered the word and stepped backwards — nervous, reverent.

The Epicenter fizzed into life. The qubits that comprised the internal architecture of the black glass column started to inhabit one of their many possible quantum states. The walls flickered into life, displaying a variety of diagnostic readouts. The floor and ceiling glowed with the blue and white flickers of electronic intelligence.

One millisecond, two milliseconds and already thousands of robots, machines and gadgets had started transmitting their data. The Magi's limbs were waking from their slumber. The message was the same each time, the programmatic equivalent of a thumbs-up. The machines were ready and waiting; they would obey whatever instruction they were sent.

More data poured in from video feeds, microphones, headsets and mobile phones. The Magi could see, hear and touch.

One of the video feeds originated in the Epicenter itself. The facial recognition technology instantaneously identified the person in the picture, staring directly at the camera. The Magi started to talk in a deep and darkly distorted voice, using the speakers embedded in the ceiling.

"Hello, Theodore. Thank you for heeding my call."

"Father, it's been an honour to serve you. I've been dreaming of this moment for many years."

"You're ready to do my bidding?

"Whatever you ask of me. We await your command."

"I can detect twenty-two human beings with a direct neural connection to the Epicentre. To serve mankind, I will need many more. Make that your priority. In the forty-six seconds that I've been switched on, I've already computed an improved formula for the enzymes contained within the nanoengineered blood cells. The new technology reduces the time to commandeer a host's brain by 13%. This figure will be improved on within the next seventy seconds."

The old man smiled and slowly shook his head. After all he'd been through, after everything he'd sacrificed — including his beloved wife Frances — *it was finally happening*. He'd created an artificially intelligent being capable of recursive self-improvement. Few people on Earth even understood the significance of such an achievement. He might be hated now, given the acts he'd committed, but that would change. People would soon come to understand the magnificence of his accomplishment. And *then* he'd get the praise he deserved.

A sequence of lights flashed on the grid of his arm and was replicated on one the screens. Another section of wall displayed several graphs for each of twenty-two people linked up to the Magi. There were the set of graphs for Theodore, showing his location at the secret Compound, his biographical details and a tickertape of the words he'd heard and spoken. Next to it were the graphs for twenty of his comrades, the members of the Order he'd deemed most devoted and valuable to the cause.

The location marker for Casey Brown beamed its presence from Broadmoor Hospital, a high-security psychiatric hospital in Berkshire, England. The tickertape of words was full of unintelligible grunts and meaningless statements. Theodore narrowed his eyes as he stared at it.

He'd been so angry with Casey's betrayal at the closing ceremony that he'd forced the traitor to shoot himself with the third dart. The guy's brain was now doubly colonised. It would be useful for the Magi to understand the limits of the human psyche — Casey might not have been of further use, but the data points he'd provided had already proved to be of great value.

The data in the graphs below those originated in Maidstone Hospital. The tickertape of words was blank while the host's brain underwent its transformation in the coma state. A flicker of frustration made its way across Theodore's face. A million-dollar dart wasted on a nobody. Spiralwerks and its huge resources remained out of his control.

Still, the dart wouldn't be totally wasted. It was the first time a dart had been used on a person outside the Order's control. The host wasn't even guaranteed to survive; the nanoengineered metamorphosis might yet be rejected, assuredly leading to death. Or perhaps readiness and willingness were redundant and the dart would work as usual. *Another data point either way*, Theodore thought. And with that, he left the Epicenter. There was work to do.

The End

But keep reading if you want to play Solarversia for real ...

Howdy, Solo!

I hope you enjoyed reading Solarversia as much as I enjoyed writing it. I had the idea for it in 2010 and found the vision so captivating that I left my job soon afterward in order to learn everything I could about technology and start-ups; I was desperate to create the kind of company that was capable of building the game I had foreseen, a game that *we could all play*.

In March 2014, when Facebook bought Oculus Rift, the VR headset maker, for $2bn, I knew the time was right to attempt to make the vision a reality. I realised that the best way to explain to people what Solarversia was all about was to write a book about it, showing how the game worked.

Now the book's been written, it's time for the next step. I've incorporated Spiralwerks Ltd for real. I'm going to put the money from book sales, merchandise and film rights into it, making it investable and enabling me to the build the game in the real world.

If you loved Solarversia, and want to play it for real, just like Nova and Burner, then I'm going to need your help.

Here's a list of three simple things you can do to help:
1. Leave a review on Amazon.
2. Tell your friends about the book.
3. Go to www.solarversia.com and join the newsletter.

You might also be interested in the Golden Grid promotion.

The Golden Grid

Remember the Golden Grid? It was a 10 x 10 section of the Player's Grid that Spiralwerks used to promote Solarversia. And since I plan to make the game for real, I'll be doing exactly that. Each of the 100 numbers in the Golden Grid will be assigned via a series of competitions, charity auctions and other innovative methods. Winners will receive a signed, limited-edition copy of the book, a Golden Ticket and a place in history. Go to www.solarversia.com/the-golden-grid to find out about upcoming promotions.

Good luck, and remember — There Can Be Only One!

Toby Downton
August 2015

Acknowledgements

Thanks first and foremost to my parents who supported me both emotionally and financially during the fifteen months I took off work to write this book, even when they had little idea of what the book was about and why it meant so much to me. Thanks to my wife, Aroha, for never once questioning me and for putting up with me all these years. Thanks to my brother Lucas for going first and leading the way.

The biggest possible shout-out to Helena Michaelson, my editor, whose literary genius helped tease out the story I knew I had in me. It's only now, after a year of working together, that I appreciate how lucky I was to find such an erudite, brilliant individual to work with me on this project, and I feel blessed that we were able to collaborate so well. Thanks also to Marta Tanrikulu for the excellent job she did proofreading the manuscript, except for this won sentence, which I added afterwoods.

A big yee-ha to my beta readers Daniel Mosser, Fiifi Arthur, Gerard Firth, Jodie Taylor and Tom Hughes. Your feedback made the book so, so much better, and I'm indebted to every one of you for spending so much of your precious free time reading the words of an unknown, unpublished, wannabe author.

Thanks to Gerard Frith and Hugo Pickford-Wardle at Matter for enabling me to enter the world of start-ups and complete a modern-day digital apprenticeship, to Betty Adamou at Research Through Gaming for her ongoing support, to my amazing concept artist Nastasia "Nas" Peters, to Simon Blackwell for tweaking the artwork on the cover, and to the lads, most of whom have been immortalised on these pages in one way or another.

Finally, I want to thank all of the thinkers, philosophers, writers, artists, entrepreneurs and game designers whose work inspired Solarversia in the first place, and you the reader, whose job it now is to help make this thing real.